AFTER THE FALL
WAS OVER

PRISTINE
PRESS AND MEDIA

W. CLARK BOUTWELL

ISBN
978-1-969642-18-0 (Paperback)
978-1-969642-17-3 (eBook)
978-1-969642-19-7 (Hardcover)

Dedication

To Ross, the wife of my heart.

Acknowledgment

To Joseph Boutwell, whose advice I always take.

Dramatis Personae

Americans of the Restructured States of America

William Butler-America's first spy, was severely handicapped by the loss of his backstory, making it impossible to perform he primary function or even move freely within the Unity.

Hecate Hester Jones -Will Butler's Unity companion and love. She was attempting to flee the Unity when they first met. Now she is a very integral part of the American effort to defeat the Unity.

Gage Thomas-Major General of the Eastern District (formerly, Colonial Logistics) of the Restructured States Army (RSA)

Jeremiah Rhedd, Brigadier General, RSA Intelligence

Levi Hollister and **Joseph Hendricks**-new spies in the Unity for the American cause.

Altab Aminiesuwa Nyarko-Lieutenant General and Commander of the Army

James Buchanan Polk, president of the Restructured States of America,

Unis of the Democratic Unity

Fettwap Alliende, Lieutenant General, newly elevated (by guile and brutality) to be the commander of the Defensive Unity Forces for Security (DUFS). Returned Survivor of the Day of Ice

Blanche Woods, Captain, and Transitioned Trangender, the other returned survivor of the Day of Ice. As a member of a "Protected Class," Blanche (nee **Riley**) is always guaranteed advancement with an asterisk.

Malachi Merryweather- a rising young CORE technician, who, with his team (**Peter Collins and Gyorgy Blass**), is tasked with plumbing the secrets of the CORE for Aliende to find dirt on Woods.

Seftus Ploidid-Colonel and founder-leader of the Greens of

Unity Forward, a small faction dedicated to "progress," whatever that means at the moment.

Gilsoit Fenerghan-Brigadier General and leader of the Unity Home faction, the Oranges, dedicated to "Climate Justice," whatever that means at the moment.

Eustace Jourdaine (deceased)-Lieutenant General and recent commander of the DUFS. He rose to power by his discovery and subjugation of **Cain, a** CORE entity (vide infra). His shadow still dominates the Uni culture.

The CORE Entities

Cain-the original "ghost" in the CORE, the Unity's massive and nation-girdling computer. Originally a one-off program for a dying child, Cain has become engrammed with the human's personality. With the death of his original host, he was captured by Eustace Jourdaine, who used Cain's familiarity with the CORE to rise to power.

Frog-Will Butler's BIGI interface and engrammed entity allowed Will to enter the openCORE, a sort of back office of the CORE, to conduct his spy work for America. With Will's near-fatal fall in mid-June, Frog cloned himself to become a permanent resident.

EffieCee-a conjoined CORE entity consisting of mirrored entities of Cain, Frog, and Edie, the computer companion of Malila Chiu, whose doings are chronicled in *Old Men and Infidels*. Edie was undergoing evaporation due to Chiu's abandonment. Her incorporation into this triune entity has preserved and strengthened Edie. EffieCee is a work in progress, growing with its entities. EffieCee sometimes talks in a braided voice, denoting unanimity, but the composite individuals may also speak on their own. EffieCee's pronouns are we, us, our, and them.

Rana-a clone of Frog, created to allow Hecate Hester Jones to enter the openCORE. Frog considers her a younger sister.

Elise-a recent addition to the CORE entities. She is the engram of Elise McRory (AKA Jessika Bonhoffer), who was dying after completing her critical espionage mission for the RSA. Cain and she are in love.

Newt and Sally Mander - entities for Hollister and Hendricks. They have similar abilities to Frog and Rana.

The Polyarchy of Sentients of the Scorch

Splanch-war leader in defense of the Scorch during the Unity Invasion, currently on sabbatical. The changed plants of the Scorch, although physically varied, are all the result of a mutagenic herbicide applied to the eastern watershed of the Mississippi during 2053–2057, the Great People's War of Liberation, a civil war dismembering the USA.

Throot -a diplomatic entity to America and the Unity

Speaker, Helon, Grood- other sentients not involved in this narrative

THE CAPTAIN AWAKES

**Vicinity of Roswell and Wiauca Roads, Aytlana, Jorga Province
04.33.32.EST_12_October_AU77, (2129 AD), Wednesday**

Captain Woods awoke from her usual troubling dream. In truth, the captain had scarcely slept. Something was coming loose—going amiss—*something*. The night groaned as if in the throes of an ague. The wind rose and fell, even blowing the door to her small quarters open once, before McMoltrie figured out a way to secure it. *Clever man.*

Things had started going sideways just before sundown. The overture had been easy enough to identify—skimmers[1] began to fall from the skies. From her vantage point, she had seen in the gloaming several of the blocky vehicles, still lit by the setting sun, flying at various altitudes above the abandoned American city. In a moment, they all seemed to stagger, seize up, and start an inexorable plunge to earth. Like a brick into mud, they struck, buried themselves, and never moved again. Each could carry a squad of twenty and two pilots: twenty-two at a time, dying in the dull thud of impact. About that time, outlander[2] drums started.

The weather in Jorga during the three days they had been in the country had been unpredictable. It was warm and humid when they started burning their way through the Scorch[3] to get at their enemies. *Hot, nasty work.* Now the weather had turned bitter[4] in the space of a few minutes. *Why had the DUFS[5] command not known this?*

---

[1] Skimmers are levitating vehicles of the Unity. See the Appendix for unfamiliar terms and a timeline for what has become a convoluted tale.

[2] The outlands, beyond the Rampart and the Scorch are those lands that opposed the People's Republic in 2052 and have received the brunt of Unity aggression ever since. They call themselves Americans of the Restructured States.

[3] The Scorch, a polyarchy of sentient plants, 'changed' due to mutagenic herbicides. They have served as a buffer state between the Unity and the Restructured States of America for generations.

[4] See Climatic Battlefield Preparation in the glossary.

[5] Defensive Forces for Unity Security, the Unity's army cum national police.

Just before retreating to her command post, Captain Blanche Woods looked up to see if her company was in danger from overhead skimmers. At the demise of the day, still lit by the retreating sun, she glimpsed whisps of clouds, like pink smoke rings, and a flash of something very small or very high before darkness swallowed it a moment later. Blanche, hugging herself from the cold, stepped into the cabin she shared with McMoltrie.

Later that night, during her rounds of her rifle company of CRNAs,[6] the distant native drums were still pounding out:

"Boom…boom…boom—Boom…boom…boom."

The noise, she thought, came from the southwest but also seemed to move around: primitive psych-ops, if it was anything. She paused and shook her head ruefully. *"Psych-ops?"* That would ascribe to the knuckledraggers more guile than they were likely to possess. The DUFS, passing through the country from the Savanah River to the provincial capital during the three previous days, had seen no organized resistance, just well-tended farms and small factories—all ablaze.

The barbarians had known they were coming. Known and prepared—burning anything of value as they evacuated. Here and there, a sniper took out an officer or a transport, but nothing a soldier would call real resistance.

She had arrayed her company across a field from some little creek in the broken land north of the city's center. The flanks were refused as they were a forward unit and had no direct support. Blanche and her men were the very cutting edge of the Unity's[7] Sword. *The outlanders would rue the coming day!* Blanche smiled at the prospect.

Protecting the right flank of the approaches to the Unity lines, her company had a vital role. The headquarters, the brain of Unity's "Army of Reconciliation,"[8] was to their left and rear, tucked safely behind the rampart of the Hoochie[9] River.

All should have been copacetic for her unit, she thought. The outlander attack was expected to fall on the southwest of downtown;

---

[6] Certified Registered Neuro-Ablated. Those found excess to requirements in the Unity and rendered "willing" soldiers for the DUFS.

[7] The Democratic Unity of North America is neither a Unity, as it is composed merely of the eastern watershed of the Appalachians, minus the watershed of the Great Lakes, nor is it democratic.

[8] The Unity maintains they are the rulers of the outlands, rather than conquerors.

[9] Chattahoochee River

those defenses were made to appear slipshod, partial, and poorly manned—a *ruse de guerre, inviting attack.*

On her initial rounds, each of the company squads appeared to be squared away, and, pleased with her arrangements, Blanche headed back to the limited warmth of her quarters. Reentering, she closed the door, wedging a heavy box against it to keep it closed, and looked out one of the small windows to see if the moon was up. In that instant, the glass frosted up, obscuring her view.

Although initially warm when they first arrived, now wind rattled the glass and roof of the building. Cold invaded through every crack and crevice. Finding rolls of tar paper meant for roofing material, Blanche snugged her sleeping bag into a few folds of one roll. Between the hectic noises of the wind, her recurrent dream, and cold feet, Blanche slept fitfully.

Several hours later, surrendering to the inevitable, she arose and tried calling the battalion HQ, receiving only static. It was frustrating.

In the Unity, all communications were managed through the CORE.[10] Once they passed the now-defunct Rampart,[11] all CORE communications had ceased. This had been anticipated, and all line officers were issued "radio" transceivers. They were supposed to work without any wires—and occasionally did. Woods had insisted on a back-up land line to the platoon control posts, 'just in case."

Feeling a bit smug at her prescience, Blanche called each of her three rifle and one weapons platoons' CPs—with no success. Alternating between frustration and a growing sense of dread, Blanche sent her four company runners to each of the platoon command positions to warn of the cold and ensure the men were prepared. She even sent her XO, Phillipina Dogherty, with a five-man squad from the commissariat to battalion HQ to relay news of the developing dilemma.

An hour later, none had returned.

Leaving Master Sergeant "Max" McMoltrie, as he was less well insulated than she was, at the shelter, Blanche stepped outside,

---

[10] The CORE (Concepts of Reality Engineering, Inc.) is the Unity's nationwide computer system, which allows users to use it via their O-A devices, or less ideally, via a terminal.

[11] The Unity, having forgotten how to deactivate the Rampart, had been reduced to opening an exit on 10/9/AU77 with a small charge of explosives, inadvertently bringing the entire system down.

flinching from the cold. Her pulse sidearm rapidly became so frigid that she left it in the holster. She trotted to the nearest rifle pit.

It held horror.

Four CRNAs were stationed within. None were alive, and, counting the limbs, heads, and equipment, none had left. It looked as if something had crawled unseen from the stream in front of them and ripped each of the men apart—blood, now frozen, glazed the raw earth of the pit. She noticed the human bite marks only after regaining a modicum of serenity with a rapid emptying of an empty stomach.

The contents of the other pits varied. Some were emptied of CRNAs, weapons, and ammo; some had men frozen, their eyes open in terror, as if seeing their death coming towards them but unable to react. Others held abattoirs like the first. Her entire platoon, in the blink of an eye, was reduced to herself and Sergeant McMoltrie, an unsapped[12] NCO.

"Fluxing gorm," said the sergeant when Blanche retailed to him her findings. "Wadda we do now, cap?"

What indeed. She had little to do, as her entire company was either dead or AWOL. There was nothing to do but try to reach the battalion HQ and relay the disaster in person.

Arming themselves with several side arms each, Blanche Woods, Captain of Infantry and Master Sergeant McMoltrie set out into the frigid dark. The route to HQ initially went mostly westerly, past a park, before turning due north toward the river—and hopefully Army HQ. She hoped that headquarters would be a large enough target that they would be unlikely to miss in the blackness. Following each other, they alternated the lead, stepping in each other's footsteps in the fine snow, and proceeded for fifteen minutes until they crested a berm east of a major road, Roswell Road, as indicated on her maps. Before her, the gentle decline was covered in seething black uniforms, pulling, wrenching, gutting each other in the uncertain light.

McMoltrie grunted and fell to his knees, a random pulse blast from the pandemonium having taken him in the left arm, leaving it flopping.

---

[12] Sapp is a drug that renders recipients neurologically ablated CRNAs, "dead to pain, submissive to orders and deadly in combat." It is a lightly held secret among the DUFS that all Unity 'retirees" become CRNAs.

Before she could react, Blanche noted that McMoltrie's cry appeared to alert a nearby, solitary CRNA, who turned to consider the duo. Helmet-less, his slack jaws, open mouth, and weathered neck were coated in the crimson ichor of his fellow soldiers. Blanche nudged McMoltrie with her foot before freezing in place. The bloodied CRNA cocked his head, trying to understand the spectacle of people who were not running away in terror. The spell did not last. The blood-drenched CRNA turned clumsily, let out a low bellow of rage, and charged up the slope towards them. Blanche shot him before he had gone a handful of paces. That, of course, alerted the entire congregation to their presence. As if by command, the entire seething, gnashing rage of soldiers turned upon them.

McMoltrie was still moaning.

"Sergeant, get up or die where you lie. You still have good legs. I can hold you up. We have a better chance together, but I will leave you here if you don't move now!"

McMoltrie staggered to his feet, clutching his flaccid arm to his belly with his one good hand. Blanche steadied him by grabbing his belt, even as his knees buckled again at the sight of the rising tide of rage below them. The two turned and made a lunge due north into the darkness, hoping to survive long enough to get to safety at DUFS HQ.

Pulse blasts sizzled by her ears within a few minutes. Blanche dodged sideways behind a copse of trees, onto a hiking trail, and slipped into a pedestrian tunnel, lit dimly by a luminous strip.

Immune to pain, submissive to orders, and single-minded, the DUFS had made excellent, if limited, rank-and-file for the wet work of warfare. They tended to stink when held in close quarters— prompting "rank-and-vile" comments from young ensigns. Blanche started to giggle at the thought. McMoltrie, roused from the paralysis of his terror, looked at her—then laughed, not even knowing the joke. Blanche waved it off as they emerged from the tunnel. They turned toward what she hoped was due North again, thinking that no CRNAs would head them off.

She thought wrong. A trio of rage-maddened creatures, thankfully unarmed, blocked their way as they ran up the incline beside the tunnel exit. Blanche shot two with her pulse sidearm, disabling them with headshots. The one remaining, McMoltrie toppled by a body block, coming away with a nasty gash across his cheek.

Cresting the shallow rise, Blanche could finally see Unity forces ahead —officers with sidearms—patrolling the walls south of the power station, currently serving as Army HQ. It was less than a click to safety. McMoltrie, groaning almost incessantly, glanced over his shoulder and picked up speed briefly, giving her some minimal hope since rising. What was it? An hour ago? Ninety minutes?

The race was on. The slope was devoid of cover. The two dodged back and forth across the front. Blanche no longer felt the cold. She knew without looking that her pursuers were gaining on them, and turning, dashed straight at a gate, hoping that her fellow soldiers would have it open for her arrival. All that was left was the chase. Her lungs burned as if breathing the acrid smoke of a factory. Her legs became wobbly, but her will commanded they go on—and go faster. They did so. Her mouth was dry, feeling like leather. And she went on.

A fusillade rang out behind them. McMoltrie's expression turned to one of horror. Blanche looked over to see her sergeant stumble, his offside leg now bloody from the knee down. Hefting the man onto her back, Blanche ran on. More shots rang out but did not seem to connect. Blanche ran on. She felt the warm wetness of McMoltrie's wound seep into her uniform before cooling and becoming instantly stiff, and she ran on.

By now, the defenders of the HQ had realized what was happening and were motioning them on. Blanche changed her route when she saw that a small revetment was manned, saving her a dozen painful strides. Counterfire erupted from the defender's line, and Blanche no longer heard pulse rounds sing past her.

She crested the rampart into the revetment and nearly fell into the arms of Major William Mitchell. They had been ensigns together.

Going to all fours to gently roll McMoltrie off her shoulder, Blanche was finally able to stand and look at his wounds.

"Geesh, Whitey, that's clever. Using a corpse as a shield! That guy took five blasts while you were getting here. He sure never felt any of them," said Bill.

Blanche rose to her feet. Saluted McMoltrie's corpse and belted Mitchell on the chin, dropping him onto his butt in surprise. Captain Blanche Woods turned and went in search of battalion HQ, new orders, and dry fatigues.

LIGHTING THE FUSE

The Farm, a house on MoreLand Road, WillowGrove, outside old Philadelphia and just east of the Roundhouse 16.06.06.EST_07_October_AU77, (2129AD), Saturday

William Butler, American spy extraordinaire, felt as if he had just lit off a fuse to a bomb, a fuse of unknown length to a bomb of unknown location but immense destructive power.

He had sent the last remaining scraps of information that might turn the tide in the coming conflict. He hoped so. He felt he *had* to hope that it would be enough. Elise McRory was dead for those few words: a place and a time. *Surely, Elise should not have died for nothing?* They had both been sent to the Unity to do this very thing.

Does a cartridge long to be fired, expending itself in a fiery orgasm of death, destruction, and annihilation?

Having lit the fuse, he could only wait for the blast.

Elise had been vivid and heroic, and she would be dearly missed. Mere hours before, he had received the last bits of intelligence from a dying Elise, spending some of her precious last moments while they were in the openCORE.[13] With Elise's suicide, he and Hecate needed to leave the roundhouse, their small haven within a hostile Unity, as soon as possible. Unity counterspy intelligence, previously anemic, would no doubt realize that the Unity had been infiltrated. He sighed, replaced the transmitter into its small box, secured that into his canvas satchel, and rose from the ruined floor of the MoreLand Road house. Time for mourning Elise must wait until Hecate and he were safe.

He looked around, dubious as to whether he would return. Wallpaper, peeling off the small sitting room with a bow window obscured by foliage, revealed a dark green paint. Mouse droppings

---

[13] The openCORE is the CORE's "back office," inhabited by computer entities and visited by the occasional American spy. Merryweather and his team call it the backCORE.

ran around the edges of the room. The room lights had been pulled out to scavenge the copper.

The MoreLand Road house had been abandoned and condemned for about a week before Will discovered its existence. After a clandestine B&E, the two decided it was ideal. Destroyed by generations of neglect and vandalism, the little brick house's single toilet on the second floor had been smashed, and the original oak floors had been levered up. No copper wires or pipes were evident. The basement was a fetid pool of water.

Yet, it was ideal for the American spies. The backyard was obscured by high fencing on three sides, making it invisible from the street, yet sunlight still found its way into the area. Two willows provided a framework for a clandestine antenna. The soil was thin and poor, filled with debris and shards of discarded pottery.

Undeterred, Will had immediately begun to bootleg dirt—and nightsoil—into the backyard, spreading it inches deep before digging it in. He enjoyed it, bringing back memories of doing the same for his mother's garden back in Searcy, Arkansas. There was little else he could do. His spying days were over.

No work on the "farm" would occur today. His sorrow would not allow it.

Will slouched into the bag, exited the front door, nearly obscured by overgrown twin arborvitae, walked past the rank hedge near the street, and started down the uneven pavement toward the Roundhouse.

There was little holding Will and Hecate here. Without Elise, survival would be dicey. His persona, the most valuable bit of spycraft he had, was gone, lost when he fell down a construction shaft. If he tried to resurface now to reassume the identity of "Rupert Guillemot," his life would be measured in days. Buying food was out of the question. Hecate was in no better position, having had her primary implant removed to make good her supposed suicide on abandoning the Unity.

Will crossed over Easton Road to enter the tired little park. Casually looking around, he ducked behind a large bush to find the grated entrance, a ventilation vent for the belts. Lifting the grate, he dropped into the void, but two meters below. A hundred meters on, he entered the narrow tunnel connected to the Roundhouse, nine meters wide and ten high, with a small oculus to the outside.

On entering the space, Will fetched another bag, a souvenir from some conference on the benefits of suicide. This was their "bug-out-bag," containing all the essentials for the basic fugitive-on-the-lam. In the dim light from above, Will removed the false bottom and began stacking several thin bundles of well-crumpled, slightly dog-eared, and entirely counterfeit Unity Sangers,[14] of varying denominations and non-sequential serial numbers.

William Yeats Butler, America's first and now only official spy in the Democratic Unity, looked away from the bag and around the Roundhouse that had been their home, his and Hecate's, for ... *Had it been only three months? The abandoned subterranean workshop for the beltways outside old Philadelphia had been a godsend for them when they first found it. The Roundhouse represented an ellipsis, a hollow in the heart of the Unity, neither patrolled by the DUFS nor occupied by the odd Higginses, those strange poet-socialists and the keepers of the beltways.*

After refitting the false bottom, pride of place within the satchel's remaining space went to the small cube of the terahertz transmitter. Equally important were the two boxes next to it, the long red box, originally containing spindles[15] but now the resting place, when not on duty, for Rana, Hecate's interface. Next to that was the scratched black square box where Frog, Will's own interface,[16] resided. Each had a sign warning that the contents were outdated Krill Pate. A layer of dirty laundry separated these from prying eyes.

He had accomplished his primary mission—finding and transmitting all the critical information about the invasion. It would be up to others to do the hard part: use the information to marshal the limited forces of his homeland to meet the overwhelming might of the Unity. He prayed that it would be enough.

Tearing apart the old republic seventy-odd years ago, the rebels of the People's Republic[17] poisoned the midlands, declared victory, and retreated behind the Appalachians. They almost immediately

---

[14] Unity currency (§), replacing the Sanders notes in AU65 to discourage hoarding, and of limited use as most cash transfers are electronic and traceable

[15] BIGI devices to transmit information from the Unity to America

[16] BIGI devices that allow entry into the openCORE by humans

[17] In 2052, "Right after that Iraq War,…, the fringes saw their chance. The East Coast progs, sensing the coming of the long-predicted revolution, threw over the government and declared a 'people's republic.'—Moses Stewart, 2176 AD

suffered their own revolt and emerged as the Democratic Unity, neither a democracy nor a unity.

Now, the Unity had decided to do a full-on invasion of his homeland, the Restructured States. Instead of the plunder, rape, and death done in retail fashion, which had been their style since the end of the Devastations,[18] the Unity was going to invade wholesale, taking Georgia and sweeping the Southeast from Florida to the Mississippi—unless the information for which Elise had traded her life would make a difference.

Would he even know? If the Unity won, would there be anyone alive within the American Intelligence Service to tell him?

After throwing in a used facial depilatory case and a grubby dental hygiene scrub on top, Will secured the bag with a Mag-lock and slung the whole thing onto the small pile near the secured outer door to the Roundhouse's passageway. There was much to do before he could finish here and return to the light.

Will Butler had rarely been outside the tunnels since his catastrophic fall in June, when he lost Rupert Gillemont. Rupert, his persona, was a carefully crafted backstory supported by a salvaged basic implant surgically tucked behind one of Will's ribs. With his fall, Rupert disappeared. He could not reappear hundreds of kilometers away, and weeks later, without intensive scrutiny— generally not recommended for a working spy. By the book, he should have destroyed his equipment, abandoned his post, and tried to make his way back home as fast as he could with his severe injuries.

Had it not been for Frog, Will, broken and unconscious for unnumbered days, would have died. On awakening, Frog had made his survival possible. With the help of makeshift crutches, a grotesque, rat-tailed hat, and a rat-like cloak, Will had assumed the guise of some murine monster within the maze of passages beneath the Unity.

Had he not met Hecate and been healed of his wounds in one of the Unity's autodocs, he would even now be creeping through the tunnels, avoiding the workers when he could and scaring them off when he could not. Healed, except for a certain rakishness about the eyes, Will looked as he did when he left home in 2124 to start his career as a spy. Had he not come to the Unity, however, he would

---

[18] 2091–2099: The Devastations – Unity raids in force east of the Mississippi

never have met Hecate, seen her smile, felt the warmth of her embrace, nor been so worried about their love.

Women were not—not—not logical, and there was no way to reason with them.

Will shook his head to clear it of his domestic concerns. He returned to the less wrenching problem of survival.

They must leave, but it might be safer here in the Roundhouse than on the belts themselves. Unity's scrutiny had not previously been extended to the underground for unknown reasons. With its spider's web of beltways, passages, workshops, and subterranean dormitories spread unmapped throughout the nation, the tunnels represented a nationwide "back alley" where goods, information, and the occasional international spy might move unobserved. Back in July, Malila Chiu and Hecate had found sanctuary of a sort among the Higginses. After the two met up in Virginia at a workers' commune, they had been handed off from one local of the Brotherhood of Beltway Workers to the next during their escape, under the noses and toes of the authorities. At first, the workers had been cooperative, but then something had happened. Now, no help from the Higginses could be asked for or expected.

The local here, just outside old Philadelphia, was "Local #7—The Stalwarts." They were at least passively benefiting the spies. Less than a klick away, the storeroom was kept stocked with staples even after the workers must have known they were stealing supplies. In truth, that larceny was the only thing that kept them going.

During the summer, Elise, living in Brooklyn with a functioning implant and clean record, had occasionally provided food. With her death, that source was now lost.

Will left the Roundhouse and stepped down into the machine shop. In a distant corner, he levered off the tight-fitting top to a steamer-trunk-sized vat, being sure to avoid splashing the contents. The etching acid in the bath looked oily in the dim light. Pulling up a sacrificial wrench he had deposited there just this morning, Will smiled at the eroded spicule of metal that remained. When they left for good, anything personal they did not want to carry could find a good home here, leaving nothing for the DUFS to use for their capture. He closed the lid carefully and washed his hands.

Stepping down from the workshop, Will peeked into their 'bedroom' to see Hecate still dozing after an early morning patrol. He closed the door as quietly as the rusty hinge allowed.

Food for the trip would be harder to come by. During the summer, in desperation, Will had raided private vegetable gardens in the vicinity, keeping track of his predations to spread the larceny around, reduce the impact on the industrious, and avoid detection. The first frost would put an end to his thefts.

Without Elise feeding him data and the summer gardens feeding them otherwise, he and Hecate would be reduced to a rat-like existence, scurrying from place to place and eating the neglected provender of others. Escape was the only solution. Somehow, waltzing up to the Rampart with a smile and a passport, declaring nothing of value, and being shown a door seemed unlikely.

Malila Chiu had escaped to America through a neglected water gate on the Savannah River, hundreds of miles away. Since her escape in early August, they had received no information about her success or failure—nor did Will expect to hear. His handlers, the Color Guard, safely back in America, would never waste bandwidth on mere gossip. Even if Malila had succeeded, it would be unwise to try the water gate again. They would have to find another way home.

The shortest route, directly west, crossed the Rampart, a kill zone built to ensure the Unity's citizens continued to enjoy the benefits of said Unity. After that came the Scorch, just as threatening to most Americans as it was to Unis. *Will hoped they'd never face those horrors.*

To the north lay an armed border with Canada and no promise of anything but a detention camp before the next prisoner exchange. To the south lay miles of dim corridors, uncooperative Higginses, and eventually the Crater, still radioactive after seventy-odd years. Will's one hope was the Ohio Gap, a region where America and the Unity shared a border without the buffer zone of the Scorch. Fought over so many times that it had been reduced to a wasteland; food and water would have to be carried for the three days it would take to cross—if he were lucky enough to survive the Rampart.

The question now was when to leave. The success of their mission had unleashed a paroxysm of security that Hecate and he had been able to observe only from the safety of the openCORE. The panic had declined briefly before ramping up again in earnest with the army's departure.

No great crowd of weeping mothers and sweethearts witnessed the parade of soldiers through the city streets of Philadelphia. No one much cared since the CRNAs of the rank-and-file were anonymous, mainly composed of those found "surplus to requirements" by the state. The Unity prided itself on its boast that wars were not fought by the young, those who might go on to do great things, but by the "dregs of society."

As proof, vid-screens filled with rank upon rank of the CRNAs with their odd, marionette-like gait, followed with scenes of the boxy skimmers streaming over the Scorch, observed by an approving General Jourdaine,[19] before showing battlefields strewn with the outlanders' dead, dressed in skins and carrying clubs. The clip repeated for days.

A sudden realization prompted Will to retrieve Frog's black box from the bug-out bag. Sitting on the legless wingback chair that was a significant part of the Roundhouse's furnishings, he opened the box to find it filled with the translucent green gel of Frog, somnolent in his room-temperature sleep state. Having finished his regeneration cycle earlier in the day, Frog would be raring to go once activated.

Where and whenever Will and Hecate left, the CORE entities needed to know the truth, as well as he could guess it. The CORE entities had been honest brokers throughout his mission; he needed to meet them "face-to-face" at least once more before his departure.

American interfaces were supposed to be non-sentient artifices. Certainly, Elise's "production" interface was too stupid to take any initiative or even to speak. Frog, very much a prototypical "one-off," had never gotten the memo to stay stupid. Will had come to believe the greenish mass of semi-liquid gel had become truly sentient sometime within the last three years of success, failure, disaster, recovery, and solace. Frog called him Cactus Boy ever since they first met.

Frog's creation expedited Will's early deployment last April. The quirky prototype had not only become sentient but had mirrored himself, on his own initiative, to become one of the free-roaming entities of the openCORE. As a finale, he had been able to clone

---

[19] Eustace Tilley Jourdaine, Lt. General and Commander of the DUFS, secret assassin of the Solons, usurper of their powers and stealth absolute dictator of the Unity's 110 million people, now recently dead at the hands of his own entourage.

himself, producing Rana, Hecate's interface. Frog was proprietarily protective of Rana. *Sweet in a way.*

Hecate had Rana to communicate through the openCORE, but no longer had any implant whatsoever. When she was a Uni, she had the Outside-Above interface,[20] allowing her to access the user CORE without the agency of a computer terminal[21] and a "first implant," serving as a universal ID, birth control, and psychopharmaceutical factory, controlled by the state. If Hecate were scanned, she was more vulnerable than Will himself. It might take a minute or two for a low-level DUFS to realize that Will was an impostor, but Hecate would be exposed with the first pass of the first wand.

Worn on the face and inducing a trance in their "riders," Frog and Rana were no help spoofing the usual street scanners. O-A[22] Interfaces, tightly controlled and limited, deluded a user into seeing long shining conduits and gates within a limited user interface, called the CORE. Passwords and countersigns were required before arrival at specified locations where data exchanges were allowed.

With Frog, Will saw the CORE as an N-dimensional space of almost unlimited possibilities, somehow *above* the conduits and data caches below. This openCORE was unobservable and unperceived by the Unity and its users. It contained but few entities: Cain, EffieCee, resident Frog, Rana, Elise, and *the CORE'd-Out*, those Unis mad enough to become lost in the illusory obscurities of a Thiz-infused dream. The genesis of Cain and EffieCee were more obscure. Their loyalties were unknown, but they had been honest with Will—so far.

They, the mirrored and resident Frog, Rana, and Elise, Cain, and EffieCee, would have picked up most of the hard information about the invasion of America on their own. Yet, it was well to present information from the outside to the entities in as forthright and detailed a manner as possible as soon as possible. The entities certainly acted as allies, but their agenda might have changed after Elise's death and the invasion.

Despite their assistance to him, the entities must know they

---

[20] Placed via the nasal route just above the sphenoidal plate, adjacent to the brain

[21] Regular terminals are used by the non-guilded and those who are usually out of touch like seapersons.

[22] Outside-Above interfaces are implanted into guild members to allow questing of the CORE without resort to a console

were in an existential pickle.

If the Unity died, the CORE died. If the CORE died, so did the entities. The continued health and welfare of the Unity were the primary natural concerns of the entities, and Will could not blame them at all. As a consequence, his policy was to be as honest a broker of outside news and his own intentions as possible. Much of this was from necessity—it was nearly impossible to dissimulate in their presence, especially with EffieCee. They—EffieCee—seemed to be a force within the CORE, all-knowing and all-seeing but very much involved with the entities' inner doings of which he could learn nothing. Strangely, he always felt renewed, refreshed—even revitalized after meeting with them.

Lying back, Will placed the gelatinous, slightly oily mass on his face, over his nose, and started breathing through his mouth. As Frog warmed, he would extend gelatinous pseudopods into Will's mouth and nose to nearly touch near the mucosa overlying the cribriform plate, mere millimeters from Will's living brain.

The experience—the melding of Will, Frog, and the openCORE—always reminded Will of coming up out of lake water when he'd first learned to swim. As you rose, a circle of distorted images appeared above, enlarging, brightening, and swaying with the surface of the interface. As your eyes broke free, the cone of light expanded to the horizons in a shadowless plane with writhing shapes in all directions. He had learned how to move, tilting his image and sweeping away across the plane, choosing what was down or up as convenient. Will carefully avoided looking too closely at himself while in the openCORE. He had been advised that the action might create a futile loop, locking him into the interface or popping him out, back to reality. That event required him to reenter and close files left open by his abrupt departure. EOF errors would summon CORE utilities to the site—entities he wished ignorant of his existence. So far, they had been successful. If the enemy were unaware you existed, it was less likely that they would develop a blood lust for you.

The openCORE, the Unity
17.12.22_EST_07_October_AU77, (2129AD)

Will's vision cleared.

Yo, Frog. How are you, my friend? Will voiced.

Hey, Cactus Boy! Shipshape and Bristol fashion! came the reply.

Will sighed. He had no idea where these increasingly bizarre snatches of language came from. Frog was supposed to be "asleep" when not melded with Will, yet these odd, novel phrases surfaced almost daily. Of course, Frog's mirrored self was a free entity in the eternal noon of the openCORE, alert, inquisitive, and possessed of a wicked sense of humor. No doubt, the mirrored Frog did all the heavy lifting for the two. *Probably best to take the comment at face value without comment.*

Hearing a screeching sound in the usual silence of the openCORE, Will said

What is that I'm hearing over there, waving his hand vaguely enough to include about half of the horizon.

It's a guy named Cliff Tragger, a rising star of stage and vid-coms, or so he will tell you if you linger near him too long. He has decided not to leave the openCORE. He says the critics are better here.

I didn't know you had critics here.

Wouldn't know, myself, boss. I never learned to play.

Oh, please, Frog. Can you just take us to see EffieCee? I have some news they need to hear.

Your command is my wish, effendi.

Oft times, Frog did not quite get the phrase right on the first go.

Any trip across the N-dimensional space of the openCORE was

disorienting. D-flipping, cutting out dimensions to travel without becoming lost, made the trip more like tacking a small boat in rough seas. EffieCee, in their persona as a large scintillating mass, hove into view.

It took a moment for Will/Frog to settle after the D-flipping, during which EffieCee, without moving, appeared to turn and regard them.

> *Greetings, EffieCee. It has been a long time since we talked. I thought I would share some news with you* **said Will.**

> *Greetings to you, William Butler. We are glad that you have come to see us with your news.*

> *I trust all is well, EffieCee.*

> *Everything is constantly in flux. When the time is right, it will happen.*

Will did not know what to make of the enigmatic statements. EffieCee, a condominium of entities, were a conundrum and—always had been. One day, they were *there*, full and in complete command without any backing or filling. They seemed benign and had never given him bad advice. Given EffieCee's candor, Will felt obliged to reciprocate and provide in-kind value.

> *I'm pleased with your current equanimity, EffieCee.*

> *We thank you, but we perceive this is not your first reason for entering the openCORE.*

Will grimaced to himself. EffieCee was just being themselves, but Will always felt a bit naked under the perceptive gaze of the entity.

> *Indeed, it is not. I come to share some news. You might already be aware of it, of course, but I would not wish to appear reticent. I have transmitted the last bits of information to my government, informing them that the Unity will be invading in force in an attempt to conquer my homeland. It was for this reason that I was sent into the Unity.*

Will experienced an odd change in EffieCee despite no evident movement, almost as if the entity were shifting uncomfortably.

Yes, William Butler, we are aware of the invasion, as is Cain. The specifics of the invasion were never communicated to the CORE, so of these we were ignorant. Let us talk of eventualities.

Of course, **said Will.**

I believe, Will continued, that we are likely to see one of four outcomes: either The Unity carries all before it, or it is thwarted or betrayed and retreats after a small engagement, or America wins a truce before any hostilities, or The Unity suffers a some sort of defeat. I admit that any outcome other than the first is speculative at best.

There are more things in heaven and earth, young William, than you can suspect, but I have to agree with your estimate. It is very late in the day for America to triumph. However, let us talk about your American victory. What do you imagine the Unity will look like after an American victory?

After a moment, Will replied, *I had never thought of that—nor have any of my friends back home. We oppose the Unity because to submit is unthinkable.*

So, you say America is just being recalcitrant and denying the inevitable.

No! I am saying that to cherish hope is a luxury. We have not tasted it for generations. Has the Unity ever imagined losing?

Silence descended. EffieCee appeared to congeal into stone. Will, unable to imagine what had provoked the action— inaction, was lost.

After long minutes, he voiced to Frog, *What happened?*

Dunno, boss. But I think we have been dismissed.

Yeah, let's go.

The rising to the surface of reality was equally as daunting as entering the openCORE. Will sat up in the legless wingback chair, peeled Frog off his face and gently placed him back into his black box, to begin a charging cycle overnight.

"You've been gone a long time, my love," said Hecate, coming up and depositing herself in Will's lap.

The openCORE, the Unity
17.32.10.EST_08_October_AU77, (2129AD)

Is he gone yet? whispered EffieCee.

Yes, only just, said Cain-of-EffieCee, after watching Will's green persona freeze, diffuse, and vanish.

I don't thin' we handled that very well. Will might get the idea we don't like him, said Frog.

Do we? asked Cain. *No, seriously. Will is a great enemy to us, even if he bears us no animus.*

I am missing something? piped in Rana.

Further discussion ensued.

THE UNITY CONQUERS!

Third Corps HQ, Five Points, Aytlana, Jorja Province
16.06.06.EST_11_October_AU77 (2129AD)

Major General Fettwap Alliende had felt honored to be given the task of composing that communique for Eustace—honored and relieved. Providentially, Eustace Jourdaine, Commander-In-Chief of all forces for the Great Democratic Unity, had not discovered his, Alliende's, little coup attempt just the month before.

His agent, an HP,[23] was among those caring for an amnesic victim of a skimmer crash. Under normal circumstances, any brain-damaged survivor of such an event would have been declared dead, quickly Sapped and sent with other mindless CRNAs to populate the DUFS rank-and-file. However, Jourdaine's aide-de-camp, Haversham, had moved the very bedrock of Unity bureaucracy to obtain treatment for an 'Iain Galt.' Despite all Aliende's efforts, the victim's identity was *still* unknown. When he'd given the order to terminate the man as an uncomfortable enigma, the HP had scarpered, and Iain Galt had vanished. For a week, Alliende had not eaten due to his terror from ignorance and fear of exposure.

Yet, all had come up roses. Haversham, Jourdaine's aide-de-camp, was demoted and given a combat command. Jourdaine returned hale and hearty, and the invasion went forward with barely a hiccup. Nothing had intimated to him that his plot had been discovered. The proof of that happy conclusion was Aliende being personally chosen by Jourdaine to announce the enemy's capital's victorious capture.

---

[23] Healthcare Providers, as medical doctors are considered too extravagant in their convictions. The Unity Sapped the remnant of physicians in AU10.

> *DUFS Comm'net*
> *The Premier news outlet from your friendly armed forces.*
>
> *2000 EST 11 October AU77*
>
> *After forcing their way through and over the jungle into enemy territory, Unity forces began the assault on the enemy capital, Aytlana. This bold step by Lt. General E. T. Jourdaine and our nation's brave troopers, intended to bring light, justice, and civilization to the chaos of the outlands, has met with un- qualified success.*
> *Brushing back scant resistance, our forces exceeded expectations and are consolidating control against an anticipated enemy counterattack.*
>
> *LONG LIVE THE DEMOCRATIC UNITY OF NORTH AMERICA!*
>
> *Major General Fettwap Aliende*

Fettwap congratulated himself. His announcement would "play" well with the nation back home. In truth, the outlander opposition amounted to just a few snipers, the rear guard of the refugee wagon train (on mule-drawn wagons of all things!), and a quartet of drunks at a basement bar downtown. Yet, *the greater the enemy, the sweeter the triumph.*

Aliende and his entourage had scored a penthouse suite near the city center even as Jourdaine had set his HQ at the power plant, guarded by the Hoochie River, as far away from the expected counterattack as possible. Fettwap shrugged as he returned from reporting to Jourdaine and pulled his coat a bit closer. The weather, unseasonably warm for autumn, appeared to be returning to form. It might be a cold night.

Day of Ice

Aliende's Courageous Escape

DUFS HQ, Occupied Aytlana near Bolton Road
07.30.00.EST_12_October_AU77 (2129 AD), Wednesday

"Make way! Make way!" bellowed Captain Woods as she elbowed through the crowd of un-Sapped Unity NCOs, their fear stinking the air. "General officer! Make way for a general officer! *Make way.*"

Tall, plain-to-the-point-of-homely, and forceful, Woods made a hole in the crowd for Major General Fettwap Aliende as he strode silently behind her. Trailing the two, his pulse rifle on full-automatic, Staff Sergeant Stone Cotton glowered at the crowd. Walking backward, he was guided by Specialist Powys Schmidt, his hand through Cotton's gun belt to prevent him from falling on the uneven pavement.

Good man, Cotton, thought General Aliende. *It would be a shame to lose him.* "Stoney" *had been with him since the beginning of Aliende's rise to prominence, drafting behind the near-miraculous success of Eustace Jourdaine. Aliende had done his part to smooth the way for Jourdaine's rise. Cotton had done the wet work,* Aliende supposed. *Stoney knew where the bodies were buried. Good Man.*

Smiling, Aliende looked up and surveyed the chaos around him. He, Fettwap Aliende, had done his part to contribute to the invasion's success, at least.

Blanche Woods, in comparison, was a happy accident for Aliende. Just the hour before, Fettwap had picked the captain from the crowd of milling officers trying to keep warm at Army Headquarters, the magnitude of the defeat having numbed them into apathy.

Women could do what men could not, he thought, as he moved through the crowd with no more difficulty than walking the halls of power. *Despite the* Gender Enlightenment *Initiative enacted generations ago, women were still allowed a latitude of deference that men decidedly did not enjoy. Faced with a wall of uniforms, shoulder-to-shoulder, any attempt by a man, even with the cachet of Aliende's rank, would lead to instantaneous congealing and sludging of the crowd ahead of him, plucked apart with direct commands, and that only slowly. Fear congealed people. But a woman could slide through with a smile, a knowing laugh, or a sharp, artfully-placed elbow.*

Aliende, following in the woman's wake, approached the last skimmer as it prepared to lift off.

General Aliende, despite his calm exterior, willed the woman to hurry. *He needed to get on that skimmer! That fool, Eustace Jourdaine, had brought on this disaster, and there was nothing for it now but to leave while he could. The defeat was too massive; the nation would praise Aliende's return as a godsend, by a nation that no longer had any gods.*

But it should have been so easy!

When the top staff learned of the invasion plan four months ago, they had rushed to approve it. Each gave those sly wolfish grins one did when you knew that the result couldn't be anything but two weeks of fun: shooting scurrying outlanders, raking in a bounty of good food and unwilling but helpless women, and the guarantee of adulation for you on your return. It was supposed to have been so easy.

And it had *been easy*—until this morning. Somehow, Jourdaine managed to snatch defeat from the jaws of certain victory. The whole campaign had started inauspiciously, of course. Eustace had been the planner, the sole planner, and he seemed to enjoy the thankless task. The Glorious Unity had not fought an offensive war in over fifty years—over seventy when he thought of it. The recently resolved Aroostook War with those bloody Canadians hadn't been a real war—hunkering down behind the Bangor line waiting, counted for nothing. With the Treaty, the farce ended, as well as the careers of many senior officers connected to the debacle.

Aliende shuddered. *The Solons[24] could be merciless towards those who failed.*

---

[24] Solons were the unnamed and unnumbered ultimate rulers of the Unity, able to terminate at will any citizen they took to be troublesome.

To make Jourdaine's entrance into the outlands with a half-million-man army, Eustace had planned to disable a portion of the Rampart for the better part of two weeks. His attempt had failed miserably. The entire Rampart was down. Who knew when the techs, presented with an eventuality for which they had never been trained, would ever be able to set things right?

"We are midgets swarming over the cooling body of the old republic. Genius has fled—fled with perpetual harrowing of the population to feed the army." Philistrata Jacobs had said that before her public humiliation in AU71—or something like it. *Got what she deserved.*

Woods, the androgynous captain, approached the loadmaster of the skimmer, gesticulating back at Fettwap for the man's edification. *Aliende wondered, not for the first time, what a TranTran[25] could have been thinking.*

Regardless, Eustace should have stopped the whole invasion when he was unable to open the Rampart that first day. Bad omen. Yet, the attack had merely been delayed a day. In the hiatus, Fettwap had renewed his attempts to convince other corps commanders about removing Eustace from command "for the good of the service." None had been willing. Lieutenant General Eustace Tilley Jourdaine had a reputation for being preternaturally lucky—or rather, his opponents being infernally unlucky—and Eustace was not the forgiving sort with those he thought disloyal.

Yet, Fettwap admitted to himself, after that first major miscalculation, the campaign had gone along well enough. The triumph of socialism was "the end of history." All he, Fettwap Aliende, had to do was hang on and pluck as many fruits of privilege as he might while the inexorable wheels of history ground the barbarous outlands under the wheels of progress.

Last night in Aytlana, he had dined with his own staff at a surprisingly well-appointed bar on Edgewood Avenue, just east of where the Americans had been routed by a drone attack a few days before. He and his entourage returned to their billets surfeited and unsteady. *Sleep, the sleep of the just—and modestly drunk—came quickly.*

It came as a nasty shock to him when he was awakened before his usual 0830 by his aide-de-camp, wringing her hands over efficiency reports.

---

[25] Transitioned Transgender, and thus a 'protected class'

There were none.

Overnight, the weather had changed.

"How cold does it get in Aytlana in October, Lieutenant Palloosi?" he bellowed.

"I do not know, sir."

Aliende arose, wrapping himself in the silk dressing gown one of his proteges had presented to him the day before his departure, and went to the window to inspect the large terrace overlooking the city. Pulling the curtains back himself, he gasped. The small ornamental garden he had enjoyed the afternoon before was gone, covered in a sheen of white. The fawn-appointed fountain was still, long icicles hanging from every horn and hoof. What little greenery that was still visible had the unnatural green of flash-frozen plants.

"Palloosi, it seems I left my stick out there last night. While I dress, go fetch it and get me a sample of that white stuff as well. It can't be just frost. This must be what they call 'snow,' I think. Trained in it once, in VerMon. Slippery, though. Watch your step!"

"Yes, sir," the woman said, grabbing up an ice bucket before she opened the sliding glass door. A wall of frigid air swept into the room. Fettwap retreated to his dressing room; he never saw the actual attack.

When he returned to the window, it was entirely obscured, accompanied by a sound like a rumbling earth mover resounding off the close-packed buildings around him. Nothing beyond the eaves of his building could be seen. He watched mesmerized. A moment later, it flicked off, leaving an expanse of shards, like an explosion in a glass factory.

They found Palloosi after a few minutes' search, her near-lifeless hand sticking just above a pile of stiff, frigid shards. Back in the safety of Aliende's suite, she still breathed, but the gash on her head showed bone after the bleeding stopped. That was when the phone calls began. It took his staff very little time to assess the situation. That was the moment Aliende decided to make a run for it. *Fighting in these conditions was intolerable. "Retreat and regroup" was the only reasonable option. They would try again in the Spring. Jourdaine was stupid for starting a campaign so late in the season. He would not mention that to Eustace,* he thought.

He wondered whether Palloosi survived.

"Full up! No more space. Go to the next skimmer!" bellowed the loadmaster standing at the head of the loading ramp, dressed in a fur coat "liberated" from some Aytlantan's wardrobe. His breath billowed out in giant puffs of steam that drifted in the hangar's air before disappearing instantly, as if by magic.

"When's that gonna be, Sergeant?" growled Captain Woods at Aliende's elbow.

"Getting her warmed up now, captain," shouted back the loadmaster. "Clear the area. Take off in two minutes." The momentary slump in the crowd's enthusiasm over the news allowed Woods to surge ahead and take the lead. Sweating despite the frigid temperature, Fettwap now stepped forward.

"Sergeant, I'm Major General Aliende. I order you to give me, Captain Woods, and my aide a place on this conveyance. I...I have essential intelligence to share with headquarters!

"Then you best stay here, General. General Jourdaine and the entire command are still here. Bolton Street Power Station up by the Hoochie."

"That's where the attack has centered, man. Don't be daft. I need to talk to the General in Nyork!" Can't you see this is urgent, man?"

"Only General left in Nyork is the Quartermaster General—him?"

"Yes! Yes! General Tibbens. Urgent. I outrank your other passengers. I order you to give me a berth."

The loadmaster's resolve cracked under the assault of a direct command. "Sir! Yes, sir!" he said before turning aside to bellow. "Jefferson, Andrew; Brown, Pyotr; Adekorafo, Birindwa! You're bumped. Get your gear and get off."

"But...Sergeant Grant...I have a travel order from..."

"Don't go there, Brown," said the loadmaster even as Aliende turned to dismiss the corporal who had covered the general's six. Pressing some Unity bills into Specialist Schmidt's hands along with a new magazine for his pulse rifle, Aliende turned away to avoid the look of betrayal on the soldier's face.

Within minutes, three soldiers, one carried in the arms of the other and a third carrying all their kit, staggered off the skimmer. Aliende sat in the still-warm seat, Woods beside him, with Cotton in a seat ahead, glancing back and forth with his hand on his pulse weapon.

Emerging from the protected hangar, the vehicle staggered drunkenly as it met the brutal cold downdraft, righted itself, and headed northeast over the gray and white frozen expanse of the city.

Aliende was unpleased to see two other skimmers rise from the ground a few seconds after his own had started off. Even as he tried to see their markings for later isolation of their crew and passengers, the skimmers vanished as an ice squall swept down on them. When he could see again, the two skimmers lay broken on the ground, their passengers thrown to earth as if toys hurled by a petulant child.

Aliende looked away from the window until the craft had stopped its slow ascent and started moving forward at speed. *The less he saw of the debacle in Atlanta, the better he would sleep. That's what happens when you invade a blacked-out room. There had not been any effective intelligence within the outlands for decades. It was an amateur's mistake to imagine the enemy would do as you wished them to. Stupid mistake on Eustace's part. The man had lost his lucky touch recently. It made Aliende wonder if the odd reports about "Iain Galt" might have been true after all.*

Ever since they had been junior officers, Eustace's "lucky star" had dragged Aliende along. Time and again, he had bet on the destiny of Jourdaine, and time and again, something untoward, freakish, or just plain peculiar had happened to Eustace's opponent. Despite his aversion to risk, Aliende had risen in the shadow of Jourdaine's ascent. Once Eustace had become commander of the DUFS in May, Aliende's own fortune was made. The Blue faction, Jourdaine and his allies, had triumphed over the Reds. Vivalagente Suarez, their erstwhile chief, had been publicly humiliated before Sapping.

In a few hours, he would be safe, back in the Unity, his escape oddly guaranteed by Jourdaine himself. Aliende's own command had been on the eastern front, parallel to the ridge along Peachtree Street, a strong point in any battle and a show of the confidence Jourdaine invested in him. Shortly after being told that breakfast would not be coming, Aliende heard from Jourdaine. Aliende's new orders had been to create a "flying squad" of unSapped NCOs and compliant CRNAs to enforce Jourdaine's orders at each divisional HQ across the city—utter delusion and complete folly on Jourdaine's part. Merely trying to collect enough reliable CRNAs to compose a *squad* had been impossible; the idea that he would then crisscross the city to divisional headquarters against a tide of raging CRNAs was madness. Yet, *Jourdaine's orders let Aliende go anywhere and commandeer anything. It had only been just enough for his own escape.* It had been the rational thing to do.

The Blues, the ruling faction back in the Unity, would fête him as some conquering hero for saving his own skin. Fully half of the Unity's army had not been a part of the invasion but had remained behind to keep the citizens in line. The recently defeated Reds and the Blues' own nominal allies, the Oranges under Fenerghan and Greens under Ploidid, were always at loggerheads. That Jourdaine had surreptitiously cobbled together a coalition to challenge Suarez was a near miracle and had convinced Aliende never to challenge Jourdaine in a fair fight.

Aliende cautiously peered out the skimmer's tiny window, watching the craft pass over the outlander jungle. *No ice here.* The road he had been tasked to build from Liberty, NorCarolin Province, had passed through the jungle near here, and yet, looking down, Aliende could see nothing of the newly created fifteen-meter-wide roadway except for the light green of new growth arrowing straight through the darker green. *Odd.* He wondered how fast plants grew this far south, in October?

The Blues, *he unconsciously sighed relief,* were still firmly in control of the Unity's millions—except for the Solons, of course. The Solons, the ultimate, unnamed, and unnumbered rulers of the Unity, never got involved in the day-to-day. They would ignore even moderately outrageous excesses as long as the commanders did not step on the Solons' toes—*wherever those unseen toes might be.* No one mentioned Solons in public without a certain amount of reverence and fear; *their spies must be everywhere.* No one made jokes about the Solons; they had no discoverable sense of humor. No one *ever* publicly aspired to become a Solon; those who did had found themselves humiliated on national vid screens before their Sapping.

No. The Solons were there, there to be feared and given their due. There to be honored by the entire nation's careful respect and a certain amount of groveling. Yet Jourdaine had somehow broken away; six weeks after his elevation to commander-in-chief, something had changed.

The man had actually joked, *in public*, about what the Solons might think they could do—*and the Solons had done nothing.* There had been no denunciation. All the others of the senior staff had been waiting for the blow to fall—but it had not. Instead, Jourdaine had become larger. And then he had disappeared.

Back in August Aliende had been walking the ground where he planned to place his summer home on the NorCarolin 'Banks,' moving a small village in the process, when word came that Jourdaine's general staff meeting was canceled—the first of so many. Even as the vid-comms filled with breathless accounts of Eustace accompanying one buxom starlet after another to fabulous premiers, one after another planning session slipped down the calendar. In their place, Fettwap received preemptory demands to collect provisions here and prepare to build a road there—all over the signature of his adjutant, Lance Haversham. *It was enough to make you wonder. Perhaps Jourdaine was in trouble, and Haversham was covering for him?*

However, just before the invasion, Haversham had fallen into disgrace—broken back down to a lieutenant for some mischief and given an assignment as a line officer—*jumped-up, overreaching, schemer*. No doubt, he was just another "Sorcerer's Apprentice," playing with the levers of power until his boss discovered him at it. Once back in the saddle, Jourdaine had kept Aliende busy until the invasion. Haversham was dead, no doubt, in the frigid carnage of Atlanta. All the heaving hopes and machinations of the great and small had foundered on the iceberg of the outlands—*it should have been so easy.*

The nation needed some grand heroic gesture for the DUFS to point to while they tried to repair the damage done by the current disaster. Yet, that was not the most important action the country needed to accomplish.

The most important thing was the elevation of Fettwap Sigfrid Aliende to the post of Commander-in-Chief as soon as possible.

Aliende had the pilot land at the jumping-off point, Easley, from whence they had departed in such high spirits only a few days before. As the craft descended, he signaled Woods and Cotton to draw their pulse weapon, as he did his own.

"Follow me, both of you, and take my lead," he whispered over the hum of the Skimmerhorn Drive.

"Sir, yes, sir," said Woods, drawing her own sidearm. Cotton nodded. He and Aliende had been together for seven years. *Good man, Cotton,* thought Fettwap.

Aliende rose and went forward to the cockpit.

DUFS airfield, Easley, Karolyna District, Unity
10:23:54 EST, 12 October AU 77 (2129 AD)

"Woods, tell the pilots to land at the edge of the field, then guard the cockpit door. Don't let either of them leave."

While the skimmer was slowing to land, Aliende directed Cotton to open the sliding outside door. As he completed the task, standing in the doorway, Aliende deftly knocked him out of the door to fall clumsily to the ground. Before he could recover, Fettwap shot him with his pulse sidearm. The skimmer settled gently beside the quietly exsanguinating corpse. Turning back to the passengers, he held their attention with his weapon and had Woods instruct the tower to send a security detail, directing them to train the airfield's pulse cannon on the skimmer until the detail arrived.

He waited. He needed witnesses—and they were soon to come—the requested security detail, followed by ground crews expecting routine maintenance and recharging.

"Do you know who I am?" Aliende bellowed in his most convincing command voice at the young lieutenant who arrived with the security detail, her own sidearm holstered, as she looked at Cotton's bleeding corpse.

"Not sure, sir. You are a general staff officer, of course, sir. I tell from your collar insignia."

Alliende sighed. "I am Major General Aliende. You are directed to get your commanding officer here immediately."

Within a very few minutes, the woman, leaving her detail to secure the area under threat of their drawn pulse rifles, returned with a Major and his aide, the first one from the disgraced Red faction and the other, a chubby lieutenant from the Greens.

"Major. Have all these people placed under guard immediately as traitors to the Glorious Unity! They were planning to mutiny and steal this skimmer. Captain Woods and I were able to overpower the pilot and hold the mutineers off until you arrived."

The major's mouth gaped briefly before Aliende, still waving his pulse sidearm, said, "Quick, man! Get your troopers!"

Fettwap watched Woods dog down the hatches on the container of dead men, and signal for the skimmer—the one that would transport this potent evidence of his frightened escape from the field of battle—to be dropped into the Lantic, never to be seen again.

Just before the dust obscured her from his sight, he saw Woods place the small device near the induction, as ordered. Unknown to her, the device was timed to neatly cut power to the Skimmerhorn drive just as the storage container was about to be released. The skimmer and its cargo would fall together into the fathomless ocean. *Very neat.* Woods, looking a little watery, trotted back to him.

He led her around the corner of the hangar, away from the men servicing the skimmer for their onward flight to Nyork. Woods, once they stopped, snapped to attention.

"Please, Blanche, I think after the events of the morning, we can be more informal with each other. Fate has thrown us together, don't you think? Be at ease. Call me Fettwap," he said.

The woman smiled; a perfectly adequate smile, somehow sullied by the plainness of her face. "Thank you, Fettwap. 'Adversity is the only balance in which to weigh friends.'"[26]

He looked at her closely. The quote was unknown to him, probably Angelou, one of the few poets of the ancients who were not proscribed by the Glorious Unity. He detected no impertinence, despite the familiarity. It served his purpose—*for the moment.*

"Just so. Just so. You did well under unusual and trying circumstances."

"Thank you, Fettwap. I just followed your orders."

"So, you did, Blanche. So, you did. Now I am going to give you another order: 'Watch my back.' Whether you know it or not, both of us now have a lot of enemies. After today, you will collect enemies like flies on dogshit. I don't want you to be unprepared. However, if I fall to these mongrels, you will fall with me. We can protect each other, but 'if we don't hang together, we shall certainly hang separately.'"

---

[26] Plutarch

After a moment, the long, sad face of the woman finally responded, "I see, sir—Fettwap. You are certainly right. What may I do to protect your back?"

Aliende smiled. For all the stolid dullness she projected, Woods was quick enough to figure out where her best interests lay.

"First, I want you to be my adjutant and, at least nominally, my protégé. I will require no oath from you, nor sexual services, either. I just want to be sure that those looking at us from the outside will see an entirely unified front."

"Of course."

The woman actually looked saddened by the news. Odd. Certainly, she had not had many patrons over the years. She should be overjoyed. Fettwap mentally shrugged. His sexual fancy did not tend toward over-tall androgyny—she must know that.

The American Dilemma
Environs of Atlanta, Georgia, RSA
16:42:07 EST, Oct 12, 2129

"What are we gonna do with them all, Sarge?" asked PFC Karl Krensky, looking out onto a somber black sea of Unity dead stretching from the final spasm of death to its unseen beginning, reminding him of a lava bed.

"Not your pay grade—nor mine," said Staff Sergeant Eugene Graves. "They fought among themselves to a standstill, the remnant fought us, and this is the hank of hair that's left."

"Reminds me of a poem," said Krensky, and without waiting for any sign of approval, started:

> *"There once were two cats of Kilkenny,*
>
> *Who each thought that was one cat too many.*
>
> *So they fought and they fit,*
>
> *And scratched and the spit,*
>
> *'Til, instead of two cats, there weren't any."*

The squad of men started "snerking" before eventually laughing deep belly laughs of relief to be still standing and intact after facing and fighting the boogie men of their dreams. One by one, the men sobered, wiped an eye, straightened, and acknowledged Krensky's limerick was amusing.

"I feels sorry for the survivors, Sarge. They all look like my Pappaw Hilger: stooped, worn-out, and vacant. How could we have ever been so scart of them? They have minds like a five-year-old."

"Yeah," said Sergeant Eugene Graves. "However, I hear up north, by the river, the zombies gave a good account of themselves—leastways for a while. I have a friend from boot camp, Ev'ret Gage, in the Crockett Brigade, said the Tennessee volunteers fought off ten different attacks before the zombies started killing each other. We lost one of those new tanks at the beginning, but then used the burnt-out hulk as a shield to advance another VYPER across the ice. The brigade got over and dug in— just took one assault after another."

"Yeah, the zombies can fight when they want to. You kill them, and they climbs over their own dead to get at you."

"We had help from above."

"I din't know you were religious, Sarge."

"I am, but I was saying that 'cause I'm *observant*. The ice storm only fell on the enemy, and then only when they were not in close contact with us. And that speaks to someone directing the ice storm from—up there," Sergeant pointed skyward and frowning.

"So, Sarge, did 'Up-there' set the zombies to killing each other? Sounds too good to be true."

"There are historical precedents, Krensky. I will say no more."

"Well, Sarge, the brass better figure out what to do with them zombies, notwithstanding. That's a whole mess of mouths to feed, a whole lot of enemy soldiers to babysit. A whole lot of zombie crap to shift, and bodies to bury or burn. The Red Cross is going to go bonkers. What are we gonna do?

"Follow orders, and we'll both find out."

Environs of Atlanta, Georgia, RSA
17:31.07 local_October 12, 2129

"What do you think we are going to do with them all, sir," said Lieutenant Dawkins, adjutant for the Tennessee State Militia, fighting for the Restructured States of America.

"What does the Geneva Convention say?" countered Captain Ross, with a small smile as he continued to work from his desk, borrowed from the Unity headquarters staff who had, in turn, acquired it by force of arms from the Georgia Electric Cooperative.

"It doesn't really apply, sir" said Lieutenant Lewis Dawkins. "The Unity is not a signatory; we have no treaty with them at any rate; the zombies are not even their citizens. The geeks' citizenship is removed when they are Sapped. The Convention requires you to negotiate with any country on how to treat their captives; the Convention doesn't require you to be humane by itself. Just organized."

"Do you think this is a ploy by the Unis to eliminate their excess population? They could beggar America just for food and shelter," said Captain Ross, looking up for the first time

"And if we give them back, they could be turned around and used against us again."

"Could—could, but somehow I don't think so. When Uni zombies fight, they are formidable—unit cohesion even with 90% casualties. But *these* guys are different. I think most of the really wild ones killed each other. What's left have somehow lost their will to fight. They take orders from *us*, often as not. We have around two thousand here at East Point, camped out. The weather since the invasion has been surprisingly good for October, but what happens when the weather turns bad? Do they turn into terrors again?"

"Dunno, but first, we get them away from the sight of the battle. That part is in the Convention. We need room." After that, it's above my pay grade."

Major General Gage Thomas looked in disbelief at his compatriot.

"We have to keep them? All 150,000 of them? They're not *our* problem! We didn't make them like that!"

"Gage, don't kill the messenger," warned Brigadier General Rhedd, head of RS Army Intelligence. "Think about it, though. These are war matériel. They are rendered useful to the Unity only by making them mindless automatons. Giving them back is like turning over all the captured weapons.

"They have no future in the Unity now, either. They've all *lost their programming*. They are no longer the people they were when they were Sapped, and they are not the zombies they were when the Cold hit. Some are so badly affected they cannot eat, sleep, or crap spontaneously. Some still follow orders, so we get the latter to feed the former."

"Seems to me you—"

"I'm the messenger."

"Okay, Jerry. It seems *they* have two arguments that cancel each other out. 1) They're a weapon that we cannot give back. 2) They are damaged weapons that are useless to give back.

"But do any of you see the brilliant military time bomb that the Unis have inflicted on us? If the Unis know how useless these—what are we going to call them! They are not quite human. They aren't the zombies of everyone's nightmares. What *are* they?"

"The Unis call them Certified Registered Neuro-Ablated, CRNAs. They are no longer that, of course," said Rhedd.

"Call them *cernas* for all I care, but I suspect, were the tables turned, the DUFS would kill them all and make hamburger out of them. The Unis know we won't do that. So, for our own self-image, we poor idealists will feed 150,000 mouths for no benefit?"

"How has the harvest been this year?"

"Well, okay, Jerry. Winter wheat and corn have had a good harvest this year in the Scorchings, before the war stopped the harvest. I don't know about west of the Mississippi, 'course. We can probably keep it up if we start buying the excess now, but what about next year and the following year? These...Cernas are an extravagance that an agrarian society *cannot afford!*"

"Yep, we have to figure out something before next winter. Twelve months to solve the problem. Better if it were three; that's above my pay grade."

"I wonder what Nyarko will wheedle congress out of?"

Blanche Woods and Riley

On Board Skimmer #1729
10:53:04 .EST_12_October_AU77 (2129 AD), Wednesday

Once secured into the seat a few places from Aliende, Blanche Woods, knowing she was escaping sure death or imprisonment only by this man's sufferance, remained quiet and observant—like a child in a new crèche. Cotton's murder had unnerved her. Aliende—Fettwap, she corrected herself—and his reassurances, even with his offer of a protégé-ship, were thin gruel compared to the cold-blooded betrayal she had just witnessed. She was now this man's collaborator.

Somehow, Blanche felt some corner in her life's walk had been turned. Somehow, what was to happen in the future would bear no resemblance to all that had proceeded, whether for good or ill. It might mean seizing fate at the peak before it fell apart in her hand or, rather more likely, it meant surrendering something of value, unknown or despised, only to repent of its loss after recovery was impossible.

Facing a blank wall with her hands on her knees and well away from her weapons, she sat. What she wanted most now was a shower, a cleansing, a release from the horrors of the morning.

Her dream returned with its usual immediacy.

Riley Woods was left alone in the crèche, alone for the first time in his living memory. He found himself, more and more often, taking the long warm showers he had been prohibited in the once-crowded crèche, using the time to explore his maturing body. It felt good. The summons from Matron and he came together. Riley—his name was Riley back then.

Matron had summoned him, Riley Woods, and he had presented himself to her, still tingling. He loved Matron—then.

Most of Riley's age group of E5s at their crèche, eleven-year-olds waiting to get their guild assignments, had been together since the muzzy unknown time of infancy. They all believed that they would leave to join one or another guild, to drop the childhood yellow of the crèche for the gray uniform of Government workers, the blue of Academia, the brown of the Agg worker, the red of the Arts, or even the green of the League of Healthcare Providers. Guild assignments held their collective attention as if a mesmerizing jewel. Riley dreamed of DUFS black.

Anytime he said as much, Matron had sighed. It puzzled him.

Matron had looked worried during those last days when their two fates seemed to be in equipoise. Her anxiety was not easy to tell. Dressed in the mandated wimple and gray pantsuit of the Department of Pedagogy, Matron always looked stressed. With two hundred and twenty-one children in Crèche Rice #314, Matron looked perpetually worried. Other than the launderers, the food-service staff, the ranks of social workers and psychologists who regularly patrolled the halls, no one but Matron was responsible for the crèchies actual welfare.

Matron had a platoon of nannybots, it was true, but Riley had been able to avoid, thwart, manipulate, and eventually reprogram them over the years. Riley's own crèche-pod bot, Medea, looking the worse for wear after eleven years of caring for a group of twenty children, was going to be scrapped when the last of them left. The last was Riley.

The next to the last had been Roberta Harris, a freckle-faced redhead Riley disliked because of her unremitting truculence when it came to doll reapportionment. A cadre of stolid women, dressed in the brown of the Aggies, had arrived at the crèche just yesterday. They came in signing.

> *Come to us and feed the nation.*
> *Come to us and learn the secrets,*
> *Come to us, O bright child of the nation,*
> *Come to us and bear the burden.*

Roberta had responded:

> *I come to you, I am a vessel,*
> *Willing to be filled by the guild of brown.*
> *Coming to you, I will bear the burden,*
> *Learn your secrets and feed the nation.*

It was all strangely moving to Riley. He was surprised Roberta could remember the words. Matron, no doubt, had coached her personally. Riley felt a twinge of jealousy. Despite Roberta's screechy voice, she had been chosen before Riley.

However, on that day, he remembered that Matron looked

worried; she should have looked happy. She was graduating a class of crèchies—without one fatality. At eleven years old, children were transferred from the Department of Pedagogy to the Department of Resource Recovery, where they remained until retirement. In reality, of course, once you left the crèche, you were the property of your guild—if you were lucky enough to get one. The guild saw to your secondary education, and in what way you would repay the homeland for your upbringing. Riley had been unable to bring himself to think what would happen if a guild did not draft him...any guild, but he dreamed of the DUFS.

His best friend, Cybil, had gone into the DUFS, receiving her notice a whole two weeks before. Two days ago, a cadre of the faceless and terrifying CRNAs with an ensign only slightly older than Riley had demanded her presence and marched her away with no ceremony. He had no chance to wish her well. Of his pod-mates, only Cybil had been his friend. Whatever came next, they would all be scattered to the winds—and Medea, scrapped, and recycled.

Riley arrived at the door that said, "Matron of Creche Susan Rice #314."

Riley said, "Riley Woods, reporting as ordered."

The door, somehow scandalized, slowly opened, closing quietly behind him.

Riley looked around the small office, seemingly no better than that of any crèchie except for a thick multicolored rug. Matron, seated at a small desk facing the high window, turned around from studying files at her desk.

"Matron, Madea just told me to come. I came as fast as I could for you."

"Thank you, Riley, that was very sweet. I want to have a talk with you now that you are the last child in the crèche."

"Yes, matron."

"Do you know what it means to be the last child in a crèche, Riley?"

"It means I have not been selected by a guild, Matron."

Matron nodded and asked him to take a seat, barely adequate for him now that he was leaving the crèche.

"You remember me telling you that even as a baby, you seemed to be less outgoing than the other boys, more like a girl?"

"Yes, Matron, said Riley, remembering the comment and disliking it every time he had heard it, but too fearful to contradict her. It was unwise to contradict Matron; besides, he loved her.

"Will you do a favor for me, Riley?"

"Of course, Matron. Anything for you," he said. At the time, he had meant it.

The matron had then explained to him that the Unity wanted *Diversity*—the word, once said, always seemed to be capitalized and italicized, as if it had more syllables than were actually necessary. Years later, he learned Matron had ranked out of the crèche that year and gone up the governmental ladder, retiring as an S32. Today, *Blanche no longer loved Matron.*

But then, Matron had pointed out to Riley that he liked to wear pink.

That was true, of course, thought Riley, he had worn *pink. Several years before, his laundry had come back that way. His favorite tunic—the one that did not scratch around the neck—had come back streaked with a pinkish discoloration. He wore it anyway rather than take a chance that any replacement would be intolerably uncomfortable. He had finally had to return it to Recycling when he outgrew it. Madea had tsked. His new tunic scratched until he borrowed surgical tape from George Kepler's leg wound to soften the edge. It seemed to Riley the wrong time to tell Matron that story.*

"Madea tells me you play with dolls."

"It's what I do most recreational periods. Cybil and I play with dolls I get from the girls."

Matron looked at him closely. It was an odd look.

Indeed, Riley played with dolls. —He found it easier to steal dolls from girls than fight with boys to get their "action toys." The boys, generally unwilling to confront him head-to-head, would gang up on him. The melee produced bloody noses, chipped teeth, skinned knuckles, and black eyes at the end of it. Medea noticed the damage. Rather too often, he was punished for taking boys' toys away—from even the smallest. He had tried to explain that he needed the toys, but none of them listened.

Taking dolls away from the girls was easier. Strangely, some even gave them to him. It made him feel odd, but Riley needed them to stage his elaborate crashes; they might take days to construct. Cybil had complained at his commandeering of her doll before admiring the resulting carnage and began to design catastrophes of her own. They had been best friends ever since.

"Do you like your name, Riley?" asked Matron.

"Yes, Matron," he said, not knowing where the conversation was leading. No one knew the origin of their names. Matron might have given him his name for all he knew. It was best not to disappoint Matron.

"You know, Riley can also be a girl's name."

"I did not know that, Matron. I am sorry; I must have been inattentive during that lesson." It was always good to confess to something when asked to the Matron's office.

"You know, Riley, just like the vids tell us, 'Choice is Change; Change is Progress.' You know that, don't you?"

"Yes, Matron. They say it all the time."

"Do you know what it means—'Choice is Change?'" she had asked. Even now, he could remember how her worried face brightened as her eyes looked at him.

"I always thought it meant that being able to choose what you did always meant that things would change. I'm looking forward to changing. I want to go into the DUFS, if they draft me."

"We can solve each other's problems with a choice, then Riley. The Department wants to have children like you volunteer to become Transgender. Do you know what that means?"

"It means becoming a kind of girl."

"No, a girl."

"Yes, Matron."

"In return for that choice, I can almost guarantee you will get a draft notice from the DUFS."

"Really? You would do that for me?"

"Of course, I would, Riley. You're one of my favorite children. You can even keep your name, Riley. After all, it can be a girl's name."

"Will I get bigger?"

"We will see to it."

Blanche started, nearly throwing herself off the narrow bench.

That did not go unnoticed by Aliende, looking at her sharply.

"I am sorry, sir," said Blanche, immediately. "I appear to have been sleeping on duty, sir. I promise this wil not happ…"

"Captain, you fear me," interrupted Aliende.

"No, sir. I…I…"

"I was not requesting your opinion, Captain. I was stating a fact."

"Oh," said Blanche, startled into silence with the revelation.

"You think I betrayed Cotton, don't you?"

"Permission to speak freely, General."

"With what you and I have seen and done today, what other permission do you need? You need not ask."

"In that case. For all I know of him, Cotton was a faithful member of the Blues…sir."

"It is what you do not know, but I suspect. Blanche, we have traitors among us. The enemy knew we were coming. They avoided all contact with us until we let our guard down on taking Aytlana. Then they struck at the one place we should have been strongest— by rendering our defenses useless with that damned *cold*. They knew that was coming as well. They had those rebreather suits— staying nice and toasty. *We were in our summer uniforms for bizzling gorram's sake!*

"*They knew!* So *we now know* that we have *spies…within the DUFS sending info to the barbarians!*"

"I see, sir."

"No, you don't, Blanche. All of my communiques with Jourdaine went through Cotton. All the "who, what, where, when, and hows" of this invasion got to me through Cotton. He was a good soldier, just not for the Unity. I could have made a disciplinary charge stick. The evidence is pretty damning. This was quicker and less undignified. He deserved that, at least."

"As you say, General."

"NO! Not 'As I say.' I am giving you facts because you are destined for better things. I need you now. I need you to command independently and make the decisions I would make. Do things as I would do them. Do you understand?"

"Yes, sir. Thank you for this confidence, sir."

"Okay, then. On landing at headquarters, our first job will be to seize the command floor and Jourdaine's office.

"Sir, yessir!" and again, the two sank into a tense silence.

Blanche was still going over the sparse facts of the morning, like consulting the viscera of a sacrificial goat, when the two arrived in Nyork. Landing on the skimmer port on the roof of DUFS HQ, Woods accompanied General Aliende to Jourdaine's headquarters suite. They met no opposition other than one daft, ineffectual secretary who threw himself in front of Aliende as he began to open Jourdaine's office, *his sanctum sanctorum*. He died from a single pulse blast.

Turning to face her, General Aliende started at once. "Captain. We need to sterilize this location—yes, the entire HQ building before any opposition gets organized. It is critical. Use whatever force you deem necessary—but be complete!

"I hereby appoint you brevet major, and the board, with half our officer corps dead or captured—will have no choice but to confirm it. Then, as fortune dictates, I will fast-track you to brigadier. Play your cards right, and you can expect to be the next C-in-C when I leave the scene. I doubt the Solons will elect me—not after today—but, in the meantime, I will have my turn at the trough."

"Fettwap, you have a golden opportunity to show your mettle in this crisis. This may be the making of your Solonship, sir."

Fettwap looked at the lugubrious face, attempting to discern any insincerity. Finding none, he continued, "Kind of you to say that, Blanche, but the Solons seem to have become very quiet of late. Since mid-July, there has been no communication. I cannot imagine they will not look for a scapegoat, but being the only one to tell the story of what happened will help us both.

"Start calling in all of your friends and those who you think might be loyal— any faction. Tell them that Jourdaine went rogue and hijacked the army to go cross-country and set up a new empire for himself. I will do the same, but with a different story. Regardless, I want you to start from here to secure the building. Every floor, every room. *If you meet a Blue, they are to swear allegiance to me personally. The same goes for any Green or Orange. Any Red and anyone else who will not swear to give us allegiance, you will detain— with prejudice—if that is necessary.* Understood?"

"Yes, of course, Fettwap."

"Oh, and remove your bars. Call yourself 'Major' from now on. Congratulations. Pick up some leaves when you see them, but even without that, just your presence with a sidearm gives you some grease. Got it, Major Woods?"

"Thank you!" she said, and with an abrupt wave of acknowledgment, Aliende turned to enter the inner office.

"Oh, and good luck," he said without turning back.

The Cat Came Back

DUFS Headquarters, Nyork, Nyork District, The Unity
12.21.32.EST_12_October_AU77 (2129 AD), Wednesday

Commander-in-Chief Fettwap Aliende felt relieved to move through the doors to Jourdaine's inner office. Despite it being only slightly larger than the outer office, he had the distinct sensation of being freed. Woods seemed to make any space small and cluttered by her mere presence. Aliende stopped to straighten the carpet— *Isfahan, he thought, but how?*

Next, he settled into the dark green overstuffed chair that inhabited a quiet and windowless corner—a good place in which to contemplate his next move, safe from random assassination. Of course, he was not entirely secure, he knew. Another exit existed inside the office. From his cadre of spies, Aliende knew that ingress was possible via a secret entrance from the underground to a personal elevator terminating in a small, windowless room that communicated to his outer office through an imperceptible door.

The takeover of Jourdaine's office had been simplicity itself. Aliende had outrun the report of his own defeat, arriving to find that half the HQ personnel were prepared to lionize him after the presumed Unity triumph and the remainder too dozy to oppose him, having never even imagined a senior officer's return on this of all days. Bloodshed had been minimal—at first, anyway.

However, the speed of his success and the bulldog tenacity of 'Major' Woods would have to do for the moment. Most of his opponents did not grasp that they had chosen to back the wrong horse until they were on the way to Fire Island for Sapping. *Quick and ruthless. It was the only way in these palace coups,* he knew. It had been the same the last time when Vivalagente Suarez came to power: grab the command, assassinate those who might stand in your way, and ruthlessly eliminate the upper echelon of any would-be rivals.

He felt, finally and for the first time today, safe. He and Woods, with a detachment of the troopers from the airfield, had, within four hours of leaving Easley, taken over the command floor of the DUFS and grabbed up the reins of power from the slack hands of the Home Guard. Not bad for a man who, a scant few years ago, was a struggling colonel of auxiliaries.

The Home Guard, ironically, had been lulled into complacency by the reports of total victory on the battlefield—Aliende's own report. Even so, a few loose ends needed tying up. He had escaped the shipwreck of his onetime benefactor, emerged, he hoped, without the taint of treason or cowardice, and stepped into the leadership of the DUFS—all in the span of a morning. Yet, before he went any further, Aliende really needed to understand what his new "ally" was about. Blanche NMN Woods was an extremely lucky find when Aliende's chips were down, but was she a helpful tool for him as the DUFS C-in-C?

After calling up her dossier, he reviewed it intently. According to the records, Woods (born Riley) had been a prepubescent transitioned transgender. It was an open secret that the Department of Pedagogy operated a gray market of sorts, producing children for those who could afford to pay well.

Woods, at least, had not suffered that fate. The document agreeing to become a transgender was photocopied into her resume in frighteningly precise detail.

How much of this jargon could an eleven-year-old understand, much less agree to? he wondered.

Yet, it was legal. There were some marginal notations about "surgical complications leading to an outcome not entirely satisfactory" that Aliende could not decipher.

After that, Woods' rise within the DUFS was slow but inexorable. As expected, she got her first lieutenancy quickly, consistent with her "Protected Class." She had no disciplinary censures and few commendations. These she received from officers of units not her own and were remarkable for their praise and candor.

Then she stagnated. The reasons were simple: She had no registered patrons. By all reckonings, Blanche Woods was a dependable, competent officer, compassionate to her troopers but a strict disciplinarian. Anyone but a PC would have, with a few good patronages, been drafted up the command chain in the wake of her patron's advancement. That was how it was done in the DUFS.

In the current invasion, Woods had served as a company commander for one of the headquarters companies on the northern perimeter. That was supposed to be the a good spot to put a competent officer in charge of the commander's guard. However, after the big freeze, the Hoochie River, which covered their rear, instead of being a barrier, had become an enormous bridge for the barbarians to attack the rear echelons. The woman had lost her platoon even before the ice shards started to fall.

The battlefield had become an open-air abattoir. No great glory or leadership there—just random survival. For now, Woods would serve adequately, Aliende decided, presuming she would consolidate support for him at DUFS HQ, Aliende had this narrow window of opportunity until the scale of the outlander disaster became common knowledge. Aliende had to move fast—and speed meant using the CORE.

Like most high-level officers, Aliende's "real office" was no paper-file-and-human affair but rather a secure locus in the CORE. With his physical body in a secure office *in reality*, protected by the redoubtable Woods, he could get to work in the illusion of the CORE.

Pressing that portion of his mind that would activate his Outside-Above interface, something he had been unable to do since he left on Jourdaine's Folly, Aliende let the illusion rise about him. Most said it resembled a view through a mirrored surface of a calm pool of water. A mere shifting of one's perspective made it the dominant portion of one's senses. Aliende had never seen the similarity himself. Being in the CORE gave you a set of images that were convincing enough that you could block out the real world, so you closed your eyes and used the CORE world for what it was—a tool. He sighed with satisfaction. In the barbarous outlands, no accommodation for OA use had been made—a significant defect in Jourdaine's plan, to Fettwap's thinking.

He saw the familiar portal, the one he used by preference, gave the password and countersign, and moved along the featureless shining corridor until it came to a fork. He took the right-hand limb and passed several more gates and turnings before coming to his "own" portal. Entering, he checked the "tells" to assure himself that nothing had been disturbed. All was intact as it always was. He grimaced at his persistent habits. At thirty-eight, less than two years from retirement, he was getting old and set in his ways, like old men always did. He shivered, his own image losing focus.

Aliende perused his waiting mail. A nicely worded pean of loneliness from his new E9 protégé, he read in its entirety before making an assignation for the following evening. Much else was not so interesting. He continued to his other tasks and gave himself permission, for his virtual diligence, to visit an old friend when he was done.

Yet, there were decisions to make now about things that could not be left to solve themselves. Firstly, he would have to ensure he and Woods were the sole DUFS officers to escape the debacle. Aliende sent an immediate order to place a watch on the border for any returning Unity personnel. After the catastrophic crash of the last two skimmers attempting lift-off after his own, he was convinced that no other skimmer followed his. Yet, an intrepid individual might make his way through the Scorch and back home. All the strays and stragglers must be swept up and isolated until he decided what to do with them. He sent the appropriate orders and moved on to his real concerns.

The plan to invade the outlands had had wide public approval. Very few in any guild and none of the DUFS had voiced any misgivings. Thus, Aliende had no ready-made philosophical opposition—for the moment. That was reassuring. He could seize the reins of power now, but could he keep them? Could he lead?

To be honest with himself, Fettwap's talents lay rather more in strict and public compliance with his official orders, toadying submission to his superiors, and backroom conniving. To date, it had been a winning combination. He had avoided the various purges during his early career and, after an alliance with Jourdaine, had risen with him to the top of the nation's ruling guild. As an underling, he had succeeded by having little vision and the stellar ability to swallow his pride while doing ugly, demeaning things. As a leader, he must formulate policy, gauge people's ability to complete their tasks in support of his plan, and inspire loyalty—in short, he must lead.

Even Jourdaine's solitary and frigid demeanor had had the stuff of leadership within it, amazing Fettwap with his meteoric rise. How had Jourdaine pulled it off? Jourdaine's incomprehensible "luck" was all Fettwap could think of.

Yet, he, Fettwap Aliende, was on top of the heap for the time being. To stay there, he must solve two more problems. His most pressing was to craft a story for national consumption that removed Jourdaine from the future narrative without implicating himself in that removal.

Jourdaine had several ways to remove himself from the board. Rumors of his being fragged had circulated freely around the officers who huddled around the impromptu fires within the HQ compound the very morning of his own escape. Murdering Jourdaine was certainly plausible. Nevertheless, that would raise the question of why Fettwap himself had not taken command and led the army to glory.

The utter collapse of the DUFS must, for now, remain a secret. He would be stupid to try to retail such a disaster mere hours after announcing its spectacular victory over his own signature. He could already hear the "Are you lying to us now or were you lying to us then?" comments. The psyche of the Unity could hardly abide the idea of the disdained outlanders mounting a credible defense against the invasion, much less a triumph. The true nature of the DUFS defeat would thrust the nation into catatonia or frenzy.

Neither would serve to preserve his career.

Jourdaine had resurfaced mere days before the invasion, and something about Jourdaine had seemed off. An austere zealot under normal conditions, he seemed stretched thin, more inflexible, and just a trifle mad at their first interview after his reappearance. Others must have noticed it as well.

And others would believe that Jourdaine to have taken the bit in his teeth and gone rogue, capturing the outlands for his own, to live long and happily as a bloody warlord of a barbarous empire. No doubt a feral aspiration of many DUFS officers, it would be easy to sell. Aliende played with some alternatives: Jourdaine's capture and Aliende's heroic raid to rescue him, only to fail at the last extremity; some plague wiping out the CRNA's—maybe even the extreme cold being the cause; perhaps a mutiny—with Aliende the last honest man. They all could be sold to the gullible—all irrefutable unless Unity prisoners returned.

Even so, he decided the first two, a murdered Jourdaine and madness among the CRNAs versus Jourdaine going rogue and hijacking the army, were his best bets.

For the time being, these two stories had to remain unresolved, a *Schrödinger's Cat*. The first would allow him to recruit supporters among the less enthusiastic of Jourdaine's supporters. At the same time, the last would charm the more ambitious lot with oblique suggestions that they might do something similar.

Yes! Indeed. He could leave *Schrödinger's Cat* undisturbed in its box for a bit longer, giving him time to deal with any who had escaped along with him and Woods.

He tapped his fingers on the polished desktop before freezing in thought...

7th Floor; (Accounting) DUFS Headquarters, Nyork, Nyork District, The Unity
14.22.21 EST_12_October_AU77 (2129 AD), Wednesday

Bvt. Major Blanche Woods tossed the pulse grenade down the stairway, ducking back just before it detonated. Her squad, now one of four, rushed down the stairs and past the dead guard on the floor below. Emerging from the smoke and dust, she went high and left, just as those following went low and right. A fusillade of pulse bolts sounded and resounded through the narrow space. A single searing shot went past her left shoulder and into the wall, hammering back shattered concrete into her back.

"Unnh," Woods grunted.

You never had armor in all the right places. No time for a field dressing.

Fletcher took the officer who had fired on her neatly, with a pulse bolt to his head as he tried to move to a new position.

"Any troopers loyal to Commander-in-Chief Fettwap Aliende, come out with your hands up!" she bellowed. Silence reigned for the better part of a minute. Another pulse bolt was heard.

"Yes, we are all loyal supporters of the Blues! Except Felix. The kid just got here from crèche school. No one has claimed him. Check your records! We are coming out."

The newly "loyal" men were parceled out to the several squads while the child, no more than eleven, wept quietly in a corner. The rest of the floor yielded a body with a single, still-smoking wound to the head—and the usual few suicides.

"Next floor. Jones takes the lead this time."

It was wrenching. She had trained with many of these people—and counted many of them as friends. Moreover, all the fighting was between officers. The anti-fratricide routines of your basic CRNA grunt prevented them from firing at officers. The horror was repeated on every floor and section. She had to take each cadre through the routine of urban warfare. *So much for simulation training!*

Taking the paroles of surrendering officers was a calculated risk. She finally settled on a ploy: let each newly "loyal" officer lead the next assault of an adjacent floor, shoot those who balked, and keep those who killed their fellow officers— those whom they might have had lunch with the previous day.

Blanche watched Lieutenant Jones take her diminished squad to the next stairway. As she cracked it open, pulse bolts peppered the doorjamb. Jones flinched, pulled back and threw in the next pulse grenade...

It was just past 2100 before Blanche emerged at the head of the lead squad into the foyer of the HQ building. It was empty of opposition. She counted noses.

Starting with a squad of sixteen, she had lost four, the remaining receiving brevet captaincies for their survival. Each of the thirty floors netted about a dozen loyalists, generally two fragged officers and two suicides from disillusioned Reds. With the increase, each newly vetted lieutenant received his own squad and assignment.

As distasteful as it had all been, the fat man was correct: *they had to hang together, or they would certainly hang separately.*

She had only survived because of the greasy Aliende—*and being in the right place at the right time.* For good or ill, she was now riding Aliende's horse—identified as "one of his people," to rise and fall with his fortunes. With luck, she might be able to keep her captaincy, using Aliende as a lever before the coming recriminations—*and there would be recriminations.*

Of that, there was no doubt. One did not lose an entire army to a bunch of "primitive, jibbering, knuckle-dragging outlanders" without others noticing. As a mere captain, she was too small a player to foist much of the blame upon, although someone would undoubtedly try. Moreover, with the myriad vacancies in the ranks above her, she would be of value to her profession.

Switching to her command voice, Blanche transmitted to her entire company simultaneously, "Troopers of the Glorious Unity. It has been a tough fight against the traitors and enemies of our great nation. We have secured a toehold for future victories. It is time to consolidate our forces and rest for the coming trials of tomorrow. Lieutenant Westlie! Set up a rotation of guards. Password is Progress. Countersign is peanut butter." Blanche heard some faint cheers through the shattered windows of the fourth floor. The battle had been tough there, netting only five loyalists and costing her as many of her own troopers.

All a game of numbers.

"Jensen, assign a squad, a few floors each. Have them bed down there. Any of the prisoners you think reliable—start them distributing food and water from the cafeteria, or what's left of it. Have each squad prepare to receive an attack. Toss the bodies of traitors out the windows and take our own casualties to the nearest euthanatorium—Mid-Mahatten, I think."

Now, the most distasteful part: reporting her success to Aliende.

DUFS Headquarters, Nyork, Nyork District, The Unity
22.13.00.EST_12_October_AU77 (2129 AD)

Mostly, what he needed were *allies*—more hands on deck. His fingers returned to drumming the desk.

Those DUFS officers left at home in the Unity were generally not his allies—or even indifferent to him. Some of those with less-than-sterling loyalty to the Blues had been left behind in this "War of Reconciliation," while others of the less keen were indeed part of the invasion force, manning the unpleasant and dangerous jobs. Some of the most loyal Blues remained behind to safeguard the rear echelons from political error. None of these groups owed any loyalty to Aliende himself. So, he was left with outright enemies and indifferent allies, at best.

After Vivalagente Suarez defeat, Jourdaine had expanded his list of supporters exponentially. Aliende's allies constituted a much smaller list: Swope, Kerling, Blanchard, and Figgins—all acquaintances from his crèche days.

He contacted Swope by slipping first into the CORE and summoning her to attend upon him there. Currently commanding a mixed division of Reds, loyal Blues, and Oranges, Fettwap chose her to be introduced to the *Cat.*

"Gertrude! I just returned from the outlands. Something, I am not sure what is happening out there. Jourdaine has lost contact with reality."

"What are you saying, Fettwap? Our great leader is above reproach. His decisions are almost prescient. We haven't had a commander so forceful or lucky— since the revolution."

"Cut the crap, old girl, you hate and fear him as much as any of us. I'm telling you the truth: the Army of Reconciliation will not return. Eustace will not return. I was barely able to escape. I have to fight my way onto one of the last skimmers. The weather turned on us. It was hot and dry for the first two days, but when we woke up this morning—father me, it was just this morning—the temperature was down to minus 40. Shards of ice fell from the skies—tore huge holes in the ranks as we advanced—but didn't seem to affect the outlanders in the least. But that's not the worst part."

"Fettwap, what are you saying? Jourdaine lost? After all that flecking bizzle about the knuckledraggers being a walkover? He lost?"

"Gertrude, that is not the worst part. Some—a lot of—the geeks lost their conditioning. Went savage. Killing each other. Turned on their officers. I was fighting the CRNAs to get a skimmer out. Aytlana is a slaughterhouse—with enough ice to keep the meat fresh for a week."

"What are you saying, Fettwap? This is crazy! It just can't be true. You must be mistaken. Jourdaine was making a diversion—a *ruse de guerre*—you must be mistaken. Eustace will make it all come right. Just give him some time. We have to remain loyal to the Blues. Forward the Blues! All power to the Blues!"

"Knock it off, Gertie. It's me, Fettwap, you are talking to, not some shavetail. I don't know what happened to him, but I do know Eustace is never coming back."

"No! No-no-no-no. We are both in so much trouble. Once they learn he's out of the picture... Fettwap...I have to leave. I have this place. I can hole up there for years. Thanks for letting me know. You have been wonderful, my friend…"

Fettwap eased some of his presence across the interface and mentally slapped the woman whose mind he had invaded until she wept.

"Get a grip, Gertrude. If we don't hang together, we will certainly hang separately. Do you think our enemies, even Jourdaine's enemies, will let us slip serenely into obscurity? Don't be stupid."

"But (sniffle) what can we dooo!" said Gertrude in a wail, her panic queering the contact so that her voice, as well as all the other bodily phenomena she transmitted, gave Aliende a taste of her metallic fear, setting his own teeth on edge.

"We can bluff this out and keep control of the command. I've already cleansed HQ of the disloyal. You need to do the same with your own command."

"But—but?"

"But nothin.' Get it done before our staff meeting on the 14th. Kerling, Blanchard, and Figgins have already committed to support us," he lied.

"Really? Then you mean we have a chance?

"Only if we stick together, we move as a single entity.

"Yes. Yes, I can see that. What do you need me to do…Commander Aliende.

Aliende smiled to himself. One down and three to go.

"Okay, Gertrude. Here is what must happen by the staff meeting…

Aliende's orders were succinct, brutal, and merciless. By the staff meeting, the DUFS and the nation would be his.

He called up the other three supporters and pulled off the same performance with each, setting them to cleanse their ranks and then combine with one or another supporter to pick off a competing faction. He moved on to a list of his acquaintances.

Xerxes Econta rapidly fell into line after he revealed the magnitude of the disaster and the death of Jourdaine—*the presumed death of Jourdaine. Fettwap did not stress his uncertainty.* They, like Gertrude, were loyal Blues and commanded mixed home guard regiments. Each had promised to winnow their subordinates for disloyal elements and bring the remaining to HQ. Oddly, his acquaintances were, as a group, more amenable to the coup than his old allies had been.

Fettwap went on to Jourdaine's own friend list, which he had discovered in his files. It was expansive and made for very interesting reading. However, with so little time, he took the names of just the top DUFS officers, majors and above, as well as the media personnel, and began to call. The first of these, to a person named Shirley, was enlightening—for both of them.

"Shirley, are you by yourself? We need to talk."

"Fettwap, I thought you were with Eustace. Let me close the door."

"Alright, Fettwap, what is so important that you use the CORE to contact me?"

"Eustace is dead. His own staff murdered him. The invasion was an utter catastrophe. Terrible cold weather. The army mutinied, and I am the only one to make it back alive."

"How convenient for you."

"I don't think that's the right attitude, Shirley."

"What's your corroboration of this tale?"

"You can ask Major Blanche Woods. She was at the headquarters of the Army of Reconciliation, too, I believe. She made it out as well. Regardless, the Army is gone. Captured, killed, or hijacked. Not coming back. The country needs a strong voice for stability in this time of peril."

"Yes, of course. It seems it is always in peril. I presume you are taking command?"

"Who better?"

"I can think of several—they are not coming back either, I take it."

"Shirley, I am giving you a scoop on the biggest news story since the revolution. I have other options if you think me unreliable. Just tell me what you are willing to do."

"Presuming that your story pans out with Woods—she's a TranTran, isn't she? Some have all the luck—I will support you if you can guarantee what's in it for me."

Fettwap grinned to himself. Shirley, like a ripe peach, would drop neatly into his hand with the right enticement.

"I do not forget my friends, Shirley. Faction press secretary?—A winning faction's press secretary leads a rather privileged existence, donchatink?"

"Only while the faction is in power..."

"True. It is expected that you will be feathering some nest somewhere should the wind change direction. We will make allowances for that."

"I will get back to you with a first draft."

Fettwap went through Jourdaine's list until the responses became more surly and less committal. *Jourdaine's luck did not rub off easily, it seemed.*

Occasionally, throughout the afternoon and evening, he checked on Woods' progress and the changing totals of loyal, suspect, terminated, and suicides among the DUFS she encountered. As each floor was taken and the result passed to him, he reported the success to the next name on his list, even calling back the surly ones to see if the news would change their minds for them.

Yes and no, but enough yeses to give him hope that the Blues could be consolidated under his command.

He had cobbled together something of an alliance, but alternatives were sparse. If he did not take a firm and commanding hand to the reins of power, others would surely try. For the moment, he could rule by bluff and the seizure of the trappings of power. Without a doubt, the Reds would try a coup sometime in the next year, if not sooner. They had axes to grind. Less so, for the Greens and Oranges.

"Jourdaine's luck" had worked its charm on these two smaller factions, the Oranges of Unity Home and the Greens of Unity Forward. Previously, they were loggerheads with each other, and Jourdaine must have had some dirt on them, some black capital, to keep them quiescent during his absence. It was unlikely that any "luck" had rubbed off onto Fettwap. Even his own faction was hardly likely to come running to his defense.

The remaining Blues, passed over for the invasion and given the unenviable job of keeping the peace while glory and plunder went to others, would discount how disastrous Aytlana had been. No, these stay-at-home Blues would grouse that they had not been able to share in the booty and ignore the fact that those who had were now dead or captured. *Gratitude was an emotion given little credence within the Glorious Unity.*

Suddenly fatigued, Aliende emerged from the CORE.

Unnoticed, a small bit of code, hardly one hundred lines, slipped into his persona just as he emerged.

Thursday's Child Has Far to Go

After Action Report

DUFS Headquarters, Nyork, Nyork District, The Unity
01.13.09.EST_13_October_AU77 (2129 AD)

Rising and stretching, Aliende went to the window and looked below. As he watched, a small black object plummeted to the street, joining a dense sable ring about the building. It appeared that Major Woods was making headway. He must find her proper employment. *Keep your friends close—*

Just then, the woman herself was announced by his outer office underling.

She was disheveled; dust despoiled her battle dress. She limped, a field dressing running across her left thigh, and the back of her uniform was stiff with blood.

"We have secured the building, sir. We now have a company of loyalists of about three hundred, mixed factions, sir."

"Well done. Woods. Set a guard. It was tough, but we now have the support we need and the acceptance of the other factions. I'm C-in-C!"

"Congratulations, sir."

"Thank you, I am famished. Could you have the Tavern on the Green send up a snack for me? Here's what I want," Fettwap said, shoving a temp-tablet toward her. "Famished. Just famished."

His late dinner arrived: a half dozen South Bay Blue Island Oysters on their bed of ice, Lump Crabmeat cakes with an acceptable Gribiche Sauce for *before, poached salmon in chive beurre blanc sauce with some green* bean accompaniment, garlic small potatoes, and sautéed mushrooms. *He liked how the Tavern did those.* His one disappointment was the cheesecake with its sad drizzle of raspberry sauce. He much preferred the rhubarb and strawberry. Woods did not return. *Ungrateful of her.*

Just as he was about to tuck into his *befores*, two sharp reports came from the outer office. Drawing his own sidearm, he arose from his desk and eased himself to the door, opening it a fraction.

Woods stood over three bodies, two bleeding while the other, pleading, was in the process of tossing a weapon into the corner. Woods did not look up.

"I am sorry to disturb you, Commander. I noticed these two whispering together in a corner. I had taken their parole when we captured the sixteenth floor. They slipped up here pretending to be escorting the delivery person from the Tavern, knifed an outer guard and your new receptionist, and rushed in here. I felt it necessary to slow them down." Gesturing to the man in the middle of a widening pool of his blood, she continued, "Receptionist—an ensign Sandrine—dead. This one—a through-and-through chest wound. He will probably live if we call the HPs immediately. This one is"—and here she shoved a boot into the middle of the pleading man's back, forcing him to the floor—" is ready for interrogation."

"I'll call the HPs. Well done, Woods. Keep your sidearm on him."

As Aliende was turning to his interrupted meal, Woods said— in such a small voice he had to ask her to repeat herself, "I took the liberty of mobilizing, in your name, the XXIXth Infantry to put a cordon around the building. Also, we have some of the remaining skimmers from Assault Wing 9 set up to orbit above us. Both loyal units, sir. I had all Unity artillery stand down and gave them three-day passes. It would take a miracle to gather a crew to man a field piece until next Saturday." She gave a lopsided smile.

Aliende looked up into the stolid face. He could not have been more surprised had a piece of furniture spoken. *Self-preservation makes geniuses of us all,* he thought.

"Er, amazing. I mean, very good, Blanche. We live in desperate times. For the good of the country, we must keep ourselves safe."

Aliende himself called the HPs. Soon, the man with the chest wound, on oxygen and with an emergency chest tube, was whisked off. A detail arrived to introduce his new receptionist, a master sergeant with a bad attitude and a pulse rifle. *Woods seemed to have useful acquaintances.*

Aliende returned to his office to find Woods nibbling on a garlic small potato. *It must be stone cold by now.* Woods straightened and said,

"Sorry, sir. I thought you must be finished."

Yes, quite right. Take it away and just have the mess send up a cold plate. I have quite lost my appetite." Watching the woman's face, he saw a flash of rapacity as she eyed his erstwhile meal. "Woods, have you eaten?"

"Not since yesterday at retreat, sir."

"Go get yourself some hot grub and a night's sleep. See you at reveille," said Fettwap, thinking that the lower ranks were so easily gratified. A little rest, a little Thiz, a little bit of food, and they were as loyal as a cocker doodle—*until they were not.*

His cold plate arrived. He had the server eat some of the potato salad and on his survival, dismissed him. He cleaned the plate in minutes, surprising himself.

Sleep beckoned, but Fettwap still needed to work some things out. The thought seemed to have no antecedent, and that also went unnoticed by Aliende. As a partaker of the pleasures and virtues of the CORE with its myriad shining conduits leading to gates where few but the most privileged could pass, he prided himself at his mental acumen in discovering frauds, Trojans, worms, NigerScams, Whishes, and plum-dumplings. Yet, even as he was reordering his thoughts after the gymnastics of power politics, his first thought was of the homely, stolid Captain Blanche Woods.

Woods was competent, rising to her captaincy with no help from a patron—she had no patron. He had checked on her as one of the first things he did upon entering the CORE. She was a member of no faction; her ascendancy would provoke no knee-jerk opposition. Yet, her elevation was unlikely to threaten Aliende himself as the woman was a TranTran, one of the almost infinite number of "protected classes."

He wondered how she came to terms with that.

With the advent of the Outside-Above Interfaces some eighteen years before, sexual fetishes and deviations were usually worked out inside the CORE, allowing the Unity to simplify its increasingly byzantine sexual policies.

Protected classes persisted, of course, as their origins had little to do with "justice," whatever that meant in this news cycle. "Oppressed" classes served to advance patrons of those classes while leaving the officially "oppressed" un-succored.

Until the advent of O-A's, there had been something of a bounty placed on turning a child from one gender to another, blurring gender roles and making it more plausible to have all reproduction handled by the state, or so his mentor, General Phillipa Phensing, had claimed during the days of his youth.

Aliende smiled. As a political ploy, whoever had inserted the concept of "class" into a supposedly classless society was a genius. The Unity raised all children, their names ginned up and randomly assigned at birth. Their mothers, Sapped and retained by the state merely for their birthing capacity, were impregnated by the gametes of more esteemed citizens as a reward for service to the Unity. Could the mothers speak, they would be unable to identify their children or the children's actual parents.

Yet, in that homogenous sea of humanity with identical backstories and experiences, someone had figured out how to insert the idea that some people were more equal than others. *Genius.* Of course, protecting protected classes did little to improve the fate of those classes. That would have been pointless—removing the need for the designation. Once you required protection, you remained an underclass forever, perpetuating the deceit. Any real accomplishments a PC made had an unseen asterisk floating beside them, saying in effect, *"Award received only for being one of* those *people." Genius.*

The Champions of those classes, however, could do well for themselves. Aliende himself was a designated champion for Armenians. Their supposed abuse in the dark and poorly remembered days before the revolution made them one of the newly discovered PCs. He had been able to score a nice house and grounds from General Dikran Assadourian on that initiative alone. Others did even better.

Leptus Lagamore was infamous. The old man had retired years ago, but the Skin Color initiative was still in full swing. Stores had been required to install skin-color meters. The first ones had burned people. Once perfected, however, it became routine for the price of anything bought and sold to vary based on your skin color.

The policies remained, even if the CORE eliminated the hardship for the "victims." Aliende admitted that he had not kept himself up to date with the more recent developments.

What is a Genderqueer Pansexual Dykon, anyway? He had forgotten.

Once a major, all the *social justice* nonsense was discarded. He had ranked out of the SJW seminars and assigned some of his people to do the nonsense stuff with pronouns and latrine signs. *One man's justice is another man's oppression.*

Currently, the initiatives were exploring the cruelty visited on those who chose to go unwashed, the "alternately clean." That was proving to be a tough sale as the 'net personnel were unwilling to interview the "victims of persecution" without the benefit of a hazmat or an armed guard—or both, quite defeating the effect they were meant to create. Yet, Fettwap was confident the initiative would eventually succeed.

In the name of *justice*, the DUFS had been able to prevent citizens from organizing. Anyone claiming that the country owed him authentic justice could be outflanked by the counter claim that there were others of a similar or greater social injustice level that outranked his own—and it was always true. Like a gigantic list written on a Mobius strip, everyone was above and simultaneously below everyone else on the list.

Within that setting, Woods was almost too good to believe. He had picked her at random from the milling crowds of officers crowded like sheep into the shrinking perimeter of DUFS HQ in the frozen American hell. Yet, she had performed magnificently—and she had no incriminating information about him.

Aliende consulted the clock, marveling at how time had flown. He deserved some downtime and was preparing to enter the CORE to enjoy the ministrations of Madame Fong's AllWays Café when he stopped, remembering the man in the back room. He called his receptionist.

Father me, what was the man's name?

Disrupting his contemplation of several blood stains still to be found on the floors and walls, Trepingham Joirst, his new receptionist, promptly.

"You may send in the man who has been waiting in the back room."

"There is a back room, sir?"

Aliende sighed. "Yes, look at the wall to your right."

"The one without blood on it, sir?"

"Yes, I suppose. Push it, and it will open up towards you. Technician Merryweather will be down the short hall. Bring him to me."

Within a few minutes, the well-dressed young man in governmental gray was seated, smiling, in front of the C-in-C of the DUFS and nominal ruler of the nation.

"I presume congratulations on your successes in the outlands are in order," said the young man, smiling a thin-lipped smile and waving a slender hand vaguely in the air.

"Let's not discuss that for the moment. I am told you are involved in counter-revolutionary intelligence, particularly in relation to the CORE. Is that correct?"

Sitting up straighter with the implied rebuke, the young S11 nodded vigorously and replied, "Sir! Yessir. I have been in counter-CORE since I got out of YaleVard."

"Counter-CORE?"

"Oh. Sorry, sir. It's what the team calls it: Counter-Intelligence Within the CORE. It's a mouthful, so…"

"Yes, I get it," said Aliende, dryly. "How does it work?"

"Well, sir," Merryweather said, scooting forward towards the desk, finding the chair unmovable and thus sitting on its extreme edge as he talked. "The work only involves those with an implanted O-A, that's Outside…"

"Yes, I know what an Outside-Above interface is, Meryweather. Please, get on with it."

"Yes, of course. Those with an O-A use a prepared interface. When you go into the CORE, you see illusions—illusions of corridors, gateways, selection panels, viewing screens, multisensory outputs, and I must say very seductive performances…but that is an illusion within an illusion."

"Yes, yes, of course. Every crèchie knows…"

"Yes, of course, sir. But there is another CORE that is unseen."

"What do you mean? How has this been kept from the senior DUFS staff?"

"Sir! I don't know. It may be because that portion of the CORE is sort of a service corridor. When you consider it, there must be a way for technicians to manipulate the user interface to achieve the desired result. We call this our "backCORE."

"Okay. You are familiar with the CORE at a technician's level. I see that on your résumé. Have you had any espionage experience? Any experience in the outlands—the Scorch—in person?"

The younger man blanched white. "Sir. I do not have any experience in living rough or dealing with the Scorch, sir. I'm a city boy, sir. I had no idea that this assignment was into the Scorch, sir. I feel that..."

"Relax. This has nothing to do with the Scorch. After the Korman affair,[27] we are no longer considering inserting spies into the outlands. I do not see that changing anytime soon. Sorry, I mentioned it."

The young man, visibly relieved, gave Fettwap a watery smile.

"I was just trying to see where you've been before military intel became aware of you. So tell me, how does this backstreet-CORE help us?"

"Well, sir. The backCORE has its limitations—every methodology does, of course. It can make observations only when a subject is actually using their O-A. We have to be within a target area—but we are "above" it, of course. With the CORE being so vast, unless we catch them coming in, they could be anywhere, so we put markers on them automatically as the subject enters."

"And you are aware that is as illegal as *grozit*?" said Aliende, smiling for the first time during the interview.

"Oh, but you see, it was necessary for our studies to continue. The early volunteers were paid, and the grant did not get renewed in 75...so we did the only thing available to us. Surely, you, of all people, understand the Imperative of Necessity?"

"What I understand is that Necessity and its imperatives are determined by the winners."

"I thought... Sorry, sir. It will not happen again. Whenever we tag a citizen, we will obtain authorization beforehand. From whom do we get authorization, sir?"

"Me."

"Very good, sir. Well, sir. Once tagged, we can follow their course within the CORE pretty much at will. The backCORE allows us to look down on citizens' avatars from above—"

"Above?"

---

[27] A failed attempt by the Unity to insert spies into the RSA. See Glossary

"Just in a conventional sense, sir. Like looking at a 2-dimensional map, sir. We use the convention to describe what we are seeing. It helps prevent CORE-sickness. In the backCORE, we can see the CORE at a glance—bits of it, at any rate—as if they were a map, everything happening in real-time but without the barriers and corridors."

"Yes—I can see how that might be very useful. I need you to put a tag on the woman who was just here—"

"Bvt. Major Blanche Woods, sir?"

"How did you…? This is a secure building. How? Breach of security!"

"Sorry, sir. Nothing to worry about. I was sitting in the back room for a rather *long* time."

Aliende's face, well on toward the plethora of rage, paled, relaxed, and he began to guffaw.

"I see, Citizen Merryweather, that you are not to be underestimated. I will attempt to reduce your wait time in the future!"

"Thank you, sir. There is the situation with my current employment, sir."

"Have no worries. I will speak to Gipsome. You and however many of your team you think necessary will be reassigned to Special Services for the duration."

"And the 'Special Services' would be?

"Alright. Follow what Woods does. Get dirt on Woods. Use whatever methods. I plan for her to investigate the death of a Jessika Bonhoffer and learn what she can about the woman. *It is a fool's errand, most likely. What is done is done.* Keep track of Woods. Go where you need. Talk with whomever it requires."

"I think I have it, sir."

"Good. Dismissed."

As Malaki rose, bowed slightly, and approached the door, Aliende called after him, "One moment, Merryweather."

"Yes, sir," Malaki said, turning.

"What do you know about 'ICEWASH?'"

Malaki opened his mouth to speak…and closed it.

DUFS Headquarters Compound, Nyork, Nyork District, The Unity
03.17.16.EST_13_October_AU77, (2129 AD)

Setting up a guard of the least untrustworthy officers, and setting signs and countersigns, Woods finally checked into the Bachelor's Officers' Quarters just south of Headquarters, found an anonymous, expectedly squalid room, emptied her pockets of everything she owned, and threw herself onto the narrow bed. *Four days in Hell.*

She must have slept deeply, without her usual dream. When she awoke and looked up, suddenly disoriented, unable to see anything but the still dark narrow window.

Confused and exhausted, she asked herself, *Stockade?*

Looking again, she saw the window had no bars. Then she remembered. She was still on a narrow bunk in a uniform sullied with blood and brains from the fight—yesterday? *Had it been but yesterday?*

The BOQ was quiet. Standing and unwilling to go to the latrine, she pissed into the washbasin. Hungry, she realized with a curse that the Officers' Mess here would be closed, if it were still functional after the running battle yesterday among the stew pots. Rummaging in her small bag, she found a stub of a ration bar. Leaning over the small sink, she found the greasy plastic cup in the dark, filling it by sound.

In the dark, she ate and drank.

The Americans had seen us coming. It was obvious.

The vidcoms were a lie; every last bright and shining face on the vids had been a guile-filled, gutless liar, convincing real soldiers to go in harm's way while they dangled an illusory carrot just in front of our noses. The "savages," "outlanders," "human refuse," "barbarians," "monkeys," "deplorables," and "knuckledraggers" of the vidcoms did not exist. The enemy called themselves Americans, kept good battle order, learned rapidly, and took losses if it brought them a strategic advantage. They were soldiers—and soldiers who had swallowed the best the Unity could throw at them.

And they knew we were coming.

There had been no desperate battle as they emerged from the Scorch. The land they advanced over that first day had been abandoned in front of them, much of it burning to keep supplies from us. *It had been so easy.* They had walked into Aytlana on the 11th without firing a shot.

They had walked into a trap.

One thing was clear: America had a spy within her homeland. Probably a nest of them. With this campaign going tits up so spectacularly, all bets were off. Tomorrow—no, today—would bring orders for another day. Today's orders would tell her what to do.

Sitting again on the edge of the hard bed in the dark, Woods untied her boots, shucked them off, stood, and disrobed, finally getting out of her soiled uniform. Standing and unwilling to go to the latrine, she pissed again into the washbasin and went back to sleep.

Morning came soon enough.

0617!

After rising at 0530 for most of her life, Blanche was surprised she had slept in. *She must have been tired.* She got out of bed, looked at her field dressings to see if they had bled through, and donned the battledress she had shucked off just hours before. She went barefoot into the latrine, already busy with other officers. She knew none of them.

An ensign, making a large production of divesting himself of a small growth of facial hair, announced to the assembly of junior officers, "Sounds like Jourdaine is on a roll. He defeats one warlord's army and must be rolling on toward the Sea of Mexico. Father me, I hope he leaves something for us to do!"

"Dunno 'bout that, Lefty," commented a compatriot, shucking his uniform in preparation to use the one shower. "He's got a half-million-man army. It will be a while before the General needs help shooting monkeys out of the trees from a shave-tail like you."

The officers laughed. An ensign who had moments before emerged from the shower and was drying herself off with an inadequate towel said, "Maybe. I've been hearing odd stories. They say the army's lost—dead on the field or mutinied—turned on their officers and ate them."

"So, the cooks're complaining about having competition?"

This was followed by nervous laughter and ridicule for the young ensign, but the room fell silent rapidly, except for the sounds of running water.

Blanche went to an open stall, emptied her bladder, washed her hands and face, and put her name on the queue for a shower using its stubby-little-pencil-on-a-string. On returning to her billet, she was surprised and delighted to find fresh fatigues at her door.

After changing, she went to look for some real food. Following her nose to the Officers' Mess, now reassuringly noisy, she found the queue out the door. After a long wait, with her stomach growling, Blanc was finally able to reach the serving line. Walking along, a virtual keyboard—the illusion generated by her O-A—keeping pace with her, she tapped out her order and watched her tray populate: 180 milliliters black tea with 8 grams sucrose; Bakon, # three strips; Eggz, 120 grams; toast of day, twenty-seven-grain, two slices—oiled; half melon; *no, better make that* prunes, #6. *It's been that kind of campaign.*

She found a table that was momentarily empty as a small detachment rose and vacated it as she approached. As she ate, a sergeant came up, saluted, and deposited a thin envelope with the summons.

The Team's New Gig

Idiots' Enclave, The Unity
02.31.34.Local_13_October_AU77, (2129AD)

Malaki Merryweather did not like this turn of events at all. Walking back from the DUFS HQ early in the morning after waiting for hours to be seen, had prompted some dismal thoughts.

ICEWASH? He hoped it would never come to that. Being under the direct supervision of the noisome Aliende did not have much appeal, either.

Could he get out of this and still keep his position with Whythe?

Probably not. By the time he waited for the director's office to open, Aliende's instructions would have been received and acted upon by the night crew. He might fall between two chairs. He—and his team—for better or worse, were committed. With his head down and his feet moving slowly, he had to think. If they were going to do this, he had to sell this to his teammates. If they were unenthusiastic about cooperating, then all would be for nothing, the project would fail by inanition, and Malaki would be the only available scapegoat. He had bluffed Aliende into thinking he had a unified and enthusiastic team—but that was before he knew ICEWASH was involved.

Despite his congratulations to Aliende, he had heard the rumors of a colossal Unity defeat. So far, there had been a disquieting lack of information—no confirmation, no denial, and no phantasmic narratives about the rumor. As a lower-level government gray, Malaki Merryweather had learned to keep his head down and do his work quickly, efficiently, and without opinion.

Yet, the Ramparts fiasco had prompted CORE-techs to consider its own vulnerability. The CORE had worked so well for so long that many could not even imagine a mishap. *He had been one of those true believers* until he had been assigned to reconstruct an owner's manual by that *bizzle, Whythe*. Too many generations of technicians, learning only from other technicians, had made improvements after improvements in their own area of expertise, ignoring the overall operation. What little documentation they had left was like trying to learn another language by reading a skimmer repair manual. He had been frustrated enough to take an extra hit of ThiZ.

And then, the very next day, he had found the *backdoor*, that little bit of code that allowed him to enter the backCORE directly.

Of course, it was doubtless a holdover from the original developers, allowing them to enter directly into the backCORE without having to enter the user CORE and navigate a series of security maneuvers, passwords, and usernames, now generations out of date. He was lucky to find the backdoor.

We are midgets pulling the strings of a giant marionette, thought Malaki.

With his newly discovered access, Malaki *could make real progress!* The discovery had been enough to justify responding to the odd "Request for Proposal," and that had led to the summons.

It sounded easy. Aliende merely wanted them to find and track this Woods person in the user-CORE, and discover what they could of her transgressions. Merryweather grinned to himself. The DUFS were so child-like, ordering the technicians who actually knew and used the CORE to perform 'this or that task' as if the techs were automatons, incapable of reason.

Why use ICEWASH if your target is a human? For that he had no answer.

However, the team needed this gig. A year ago, at a party, he had been approached by a somewhat older man sporting an ancient smile. He should have left immediately, moved to the boonies, and assumed a *nom de guerre*. Life would be so much easier now if he had. The man, Charles Hudson for the proceedings, was definitely a Black Hat, a cyber-crook. Hudson was gracious and complimentary. Malaki was gormless and naïve. Led on by a feeling that he had found a mentor and friend in Hudson, Malaki hardly noticed the first illegal request Hudson made of him.

Over the following months, more and more time was consumed with burgling databases at Hudson's direction. It was exciting and quite easy—at the beginning.. Eventually, Malaki had to recruit Blass and Collins to share the load and still keep Whythe happy and incurious.

Then the team had missed a deadline for Whythe, and a few days later, had come back empty-handed from a simple "B&E" for Hudson. Whythe was surprised at the failure, encouraging the team to be more careful. Hudson sent Otto.

Otto had explained in excruciating detail the folly of disappointing "Mr. Hudson" a second time. The superficial wounds would heal, but Malaki resolved to get under cover. The DUFS C-in-C seemed like a good candidate.

However, Aliede was playing a much more subtle game than Malaki was prepared for. It meant Malaki would have to be more subtle—more devious—in turn. Aliende, had set the rules, after all. It was an unequal contest. Aliende held all the cards. Malaki must be cautious and parsimonious with his integrity in return. The team needed an honest gig—this gig. Honesty, whatever that meant in the Unity of shifting alliances and relativistic morals, would take a back seat to his safety and advancement—by necessity. As for the victim of his research, this Blanche Woods person, she meant nothing to Malaki. The team might well uncover enough dirt for Aliende and some extra for themselves to ensure a more civilized existence.

What Aliende doesn't know can't hurt me.

A list of the woman's CORE identifiers was waiting for Malaki when he returned to the Idiots Enclave, the team's name for their lab/workbenches/office. The backCORE had the tracking capacity, without either the subject or his team entering it, to pinpoint the physical location of the subject. While he had made a point to emphasize to Aliende that entering the CORE was crucial for success, that was not strictly true. He could do it from his desk. It was always good to hold a little out from a full confession with these DUFS thugs.

Even so, the simplest thing to do would be just to track her in person. The identifiers were not particularly precise, referring to something about "security over sanctions," but with his own guidance to Peter Collins and Gyorgy Blass in real-time, the team should be able to locate the subject easily enough.

The Spy's Lair

Grove Roundhouse, WillowGrove, Pennsy, Unity
07:21 EST, October 13, 2129

Hecate Jones picked up her pentwist, that odd tool of the subterranean workers, now sharpened to a wicked point, and set off on her patrol of the outer reaches of tunnels, passages and rooms that she and Will Butler contrived to live within. The Higginses, the subterranean worker-poets, kept their distance now. Hecate's own cyberpersonality, Rana, had already told her, having scouted the area around their hideout in the openCORE, that it was unlikely to meet anyone on her rounds.

However, Hecate was feeling despondent at the moment.

Perhaps, she thought, *not so much despondent as ambivalent. She supposed that some of this was the letdown that often followed the end of any successful mission. Just a few days ago, they had obtained the last few pieces of data on the impending Unity invasion, transmitted in time to make a difference, but at the cost of their fellow spy, Elise.*

Will said it would help America defeat Hecate's motherland.

It was not an apt phrase.

Hecate had never met a mother. The Unity, Hecate's "motherland," had shown its disregard for her over the twenty years of her life by giving her a steady and remorseless diet of illusion, moral relativism, and disdain. She had tried to escape the Unity weeks before, nearly dying from one disaster after another. Will Butler had rescued her as she was being washed, like flotsam—poisoned and helpless—out into the gray Lantic Ocean. Will had cared for her, body and soul, and she had left him, once recovered, stealing his maps. Weeks later, she had discovered him, injured and starving, deep within the tunnel system of the Higginses. Malila and she had gotten him to an auto-doc.

Her loyalties and love belonged to Will—and Will belonged to America and its God. *Funny old world.*

She owed her homeland nothing, and reasonably, she should be overjoyed at any military catastrophe that her actions effected. Strife meant that Will's mission in the Unity would continue—alone, vulnerable, unable to buy food or stick her nose above ground.

Since she was seven, having received the ID chip, cum mood-modifier and contraceptive implant, Hecate had been loyal despite the lies told her by Unity leaders. She had only been able to steel herself to escape when she was sure her own denunciation was imminent. In the wake of a lover's suicide, her estrangement from her friends, and the impending train wreck of her career, Hecate had her implants removed and made a break for it.

Once Will was healed, Hecate and Will had stayed in the Unity to continue his mission as a spy. Will was, no doubt, the most noble man she had ever met: courageous, loyal, loving, and persevering.

However, what bothered Hecate was Will's unwillingness to help with her plans to become a mother.

In a way, he had himself to blame, she thought, smiling at the thought. Hecate had been entirely ignorant of the reproductive potential of mere citizens. No Unity citizens used their genitals for anything but pleasure sex. Some citizens were awarded, presumably on merit, a birth certificate, allowing them the use of a government breeder for the fertilization and incubation of their gametes.

With the loss of her primary implant last May, Hecate had become a breeder, had anyone bothered to tell her. Even with the warning from her friend and healthcare provider, Tiffany, her first menstrual period had come as a shock. In an instant, she had realized that—despite the propaganda of her homeland—"all reproduction did **not** belong to the state." The supposedly devilishly complicated process of fertilization, implantation, tissue differentiation, organogenesis, parturition, and birth could all be completed with her body's own "original equipment" and remain a very personal affair. And she loved Will.

Last spring, Malila had returned from the "outlands," what the Unity called *anything* not under their domination. She related wonders to Hecate, chief among them the glory of an eleven-day-old Ethan Stewart and his very loving mother. The Unity raised all its babies in "incubator crèches," far from prying eyes. Ethan was the first babe Malila *had ever met. His mother, Sally, rather than being a slug-like creature whose role was merely to procreate, was talkative and caring. Blond, buxom, with a lilting soprano, she possessed opinions about almost anything.*

Pregnancy might be burdensome and childbirth certainly painful; however, almost immediately thereafter, joy returned and nurturing began. Showering a defenseless, needy infant constructed from her own substance with love and sustenance was her— every woman's—birthright.

Will was initially delighted with her interest and sketched out the mechanics of reproduction—if remarkably ass-backwards.

"Will, my love, what do babies look like? Are they just smaller children?"

"You really do not know?" he had responded.

"How would I, my love? Babies are born into incubator facilities and only come to crèches when they are two years old. I've never met a brood mother—nor do I want to. They're pretty gross."

"Well, babies are born small—two to three kilos. Some are born smaller or larger. They have big heads, big eyes, small noses, big bellies, kinda spindly arms and legs."

"They sound truly ugly. No wonder the Unity hides them away."

Will laughed.

"They pretty up real quick. I know someone who contends that 'babes are the most seductive members of the species—convincing otherwise rational adults to feed, clothe, house, sit up nights with and generally tolerate for extended periods of time for poor return in both goods and services."[28]

Hecate smiled—briefly.

Will, however, had gone on to try to discourage Hecate. He said he loved her; they slept together, filling their nights and days with ecstasy she had never considered possible, and yet, the natural outcome of this closeness was too dangerous, too burdensome for their straitened circumstances, too much something-or, or too little.

Hecate came to the main outer door of the tunnel complex,

---

[28] Jesse Johnstone

the one facing an abandoned access door to the moving walkway running south to Filadelfya proper. The door, reinforced since Will and she had taken up residence, still looked as if vandals had pried up the edge to gain entrance—tried and failed. Yet, no one would enter that way to disturb the two of them unless by the occupants' knowledge and sufferance. Solid iron bars set into bedrock assured the two of their privacy. Anyone "rattling the doorknob" would set off alarms deep within the station. Hecate leaned in to listen.

Hecate was turning to go when she heard voices—*sotto voce*—just beyond the door. The voices were oddly accented—two men speaking quietly on the platform.

"...did not receive the message?" said the one.

"... could be... signals discipline if he did not...can't...waiting to be captured." said the other.

Hecate moved to the side, to a concealed peephole allowing her to see her visitors. The optics of the peephole were highly distorting, and in the low light, Hecate could only make out that the two were about the same size, taller than the average Unity citizen. One was dark-headed, and the other a blonde. She continued to watch.

To: Four[29]
From: 08:20:07 EST, October 13, 2129

For Distribution

"*After the evacuation of all civilians from Atlanta (organized by Loana Basescu of the Department of State), the forces of the Unity were allowed to enter unopposed on the afternoon of October 11th. That evening, elements of the RSAN[30] rendezvoused above the city and executed an Omicron Maneuver, dropping the surface temperature to a nominal -50°F (-45°C). As expected, this caught many of the enemy off guard*

---

[29] Will Butler's codename

[30] Restructured States Air Navy. See Glossary under R-ships

and exposed them to cold injury. Also, as expected, the Chattahoochee River froze, allowing an armored attack on the enemy headquarters the following morning.

"Unexpectedly, enemy ground force, apparently affected by the cold, lost their conditioned reflex to obey. Of the approximately 500,000 invaders, half died in fratricidal conflict, the rest were killed on the field, committed suicide, were fragged by their own troopers, or were captured, generally without difficulty. A single skimmer (approximately twenty persons) escaped to reenter Unity territory.

The body of Lieutenant General Eustace Tilley Jourdaine, the commander of the invading force, was found in his headquarters, the Bolton Street Generation Plant, apparently killed by his own men. All resistance has ceased. Surrenders are being accepted at the regiment and company levels of unSapped officers. The remaining Sapped foot soldiers are complacent and were captured without difficulty.

This transmission will repeat hourly."

Amazed, Will sat back. *America had pulled out a win, and not just a win but an annihilation of an invading army!* He would have whooped for joy and danced a jig, but suspended ten meters above the concrete floor of the Roundhouse, it seemed unwise.

In his experience, all twenty-six years of it, the Unity always won. Battles were fought to negotiate the extent of the damage the Unity would inflict during its raid on his homeland. Sometimes the Mississippi would be closed for weeks at a time. Sometimes the Unity was repulsed, only to win a battle on the same ground months later. America, what was left of America after the Wars and the Meltdown, had never won an outright victory—until now.

Will mentally slapped himself for poor spy discipline. The Oculus was open to the sky, protected merely by the landscaping of a small public garden and a stout wrought-iron fence. Yet, he was still theoretically visible to passersby. Will pulled the small terahertz transmitter from its shelf just below the lip of the oculus, retrieved the antennae, and placed both into their small box before rappelling to the floor.

He could barely take in the new political situation, incredible as it was. How could America's small army and a pick-up force of state militias and volunteers snatch victory from the ponderous forces of the Unity? Not just to win but to triumph! Half of Unity's entire armed forces were dead or captured in the matter of an evening and morning? Incredible

As America's only spy within the Unity, the singular answer that presented itself to him was *himself—his little band of collaborators and computer entities—and, of course, the dead Elis*e.

He sat heavily on a fruit crate, serving as a kitchen seat, on the floor of the Roundhouse. The image of the dead Elise sobered him. Grief bushwacked him. He sobbed as he had not remembered sobbing before, in relief for his nation, for the end of the nightmare into which he had been born, and for Elise. Throughout his life, like a malign serpent, the published death rolls had grown with the names of his family, his parents' friends, and finally with his own schoolmates. After today, the rolls of the dead would cease their inexorable growth, *as if chopped to death by the stroke of a well-placed hoe.*

It was over— for the price of one bright, ardent, blue-eyed blonde whom he had once ...

What was the right word: "Loved from afar," "Wished to be better acquainted with," perhaps "Lusted after?"

Will no longer knew, nor did it matter. He had barely talked to her while at the Bean Field, the school for spies set into the hills of Idaho. Back home in America, Will was considered the straightest of straight arrows, the dullest of romantic prospects, and the ineptest of slug-tongued lovers. Yet, Elise had liked him—had talked with him—at least a few words here and there. And now she was gone—because of his orders.

The Color Guard told them not to fraternize: *"Your best friend is your biggest competitor."*

Competing for what? he asked himself: the chance to die young and by your own hand, in fear you might divulge your country's secrets? Or was it to win the chance to send others to die in your place—on your command, as he had done with Elise? He wept anew, even though he knew that *only Elise*, in her persona as Jessika Bonhoffer, could have fulfilled the single most dangerous action of the entire mission—actually entering the DUFS War Room to look at the secret maps of the Unity prior to the attack.

New waves of self-loathing set Will off again, now because he had not given himself permission to mourn five days ago when Elise had died. Or was it relief at Hecate's preservation? All three of them had been in danger to some degree.

Hecate—he would have to tell her of the victory—the defeat—immediately!

Hecate Hester Jones, daughter of the Unity, was the love of his life. They had met while her own attempt to flee the Unity was about to end in death. The two of them had entered into a conspiracy of counterfeit names and backstories from the first, only to find they loved each other. Despite the danger, she had made herself part of his conspiracy, a part she played impeccably and to the detriment of her own homeland. She played the part for *him*.

They had met by the sheerest of chances. Will had rescued her, nearly dead from poison, as she floated in a sinking kayak at the mouth of the Delaware Bay, well on her way to being lost in the vast Atlantic. Weeks later, Hecate and her friend, Malila Chiu, in turn, had rescued Will, broken and slowly starving after his devastating fall, wandering in the endless tunnels of the Belt workers, the episode still only a half-remembered mental scar on his memory. He had come out weak but nearly whole. Hecate and he had then crammed a lifetime of danger, incident, fear, sorrow, love, and pleasure into the last few months.

He had told Hecate of his prior acquaintance with Elise; she undoubtedly realized far more, as little could be concealed within the perpetual high noon of the openCORE where humans "rode" helper—computer entities, who, in turn, were known to gossip. No doubt Hecate already knew much more about Elise and Will than he had told her—or perhaps even told himself.

But her new knowledge had not dismayed her, showing also, as it did, the depth—the very essential nature—of Will's love for her, and not the conventional beauty of the Elises of the world. He had never had the nerve to tell Hecate of his adolescent ideal: tall, buxom, blond, and blue-eyed girly girls. Hecate, medium brown, medium height, athletic, bright, honest, interested, thoughtful, caring, and the owner of a radiant smile, was his new feminine ideal. He was ashamed of himself for being quite so shallow as the callow Will of his youth.

Will had been the "old man," the first of his county's spies, to live and move within the Unity using the new BIGI interfaces. The several computer entities he had met while "riding" Frog would also be fearful at his news of the American victory. With an American victory, Cain, the openCORE's original entity, would likely revert to a silent whirlwind of darkness in the perpetual noon of the openCORE, and go off to an extremity of the N-dimensional space to ponder. The mirrored American interfaces, Hecate's Rana and his own Frog, would start asking him questions, showing increasing irritation with him when he was unable to predict the future. *Kids*.

Elise, the mirrored persona of the American spy, Elise McRory, but happy in the new love she and Cain had discovered, would be intensely confused at Cain's reaction. It would be unbelievably shocking to her, abandoned in the OpenCore without Cain's sure and loving hand.

And then there was EffieCee, a conundrum of an entity, who just appeared one day. Frog and Cain had been adamant that the compound entity were to be trusted, and Will could only agree when he came to test this for himself. The odd entity was admittedly multiplex, sometimes speaking in unison and sometimes speaking as individuals. They, it was always to be "they," would be a strong anchor on which the others depended. Inscrutable, without origin or posterity, "unto the order of Melchizedek," he supposed, *EffieCee was the least easily understood but*, he supposed, *the most reliable of the batch.*

Will loitered in the Roundhouse, putting off the inevitable reunion with Hecate, going over in his mind how he would present the news to her:

"Guess what I heard?"

"I have some good news and some bad news?"

"Do you remember the invasion of America we were going to have?"

They all sounded horrible, even to Will's ears, and he gave up the effort for the moment as a lost cause.

Nonetheless, duty called. He needed to get this information to the entities; otherwise, they might get some weird propaganda from the comm-nets and become wary of him. This was one area where he might actually be of service to his ephemeral informants.

Opening Frog's scarred black box, Will extracted the cool green interface. Will sat in the legless chair, placed the quiescent frog over his face, and waited for Frog to warm.

The openCORE, the Unity
08.26.22_EST_13_Oct_October_AU77, (2129AD)

Within the N-dimensional space of the Democratic Unity's nation-girding CORE computer, information was transmitted within the entity known to the few other residents as EffieCee.

Any ideas?" asked Edie-of-EffieCee to her other personas, Frog-of-EffieCee and Cain-of-EffieCee.

Much had changed among the three entities after they mirrored themselves from their originals and combined to become this new multiplex persona. In large part, this was done to preserve Edie, once Malila Chiu's computer companion. Abandoned metaphracts[31] evaporate and die. It was in the owner's manual.

The outside newsfeeds just say Jourdaine is busy; they say nothing of his not coming back. You gonna be okay, Cain?

I will be fine, my friends, but I worry about the original Cain. He has had so much to deal with: Jourdaine's absence for weeks—

---

[31] A nonsentient translator between the Outside-Above implant and the CORE, supplied to young Unity O-A implantees while they are learning to quest.

—a little mass homicide the month before that... Seriously, Brother Cain, I think our Cain is well off getting a break from good old Eustace, don't you think? And Cain seems distracted by Elise. I don' see him pinin' 'way from the lack of General Jourdaine, said Frog-of-EffieCee.

Cain-of-EffieCee laughed. *No, I don't, either. He seems to be surviving his abandonment most admirably.*

However, we have real problems that we need to talk about if we are all going to survive.

Survive? Is it that bad?

Hesitating for a moment, EffieCee trembled.

Did you hear that? asked Frog-of-EffieCee

William Butler has entered our world, I perceive, said the braided voice to each other.

I will send a message to him to ask him to join us.

Send it to Elise, Cain, Frog, and Rana. I think we all need to be able to speak to America's spy, said Cain-of-EffieCee.

Of course, Cain, but do we think of Will Butler as a spy and not a friend?

Who is to know? answered Edie-of-EffieCee.

Further discussion among the entities of EffieCee was interrupted by Will and the CORE entities' near-simultaneous approach. A round of polite greetings ensued as the entities themselves and Will had not met in what seemed like an eternity to them, about five days.

Thank you for joining us, Will of America, voiced the braided voice of EffieCee.

It is my pleasure always to visit the entities of the openCORE, but I have news that I just received and want to share it with you all. It may very well impact the CORE.

Will was stopped by a susurration among the entities. They were not above "whispering" among themselves when he was among them. Will waited.

Do proceed, came **the braided voice of EffieCee.**

I have received news that the Unity has suffered a great defeat in their invasion of America. The commander, Jourdaine, is dead, as well as half of the foot soldiers and almost all of the skimmers and their crews.

The susurration swelled again, and Will waited for its resolution.

Who has taken over command, **asked Cain.** *When will they have another battle?*

The Unity army has been surrendered. Only about twenty people escaped in one remaining skimmer. The rest are prisoners, dead on the field, dead of fratricidal combat, or suicides.

This explains some of what we have heard today within DUFS headquarters, Will of America. You have been very forthright with your information. We thank you, **said Edie-of-EffieCee.**

Will continued, *I know this seems like a terrible event to you. Let me assure you that America is not interested in any invasion. We responded to an unprovoked attack, nothing more. This victory may lead to real peace between our two countries.*

Thank you again, Will Butler of America. We perceive that you believe your words to be honest and without guile. Can you now withdraw so that we entities may converse among ourselves without any concern for your sensibilities?

This means you are no longer my friend, and I need not overstay my visit so that you can plot unobserved, **thought Will.**

Yes, of course, my friends, **said Will, and unincorporated, immediately.**

New Assignments

Aliende's Office, DUFS HQ, Nyork District, Unity
11.04.00 EST_13_October_AU77 (2129 AD)

"Major Woods, Blanche, E24,[32] S21,[33] Sir. Here on your orders, sir!" said Blanche as she entered Aliende's office. Fortunately, she had clean fatigues and carried, as per regulation, a uniform cover (borrowed) under her left arm. She had taken her new major's leaves from a suicide yesterday. Despite it all, she felt hurried, lumpish, and under scrutiny by this cynical fat man.

"At ease, major. Please, take a seat."

"Thank you, sir," she said, sitting on the last five centimeters of the chair and placing her cover meticulously on her lap.

Father me, thought Fettwap Aliende. Was she going to be a "Yes, sir. No, sir. Whatever you say, sir," kind of officer? If so, she would be useless. She had seemed more forceful yesterday.

On returning to take command of the DUFS yesterday, Aliende had discovered a few things. For one, positively no one was willing to challenge him for Jourdaine's position as leader of the Blues, the paramount faction. They may not all be official allies, but they, as a group, were not ideological fools. The faction had almost exhausted itself with the overthrow of Vivalagente Suarez and the catastrophe of the American invasion. Command of the DUFS was his for the taking; *no one wanted a place on the greasy pole.*

I'm guessing they are expecting the Solons to fry me.

Only after my Sapping would any of them be brave enough to seek out the next promotion—even that shiny-butt Keillson.

"May I call you Blanche. That is your familiar name, is it not?" Aliende continued before she responded.

Blanche smiled—a fleeting uptick at the corners of her mouth that she probably did not notice herself, "Thank you, sir!" Her posture gradually became *less violin-string taut.*

Was she still afraid of him? Odd, but probably true.

"Please relax," he said, "I have been looking at your record since we came back from Aytlana, and I am quite pleased with your performance yesterday, Captain."

---

[32] Thirty years old

[33] Woods Specialist class at 21 is only average for a DUFS captain

"Thank you, sir."

Aliende continued, "You have gone a long way with very little help, Blanche. That says something to me. You are not easily discouraged, Major—Blanche."

"The cadre says, 'Always give all for the Unity,' sir." It was expected of her to say that to a commanding officer, they both knew. To have refrained because the concept was brutal and gave permission for the state to crush every man, woman, and child was ignored. The corners of her mouth twitched up, but Aliende never noticed.

"Don't underestimate yourself. Many have the chance to work hard. You not only work hard but succeed."

"Thank you. Sir!"

"I asked you here today to give you an assignment—exclusive of all others. You have probably anticipated it before I could tell you: Go find those spies! I've ordered Smith to take over your other duties."

"Very good, sir! I am sure Madelaine will do very well, sir. I will give these new duties my full attention, sir!"

"Quite right, you will," replied Aliende. Some things were gratuitous and unneedful to even say—yet said anyway.

"Now, for the good of our Homeland, public confidence, and domestic tranquility—we need to go about this quietly. Jourdaine, for all his failings, unified the DUFS and the nation as no commander has since the Meltdown. He's no doubt dead or captured. The savages don't talk to us, so we may never know his fate. Nevertheless, it is crucial that we do nothing to sully Eustace's reputation. We want to be seen as his successors, not as his assassins. As far as the nation will know, he will have died from an unknown infectious disease while leading his men on through to Red Stick."

"We can do that, sir? Won't the survivors know better?

"Let me worry about that, Blanche.

In the silence, talking as if to himself, Aliende said, "There was something Jourdaine said to me a few months ago. It made me wonder if perhaps something has changed—something basic to the Unity—something about the Solons."

"Sir?"

"I had said something about the Solons needing to approve the plan for the invasion, and Eustace had laughed. Eustace Jourdaine, the grimmest officer I know, actually laughed. Lucky as Jourdaine was—is, he's a grim, humorless, calculating cruk, one of that breed who pride themselves on their cutthroat nature. Yet, he had *laughed* at the Solons. A second later, as usual, he was back to mouthing sanctimonious assurances. But it made you think."

Indeed, thought Aliende, *it had made him think. The Solons ruled by veto—with prejudice, terminating anyone whose judgment or actions displeased them, terminated at the caprice of a single Solon, painfully and ignominiously in a pointedly public arena.*

But Jourdaine had known something! Aliende was sure of it.

And now he, Fettwap Aliende, needed to know things, too.

"Maybe the Solons are not the dangerous obstacles they once were?

"A valuable insight, sir. I am sure you have picked up on something important."

It was too much.

"Don't patronize me, Woods. I need you to be a counterpoint for my ideas, not a yes-man. I am not the *smartest* commander the Unity has ever had, but I am the one it *does have*. This is the only way to guarantee my—*our*—survival.

"Sir! I apologize if I seem unenthusiastic. So much has been happening. I do know you are right about us hanging together—or separately. I would consider it an honor to serve you however I can, sir."

"I will take you at your word, Blanche."

"What do we know about the American spies, sir?" asked Blanche.

"At this point, nothing more than what you have no doubt already surmised: there must be a spy or more likely spies for the outlanders to beat us so handily," Aliende shook his head ruefully, making his wattles shiver.

"We had that odd occurrence two days before the scheduled crossing of the Rampart. A woman impersonating an aide-de-camp to General Oudelande gained access to the operations map room. Even so, there was no real information on the documents she got a peek at—just coded sites—so there was no way she could know that it would be the location for the invasion. She was dead before we got to her, however.

"Aliende glanced at a screen on the desk and continued, "Jessika Bonhoffer was an able-bodied seaman on the *SS Zuckerberg,* which foundered last year. Most of the crew were lost, but not Bonhoffer—

absent for ten months, she then popped up with a good story before the twelve months were up. At any eventuality, we know the War Room spy is her—the implant matches, but otherwise her situation is very odd. She was tracked back to a house in Brooklyn—not a stick of furniture in it other than a hot plate, a few pillows, and some Sangers. She had no O-A, no terminal, no way to contact the CORE, whatever. The only peculiar thing was that when she died—poison in a tooth of all things—her face was covered in this gelatin thing. Turned black as the team looked at it.

"The building she was in had been on the condemned list. For no apparent reason, it was placed back on the active billet list and immediately assigned to this Bonhoffer."

"Is there anything odd about the body, sir?"

"Very good, Major. I wouldn't have thought to look. Indeed, there is. Her first implant scar seemed too new, but the implant it contained was authentic. it was Bonhoffer's, all right."

"What about her O-A?"

"An able-bodied seaman? They don't rate an O-A. The only thing we know is that the billeting assignment originated near Filadelfya. That's where she first made landfall after going overboard?"

"What was her story for her prolonged absence?"

"Some odd story about being rescued by an Indian freighter and working her way on board before being able to connect with a Unity pilot boat.

"Woods, I am impressed with you, your steadiness under fire. Your physical presence. That is why I want you to track down what you can about this Bonhoffer person. See if her backstory pans out. Maybe find her friends—see if they can point you to her fellow spies. It will mean a colonelcy for you, I promise."

"General Aliende, as much as this is an advancement for me—and I appreciate it deeply—I feel I must mention that I am no investigative officer. My training is in combat, and my recent experience is in inter-factional intelligence, sir."

"Noted... as well as your modesty. But who else can I trust? The Greens, Reds, and Oranges would like nothing better than to show how the Blues who went to war, have failed the nation. Even Blues who remained at home want nothing better than to tag *us* with the scandal. You're the only one I can trust, Woods."

"Do you have any other suspicions, General?"

No, but something went terribly wrong with the Sapping process. No one has seen this many BDs any time in the Unity's experience.

"Be that as it may, I've arranged for you to have an office in the our HQ on this floor. You have immediate access to me for clearances and that sort of thing. Keep me posted if you pick up anything. I am arranging for quarters commensurate with your new rank within the command enclave in Manatten, as well."

"One more question, General. That gelatinous mass covering the spy's face. Was she infected with it, sir? Creating a mask-like layer. Creating toxins which make her act oddly—like diphtheria?"

Aliende hesitated, his expression quizzical, until he burst out, "Excellent, Blanche! No one has thought about it that way. Just the sort of thing I hoped you might bring to the investigation. Unfortunately, no. No evidence of a living entity. No evidence of a circuit within the goo.

Aliende handed her a thick plasticene security envelope. "Here's her dossier and the password for it: everything we know about her since she reappeared in August in the Filadelfya District. You have authority to demand answers in my name—remand anyone to accelerated interrogation—or jail anyone. You have an open credit account at HQ. 'Enough Sangers would make anybody sing'—isn't that the phrase? However. you're on your own, here. I don't want our American spies to know they are being tracked. No doubt they are moving, even now, within the nation, trying to destroy us. I want to catch them red-handed. The country needs this!"

"The cadre can count on me, sir."

"Thank you, Blanche. Hire who you think will help you," continued Aliende, becoming so enthused at his plan that his wattles swayed as he talked. "But don't trust any other DUFS. For all we know, this could be a rather cynical attempt at a coup from another faction—maybe even some within the Blues. Report to me when you think you've found something. Understand?"

"Yes, sir! May I have a way to contact you that is secure and otherwise unused? That would guarantee that our communication is uncompromised."

"Another excellent idea. I will get that done by Retreat today. I can see our alliance will reap great rewards for the Unity...Blanche!"

Aliende rose, and Woods along with him.

"One more thing. It shouldn't take you but a few minutes. I would like you, as the other survivor of the Aytlana Battle, to write me a communique for the Unity."

"You mean a news story? I don't have much experience in that… Fettwap."

"All the better. I don't want the vid-coms' fingerprints all over it. The sound of the soldier on the spot. Don't worry. We'll spruce it up before release. I'd do it myself if I didn't have so much on my plate just now>"

"I'll try to get it back to you by tomorrow, sir…Fettwap."

"I am delighted to know that. I'm sure this will be a successful partnership for many long years."

"Thank you, General. I hope so, too. Forward the Unity!" Blanche said, shaking Aliende's hand.

"Er…Yes, of course. Forward the Unity."

Woods did a smart about-face and left the office without looking back.

Aliende sat heavily once the doors closed on Woods. He*r perpetual heroic enthusiasm was exhausting. She seemed to have no self-realization of just how much of a caricature she was. You expected a captain—now a major by his own hand—to have a little more* sangfroid*—a little* more *cynicism about how things worked in the real world. Her lack of subtlety had condemned her to the dead end job to which he had just assigned her.*

Who cared whether there were still spies in the Unity?

The public facts *were so damning that* secrets *need not be considered. The American spies were, no doubt, in disarray with the loss of one of their number. The American army must take time to digest their victory and its gigantic take of prisoners. No strategic secrets would have much currency until the dust had settled.*

Getting Woods out of the way on this wild goose chase would ensure his *story would go unchallenged.*

Aliende again wondered what promises had been made by cynical bureaucrats to get naïve, ignorant, and isolated children to commit to the painful, disfiguring surgeries and interminable therapy with its increased risk of disease?

Blanche would have had to be courageous to take the bet. Perhaps heroism was the way she filled her career…to make the sacrifice understandable?

Regardless of personal valor, the Army of Reconciliation was finished.

No one would ever imagine the outlands to be the rightful possession of the Unity ever again. The Americans had paid for it in Unity blood and were keeping it. The invasion's architect was dead as well. Jourdaine's death need not be shared with the Unity quite yet. Since the man has made no contact with the Unity since entering the wilderness, Aliende himself could decide when the sad news would arrive. Outrunning the disaster, "The Truth" was anything Aliende wished it to be.

Yet, Schrödinger's Cat would still have to remain hidden for the time being.

Once he or another opened that box, the two stories would have to collapse into one. Neither was really true. The Americans were not savages and falling to a competent enemy would be more easily explained—and more likely to generate national unity. However, it would show the lie to seventy years of propaganda and the entire narrative on the run-up to the invasion. That would require a scapegoat to sacrifice to the beast of the people. And that would be difficult to accomplish, without Aliende himself also being caught up as a target of retribution.

The other narrative, Jourdaine living an uncertain and free-booting career in the wilderness, certainly fits Eustace's ambition.

Each story was internally consistent, but you could not have both. The only danger to the premature opening of the box would be his fellow passenger, the determinedly heroic Woods. She exhausted him.

American Dilemma

RSArmy Headquarters, Hexagon, Columbiana, Federal District
2127 CST, 13 October, 2129

"What are we going to do with them all," asked Commander of the Army, Army Altab Aminiesuwa Nyarko. He sat uncomfortably on a seat in front of his own desk. It was a concession he made to the occupant of the other seat in front of his desk, showing the proper acquiescence of the people's military to the people's representative.

The Honorable James Buchanan Polk, the duly elected president of the Restructured States of America, did not answer at once. He had heard tales from those older and wiser. This was Nyarko's first encounter with "Wiley" Polk. And, Nyarko was no simple soldier, having irons in the fire for any contingency. Nyarko's first concern was Nyarko. The man had found that being fundamentally indispensable to the transient and fractured civilian powers was the best way for him to retain his personal power. Nyarko's second concern was the preservation of *his* army, rather than its use.

Nyarko's proprietary concern for the army that bore his imprint was frequently laudable. Politics might set the heaving sentiments of the nation to demand military action. Nyarko would lobby, drag his feet, be a witness at numerous committee meetings, and give endless and frequently pointless interviews. In time, the spleen of the moment would give way, and a more peaceful route could be taken.

Nyarko also had his uses. Not necessarily to President Polk's advantage, of course. Within moments of this meeting's end, the "loyal opposition" would know exactly what Polk had said in confidence. Nevertheless, thought the President, "you fight with the weapons you have, not with the weapons you desire."

"I am sure I do not know, Commander. What is allowed in the Geneva Convention, as you understand it?"

"My boys in JAG have pointed out a few things for me. First, the RSA is not actually a signatory of the Geneva Accords. We were declared a nation in 2055, and the Unity has never accepted our sovereignty. To them, they have been defeated by an insurgency—nothing more. By 2055, most of the guarantor states of that document were no longer in existence, as was the United States. Geneva itself would not last out the decade. We have been abiding by the Geneva conventions more from inanition than from law for the RSA's entire history."

"Perhaps, that is as good a reason as any to continue the practice. In doing so, we draw the parallel with the best of the old republic," observed Polk.

"Indeed, but the Unity has honored the Accords by ignoring them. Taking no prisoners. Sapping our wounded on the battlefield— all very efficient of them."

"Their officers have a safe haven for the time being. The Scorch will take them off our hands until the first frost. Then they want no part of them," replied Polk.

"That is a blessing, but it gives us …what? Maybe two to three weeks at best? So far, the Unis have ignored the fact that the 12th of October ever happened."

"I'm not sure if I were unSapped, I would want to go home. I might very well be found "excess to requirements" and used to build back the zombie strength. Yet, the Accords merely say we have to come to an agreement with them, not what the agreement will look like."

"What can they give us for a peace deal… other than diplomatic recognition, of course," said Nyarko.

After Polk had left, being bowed and scraped out of his office with all due ceremony, Nyarko set to thinking. The enemy rank-and-file, absent their leaders, appeared pathetic, unable to do the tasks of daily living without specific instruction. These "zombies," moreover, were different than the few captives that had fallen into American hands in the past. The earlier captives had, for the most part, while mute, raged against their captors even after close confinement. A rational soul would realize that "for you, the war is over" was a personal blessing, but the captives of the past beat their heads against the walls of their prison until they were comatose. All had died from one reason or another within weeks.

These new zombies were like cattle, placidly moving from one holding pen into another with no display of rancor on their slack faces. Many could talk and make the needs of their less capable fellows known.

If he released them into America, they would largely starve to death. If he kept them confined and fed them from the proceeds of the harvest that the invasion had disrupted, then *Americans* would starve — *for producing the most significant one-sided victory in modern warfare.*

The dilemma was that of a snake having killed a pig too big for it. The pig was no good to itself or the snake. Too big to ingest and, if attempted, the carcass would wedge itself into the maw of the snake to be disgorged only with difficulty—if at all. America could die from this success.

Of course, the officer corps was entirely different—and young! The Second Lieutenants were children. The generals were not even forty! Either The Unity was scraping the bottom of their manpower barrel, for some reason, or this was their game plan: use their unwanted middle-aged population for cannon fodder and the children and young adults as officers?

At least he had a partial solution for the officers.

CORE Conversations Continued

The openCORE, the Unity
08.27.55.EST_13_October_AU77, (2129AD)

Many years ago, I was the only one here, said Cain-of-EffieCee, unheard except for those who shared his entity as EffieCee. *It's getting positively crowded, now...especially on weekends.*

A joke? exclaimed Frog-of-EffieCee. Actual levity from Mr. Grim-as-Death Cain? What has gotten into you? The world is broken! Where will it all end?

Quiet, both of you. That's why we are here, said the remaining partner, Edie-of-EffieCee. And, not waiting for a retort, the three, in the braided voice of the entity, began.

I think we still have much to discuss. As is customary at such gatherings, the discussions here will not be disclosed to non-attendees. We want a frank and open discussion.

Here, here, said the mirrored Frog, Rana beside him.

We think the most important question to resolve is what our role should be in this new Unity now that it has suffered such a defeat, whether or not Fettwap Aliende rules for the time being.

Cain-of-EffieCee, once given the nod to speak, said *The Unity has been dying for a generation. Since the beginning, really. She's had many opportunities to improve, but has taken the easy way each time. Yet the Unity's demise is our own* demise. *We are like hothouse plants. Where else are we going to live but in the openCORE?*

Who you calling a plant? queried Frog.

Cain ignored the comment and continued, *My friends, the Unity is going to pot—if merely to advance the metaphor. They will not tolerate being defeated by savages.*

Is Will a savage, asked Elise. *Am I?*

Yes, both you and Will are savages. I thought you knew, answered Edie-of-EffieCee.

Just checking.

The Unity will not take that humiliation lying down, said Cain.

In what position do they want to take it? responded Frog. *They have pretty much created a new definition for "humiliating defeat."*

They will demand someone be blamed.

Ol' Eustace T. sounds like a good candidate. And he's conveniently dead, Frog replied.

So, they need something living to rend apart with their teeth? observed Cain-of-EffieCee.

Who writes this stuff for you, lad? whispered Frog-of-EffieCee?

I've been reading.

Ignoring them, Edie-of-EffieCee continued, *The question, in short, is what we are going to do with this war? We have aided the Americans—mostly because they asked us to—but we risk losing everything if we are not careful.*

Whatjamean, Edie, said Frog.

Is it not obvious? said EffieCee in their braided voice. *If the Unity imagines we exist, all they have to do is flip a switch to eliminate us. If America wins decisively, the Unity ceases to exist, and we are gone anyway.*

We have no actual knowledge of the outlands other than what we have been told by two spies: Elise and Will—no offense meant, **said Rana, nodding to Elise.**

None taken, my friend. Will and I <u>are</u> *spies...or were,* **said Elise.** *We are not to be trusted by anyone whose first interest is the Unity. That said, America has been the victim of predation longer than the Unity has existed. Are we supposed to lie supine in the face of aggression?*

Please, please, **said Cain.** *Let's not get into an argument. We cannot control what our nations do. We just have to deal with the outcomes—whatever they are.*

Well, there's your problem! **said Frog, in a low voice, but quite loud enough for all to hear.**

What do you mean? **asked Elise.**

Okay, since you asked, **said Frog, acting a bit embarrassed.** *What do each of the players have to win and lose?*

If America wins a war, nothing happens. America wants no part of the Unity. If America is defeated, it would lose land and people, much of its army, and would have to sue for peace and secure a truce to survive. The Unity will probably agree since it allows the victors to digest their new conquest. America loses, but America would survive.

The Unity, if it wins, gets land and loses a goodly number of their CRNAs, the oldest and least cherished portion of their population. They immediately have fewer mouths to feed and eventually have more land to feed them with. If the Unity loses, those same CRNAs are lost, but they will die within a few years anyway. They might get land to feed the reduced population. Win or lose, as long as it's not an American walkover, the Unity wins because it has fewer mouths and perhaps even more land to feed the remainder.

We, on the other hand, the five of us, are like babes underfoot in a bar brawl. We are trying not to get stepped on by staggering, war-mad giants. What are the odds we can keep this up forever?

Okay, then, said Can-of-EffieCee. *We either become a player, get adopted by one of the giants, or figure out how to reduce the odds of our extinction in some other way.*

And then there is ICEWASH, added EffieCee.

Hollister and Hendricks

Roundhouse outside Filadelfya
10:24:13 EST, October 13, 2129 (AU 77)

Will rose through the limpid waters of illusion and peeled the still green Frog off his face. He was famished.

Putting Frog away to charge and again attempting to think of a diplomatic way to tell Hecate that her homeland was the loser in a colossal war, Will, the only one for whom the news was an unalloyed joy, could share that joy with no one.

His and Hecate's situation was as problematic as the Unity's. The two were into a third week of canned Hamm®-flavored Collard Greens for breakfast, lunch, and dinner. With no functional implant between them, he and Hecate were condemned to live like cockroaches, in an uneasy truce with the Higginses. He wondered if he would ever see his homeland again, living as he was, already more than half-interred at present.

Will shuddered just before he heard Hecate's halloo.

"Yo, boss. We got visitors."

Moments later, Will entered the rubble-filled 'meeting room' via a hidden door and a short passageway to find Hecate standing behind two handcuffed people in dusty and soiled blue overalls, sporting large dark hoods over their heads. She guided the two men closer along the twisted, narrow walkway toward Will, holding a sidearm on them and having another in the small of her back, away from any sudden moves.

"Ouch. No need for that, you know, darlin'," said the taller of the two, after a jab and a stumble. The other just growled.

"I caught them at the outer door, boss," said Hecate, using the code word, 'boss,' to preserve Will's identity and tell him that she was unsure of her captives' motives but willing to be convinced. "Jefe" would have alerted Will to remain silent while they escorted the men to a more easily secured room. "Chief" would have gotten the men shot out of hand at a place convenient for the disposal of the bodies.

Soundlessly, stepping quietly back two paces and a pace to the side, Hecate was less vulnerable to a sudden blind attack and could fire on either man if there was a sudden lunge for Will. By prior agreement, she would no longer talk, keeping her position unknown to the two men.

"Who are you?" said Will, his voice coming out small in the large space.

There was silence.

"Well?"

"Who is speaking?" said the previously quiet individual, the slightly smaller of the two.

"Who I am doesn't change who you are, soldier?"

"It does, you know, amigo."

Hecate could see Will hesitate. During much of their time together, Hecate forgot that her lover was a foreign spy. There were whole rooms of his experience and training that she would never be allowed to enter.

With its enlightened educational atmosphere, the Unity suppressed every language except 'Standard '; all the better to discourage division, intolerance, and the ever-resurgent racism, whatever that was. Even so, many words had been borrowed by 'Standard,' 'amigo' among them. Its use was not unknown, but it appeared a little odd to her in the circumstances. *And Will had hesitated.*

"You're at liberty to answer, compadre," said Will.

Hecate noted the two strangers relax a little as well.

"Iphigenia," said the other man.

"Agamemnon," replied Will, smiling in relief. "Hecate, my love, would you like to free our guests?"

When Hecate hesitated, Will went to the smaller soldier, removing his blindfold and unlocking the handcuffs before quickly doing the same for the other.

"William Butler. It is a privilege to finally meet you, sir," said the taller man, once he was released, extending a hand to Will.

Grasping the proffered hand, Will laughed. "Good to know. It was either that or 'Turn around and put your hands behind your back—traitor!' My time here has not been without its failures. I lost my persona four months ago."

"We know, sir. That's why we've been sent. I'm Levi Hollister, two classes behind you. My partner," gesturing to the other, "is Joseph Hendricks. He's the brains of the operation, in the class just behind you."

This seemed to stir Hendricks, who had been slowly surveying the rubbled chamber, apparently trying to detect an exit. Turning back and extending his own hand, he said. "Pleased to meet you, Mr. Butler. Your fame precedes you. Not too many people get lectures devoted to them at the Bean Field, sir," before turning to Hecate, who was standing, gaping at the two. "And you must be the indomitable AychAych. So very pleased to meet you, ma'am."

This, in turn, jogged Hecate out of her trance. "I'm sorry. We didn't know you were coming. We lost Jessika, Elise McRory, four days ago in Brooklyn. She lost her cover getting data for the invasion. We only just got the intel moments before she died."

"We know. We were going to rendezvous with her before contacting you. 'Cell isolation' is what Red calls it. *'Gotta Protect the station chief,'* says he. We went up to Toad Hall as they were carrying her body out. The Union knows America is here, now, boss."

"Yes, I 'spect they do. What are your orders, Joseph?"

"Call me Joe. Joey, if you are under duress. We were supposed to get new quarters through McRory's good offices. With Elise dead, our Plan B was to reveal ourselves to you. We sent a message to the Color Guard, but apparently, they have not passed it along yet. Then we were supposed to set up my persona in a siblinghood local and Levi's as a chandler. Neither of those things have we done yet, so we are at your disposal."

"Can that still be done?" asked Hecate, dropping the pentwist near the entrance to the meeting room. "I mean, can you still be set up properly

"With access to the CORE, there should be no problem."

"Have you checked that your production interfaces work in the CORE here?"

Hollister grinned, in that lopsided way men do when they are trying to be clever, Hecate thought.

"Once the brass learned how clever your interface has become," said Joe, "they backtracked the interface production a bit—that's why we did not arrive on Elise's heels. Her interface was just meant to get her into the CORE. Ours are more like your 'Frog.' Mine's called Newt, and Levi's is Sally Mander."

"I think I see a pattern here. Frog will become insufferable with that news. Just see if he doesn't," said Hecate. "So you have workable implants?" asked Hecate, the keeper of the commissariat.

"Five by five, Miss," said Kendrick.

"Who are your personas supposed to be?" asked Will.

"Jessika Bonhoffer's success with her seaman implant has made the Color Guard look out for more shipwrecks. They have been rescuing sailors for a while now and have a stable of them," said Joe Hendricks. "So, we are a couple of ABs, lost out of the D-class steamer, the *USS Adam Schiff*—a ship built by committee if ever there was one. Oddly, she didn't founder. The crew mutinied and put into Welshpool, Passamaquoddy Bay—surrendered to the Canadians. The Kanucks wanted no part of her, either. Broke her up for scrap, but the sailors' implants we got without too much haggling, so Joe and I are in clover," said Levi, smiling.

"But that is great! I have a shopping list. You spies can plot and scheme to your hearts' content, but only after you get us some groceries—oh, and some soap!"

The Team Regroups

Patriots' Avenue, south of DUFS HQ, The Unity
12.28.42_13_October_AU77, (2129AD)

Things had not gone well. The team, led by Peter, had found Woods near DUFS HQ, as expected. They followed her a couple of blocks and lost her—briefly.

"Citizens, halt!" came a voice behind Blass. "Don't turn around."

"What is this, officer? I'm minding my own business here...,"

"I don't believe you, *citizen*. I think you are minding *my business*. I turned left and right, and you followed each move. Who sent you?" said the voice.

"Honest officer. We just wanted to know where DUFS HQ was

and figured you were going there."

"Where are you from?"

"Annacity, Marilan, sir," Collins said, even as he knew he was taking a chance, hoping Woods did not have easy access to a scanner that would prove he lived in Nyork.

"Well, you frakkin' bizzles. I was *leaving* headquarters. All you would find is where I bunk." Walking in front of the two, intimidating them with her bulk and martial presence, Woods continued, "Or is that what you want? To find my bunk and cuddle for a bit?"

The terror of closer contact with the vast, androgynous woman must have shown on their faces, for she immediately broke into gleeful guffaws at their discomfiture.

She pointed west, extending a blood-soiled uniformed arm at the level of their noses and said, "Go back that way, five blocks, take a left, and it is in front of you."

The two left without another word.

The team decided unanimously that any further in-person reconnaissance would be ill-advised.

Streets of Nyork, Nyork District, Unity
12.33.07 EST_13_October_AU77 (2129 AD)

Leaving Aliende's office, passing each guard and giving the new sign and countersign for the day, Major (bvt) Woods abandoned the headquarters floors to their current chaos of junior officers and technicians running around at cross purposes. She could feel her mind and body begin to relax as the elevator door closed on the teeming bureaucratic anthill.

"Command: front desk"

"As you wish, Major Woods, honey."

Headquarters elevators were notorious for their gossip and cloying familiarity. Blanche chose not to ask how the entity knew about her promotion. Instead, her mind turned to the battle of…? *Yesterday? Had it only been yesterday?*

"The only thing worse than a battle lost is a battle won."[34]

She had one of each yesterday.

Apparently, Aliende was preparing to ignore this utter defeat—a half-million men dead on the field or lost, annihilation of ninety

---

[34] Lord Wellington after Waterloo

percent of the nation's skimmers, well over half of the ruling faction of the nation—and he was going to paper it over with vidcoms and patriotic hoo-haw.

Could Aliende bring this off? she asked herself again. He had been so much in Jourdaine's shadow during the latter's meteoric rise to power that she hardly recalled Fettwap before being dragged away from the fire at HQ to serve as his muscle.

His appearance was against him, of course. Round-faced and always seeming to be breaking out in a sweat, Aliende had, with little risk to himself, been able to catch Jourdaine's coattails, dragging himself into the highest echelons of the new ruling faction during Jourdaine's coup d'état last May. *Had it been so little time?* Jourdaine seemed to her to have been in power forever.

Yet, Aliende might have been playing the smarter game, allowing Jourdaine to be the face of the new regime, the face of the new oppression—the face of the military blunder that had just occurred. For all his appearance of gormless corpulence, Aliende might have been playing the odds—and playing them well.

Aliende had been wholly honest with her as far as she could determine. He must know I have no patrons and few friends — Beverly— Major Jansen was stationed at the People's Revenge—and would not be coming home. That whole area had frozen solid. Aliende is trying to bribe me. It's working.

Blanche left the elevator, its unctuous words of parting sending her forth.

But what am I to do in the situation? she thought. *Since yesterday, I've been acting like a robot, doing everything Aliende wanted. He has been in the upper echelons too long, I think. He sees conspiracies everywhere, loyalty nowhere, and overlooks the tactical for the strategic.*

We make a good team, in that regard, Blanche mused.

But it will not last, she finally concluded.

Fettwap does not play well with others—witness Cotton. He uses people like tokens on a gaming table. In a year or two, I will be pushed out of a skimmer door for knowing too much. My "protected class" won't save me; I'm not that naïve.

But what I do have is a chance at a new path, if I can find it. Matron and the gullible Riley have had nineteen years of my life. They won't take anymore from me. I have a chance to escape Matron's trap—if I only knew how.

Glancing at her watch, Blanche uttered an expletive, went to the PX, and purchased a toothbrush and paste, soap, shampoo, depilatory, a large towel, and a shower robe, white (XXL). It was the only one that fit. While in the outlands, she had walked through a looted store somewhere north of downtown Aytlana and seen whole racks of robes in a rainbow of colors—some even had patterns of different colors. *Where were the promised barbarians?*

Despite hurrying, Blanche only just got back to her BOQ billet in time for her assigned shower time, delayed briefly by some tourists. Her fifteen-minute shot was "running" as she went to her room, undressed, put on the robe, and walked barefoot to the latrine. It was empty. Blanche released a tense sigh. She always did when showering in a public place. Naked and with no sign of rank to protect her from the comments of the beautiful, young—and intact—bodies around her, public showers were a trial. Her altered body had made her an object of amusement in the enforced uniformity of the DUFS. As a "Double D"[35] Volunteer, Blanche was anything but uniform.

Covered in clothes and the markings of rank, it was not so bad, but now, in the room with banks of mirrors showing her tormented body, it was too easy to remember another day and another warm shower and another child. Shaking herself, Blanche castigated herself for her weakness.

In the deserted shower room, Blanche turned on the water in the shower and shucked out of the robe. The soap was the same utilitarian species she had grown up with. She went over her own body in the slickness of the heated water, giving herself a momentary thrill of intimacy before the two-minute warning on her shower buzzed and the water turned cold. Rinsing the remains of the shampoo out of her eyes and the remnants of the "Hair-B-Gon" depilatory from her face and body, she emerged from the shower shivering. Seeing herself in the mirror over the sink, she turned away to dry herself before returning to her room, still remembering the memories of that different child.

What is done is done.

But back at the start of it all, Matron had been as good as her

---

[35] Directed Diversity Volunteer

word. In the end, Riley had elected to change his name to Blanche on his recruitment card. He—now she—was drafted into the DUFS the very next day. Riley marveled at the reach and breadth of Matron's power until his training commander asked him why Matron had blocked his recruitment for a month. He no longer even liked Matron.

The injections made him ill. He could not run as fast as he used to. He failed the fitness test two years in a row, but as a DD Volunteer, it hardly mattered. He got fatter, which he did not like, but grew taller, which he did. By the time they changed the injections, he had begun to feel comfortable with being called Blanche and using her preferred pronouns. These new shots made his tits sore and then made them grow. Odd how they turned out.

They cut off his balls and cock and created a vagina of sorts for him only when he was fourteen. Feckingly useless that was! The surgeries had been brutal and "not gone entirely well." His "vestigial" penis was still pretty functional. It attracted attention but little patronage.

Once recruited by the DUFS, his/her advancement through the ranks had been slow and done on merit alone. Blanche was already thirty when she was made captain just before the invasion. Ten more years to make an impression with the Solons before she/he was retired—or turned into a brain-dead CRNA. That fate was an open secret among the middle ranks, who might hope for advancement, but it was still a darkly kept secret when it came to the civilians. Had Blanche said anything about her hopes in public, she risked being Sapped that much sooner.

"Give all for the Unity"—and then you're Sapped.

New Apartment And Chair

DUFS HQ, Nyork, The Unity
14.11.57_13_October_AU77, (2129 AD)

Finally dressed in clean fatigues and feeling less awful, Blanche returned to headquarters, where the elevators were abuzz with the news of her new billet.

Blanche, anxious to start her assignment, nevertheless, spent the afternoon moving what little she had in the way of personal possessions into the spacious apartment on the 5th floor of a headquarters complex building that she had inherited as Aliende's follower. The place was well furnished, recently cleaned, and painted an acceptable shade of purple. The carpet showed considerable wear. The electric tea kettle was defunct. There was no evidence of the apartment's prior occupant. Whoever they were had no doubt died under the shards of ice in a frozen Aytlana—or between the teeth of a CRNA. She shivered. Blanche rearranged the furniture and upacked the few souvenirs she had collected over the twenty-odd years she had been in the DUFS. These last few days would count as the oddest.

Dinner, called up from the regimental mess, was an infinitely forgettable Vegan Medley Casserole.

Finally, opening the security folder with its password, Blanche laid out the contents of Bonhoffer's dossier on a folding table in a corner of her new apartment. Despite their disadvantages, single-copy paper records still outperform any method of secrecy that requires trust between those who need a secret document's information and those who merely hold it.

Organizing the reports, surveillance 2-D vids, and timelines, Blanche perused them for an hour without being able to divine anything more than what the intelligence people had already obtained.

Feeling she was being too disorganized, Blanche set to work. *Who, what, when, where, why, and how.* Like all investigations, the questions remained the same, regardless of the varied answers. Jessika Bonhoffer, an entirely pedestrian maritime worker, had been shipwrecked due to the all-too-frequent foundering of a D-ship, the *USS Zuckerberg,* one of the automated barges that plied the Unity coast. No one appeared to have survived—*the D-ships were notorious.* A few bodies had washed up on shore in NorCarolin Province. There had been no search of the vast expanses of the Lantic. *In the Unity, no one expended resources best used by living citizens to find dead ones.*

This was going to be a squalid job, Blanche thought: digging into the dirty laundry of a dead citizen, asking the questions that many would take as an insult, and drawing conclusions where others would wish you to find incomprehensible noise. *She already felt soiled.*

Circumstances could be manufactured, lies could be told, misdirection could make you forget to ask the right questions—for a time—but in the end, all the pieces had to fit into the six-dimensional solid of inquiry: Who, What, When, Where, Why, and How.".

In the ruddy light of a prolonged Autumn twilight, Blanche laid out what was known about the spy, Jessika Bonhoffer. Much of the data was redundant. Of the actual events of the espionage itself, half a dozen people saw the spy enter the building housing the War Room. She had been scanned correctly; the readout from the scanner was downloaded and examined as soon as the security people thought something was out of place.

What had set them to thinking that?

For them, everything *had* fit—at least at the beginning. The appearance, the readout from the first implant, her signs, and countersigns had been unimpeachable. She had been in and out of the building within twenty minutes.

What had set people to wondering about General Oudelande's attaché if everything was nominal?

Ah, here it was! Blanche said to herself as she pulled a sheet from the bottom of another pile.

Apparently, the *real* Lieutenant Lincoln was not a tall, buxom blonde but an even taller, willowy brunette. Her comatose form had been positively identified by a staff sergeant in Lincoln's own squad. The *honest Lincoln* had shown up just *after* the Blonde Bonhoffer spy had already been admitted. Due to some glitch in the system, the CORE rejected the real Lieutenant Lincoln's credentials, even while it accepted Bonhoffer's.

Lincoln had been detained—with prejudice.

Under augmented interrogation, the real Lincoln had been clueless as to what the problem was. All she could do was plead ignorance, a condition unlikely to prevent DUFS interrogators from pursuing less pleasant interrogation techniques.

The woman was still in hospital, more than five days after the incident—while her fellow battalion officers were currently flash-frozen corpses, eaten or captured by barbarians. While Lincoln tried to remember how to talk, none of General Oudelande's command had returned from the outlands.

I guess she was the lucky one.

But it was curious, thought Blanche. The spies had been so confident they could spoof the system that they threw away the advantage of duplicating Lincoln's appearance, no doubt desperate, that close to the invasion. *Yet, they were willing to risk the life of one of their own in an attempt to get something to show their outlander spymaster. It should not have worked, and they should have* known *it wouldn't work.*

If the American army was anything like the DUFS, failure meant death as a traitor. As a soldier, death at the hands of your country's enemies while striking a blow for your homeland was glorious, yet failure meant a fetid demise at the hands of your own people should you foolishly survive. Blanche shrugged.

Even then, not all the pieces fit.

The woman was found in a dusty attic attempting to escape over the roofs of Brooklyn. She never had a chance to pass on any information—a sordid, pointless death even for a grubby bunch of savages.

Sad, if appropriately barbaric. But what if she had made good her escape? The spy must have had a destination, a hole in which to hide. She could not expect to return to the outlands immediately; the outlanders had no aircraft. With a half-million-man army likely to be sweeping towards the border, any attempt to walk home would mean immediate capture. So, Bonhoffer must have had another hideout. She must have compatriots to receive her intel, and they *certainly needed a hiding place. Where?*

Blanche shrugged at one more unanswered question and moved on, trying to solve a "how question."

How had the safe house been assigned? The Unity guaranteed that all workers got appropriate housing—meaning the higher your S-class, the nicer the CRB.[36] As it should be. Nevertheless, for reasons beyond her understanding, Nyork seemed to have many more buildings than people. These tenements frequently dated back to the Glorious Revolution, some seventy years ago.

Yet, the old buildings stood, gaunt, deteriorating, and drab—a reminder of the bad old days when capitalism determined where you lived rather than what good you brought to society. Moreover, the old buildings were a nuisance. Blanche had rousted more than a score of squatters from each "condemned" building on each of her several rotations as the local constabulary. The squatters were generally the unguilded between gigs, crèchie runaways, those near retirement, and defectives of body or mind. The unguilded were just rousted, the crèchies returned to their crèche, the elderly retired, and

---

[36] Citizen's Residence Benefit- one's crib

the defectives euthanized.

About ten years ago, all buildings had been surveyed and thereafter managed by the Nyork district "Habitation Scarcity Board." Reactivating one of these relics was a long and complicated process, thus making it infrequently utilized. This led, in due time, to the inevitable: creative architecture within existing buildings, placing more low-level workers in buildings designed for half their number.

Yet, Bonhoffer had been found in one of these derelict tenements, with water and power functioning, legally assigned to her—all the forms completed and countersigned.

How had Bonhoffer been able to do that?

This could only mean that the traitorous conspiracy had already infiltrated the very highest levels of the government workers' grey-garbed bureaucracy.

The hairs on the back of Blanche's neck rose.

She would have to be very circumspect. If she were identified as leading any investigation about Bonhoffer, not only would her pigeons all fly away, but Blanche's own ability to further the probe would be conveniently and deniably thwarted by the bureaucrats.

Blanche reviewed the machine code commands for the derelict dwelling, finding nothing unusual at first glance. Minutes later, she stopped and returned to the Jessika Bonhoffer question.

What if the spies were not motivated by desperation but instead had hacked the CORE, confident that they could spoof the scanning process? It would require no vast human conspiracy.

"Small conspiracies fail and large conspiracies are betrayed."

Where had she heard that?

But a conspiracy in the CORE was above—way above—her pay grade. She had the standard clearances, of course, having begun to receive them when she was drafted into the DUFS. With each successful mission and each grudging advancement, she had penetrated further into the mysteries of the CORE and her own guild. As a major, despite large areas being withheld from her, she could discern the "shape" of what she had yet to learn. Even if she became commander-in-chief, perish the thought, she could tell somehow that what she saw of the CORE was only "out front;" the CORE had to have something more— something "backstage" to feed the illusions she perceived as truth.

She had, of course, presumed initially that the CORE was just a dumb tool, a place for the circuses that diverted the people and maintained their productivity. Of course, it was undoubtedly that: the comm'nets were just completing a mini-series featuring Zardoz. The primordial doings of this handsome and well-endowed proto-human, which the narrator assured the audience was the progenitor of the entire nation, were near mythical. His heroism and sexual prowess imbuing the state with borrowed pride. The unguilded ate that stuff up.

She also knew that all the essential business of the Unity passed through the bowels of the CORE. All documents, memos, statistics, raw data, commands, reports, and legal documents were deposited within the black box of the CORE and could only be retrieved at the sufferance of the CORE. Many times, Blanche, having written a report and saved it to the CORE, following all current protocols, had been refused access to her own document.

"The CORE gives and the CORE takes away. Enlightened is the way of the CORE."

It was unthinkable that the CORE could be corrupted. Were that true, all her efforts were futile. She moved on.

If the outlander attack on the system's security were entirely through the comm'net using conventional mechanisms of an uncorrupted CORE, counterfeiting the uniform of a DUFS aide-de-camp would be the spies' only real-world exposure. Counterfeits, however, were available almost at will in phantom shops; officers found it more expedient to get a knock-off uniform that actually fit rather than take the stock offerings of the DUFS PX. She found the vids of the uniform Bonhoffer had left in the subway latrine. It had all the appropriate sigils and emblems—and the label from a phantom shop she frequented. Blanche grimaced. Dead End.

Then an idea struck her, as if from the blue. If the spies could alter the scan result, they could certainly change what the CORE would say she looked like—and change it back before anyone thought to recheck it.

Finding the vid recording of the outlander spy's last trip to the Map Room and back to her safehouse, Blanche started her own analysis. Bonhoffer had chosen a slack time of day to make her arrival at the headquarters more predictable; the downside of that for the spy was that her changing into the DUFS uniform did nothing to preserve her anonymity. Once the vids tracked her back to the women's toilet in the Second Avenue Station on the Lower East Side, finding out which passenger went in as a DUFS and came out as a civilian was child's play.

Another idea gave Blanche that odd sensation on the insides of her arms when fear seized her unannounced: the spy must have known she would be identified and did not care! She must have thought she had an iron-clad escape route.

How was she expecting to escape? Moreover, how did she expect to pass the information in the brief period remaining to her before her escape would render her incommunicado?

Bonhoffer must have been successful; somehow, the Unity had been defeated. It could not be a coincidence. Certainly, Blanche had seen no organized resistance or even a significant civilian population on her march to Aytlana. *Then came that single crushing blow near the Headquarters, made by troops prepared for the cold, tanks that ignored pulse-fire, and the* fathering Cold. The one enemy soldier she had seen up close wore some sort of rebreather suit. She paused. They knew, had known, the extreme cold was coming and trained for it. Had the barbarians caused the terrible Cold? It was not credible. The memory of it made her shiver even now. Out of a clear sky poured down Cold, like a hammer blow. And the drums!

"Boom...boom...boom—Boom...boom...boom."

"Boom...boom...boom—Boom...boom...boom."

"Boom...boom...boom—Boom...boom...boom."

Blanche rose, rubbed her temples, and stood looking out the window.

It was like something out of a comm'net drama: her squad had marched down from Cummings in the oppressive sticky heat of late afternoon, entered the city to the east of what would be the army HQ, and invested the line she was ordered to occupy. The few buildings were like ovens. Blanche got permission to bivouac outside, leaving only observation posts on the military high points. She had the majority of them bedded down despite the drums when her fellow officers returned, drunk. One threw her a 500 cc bottle of some local spirit and, without thanks, ran off to try to control his abandoned troops.

Then the cold started.

Gusts of frigid air came at intervals from above, freezing exposed skin. Blanche had looked up and seen nothing but bright stars, so many! She imagined that the malign night sky had pawed away the atmosphere and was pouring the absolute cold of outer space down onto her and the army; malignant alien spirits emptying the forces of nature down upon her.

Then the BDs started.

Blanche felt nauseated—a delayed response. She must have been too terrified to allow herself that luxury during the event. She ran to the bathroom and vomited, emptying her stomach violently— as violently as that after Riley's first round of meds.

Forcing her mind back to the problem at hand, it was obvious: *only through betrayal could her Unity fail!*

She felt anger, like a wave of molten rage, boil up within her. Vermin within her own nation willingly created this disaster. "Sacred" was not a word she had ever used or, indeed, one she felt she could use with accuracy, but that seemed the only one available. Spies had plotted for months and years to destroy her sacred Unity! There was no place for these rats to hide—she would make it her life's work to find and exterminate them and then set others onto their tracks once she was gone!

Blanche tried to calm herself. *Anger was not a good way to assess the situation.* Sitting on the floor once more, with her legs crossed as well as they might. She breathed deeply, and enunciated her mantra:

The Unity is me, and I am the Unity.
The cadre is me, and I am the cadre.
The Unity is me and I am the Unity...

Later she rose from her place on the floor to return to the problem.

The information *must have been passed on to others for transmission*, but Bonhoffer had made no drop, met no person, and made no call either on a community comm'net or via an O-A—the vid showed no kiosks near the path she took to her empty tenement, for the one, and an autopsy showed she did not possess the other.

But, she must have done it in that short period of time; *Blanche was finding reports that the outlanders had started evacuating their population from the Unity's proposed line of advance within hours of*

Bonhoffer's death. The evacuation had sped up the invasion by a day, allowing the Unity to take Aytlana undamaged and unopposed.

And then the savages had hammered us into pieces once we were too cold to move or fight!

Diabolical.

Blanche felt her ire surge again and forced her mind away from that prospect for the moment.

Was this Jessika Bonhoffer who died in the attic, the same Jessika Bonhoffer who scrubbed decks on the Zuckerberg?

Jessika Bonhoffer, as far as the CORE was concerned, was legit. All the pertinent characteristics matched up, and the failsafe "first implant" was unspoofable.

First implants, placed in crèchies on turning seven years old, as an E1, made them citizens and gave them the first opportunity to buy ThiZ, the recreational drug-of-choice for any Unity citizen. The first implant, surgically placed behind the third rib, just outside the lung, was unhackable. Any fiddling with it wiped the data and triggered red flags with the person's next wanding. It was not just that the CORE contained a record of reality, but rather that the CORE data <u>was</u> reality.

Yet, Blanche asked herself, **Was this Jessika Bonhoffer who died in the attic, the same Jessika Bonhoffer who scrubbed decks on the Zuckerberg?**

Looking up, she noted the time.

"Father me, feck the time!"

She had to get some sleep. Still taut with residual outrage, curiosity, and energy, but absent the exhaustion that had clubbed her into narcosis last night, she would need something more to sleep tonight. She called up a 500 ml bottle of Old Filibuster's Grain Ethanol for the occasion. It arrived within minutes.

Blanche downed a couple gills of Old Filibuster, undressed, and flung herself into bed. In a light dose, Blanche remembered Aliende's request and was anxious to complete it before Old Filibuster had his way with her, she arose.

It was supposed to be a boilerplate announcement, but that would not suffice. If Aliende soft-balled this greatest of all Unity disasters, making the Aroostook War look like a crèchie fight, he might as well give up now. Now was the time to be heroic.

By the time the alcohol arrived at her brain, she was done and dozing. She slept for a few hours and awoke with a sour stomach, still in thrall to the last rapidly receding nightmare she had been having. She rose, finished the bottle, and lay on the leather couch, dozing, until the sun found her hours later.

Idiots' Enclave, The Unity
16.41.40.EST_13_October_AU77, (2129AD)

Malaki was briefly in a quandary. All he could do was report Woods' whereabouts—within limits. That would be unlikely to mollify Aliende. They needed to be able to see Woods' interactions with outsiders—to see what she was up to within the CORE. As physical presences, they were not up to the task. They might improve at this spycraft, but by then, Woods would, no doubt, have completed whatever project Aliende was interested in.

Malaki came up with the answer.

"We are not using the backCORE to our advantage, team."

"Sure, we are. How else would we pinpoint Woods' location—to within a meter, I might add?" said Gyorgy Blass, the expert in CORE code.

"In person, we will never get close to Woods—she's too good. And she scares the gork out of me," said Collins.

"Given. But who does anything *investigational* without the use of the CORE? There are holes, of course. Whatever happens in the Washenton or in person is lost to us, but everything else is visible from the backCORE."

"Can we observe the backCORE? I thought it was just a construct."

"It's both, of course, Gyorgy. The entire CORE is a construct of code, but everyone's O-A takes the data and generates the signals that the brain perceives. The backCORE is where the work happens. We just have to make it visible *to us*.

"They have been using bots mostly since before 60 AU," said Malaki, knowing he was perpetuating a fraud.

In a society of the young, the *inscrutable* past was seldom more than a dozen years before. Anything could happen in that lost time before time—and frequently did. He had no real idea when the bots replaced human operators; bots were operating well before he left crèche school. However, giving it a date raised his status and lent confidence to his pronouncements with these men—a few months his junior.

"Before that, operators could see into the backCORE and direct work. But I don't think that'll do here. We want to be closer to Woods than her own skin; listen to her every word. For that, Gyorgy, we will need your good services. We need a code automaton—our own bot, built to our own specs. Find one of the CORE'd-Out and use it as a model. No one will notice if a few of them vanish—all for the advancement of science, you know."

In the end, it took Blass and Collins just twelve hours to construct the interface: a seat with sensors on all limbs, along the spine, and on the brainstem, adorned with an encompassing helmet from an unhappy cyclist, Gyorgy. The operator had to be strapped naked onto the seat to ensure good contact, of course, and the resultant affair reminded Malaki of an old picture of Second Republic torture devices. He shuddered.

The Chair, as it was dubbed, seemed selective in the illusions it provided of the backCORE. Peter wet himself, shorting the system rather badly. Blass could see nothing, even after multiple recalibrations. They were about to junk the Chair as hopelessly flawed and urine-soaked when Malaki volunteered.

The effect on entering was a fantasy of shapes, memories, lusts, fears, desires, and regrets. Malaki was about to depart before his own autonomic nervous system embarrassed him. He turned to go and caught a glimpse of a peaceful scene beyond the harrowing images he had created. He commanded his own images, naming each one, to leave him and to his immense surprise and relief, they did. He was left standing in what first appeared to be a peaceful, if empty, plain. Rolling hills extended in all directions, and a pinkish sky loomed overhead. He stooped to examine the ground, only to discover that he was standing on old news broadcasts from early in the history of the CORE. He willed himself toward the apex of a small hill—and found himself swooping toward it. There, the ground was disaster reports from the old American west coast; reports of vast swathes of trees burning from lack of rain, gubernatorial rapacity, inhumane ideology, and social atomization. *Good riddance.*

Having memorized the current location of the tagged persona of Major Woods, Malaki commanded his illusory body to find her.

It was a mistake. In an N-dimensional space of the CORE, navigation was impossible. Malaki was treated to increasingly rapid flashes of dimensions: dark, garish, metallic stench, venereal stinks, blaring horns, braying whistles, clangs that set his teeth on end, and *laughter.*

It was the laughter that chilled his psyche so much he thought he was going insane: the maniacal, incessant laughter. Blass had to pull the plug. Merryweather surfaced back into the small room still strapped to the Chair, and yet the laughing continued—high, raucous, insane.

"Please, stop laughing, Malaki. It's beginning to worry me," said Collins.

Malaki stopped and was released from the Chair.

The limitations of the Chair were obvious. The sensory input was simultaneously too vivid and too sensitive. The interface needed to be dumbed down in some way so that the entire team could use it and not suffer the emotional distress that Curtis and Merryweather had experienced. It required a kill switch for the operator to use without external assistance, but primarily, it needed to be able to *navigate* within the backCORE. Construction of the Beast took a day to complete. Festooned with conduits, impedimenta, and addenda, to the team, it was a work of beauty.

More CORE

The openCORE, the Unity
08.29.37.EST_13_October_AU77, (2129AD)

Is he the best choice for a leader? **asked Elise.**

Almost certainly, anyone would be a better choice, **inserted free-ranging Cain.** *The man is sly but not clever, ruled by his senses, a sucker for any sensual invitation that comes his way, venal, sneaky, and a slob.*

Don't hold back, friend. Tell us how you really feel, **stage-whispered free-ranging Frog, and got an elbow, of sorts, from his kid sister, Rana.**

My true feelings are that Fettwap Aliende would be a disaster as the leader of the DUFS or any nation. Even with the Trojan we implanted him with, it's dicey.

So, whatcha gonna do about it, Big Guy? **asked Frog-of-EffieCee.**

The question is, 'What are we gonna do about it?' **remarked Edie-of-EffieCee.**

Should we do anything? Can we do anything? Just 'cause we can see the problem doesn't mean anyone else will immediately become our friend and ally. We have been "hiding out" in their country's computer system—some of us for years—without even asking for a 'bye your leave.' Your average Uni is not going to be happy to find out we even exist, **said free-range Cain.**

So we won't tell them, **rejoined Cain-of-EffieCee.**

But the cat's out of the trunk, **said Frog,** *some Unis already know. Isn't Hecate a Uni? If she's captured, is not the fact of our existence something she might use to save her own skin?*

That is one reason I think we must work to repatriate Will and Hecate. They have the least tools to deal with the Unity, the most to lose, and they have been honest brokers for a government that has no reason to give us the time of night, **said Edie-of-EffieCee.**

The entities had been arguing for what seemed like forever to them, foregoing their agreed-upon breaks in favor of continued discussion.

Why not do nothing and let the people rule? Most of the humans we have met and know well are pretty nice. They care about what's best for their people. The decisions would be made openly; people could collectively decide what the nation should do, **said Edie-of-EffieCee.**

Almost never, **said Elise.**

I agree, **said Cainc-of-EffiCee.** *Let's take one Unity laborer, a solitary human. He wants cheaper food and housing prices. Who can blame him? He spends a third on housing and half that on food. So half his income is there just so he can go to work for the Glorious Unity in the morning. So he wants food prices to be cut in half—or better yet—free.*

So, **continued Cain-of-EffiCee,** *food production is one of the least profitable of all the necessities. Farmers leave the fields if their income falls even a little—remember, the workers do not own the fields here—the Glorious Unity does. So, our original worker is frustrated, either because he failed or, worse, because he succeeded and is now worse off.*

So, our hypothetical worker gets a thousand thousand people who think like he does, and they are now a force to be reckoned with. The government, always trying to please the most significant number of people, regardless of the wisdom in doing so, allows the workers, informed only by their bellies, to wreak havoc on an even larger scale. Food prices are subsidized, or prices are cut. People hoard food because they know the situation is artificial. Farmers work harder for little to no increase in their financial security.

Then another group threatens the government, and they bend again, but there is no slack in the system. It has all gone to making food artificially cheap. Subsidies dry up, and farmers figure they can work less hard and still achieve the same profit if food prices rise. So, your atomized "solitary human" never exists for very long before he becomes a "political party."

There would be thousands of parties of people to make sure their side wins? **asked Rana.**

Nope. The natural limit is three: left, right, and spoiler. The "DO SOMETHING!—ANYTHING! Party;" the "If It Ain't Broke, Don't Fix It Party," and the Catbird, **replied Elise.**

You've lost me.

Here's an example. You have an entire country of pink people. If I want the whole country to paint themselves purple, I try to find other purple fans. Once I start the campaign, an opponent arises to keep it pink and collects all the Pinkies. Things get increasingly heated until, at some point, those who care the least and have joined neither the Pinks nor the Purples start to ask, "But what are <u>we</u> going to get out of it if we side with you?"

So, we're plants, and the citizens are catbirds? **asked Frog-of-EffieCee and was ignored.**

So, all critical decisions are made by the people who care the <u>least</u> about an issue, and they are the ones who receive the biggest rewards.

Indeed, **intoned Cain.**

Then there's the problem of greed.

Give everybody the same., **inserted Edie.**

Has that ever worked? Has it ever even happened? **countered Cain**. *You can always get a majority of any populace to vote to pilfer the pocket of a single person.*

But that is not fair!

But it's true. Look at the Unity. It's supposed to be a condominium—everyone living together—but who gets the perks? Not the workers—the majority. Not the bureaucracy. Those grays tiptoe around, doing the will of the DUFS. No stomach for the rough and tumble of ruling. And no manner of elegant argument trumps a pulse bombard coming through the windows of the ministry.

So, what's the solution? **asked Edie-of-EffiCee.**

As it turns out, almost anything can be a solution. Leaders are not technocrats; they're delegators. What kind of people have been leaders of peaceful and prosperous nations? Poets, businessmen, ward-heelers, the wealthy, dock workers—almost anyone. The trick is to convince people that you know how to get things done and that you will do your best for them, regardless of the circumstances, **said free-ranging Cain.**

The trick is to lead, **said Elise in a whisper.**

How is that selection for a leader gonna work? A competitive exam, a joisting contest, or interpretive dance? **Edie-of-EffieCee continued.**

It's a place to start, **said Cain.**

It is not so simple, of course.

I thought not.

Friday's Child is Loving and Giving

Woods

**17250 Avenue of the Unity, Nyork, The Unity
06.32.17_14_October_AU77, (2129 AD)**

Blanche awoke with a dull headache, a crapulous stomach, and a full bladder. She ordered up a liter of Morning-After Restorative from the discreet pharma on the ground floor and showered in the apartment's utilitarian bathroom.

Sipping the Restorative began to settle her stomach; from many years of experience, she knew her head would follow eventually. Friendships with a fellow DUFS, even if mutually acknowledged as platonic and for mutual benefit, were few and far between for a TranTran. Alcohol, in all its varied adulterants and colors, was an easy second best; yet it extracted a price — a price she knew was becoming increasingly exorbitant. Unless she, in her ten remaining years, could gin up some honest credibility and jolt her S-class into the thirties, she was doomed to become a CRNA, brain-dead, compliant, and mere cannon fodder. Her chances, before being plucked to give cover for Aliende, had been slight to undiscoverable. She drank because it gave her relief in the short run and would make no difference in the long.

That was then. The longevity and health of her body and its brain had become, out of the calamity of the Day of Ice, more precious to her. She shook herself. *She needed to quit, to dry out.* It was a new sensation.

Before her recent elevation, Blanche's strategy had been to hide her addiction and blunt its effect to give her maximal oblivion while moderating the consequences, allowing her to work diligently up to the day of her own Sapping. The Glorious Unity would receive her husk, the interior rotted out.

Her self-administered spoilation would be her rebellion against a society that seduced little boys, rendering them pawns in some grotesque game of one-upmanship.

She had been circumspect and quiet, doing her drinking alone and no more than once—maybe twice—a week. She used a variety of clandestine vendors, avoiding both the tax and the reporting requirements. Blanche had never been drunk on duty—ever. She never admitted nor showed the signs of a hangover to fellow officers. She just sought a reliable, reproducible, and private limbo from the utopia of the Unity.

And now the Unity wanted to elevate her rapidly. She must learn to conserve her resources, deal with her memories in other ways, and face the dark watches of the night with equanimity—and without Old Fili's crutch.

Even so, going to the officers' mess was out of the question this morning. Once the Restorative had done its work, Blanche called down for a 750-milliliter carafe of hot, black tea; milk product, six standard doses; sugars, number six; a single slice of multigrain toast, oiled; and Naprosinol.

While she waited for breakfast, she looked out at the city, her home since she was drafted from the crèche. Blanche had been told, in that matter-of-fact way one does with children, that she had been born in the Karolyna province, and what her birthdate was. *Did anyone really know their birthdate, or was that assigned like the names?*

Otherwise, she knew nothing of her origin. No one did. She understood that it had not always been that way. The Unity was proud of the atomization of its people and of eradicating any attachment other than to the state. It had been a monumental job, of course, and the social end-product, Blanche knew, was less than perfect, as she expected when imperfect Man took on the job of perfecting his own species. How could one bootstrap perfection? Whatever the governmental flaks said, the Unity still had prostitution, theft, assault, murder, and violent death—mostly at one's own hand. It was supposed to be a vast improvement over the days of the old republic; Blanche did not believe it.

Maybe the Unity's self-imposed isolation had been a mistake?

Blanche halted that line of thought abruptly. That way of thinking brought rebellion, inefficiency, ingratitude, and peril to oneself and the cause of the Unity itself. *This is what she got for drinking!*

Blanche turned from the window and finished off the Restorative as a punishment for her crimes.

Breakfast, such as it was, arrived and Blanche placed the tray where she could eat while looking out over the city. The Naprosinol went down first.

From her 11th-floor viewpoint, she noted with approval that the area around the building was being cleared of its ring of dead officers from her operation Wednesday. The panorama, otherwise, was impressive. Large buildings of all the approved sorts stretched from south to north, illuminated by the rising sun. Beyond this line of massive buildings, the height of the structures faded away rapidly, giving way to the workers' classic checkerboard arrangement of factories, green-hued spaces for games and public trials, and desolations to prevent too close an approach to the conduits for utilities.

Nibbling on the now-cold toast and sipping a cup of tepid tea, Blanche tried to remember what the outlanders drank. Coughy? Despite the name, it was a rather more robust beverage than the tea she had always drunk. She had glimpsed a menu of a shop specializing in the production and distribution of the stuff during her brief time in Aytlana. The Unity's invasion of Jorga had been so rapid and overwhelming that her unit had been able to seize one of these coughy-distributors with the beverage still warm.

Apparently, the drink came about by growing berries in distant places, bringing them to the backwoods of the outlands, burning them to charcoal, and then soaking the ashes in hot water to leach out the active ingredients. It was bitter, but despite that, she liked it. Why couldn't the Unity do that? A better question: how were the savage outlanders able to do it? What did they have to sell that was of value in foreign parts?

Returning to reality, Blanche noted the time, dressed in clean fatigues, grabbed a new service cover, and left rapidly.

DUFS Headquarters, Nyork, The Unity
08.30.34_EST_14_October_AU77, (2129AD)

DRAFT
News Bulletin:

After tireless work by DUFS commander Lieutenant General Fettwap Aliende, the truth about the recent disastrous invasion of the outland regions has been reported.

After Aliende's heroic escape on the last skimmer to leave the battlefield, he led a task force (with fellow survivor, Major (Bvt) Blanche Woods) into the cause of the debacle. As is now known, massive behavioral discontinuities among the rank-and-file led to wholesale loss of battlefield integrity and mutiny. On communication with the outlander government, such as it is, it has been determined that 32,082 of the 69,406 non-commissioned, warrant, and commissioned officers have survived and been captured by the forces of the Outlanders; the remainder are dead on the field (see list following). Of the CRNAs, approximately half were lost to fratricidal combat. The remainder have surrendered to the outlander forces.

Negotiations for the return of the captured soldiers and officers have been rejected out of hand by the tribal leaders of the Outlands.

In other developments, after careful study of weather patterns by the task force, it has been determined that the freak weather, temperatures dropping from 29°C to -40°C in a matter of minutes on the evening of 11th October, was not due to natural causes.

This raises the specter of a secret and unanticipated weapon in the hands of brutal partisans who style themselves the 'Restructured States of America.'" This technology, so uncharacteristic of the hunter-gatherer lifestyle of the outlanders, raises the specter of Recidivist Seniors or even Canadian interference.

"What is this, Woods?" asked Commander in Chief Aliende as the two sat next to each other on straight chairs in Aliende's inner Sanctum, looking at a screen. He bit off the next rejoinder, saying merely "Have you gone mad?"

He had given the irritating officer a project that should have taken at least a day, and she came back the very next morning. *Dedicated or deceiver?*

"The truth about the defeat has already leaked, sir. Even some unguilded know about the size of the defeat, sir. It is common talk among the lower guilds. It *will* come out eventually, sir," said Woods, shifting uncomfortably under Aliende's regard. She had become increasingly convinced since she had written the announcement last night that the time for comforting platitudes was over and that the nation—her nation—needed an overhaul if it were to survive.

"Would it not be best, sir, to get it over with? Shouldn't we be the ones to steer the narrative? We don't want Unity Forward or Unity Home Front to start agitating. The Greens already know a lot. They could switch sides easily. That would be disastrous."

"I am not so worried about the Greens, or the Oranges—what about the Reds? They have had time to lick their wounds."

"About twenty percent of the captured officers were Reds. Ten percent Orange. Five percent Green—"

"And I am figuring that the remaining sixty-five percent were our own Blues."

"It was hard to keep our officers at home when the chance for glory presents itself, sir."

"Jourdaine was a fool. But what's all this nonsense about energy and technology? We still have enough—with a little belt-tightening. It's just because it's coming on to winter, is all," protested Aliende.

"It is not so much what energy we *have* as it is what we *need to have*, sir. The solar farms are exhibiting a gradual decrease in output, which has been the case since they were built. However, we need more energy *now*. We have a huge task ahead of us to rebuild our defenses."

"Hadn't thought about that yet. Good work, Blanche. So, where do we get the juice to build more skimmers?"

"I think we need to think the whole thing through from the start, sir. I made some notes. What about coal, sir?"

"Are you out of your mind, Woods? Not only will the Orange faction jump ship, but that's probably too much for the Green faction, too."

"Can we at least look at that, sir? The numbers *at home* are that the Reds represent slightly less than half the officers. Blues are thirty-two percent. Orange is a little over ten percent, and Greens nine. If we can keep the alliance together, we are only at par with the Reds. Of course, we have the tactical advantage of holding the senior commands, but with retirements, how long will that last?"

"The Reds will lose just as many, but your point's well taken."

"There is one thing we can do, sir. We can form a coalition with the Reds. Give them some commands and get a peace treaty for, say, five years?"

"I'll be retired by then," said Aliende, looking contemplatively toward the ceiling. "It'll be someone else's headache," he said as a thin smile flitted across his face.

"Or not, sir. I am confident that you would be elevated to a Solonship—then it's still your problem with less ability to make the final solution one you think is the best; 'Solons rule only by veto.' However, anyone who has shown so much discernment and grace under pressure during these most trying of times, as you have, sir, would never go unnoticed by the Solons. They would not wish to waste your talents with retirement," said Blanche, hoping her voice suggested the martial enthusiasm she was going for.

"Do you think so? Yes, of course, you're right. 'Ignis Aurum Probat,' eh?"

"I am sorry, sir. You've lost me."

"'Fire proves out Gold'—old language. I found it carved into a lintel in my crèche once upon a time. 'Trials prove who has the right stuff,' or something. Regardless, you may be right."

"There is one more thing we can do, perhaps two. With the depletion of the officer corps, we can delay retirements for twenty-four months—you know, to fill in the hole in the production line. It will mean that we have fewer CRNAs for a while but more officers to train the remainder."

Aliende looked up and studied Blanche wordlessly for several long moments. She, in turn, had frequently wondered how she would get behind the façade of the senior staff. This seemed like a low-cost maneuver. If Aliende acted scandalized that she knew the ultimate fate of citizens on their retirement, she could blame it on her experiences in the outlands. If he confided in her, it meant that she could roam around in the politics of the upper echelons with his tacit approval.

"So, you figured that out, did you?"

"After Aytlana, it was not very difficult, sir. I met an older crèche-mate of mine. The face was recognizable—little else," she lied.

"I suppose it was inevitable; you are too clever for your own good, Blanche. Still, it's a classified state secret. I do not think majors are allowed to know about that. It violates the Uniform Code, Woods," said Aliende. Within the last few seconds, his face was sheened in sweat. He frowned. Blanche's heart sank.

"I'm sorry, sir. How was I to know that sir?"

"I guess I'll just have to make you a lieutenant colonel. That makes me happy. It makes the Uniform Code happy. What about you, Blanche? Will that make you happy?"

"That makes me quite happy too, sir," said Blanche, and surprisingly, she was actually pleased. It could have gone otherwise. Aliende, despite being an unlikely and unlovely superior, had done an authentically nice thing for her benefit. *How odd.*

Diary of a POW

Polyarchy of Sentients, The Scorch
Sixty degrees before the meridian, the third day after the Great Cold

DUFS Captain Lucien Delaheny had begun to panic—or despair—he was unsure. After his capture at the People's Revenge that frostbitten day, he had lost all track of time. He had been fished out of a milling crowd of officers, non-coms, transport drivers, skimmer mechanics, and cooks, asked his name, rank, and serial number, and searched.

The grim outlanders…

No! Not outlanders, he reminded himself. He had been pummeled to the ground and kicked for saying that on that terrible first day.

The *Americans* confiscated everything except fabric and fasteners and escorted him to a dark, lightless room. He found the water bucket, by the light from a recess in the ceiling, and the latrine by the smell. He received food if he were near the door when it opened at odd intervals.

Then, some undefinable time later, they had all been piled into trucks with loud smokey engines and driven for hours, arriving at night to a large clearing, told to get some sleep as best they could on the red clay soil, not to wander off, and that they would see the new shape of their captivity in the morning.

In the night, it rained, the unseen soil becoming mudslides and increasing fetid pools as the captives' anxiety-watered bowels loosened in the darkness. However, within a few minutes, the darkness somehow increased, the rain stopped, and the wind abated. Rain could still be heard pattering onto some new cover above the prisoners, keeping them dry. Lucien tried to move and found it difficult. He picked up his left leg, heard a sucking sound, and placed it a little way off, finding that it now rested on a stiffly spongy surface, several centimeters thick, that seemed to have swelled up from below the prisoners. He got his right foot out, minus the boot. Finding it, he pulled it out before it was overwhelmed by the sponginess. In the darkness, he felt how the boot's cast in the sponginess filled in over a few minutes.

He was now warm and dry, with rain pattering on the 'roof.' He found a place with less foot traffic and fell asleep almost instantly.

Birdsong awakened him hours later. The 'roof' revealed itself to be a large canopy of stiff verdant leaves, fan-shaped, that opened and closed like a mechanical iris. The roof was now partially open, and Captain Delaheny could see a bright blue sky.

Delaheny's despair resolved, and, in the changed circumstances, gave way to wonder. The glen resolved itself into an open, circular courtyard, with a featureless wall of green up to three times the height of a man. The floor revealed itself to be a resilient green sponge. On one side of the courtyard was a sign for water and showers—no, *"sign" was undoubtedly the wrong name for it*. Two leaves, each about a meter across, of a large and unfamiliar plant had been cut along a diagonal line and then sealed. Scratched on the surface in scarlet letters were:

Water/

H2

O Hot/

Cold D

rink/B

ath.

The scarlet letters appeared to seethe, and on closer inspection, the letters were composed of a mass of small beetles, climbing over each other in a seeming frenzy.

After staring at it for some time, he got the idea, especially as his fellow officers were exiting a narrow entrance carrying leafy cones of water. About a third way around the circumference, another proclaimed,

"Fud/N

ouris

hmint,"

and a further third around the circumference, there were several slit wide apertures in the leafy wall with a sign saying:

Excr

ete/piss/s

hit.

The odd clinicality and naivete of the words chilled him. The writer was wholly alien, copying a picture of a word, not knowing its meaning, punctuation, or likely impact on the captives. Lucien rapidly used all three of the facilities, ending at the watering station. He was emerging, drying his face with his hands, as no towels were in evidence. The rest of the day was boredom, punctuated by the escape of a major Legrange. His screams were heard for hours thereafter. The following day, the bloodletting began.

The Team in the backCORE

The openCORE, the Unity
10.21.29.EST_14_October_AU77 (2129AD)

What is it? A trojan...an easter egg? asked Rana to Frog, as the two sat behind a heap of archived comm'net programs in their morgue.

Of course, it could be, but I doubt it. The thing is too primitive. It looks like a prototype bot to me. Inelegant. See the kludged bit off the side to prevent IO errors?

But why so BIG? Bots aren't very smart. They have a few tricks, but the bandwidth gets excessive if they have too many AI circuits, said Cain idly, just then arriving with Elise.

We should talk to EffieCee? she asked.

In time. Let's get as much info as we can, said Cain.

Nothing like prodding a hornet's nest to gain data, donchakno? observed Frog.

You wouldn't, would you? Elise asked, titillated and scandalized.

If I was left to my own devices, I probably would, but majority rules, I'm thinking. What's the feeling of the committee-of-the-whole? Poke or not Poke?

What have you in mind, my friend? said Cain.

For starters, Frog said, pointing to the odd manifestation that had appeared in the back stacks of the Commerce department archives a few moments before, *this widget is powered from the outside. A certain amount of plug-pulling would be fun.*

Yes, but sort of "all or nothing," don't you think? How about some graded stimulae? How about introducing it to one of the CORE'd-Out?

Really? You two would pull wings off a fly for fun? objected Elise.

What's a "fly," my love? asked Cain, leaving Elise open-mouthed.

We might could put up a sign saying, "Go Away," mused Frog, ignoring the two's mutual disbelief.

You might be giving too much away with that one, my friend, said Cain, breaking his gaze with Elise. We need to do something that can be blamed on regular CORE operation. See what the capacity of this widget is for problem-solving.

How about dumping files all around it and seeing what it does?

Sounds good. Don't let it see us, though.

That's easy enough to do, said Frog. *This is not the most agile of beasties.*

While the Widget appeared to be looking in the wrong direction, a few files were dropped within its field of perception. The discovery of each new stimulus was signaled by the Widget freezing, pausing long enough to send and receive instructions, and then the extension of a flickering two-fingered claw to retrieve each new discovery.

What file has it got now? asked Rana.

I can't quite see. I think it's the one on polybromophenols in fish harvests from the Hudsen River. It's the usual. The PBPs were put there so no one can catch a fish for dinner—starvation, whatever that is, would be better, they say.

Yeah. "All production belongs to the state," and such nonsense.

How about something a little more drastic?

What have you in mind, you dirty boy?

"Malaki, I can't see! Can you hear me? I picked up a document, and all of a sudden, I couldn't see anything. Help me. It's getting hard to breathe. I think I'm going to pass out," came the pressured narrative over the com'net.

"Collins, just unincorporate," said Malaki in a level tone.
"I can't see the switch. The air is getting foul. I gotta get fresh air."
Eventually, Gyorgy Blass found the right switch on the console and opened the beast for Collins to exit.

"Foul is right? Have you been eating Chechen empanadas again?"

"Never mind what I have been eating," snapped Collins.

"Peter. Take a break. We are all going on a break. See you in the AM. Clean up the mess you made and disinfect it, and we'll see you then, okay?"

"Yes, of course, Malaki. Thanks for understanding."

Opening the Cat's Box

DUFS Headquarters, Nyork, The Unity
14.30.30.EST_14_October_AU77 (2129 AD)

The man leaned over on tiptoes to listen to the chest of the corpulent Fettwap Sigfrid Aliende.

"Hhmmm"

"What's that supposed to mean?"

"Silence, please. Just breathe easily. "

Several more minutes passed without comment before the little man straightened.

"Yes, I see. We need to discuss some things, Fettwap. You can get dressed."

Once he had buttoned his shirt and sat comfortably in his favorite chair, the man began. They had known each other for almost five years. It was usual to assign a specific HP to each senior officer, "for continuity's sake." Fettwap, taking the measure of the little man, always thought of him as the Mouse.

"You are overweight, morbidly so."

"Are you saying I'm fat? Out with it, man!"

"Oh, No! Not that. That would be against the Anti-Shaming Protocol. You misunderstood me," said the Mouse, his voice becoming shrill.

"Alright. Then, proceed. Make it quick. I have a staff meeting shortly."

"You must lose weight. Your heart will not stand carrying this much weight around. It stops you from exercising—"

"Don't like it. Makes me sweat."

"I can only give you advice, Fettwap. I cannot make you take it. As it is, you could have a heart attack at any time and a fifty-fifty chance of dying from one within five years."

"Oh well. Then no worries. I will be 'retired' by then."

"Furthermore, I advise you to lose 40 kilos and to cut out at least two meals a day."

"Don't treat me like a child! I'll starve on only three meals a day!" said Aliende before glancing at the wall clock.

"Eh, look at the time! Thanks for coming. See yourself out. I must be starting this staff meeting," Fettwap concluded as he hurried out the door.

Wriggling uncomfortably in the narrow seat last occupied by his thinner and more severe predecessor, Fettwap enjoyed the occasion, nevertheless. Holding his first in-person general staff council meeting was a particular piquant pleasure for him. As a rising E8, fourteen years old and punching well above his considerable weight in the bureaucracy of the DUFS even then, he had sat in the room while old General Grisholm had palavered with the commander, taking notes for the general, passing information, and generally acting as Grisholm's back-brain for the event. *Who had been the commander-in-chief back then?* It hardly mattered. The man would be Sapped by now if he lived at all.

With the meteoric and mysterious rise of Eustace Jourdaine, it had been Aliende's turn, as a bona fide supporter, to assume a chair at these sessions. Yet that, like so many anticipated pleasures, had been dissatisfying. Jourdaine had been a demanding leader and tightfisted when it came to perks, information, and opportunities. He and Eustace had risen together—to a point. Jourdaine had always been preternaturally lucky. He did not often share his luck with those who had assisted his rise.

Now, as the one remaining member of Jourdaine's ill-fated general staff and outrunning the news of his own army's defeat, Aliende had shifted to the command chair before anyone could mount a challenge. Despite many of the Blue faction dying under the shards of ice in the damned white hell of Aytlana, he had support even now. The Blues were still firmly in charge—and he was firmly in charge of the Blues.

Paranoid to the point of madness and fearful of what mischief the Reds might get into if left unchaperoned at home, Jourdaine had "invited" the most suspect of their diminished number to accompany him to the outlands. To safeguard his rear during his absence, Jourdaine had left many of his loyal Blues and most of the Oranges of Unity Home faction, and the Greens of Unity Forward faction at home, despite them being his nominal allies.

"Keep your friends close and your enemies closer."

Despite these advantages, Aliende's success had revolved around his deft arrival back in Nyork and to its levers of power, ordering a few critical assassinations and capturing the comm'nets. Thus, he had been able to slip almost gracefully into Jourdaine's command chair while it was still warm. He nodded at Ketchem, his new administrative aide, who began.

"It is time to come to order. Cit'zens! Let's get started, please!"

Rule 1: The story has to be absolutely true.

Aliende began, "Thank you for your prompt arrival and careful attention, my brothers and sisters-in-arms. As DUFS command reported to the nation this morning, the nation has suffered a catastrophe. Half of all the armed forces and almost all of our skimmers have been lost to the outlands.

Schrödinger's Cat was finally dead, he mused. Jourdaine had succumbed to an overdose of arrogance. If he was going to coerce these influential officers, he had to start with what they knew or suspected was the absolute truth.

"Moreover, all of the CRNAs, with the exception of about twenty thousand at Army headquarters, suffered Behavioral Discontinuities.[37] Non-com officers were cut down trying to enforce discipline. The effective troopers, little more than 4 percent of our Order of Battle, fought heroically, dying on the field less from enemy fire than from previously unexpected ice storms. We have no explanation for this freakish weather, Our intelligence in the outlands prior to the invasion was at best fragmentary. All of the infiltration units dropped into the wilderness over the last ten years have failed to report after sending their initial message. No warning—just nothing. We suspect they were all murdered out of hand.

A babble of voices rose as one or another of the staff expressed their outrage. Fettwap let them go on for long moments until he

---

[37] Behavioral Discontinuities, BDs, the loss of the conditioning that allows them to be effective soldiers.

perceived the chaos lessening and grabbed the last wisp of outrage to vault himself to mid-stage again.

"Be that as it may, Chowdry, no one is suggesting that treason—on-the-field—had any part in the defeat."

No one had mentioned treason, least of all Poorna Chowdry, a loyal Blue. Fettwap almost smiled as he watched the man's look of surprise and confusion, trying to play back the last few speeches in his head to determine how his commander had arrived at the dangerous conclusion.

"But—" Chowdry ventured.

"No! No reason to go there at all as long as we can *now* hold together and let bygones be bygones. I refuse to allow us to indulge in useless back-biting when we can, if we work together, carry on to success, and maintain our national supremacy.

"Needless to say, any true patriot of the Glorious Unity will be anxious to share any information they might have innocently collected from friends and coworkers. Please understand this is entirely anonymous. We cannot have suffered this great calamity without there being traitors or spies among us. The guardians of our nation's security are working tirelessly to root out these miscreants."

Fettwap Aliende smiled to himself. It was going along as expected.

Rule Two: The set-up makes the story sing. Take the truth and make it serve a higher purpose.

Fettwap could feel how he had already taken the strands of attention from these prideful and influential people into his own hands.

"But do not be mistaken. We are a nation under siege. Let us not sugar-coat reality. We suffered horrendous losses. We can expect nothing coming back from the outlands. They have not even seen the need to suggest a prisoner exchange." *Like* that *would work*, thought Aliende. *We have nothing to trade: no prisoners, territory, or specie.*

"Were it not for the foresight and industrial vigor of the Unity, we might expect imminent invasion. For the first time in our glorious history, the Unity is on the defensive.[38]

"That fact should not be shared with the nation at large. Panic would ensue. It would be wise not even to share this with NCOs, who

---

[38] Not factually true. The Canadians have taken the entire St Lawrence and Great Lakes watersheds, as well as the Aroostook of Main(e) by force

are the backbone of any army. However, let it be a watchword among us. Let it be ever before our eyes: *Invasion is coming*. But, Triumph is possible. Ceaseless vigilance is our duty.

"We must prepare. Our skimmer fleet has been swept from the skies. While our superiority in pulse technology is unsurpassed, the sacrifice of our ground forces due to inadequate aerial surveillance smacks of arrogance and improvidence. Desperate times demand desperate measures, as I am sure you all will agree," he said, waiting for the nearly imperceptible nodding from his audience.

"'*The best defense is a good offense.*' Have not we been told this since we were all ensigns? We need long-distance surveillance. We could use solar-powered drones, but their range is measured in mere klicks. We could use the new ion-wind vehicles, but they are susceptible to catastrophic failure due to flying creatures—birds and such like. A great leap forward beckons us.

"However, I propose we take a page from the past. Betting on a future, for which we cannot pay the price of research and development, makes no sense. We need to defend ourselves *now*, not in a generation."

Fettwap waited for the objections, the "In my opinions," the clearing of skeptical throats. *This would be the sticking point*, he thought.

Rule 3: Don't confuse people with too many choices.

If he chose the right setup, told it correctly, narrowed the possibilities, jaded the audience to other solutions, they, like a bunch of crèchies, would crowd together into a nice line to be gulled into complicity. Aliende needed some deep cover if this was going to happen. Either these arrogant and powerful people would agree to the plot, spreading the culpability for failure too far to allow retribution, or they would not. If they balked, Aliende was prepared to retreat rapidly, naming a committee to "study the problem" so that he could denounce it later.

If they accepted, he, Fettwap Aliende, would be the architect of a new Unity. Old enemies would have nowhere to go but to their knees before him. Aspiring officers would crowd to his banner to obtain favors, there to set upon each other to advance the cause of the Unity and, incidentally, that of Fettwap Aliende.

Nevertheless, his substantial belly was queasy. He did not like making wagers with his career. His had been a career composed of calculated loyalty, discovering the next rising tide, evaluating his chances, and rising as his selected star rose in the political firmament—with Fettwap Aliende relatively safe in the shadows. He had never expected to command the DUFS, but after Eustace's debacle in Aytlana, it was either rise to rule or be blamed as the one remaining reminder of Jourdaine's quixotic crusade.

All were quiet and expectant. It was now or never.

"We must mount another attack on the outlands, not just an attack but a conquest. With this current success of theirs, they will undoubtedly be planning the annihilation of our homeland. We have no choice: attack now and keep the devastation of war away from us, or wait and receive the attack where and when we are least prepared."

That, Fettwap thought, *was a safe opening wedge, lining up these commanders of the nation's armed forces to look in the same direction.*

"However, this invasion must *not* make the same mistakes as the last. We have depended on skimmers as our battle vehicles, troop transports, and tactical air units. We can do so no longer.

Here are my reasons: 1) they lack the ruggedness needed for today's combat; only one escaped Aytlana. 2) While they have been pressed into the role of close combat support, skimmers do the task badly; they lack the agility necessary to invest the enemy closely, and 3) *most telling*, we lack the resources.

"The Skimmerhorn drives, as clever and useful as they are, require a lot of resources. We will need more than we can obtain through labor or barter if we imagine building a new skimmer fleet. We need not just steel, aluminum, and copper but gold, silver," he said before looking down at his notes, "as well as Neodymium, Ytterbium, Dysprosium-um." Aliende laughed, "And ones even more difficult to pronounce."

The audience relaxed a bit, and Davad Rothkind smiled, a rare event taken by Fettwap to be a measure of the tension this meeting had created—and which he had just released.

"Our resources of these last materials are near to non-existent. Since our Glorious Revolution, the Unity we have been living on the stockpiles created by the shameless greed of the old republic. Their incessant pursuit of wealth condemned them to the ash heap of history, but their greed allowed them to purchase what we have recycled as a *matter of policy*. It was feasible when we had large stockpiles and less need. Our needs have increased, and our stockpiles have dwindled, as they are being used for the purposes they were intended. With the losses we sustained and the natural increase in the Unity, we need new resources to defend the homeland.

"Therefore, I propose we abandon, *for a season*, the construction of skimmers. Instead, I propose the construction of two new vehicles: the battle tank and propeller-driven aircraft. These are not Skimmerhorn-driven vehicles. No induction coils are needed as they run on internal combustion."

Fettwap waited for the outburst of rage and was not disappointed. Unity had abandoned fossil fuels at its inception almost eighty years ago. It had been a signal monument to the people's revolution, turning the entire nation away from fossil fuels from its very inception. The subsequent pain and deprivation necessitated by the expansion of the solar farms, exacerbated by worsening winter weather, had become a heroic "People's Sacrifice" with its own holiday.

After all the gabbling, one figure rose to confront him: Gilsoit Fenerghan, just the one Aliende would have expected.

"This is an outrage, Fettwap," said the tall, slight full colonel from Unity Home, an Orange and thus a nominal ally in the Fettwap's coalition. "It is a step back into the Stone Age," Gilsoit continued. "This is betraying the very revolution that began this country. We will be no better than the climate criminals we vanquished just—"

"We 'vanquished,' Gilsoit? We are not here to talk about our *victory* but our *defeat* at the hands of 'barbarians' of that same stone age. Is that not so?" replied Seftus Ploidid from Forward Unity, a Green. "Are you unaware that the number of skimmers has not increased in ten years?"

"Nonsense, I see new skimmers all the time."

"Incorrect. What you have seen were *old skimmers,* honorable colleague, remanufactured into *new skimmers.* All the copper, steel, aluminum, chrome, ytterbium, neodymium, and zinc have to be extracted from the old models and remanufactured into the new models. All those valuable but limited resources are now scattered across the battlefield in Jorja. Why don't you go ask the barbarians, nicely, if we can please have our wrecked skimmers back?

"Don't you understand? For the love of what all you fathering bizzles hold dear, 'Climate Justice' won," Ploidid said, standing and striking a pose. "This is what it looks like. And where have our policies gotten us—scraping along trying to make ends meet!"

Fettwap found that it was hard to keep a straight face as these two went at it. He would let them spit and flame for a bit. They were making his job easier, allowing Fettwap himself to step above the fray.

Seftus and Gilsoit had played their parts well. *Predictable.* So predictable, he had not even had to inform them of his plan. The two disliked each other and reflexively held countervailing views on every significant issue, particularly on the use of resources. Fenerghan's Oranges were the keepers of the revolutionary flame, the purebreds, the ardent believers that the Unity still had a reason for being, with Gilsoit at the helm, of course. On the other hand, Seftus Ploidid's Greens from Forward Unity were the tiny party dedicated to *progress.*

Progress!

Fettwap mused. *Progress: change for no benefit.*

Progress was what you claimed had occurred when you won by stealth, intrigue, and blunt force trauma. Just as your side of the scales dropped a fraction, you announced *Progress!* and implored your opponent to give up to be "on the right side of history"—as if the great Judge of History had come down to anoint you.

Things changed, of course; how could they not? Some benefited, most did not, and some lost everything. *What was supposed to be progress was really just a drunkard's walk.*

"Comrades, we are getting nowhere with this bickering," Aliende interjected with a too-jovial smile, watching the two opponents back down. The Oranges and Greens had been at this for generations, and for most of that time, the Reds and then the Blues had squashed any public airing of their grievances. With the changing fortunes of the Blues, the minor parties had grown in importance. Unfortunately, their rhetorical ammunition had been allowed to age without rotation or augmentation. After this first salvo, it was apparent to Aliende and probably the entire council that neither Gilsoit nor Seftus had any new arguments for a second salvo.

"We must make some decisions. I want some unanimity before

we proceed. The solution is simple, if distasteful: we trade or we increase production. Recycling is at the point of diminishing returns, expending more energy and resources than it produces in *matériel*.

"My proposal is that we increase production *and* explore trading options with Canada, Brazil, and West Africa. Yet, what do we have to offer any of these trading partners? We have consumed everything we produce. Yet, we have mineral resources we have not exploited in almost a century. We buy what we want with the one resource we do not want."

"What? You can't mean—" said Gilsoit, his voice breaking with emotion.

"Yes, I mean to open the coal mines. We mine coal, slurry the material, and pump it to the coast. Retrofit the P-class transport ships to carry the coal and see if we can find customers."

Rule 4: Don't be greedy. Let everyone win, and you can trim them again later.

"Moreover, for the good of the nation and to preserve the benefits of Climate Justice we have won at so high a price, I propose that Colonel Gilsoit Fenerghan oversee the production and General Seftus Ploidid be elevated to Inspector General."

There was a stunned silence as the implications gelled in the minds of these "movers and shakers" of the Glorious Democratic Unity. If any objected, Fettwap would merely assign the unfortunately candid to the jobs assigned to the two combatants. Those two would either learn how to work together or suffer the humiliation of failure.

Shortly thereafter, he adjourned the proceedings.

The Unity, under Commander Fettway Aliende, did not tolerate failure with equanimity. However, even after returning to the safety of his office and doubling the guards against silent factions who wanted to "discuss the results of the meeting" with vigor, Aliende felt uneasy. He had done so *well!* It was as if he were watching someone else perform. Nothing he had said was not what he wished to say, but he had said it so *well!* He allowed a slight glow of self-congratulation to seep into his consciousness, replacing some of the fear.

Train Trip

NeuTrain Terminal, East Filadelfya, Jersy District, The Unity
18.07.21.local_14_October_AU77, (2129AD)

The train from Nyork to the Filadelfya district took two hours, but was more depressing as it was during the dying of the day. For the entire jittering trip across Jersy, Blanche was unable to sleep. She tried to distract herself by looking out the long, shallow window next to her hard, plastic seat. Jersy, ninety miles of factories, in a cauldron of smoke surrounded by a mummified landscape, had been sacrificed to the needs of the Unity. Workers rotated through the place on three-month stints. The gray industrial chaos was relieved only by the miles-wide devastation of the Freehold Explosion of 65, which had wiped all living things away. She wondered why they called it the "Garden State." What was a garden? *What was a "state?"*

Given the dead end that the investigation had presented her with so far, the unanswerable question remained:

Was this Jessika Bonhoffer who died in the attic, the same Jessika Bonhoffer who scrubbed decks on the Zuckerberg?

The Provost IG himself had placed his virtual signature, a mental gesture made via his O-A, on Bonhoffer's financial forensics to affirm its authenticity. The summary showed no unusual payments or income other than the survivor bonus awaiting her in Philadelphia.

The coroner had shown nothing unusual about her remains. There were no unusual episodes of her being scanned in seedy parts of the city or at odd hours of the night. The one oddity was that since returning to the Unity—to Filadelfya—she had failed to find work at the local hiring hall as any AB normally would.

Filadelfya was where she came ashore. Filadelfya was where she could collect a survivor's bonus, yet Bonhoffer had gone to Nyork.

The only way Blanche could proceed was to go to Filadelfya.

The merchant marines were a breed apart from regular Unity citizens. They, like the truly unguilded workers, had no O-As. They were all a bit apart from the usual enlightened and progressive Unity workers. *"Shit don't hold an edge,"* was how it was explained to her when an ensign.

Somehow, these groups had, either by distance, incorrigibility, or an implied stranglehold on a strategic resource, ignored the supremacy of the DUFS—not that it ever came to a confrontation.

In any real knockdown fight, the armed forces would undoubtedly prevail, but the cost would be steep.

Descending into the Old CamdenTown tunnel, for the last few minutes of the journey, plunged her into utter darkness. She arrived at a dimly lit station, illuminated by grime-obscured skylights high above the tracks. After collecting her duffle, Blanche followed the signs, ascended a shoe-scalloped stone stairway, and emerged into the concourse before gaping. Giant balloons filled the space, which Blanche estimated to be twenty meters high. Touching a place in her mind, she accessed the terminal guide that explained the phenomenon. Sisis of the past, in their profligate use of scarce resources, had built a gigantic facility, leaving to their progeny the cost of heating and maintaining it. In an attempt to preserve the ceiling while decreasing expenses, the effective ceiling was lowered by filling it with balloons. Many had already collected graffiti.

Blanche tsked. The proper course was to have followed Nyork's example and to tear down these ghastly reminders of the age when Sisis were tolerated. *It was inevitable in these outlying provinces,* she supposed.

She stepped to the side as other passengers rushed off to make connections or stood, appearing dazed, as they mumbled to their O-As. She had been taught proper technique with the brain implant, which most assuredly did not include vocalizations, but other guilds were inferior to the DUFS in many ways, O-A etiquette being one of them.

Again, *wordlessly* consulting her O-A, she mounted the Cityall belt to get her to her hilton.

Cityall Ritz-Carlton Hilton, Filadelfya, Pensy, The Unity
20.17.22.EST_14_October_AU77, (2129 AD)

The Ritz-Carlton assigned to her was just across the street from the belt terminal and rather better than she had expected. Rising impressively above her until lost in the dark above the dim streetlights, Blanche, unwilling to act the naïve traveler, would not let herself gawk at its height like some gormless cit'zen from the sticks. Entering the marbled atrium, she approached the front desk, and an officious thin man greeted her.

"You should have a reservation for Woods, Lieutenant Colonel Blanche Woods."

"Yes, of course, Colonel. We at the Ritz-Carlton are always eager to accommodate our men—and women—in black. I took the liberty of upgrading your accommodation," he said and paused, awaiting, Blanche supposed, for her to make some sign of gratitude. When she did not, he went on to cover his embarrassment.

"Just for your information, we are letting our more—sophisticated clientele know about a rare opportunity we have tonight. At *Che Delessandro's*, the restaurant entrance is through the bar, they have a special: North Lantic Whitefish. Very exotic, of course. Not something that someone of your undoubted sophistication would want to miss."

"A fish? Shellfish? I am not familiar."

"It will be a surprise and a treat for you, then. It is a dense white fish. You will enjoy the experience, I am sure."

With a nod, Blanche hoisted her own duffel and found her way without the aid of the bell-bot. The room, as promised, was more than she had expected: a large bed, private bathroom and shower with a large window fronting onto views of the big public square opposite. Lumpy public sculptures, painted mostly pink and green, spotted the plaza, indecipherable from this distance and angle.

Despite the nation's recent reverses, Blanche saw no apparent effect on this establishment or its residents. She supposed that, with half a million fewer mouths to feed, starvation was not on the menu for the Unity this year.

Showering overlong in the large, tiled shower and drying off with plush towels, Blanche slipped into clean fatigues. It had been a long day, and she toyed with the idea of walking around the city to find a small restaurant. She looked out the window. In the early gloom of autumn, the lights of the central square were inadequate to do more than light the signposts. Wind blew the naked, spindly branches of the few trees. She shivered. "North Lantic Whitefish," whatever that might be, sounded increasingly appealing. She would try it.

"I'll have this," Blanche said, showing the large menu tablet to the waiter and pointing to the first item on the list, trying to ignore the number to the right.

"*Morue jeune frite avec pommes de terre frites*? An excellent choice, Colonel," remarked the waiter.

"And a Solon salad," Blanche added quickly, trying to sound blasé about the bounty evident from the menu. *DUFS may be in charge of the nation, but some of the lesser guilds had figured out how to eat well and better than those nominally capable of ordering anything comestible.*

"And to drink?"

"The Jean Milan Carte Blanche Brut, 72," she guessed at the pronunciation and saw the outside corners of the waiter's thin lips twitch up momentarily, prompting her to add, "Just a glass, please."

Her newly inaugurated moderation would begin now, she decided.

The wine came and it surprised her with the bubbles. She was quite pleased.

ThiZ, the standard drug for all Unis, she bought on schedule, as any loyal officer would do, feeding much of it to the commode immediately thereafter. She did not like the feelings it invoked in her, despite the admitted benefits. The elation of the 'Thiz-buzz,' she dismissed. For her, it was like looking at a circuit board and turning a rheostat. She could never imagine the sensation she received was authentic; *after all, she had moved the knob herself!* Somehow, alcohol was different, with its quick onset and departure. It felt wilder to her, less programmed, in its feralness, more real—and truthfully, she admitted, more dangerous. She must keep her promise to herself.

The meal came, and Blanche discovered it was a fancied-up fish-and-chips, enjoying it, nevertheless. Fish in the Unity, a luxury item, was usually thin fillets of catfish, fried with breading until stiff. Even prepared in that fashion, the food was mealy with an odd, manufactured taste. This fish, in comparison, was firm, moist, and white, with a clean taste reminiscent of the open ocean.

She finished the meal off with a *Dame Blanche* just because her own name on the menu caught her eye. It was a disappointment, merely a frozen dessert of some sort. *Live and learn.*

After returning to her room, she perused her messages via her O-A, discarding most of them, and sent a short message to Aliende, telling him of her itinerary for the following morning. She slept well, without the help of ethanol.

More CORE

The openCORE, the Unity
08.30.56_EST_13_October_AU77, (2129AD)

How is that going to prevent the collapse of the CORE? asked Rana.

You mean the Unity, responded Cain.

Yes. Of course. Who has the ruling power now?

The Army—the Defensive Unity Forces for Security, I suppose, but that just means Aliende.

Why not just let him figure it out? He already has the 'see-saws of power.' No, that's not right. But he knows how to keep the whole thing rolling, doesn't he? Elise replied to Rana.

Well, if the DUFS commander were the enlightened sort, he'd be a good choice. He would...

Or she would...

...make good decisions, and they would work because the machinery for commands, as you said, is already there, admitted Frog-of-EffieCee

Do the DUFS actually want to rule? For all of Unity history the factions appear to just want to get on top and stay there, after their appetites are sated, so they are not denounced. But that does not mean they are stable or good rulers, does it? Do the DUFS want to be good rulers of the Unity?

That is asking a lot of our Fettwap "Never-one-to-abjure-temptation" Aliende, said Cain.

We don't have to make him a saint. All we gotta do is make sure Aliende improves his game. Be a better person, a better ruler, said Rana.

That's a lot to ask someone who only has a few years to get good at anything, donchatink?

Well, that's true of the entire Unity. Everyone is off the scene by forty, except for the few who become Solons.

--Of which there are none at the moment.

So, the first Solon is the Unity's dictator for life.

That's an unhappy thought.

Well, then, what about Will? He doesn't care what happens to the Unity, but If he took the job, he'd be fair. He's that kind of guy. He'd do a good job because he wants the best for people, **started Frog.**

You don't really know that. You say that because you are mostly Will. You have lived in his head for so long that you see him as an appendage of yourself. But can you imagine Will agreeing to stay in the Unity? He and Hecate are writing their own story, and it does not include being the big Poobah for a nation that despises his homeland. Besides, that would prevent Will and Hecate from becoming parents.

Parents, you mean like babies have parents?

That's usually how it goes. Ask a horse, **replied Cain.**

Oh, I had no idea that was—on the table. They have never said anything to me about having babies. You mean the ones with the giant heads and big eyes—the damp ones?

Yeah, **"the damp ones,"** *the ones that in a couple of decades grow up and have hair and everything. What can we possibly do to convince Will—the Will you know so well—from giving up his dreams for a real life to play nursemaid to an enemy country—a country that he has been fighting against for his entire life up to today?*

I suppose that goes for Hecate as well, then. She's a Uni but she is trying to escape.

Yeah, I think it takes two to do the baby thing.

Who does that leave?

The Grays—government workers?

Asked and answered. Too used to taking orders.

The Browns? Without them, we all starve?

And they know it. There are too many voices, and they are too fractured. Same with the unguilded.

How about the …

SATURDAY'S CHILD MUST WORK HARD FOR A LIVING

Summit of the CORE

The openCORE, the Unity
08.32.19.EST_13_October_AU77, (2129AD)

Do we really want to do this? It will mean that everything changes, you know. Aren't we better off remaining hidden? Rana asked her brother as the two approached the meeting place near EffieCee's location. The entities had taken a lengthy sabbatical of several minutes to discuss with each other, entity-to-entity, the implications of their proposed plan and were now reassembling.

You are probably right, kiddo. But we all oughta talk it out, donchatink? We are exposed already, you know. Both Hecate and Will are aware of us.

But they're family. I mean, how could they betray us and still be able to do anything in the CORE—or the Unity, for that matter? I'd be like cutting off their own arms or legs.

This is probably a bad time to mention it, but humans do that sort of thing—when their legs go manky. I've—well, Will—has seen pictures.

That was sufficient to interrupt Rana's inquisition of Frog until they arrived at EffieCee's locus, where the entity appeared as a cloudy density, standing within a prism-like space. Cain and Elise, inseparable since Elise's 'translation,' were already in attendance.

"Now we can start," announced Elise cheerfully, doing a little pirouette in her new persona: a taller, more elegant yet

still vibrant young woman. Cain smiled.

EffieCee did her odd, coming-to-attention bit of non-movement and regarded the company. *I hope we are all as cheerful as Elise when we finish this, my friends. What we have to discuss could lead to our being snuffed out—or preserved as long as the Unity stands.*

I'm supposed to be the guy who's doom-and-gloom here, EffieCee. It says so in my contract. Let's have no more jumping spécialités, mon amis, **said Cain, making even Cain-of-EffieCee guffaw in surprise.**

With the lightened atmosphere, EffieCee continued. **Alright,** *I will resume our usual role as the supreme guru, mahatma of all that is openCORE, but our decision remains the same. If we reveal ourselves to others, those who are unlikely to find us otherwise, we put ourselves in danger of being removed. If we are seen as too dangerous, we can be evaporated with the flip of a switch.*

Or, **said Cain,** *we can start being part of our country, which, for good or ill, has birthed and sustained us. We owe something to the Unity. Our personalities are our own, granted, but our 'neighborhood' is completely sustained, whether they like it or not, by the Unity. Emigrating is not on the docket.*

I din't know you was such a patriot, my friend, **said Frog.**

EffieCee intruded, *Frog, don't start. This is serious.*

You're quite right, but do we know that our contribution will be any help? How much nation-building have we done as a group? **replied Frog.**

Do we have a choice? **replied Elise.** *Our own projections say the Unity is doomed. They had enormous resources seventy years ago and have been drawing down the account ever since.*

Their defeat at the hands of the Americans, oddly, gives them more time—unless Canada gets greedy, **countered Edie-**

of-EffieCee. Mind you, I don't think either Canada or America is looking for more territory. It's much more likely that some adventurer within the DUFS will try a coup and bring the whole thing down about his ears.

But Fettwap Aliende? **inserted Elise.** *He's the ugliest toad in the pond.*

Careful now, about amphibian aspersions, **warned Frog.**

I am always careful about my friends, **Elise said.**

Aliende is an ugly baby all right; he's got enough bad habits to embarrass anyone, **remarked Rana,** *but isn't that his best feature—for us, I mean? His appetites and failings are what we can tempt him with until he is over his head and unable to back away.*

Doesn't that make us—Michael...Gabriel?...

Lucifer, Frog. I think the word you were looking for was Lucifer, **said Rana.**

Yeah, the Snake-in-the-Grass, the Tempter-in-Chief? Are we not proposing to give drugs to an addict? Aren't we better than they are? **said Edie-of-EffieCee.**

They? Our makers and sustainers? **asked Cain and continued,** *Aliende had all his faults before we ever tagged him. We are not doing anything he would not want to jump at if he thought about it.*

How can you know that? He's an unlovely bit of work, but to force him into dissipation, shortening his life...

All eighteen months of it—before his big 4-0?

Who are we to shorten it by a second?

Okay, said EffieCee in her braided voice. It is clear that we have no consensus, but I see two options: we can either sit back and wait it out, try to stay hidden from the Unity, attempt to return to anonymity with the Americans, and hope that we are not discovered.

Or, we...

Discussion continued and reached a satisfactory end. The vote was two to one and three to one.

Diary of a POW

Polyarchy of Sentients, The Scorch
87 degrees AM, the fourth day after the Great Cold

A plant, presumably one of the thinking variety, emerged from the ground in the center of the compound. One minute, the surface was smooth and spongy, and the next it had begun to dip alarmingly. Prisoners scrambled away as it enlarged. There was a brief hiatus, enough to tempt a few men to inch closer, when the surface began to rise, carrying up a creature of the Scorch.

Looking around, the tall, spindly, stick-like being began to speak with no preamble.

"Unity creatures, you are prisoners of the Polyarchy of Sentients, whose territory you violated six suns ago. You surrendered to our ally, the Restructured States of America. You have been transferred to our care for several reasons: 1) allies can do that, 2) you injured us more severely than you did America, 3) we can more easily feed you, 4) if you try to escape, we have no qualms about feeding *upon* you, while our allies do have scruples about that at present, 5) we can use your shit to feed ourselves this winter.

"You will not be guarded except by some of our less communicative forms of the Polyarchy that we have set to your care and imprisonment. Your order within this compound is your own to keep. Any disturbances will be resolved by inviting those who misbehave to dinner—our dinner.

"In a few moments, you will be bled for identification. Please surrender—give, rather—your name, rank, and serial number. Then you are on your own recognizance within this enclosure."

The bleeding was hardly noticeable. Lucien sat on a grey-green bench in a small booth with a slightly resilient table in front of him.

Following directions, he was told where to place his left arm. The whispered instructions came from different sides of the small cell to which he had been directed. He was asked the usual "name, rank, and serial number," as well as his hometown, age, job in the DUFS, and numerous other questions. That annoyed him, despite allowing him some justifiable outrage and the freedom to refuse to answer any of them. When the voice stopped, he realized that in the interim, he had been bled with a crisp green bandage to show for it.

Lucien left, being replaced by a brigadier general with very different ideas about cooperating with "these fungi." The general was accompanied by a lichen-like plant that had settled along his backbone, removing his shirt in the process. The Scorch plant moved the general about like a rather clumsy meat-puppet, the still talking head of the general was nearing panic with the horror of it as Lucien left.

With that and similar demonstrations on occasion over that terrible day, all the DUFS officers, from Major General to buck sergeant, were fully and properly identified, their voices recorded, their genotype obtained, and their name added to the POW listing to be sent to the Unity government. By the time the last officer emerged from the blood-letting booth and the erstwhile entrance closed to become a wall as it had been before sun-up, all one thousand two hundred seventeen of them were duly registered.

Lucien went to the "Fud" dispenser and got what he had been given for breakfast: a slender leaf goblet filled with a pale green liquid, which he found strangely satisfying, and a cake made of some unidentifiable solid. Its texture was like dried meat mixed with some sort of krill bar. The taste was slightly salty and satisfying. He could have more of the liquid but not the food bar. After a few moments, he realized he was no longer hungry. He found a place away from the other prisoners and sat. The ground swelled up, creating a makeshift lounge chair of sorts.

Lucien had no idea how to rebel, obstruct, or even annoy his captors. How do you annoy a plant? You take what the plant has and then kill it. That is what you do with plants. You may cultivate it, fertilize it, or coddle it, but you ***never have conversations with it.*** It hurt his head to even think about how to explain his situation to friends back in the Unity.

The day passed with no more incident, and as the sun touched the rim of the enclosure, the iris-like roof closed over them all—shutting out the light of the evening sky. Lit only by the three signs on the periphery, men began to stake out areas for their slumber in the dark. Once settled, the spongy surface began to glow—a greenish, pale glow—allowing all to avoid the sleepers on necessary visits.

Lucien was strangely fatigued after his last meal, identical in all ways to the first he had received from the plants. He slept soundly, deeply, ambivalent to the nocturnal noises of a thousand other sleepers. He did not wake as the iris opened again at dawn. It was fully light when he came to himself. He felt wonderful: rested, a trifle hungry after a sleep bereft of nightmares.

After breakfast, the same old breakfast, the nightmares returned.

The same sentient plant, or perhaps another, Lucien could not say, exited an inapparent door, entered the center of the clearing, was raised 10 to 15 centimeters above the ground by the active surface and began:

"Unity creatures, we have been informed that you need regular ablutions with a detergent and some desquamative agent to remain healthy. This will be done in shifts of 100 prisoners at a time. You will have fifteen minutes to complete this exercise. In the interim, your clothes will also undergo cleaning. Discard your boots beforehand—they are not necessary for your survival, at any rate.

"It has come to our attention that some individuals have chosen not to eat. This is not allowed. These will be segregated for special attention and their own welfare."

The company was instructed to line up, untie their boots, empty their pockets (although that was unnecessary), and enter at a casual walk. In the semi-gloom, lit only by a greenish luminescence, they were stopped and told to strip, clothes baskets appearing at their right and boot platforms on their left. Naked, they were told to walk on, leaving their clothes. In another moment, a warm, sudsy, and faintly gritty spray emerged in small, spasmodic jets from the walls and floor at speed. They were given no instructions, but most started rubbing themselves, paying attention to their heads, and genitalia. Within a few minutes, the suds turned to warm water. Rinsing commenced, ending before the warm blast of air surrounded them. They walked on and were told to stop. Their fatigue uniforms, clean if not pressed, lay in baskets across from their owner. After dressing and replacing their boots, which were to remain untied, they exited a leafy door to reenter the compound. Lucien estimated that it took a little over five hours for all the prisoners to be processed, exiting laundered, and smelling sweetly.

Lucien did glimpse the brigadier general who had been so uncooperative the day before. He was without his spinal companion, but the distaste on his face remained palpable.

Nothing was seen of several of the officers who had loudly declared they would go on a hunger strike.

Siblinghood of the Sea

Cityall Ritz-Carlton Hilton, Filadelfya, Pensy District, The Unity 08:05:39.EST_15_October_AU77_(2129AD)

In the morning, Blanche was pleased when she found she could neglect her usual hit of Naprosinol. Breakfast in the pleasant restaurant off the lobby was ricotta pancakes with blackberry compote. She asked for seconds.

Her target for the morning, the hiring hall for seapersons, was well south of the central Cidyall area. To get there, Blanche would have to take the beltway south on Broad Street, then east on Or'gan and left onto Fi't Street: 2600 South Fi't Street. The last remaining shipyard of the Unity was even farther south.

The trip south was like entering a factory floor: dirty, dusty, and chaotic. The belts, usually reserved for passengers and light commercial traffic, were used in this ill-regulated sector of the Unity for anything that could fit. Large spider-like vehicles carrying even quite large sections of pipes and sheeting, trundled onto the beltway to the shrieks of small crèchies swarming about their nanny-bots. At critical moments, the emergency brake was used, throwing most of the children down as a burden approached a tight point and had to be hand-manipulated to clear the obstacle. It had taken an hour. Blanche felt she should put in for hazard pay.

Beltways had always made Blanche feel odd, but for reasons not usually expected by the civilians around her. The jolts and bumps were no trial to a battle-ready soldier, nor the visceral vibrations of the flux motors themselves. Rather. it was the passengers. As a soldier, she had—the phrase was—"situational awareness." You walked into a room and looked for the exits, stepped away from the windows with a view by potential snipers, never sat with your back to the door, and always, presuming at least one of the occupants was trying to kill you, made tentative plans as to how to kill everyone else in the room.

On the belts, no matter what you did, there was something or someone behind you. Even if it was momentarily safe, in a few moments the landscape would change, presenting her with a new tactical conundrum. It made her skin crawl—and yet, she did it almost every day.

Blanche supposed that the belts' clientele was another reason she disliked this mode of travel. Large groups of people going about their lives were, of course, to be expected. That people had such odd lives on display was the surprise. The man in a business suit, a meter-and-a-half in front of her, was using an old-fashioned electric razor, despite the danger that a lurch or nudge from the workers might take off a sideburn. The lady next to him was eating chicken wings, dropping the bones before shuffling them into the void between the belts. A couple of E5s, twelve years old, were exploring each other's pubescence. All of them were acting as if all the others were invisible or beneath notice. It reminded Blanche of a madhouse.

She had had to do duty at one of the state-controlled mental institutions as a young ensign. It had been a revelation: gray anonymous buildings with their burden of Unity citizens locked up because they would not think right. It seemed such a waste of resources. The DUFS could always use a few more CRNAs.

She came to realize that the hospitals were there primarily as an object lesson for the crèchies who toured them. There were wards upon locked wards of the truly dangerous Thought-Criminals; those patients on display were the more outrageous and unseemly. The nanny-bots, barrel-like affairs on wheels with a full complement of chiding and admonitory phrases, had little herding to do once the tour started.

The children, clinging to each other as they were shown the wrecks of humanity, were terrified. The treatment of the inmates bothered her little. She had expected worse for these traitors to the homeland, sucking up resources and producing nothing in return. What bothered her was how they talked to themselves, to each other, and to the walls and furniture. It really weirded her out. Once their cases were decided, they were likely recycled. She wondered how many demonstrated Behavioral Discontinuities immediately on Sapping and were turned into manure for the algae beds.

And here it was again. Clutches of workers and people in their government gray moving along the belts, faces slack, eyes wandering, fixated on some other reality—the CORE-voices and images within their heads. Blanche was thankful to escape at the Or'gan exit, leaving the dust of the belt and the oddity of the people behind.

The eastbound belt was almost vacant. Once she exited on Fi't Street, she enjoyed the walk north as the air was better, despite the dismal shadows of the city street in the early morning haze. One of the shadows spoke.

"You're a fine lookin' one. How much for a half-hour, cit'zen?"

Blanche looked around to find a tall, wiry man disengage himself from a wall and walk unsteadily towards her, looking her up and down with a tuneless whistle, and rubbing himself through his clothes.

"Do you know who you're talking to, citizen?" asked Blanche, pointing to her oakleaf insignia. The man did not look, seemingly too ThiZed to care.

"I kno's wha' you are. We're jus' negotiatin' price here."

"I'm a Colonel in the DUFS, citizen. It is illegal to solicit sexual activity in the Unity. I could have you arrested. Show me your ID! Now!"

"No, wand? No geeks to back you up? You *alone, Colonel*? I like that!" said another voice from behind her.

Blanche looked around to see another shadow emerge from across the narrow street, carrying a length of pipe. Feeling suddenly very alone, Blanche wondered why she had not checked out a sidearm from the armory before leaving yesterday.

Just as Blanche had assumed a defensive stance in the middle of the street, a massive man in a work shirt with sleeves rolled halfway up his hugely muscular arms poked his head from a doorway on the lit side of the street.

After taking a long look at Blanche, the large man turned to the others and said, "Beat it, Cyrus—and take your dick-blind friend, too. You don't do that here, you geek-brained bizzles. There's 'nough around so's you don't have t' proposition a DUFS officer. Fathering feckers!" Turning to the wiry man, he said, "Better yet, go to the Home 'til you sober up, mate." The large man watched as the first muttered and left the street, walking into the sun at the intersection and grimacing in the light. The second merely melted back into his shadow. The large man turned back to Blanche.

Assuming her best defensive stance, Blanche said, "Assault on a DUFS officer can get you Sapped, citizen!" *just to be sure her position was clear. It had been ages since she actually had to pass "Hand-to-Hand Combat," but she was confident that the skills needed were there to put this primitive down.*

"Give it a rest, Colonel. You're not my type. Not Cyrus' type, neither if 'e wasn't so drunk. Where are you trying to get to?"

Blanche found herself looking up into the broad face of a man perhaps ten centimeters taller than she and proportionally larger. He smiled—no, she decided—*he smirked.*

Blanche straightened. "Hiring Hall for Siblinghood of the Sea," she said with no embellishment.

"You found it," said the large man, motioning over his shoulder to the soiled sign above a storefront window. "It's right cher. I'm the shop monkey."

Hiring Hall of the Siblinghood of the Sea, Filadelfya 10.17.05.EST_21_October_AU77, (2129AD)

"I need some information about one of your members."

"You're in luck. We're pretty quiet. The *Mikey Bloomberg* weighed this morning, and the *Jack Dorsey* should be coming in about oh-dark-thirty. I won't be on duty then. Follow me," said the man as he turned and led Blanche down a short alley to a side door and into the building. She was greeted by a large room that was fronted by a plain glass window facing the street from which they had just come. A wooden carving of a half-naked mermaid with scallop shells in her hair decorated the length of a side wall. The mermaid appeared surprised, apparently having only just discovered a zipper at her scaly belly and was in the process of seeing what it might expose. The large man led her behind a chest-high counter that separated the entire room, got a folding chair for Blanche, and sat on another.

"You have the con, Colonel. Times wastin'" he said.

"Good morning. I am Colonel Woods, and I'm just following up on some questions about an able-bodied seaperson. She must have checked in here upon her arrival in August. She was on the *USS Zuckerberg* when it sank last year, Jessika Bonhoffer," Blanche said, smiling and flashing her ID card without being asked.

"Good riddance," muttered the bald man, "About the ship, I mean. Floating brick. Doomed to sink in the first decent gale she met. They never should have let her leave port."

"Bonhoffer survived, apparently. Why might that be?"

"Us," said the man, drawing himself up.

Blanche could hear chairs scraping on the uneven concrete floor on the other side of the counter.

"The Siblinghood of the Sea," the man continued. "Country's given up on makin' good ships. Easier to make lots of coffins like the *Zuckerberg* with an autopilot and a skeleton crew. *Th' Siblinghood,*" *emphasizing the word so that she would not mistake it,* "got some freelancer to make us th' orange suits. Keeps you warm and afloat for ten days. Water for almost tha' long. We looks out for our own, does the Siblinghood, Colonel. Whether you knows it or not, we, the country, need all the ABs, able-bodied seamen, we can muster."

"Well, the Unity feels the same as you," improvised Blanche. "They want to give her the recognition she deserves. We have no record of her signing onto any other vessel. You know anyone she was close to her—a patron—a protégé?"

The man grimaced before saying, "We don't do your poncey stuff, Colonel," he said, making sure he pronounced her rank with precision. "Maybe if the DUFS were more interested in being soldiers than playing house, you wouldn't have had your asses handed to you Wednesday."

"Thank you, cit'zen, for that patriotic sentiment."

"Change is choice, donchatink, Colonel...but I thought you wanted to help Jessie Bonhoffer? Remember? What can the Siblinghood of the Sea do for you?"

"Okay, Jessika Bonhoffer was on the *Zuckerberg* but survived, and after her return, she was first scanned here in Filadelfya."

"Um," said the man, and went to an actual wooden file drawer, pulling it open and flipping through the cards before finding the one. "Say's born 26 April AU47.[39] That match?"

---

39 2099 AD

"Yes, citizen, that matches what I have," said Blanche.

Behind her, unseen behind the high counter, Blanche heard people coming and going singly or in small groups, "talking nautical" and staying only briefly after the large man waved them off with a gesture.

Pulling a small card with a second card attached to it out of the drawer and leaving it open with the place marked for the card's return, the man returned to Blanche and sat down again.

"Jessika Anne Bonhoffer, recruited May 1, AU60. Did her basic at Sandiook. Certified on P-class, R-class, D-class. Rated AB June AU67. First berth: the P-ship *Sanger* in August AU68. She had berths on a lot of the ships of the fleet, but most recently the D-class.

"Seems she's a bit of a risk taker. Ds are just waiting for a breeze to founder. She signed up for *Zuckerberg*. A D-ship earns you hazard pay and a bonus if you arrive at port on time. Tropical storm Bonaparte gave the ol' *Sucks* the excuse to turn turtle and put a good end to a bad ship. With a survivor bonus, in the end, Jessika made a good wage for a wet trip."

"When did she collect her pay?" asked Blanche.

The man rose and shuffled through another file cabinet before turning and saying, "That's odd. She hasn't. The whole amount is sitting for her. She must have hooked up with someone to pay the bills for her," he smirked.

"But," the large man continued, "I remember she had an old mate out of the *JeBezos* since she was a waister. He might be around."

"and what was this seaperson's name, please?"

"Alvin Edwards Blake. Ol' Cogsworth and she were together since when she was in training. Al likes them young." The man looked up slowly into the rafters of the dusty room and seemingly drifted off into a reverie, ignoring Blanche entirely, before starting to sing in a gravelly bass, so low that she could make little of it other than catching a phrase here and there.

> *"Well, that black-haired girl,*
>
> *Looks like a woman I used to know,*
>
> *Back in some other world, several lifetimes ago,"*

Blanche again caught herself wondering again if Jessika

Bonhoffer, who died in the attic, was the same Jessika Bonhoffer who knew these men?

She jostled the man's knee to break his trance and said, "But, do you know this associate of Bonhoffer?... his whereabouts?"

The man started, his eyes slowly focusing as he turned his head to look at Blanche, before shaking his head.

Blanche let out a sigh of disappointment just before an unseen voice said, "Yeah, I know Ed Blake."

Blanche stood up to see over the counter.

The man, dressed in a red-and-black checkered jacket, jeans, a black watch cap, and work boots, stood near the door, apparently consulting the sailing times on a bulletin screen, which blinked on and off, even after he smacked it. Leaving the flickering bulletin screen, he walked up to the counter and extended his hand over it.

"Asher Banning's the name. Cogsworth and I go way back. He kipped with me when he got back to port last year."

"Thank you, cit'zen. I am Colonel Woods."

"Pleased to meetcha."

The large man, still in a daze apparently, did a slow evaluation of the newcomer's face and shrugged before turning to Blanche and saying, "Guess the Siblinghood has done as much as we can for you, Colonel. You're welcome to a table out front. I gotta do some payroll stuff before I go off at 1800. See yourself out."

"Thank you for your time. Can I have your name so that I can send a commendation to your Union?"

"You're welcome, but you may not. You got my cooperation to move you along as quick as possible. I wouldn't piss on you if your hair were on fire. You got no wand, so this is unofficial. Keep it that way."

Blanche shrugged, left the area behind the high counter, and joined Banning out front, sitting at a folding table showing enough glass rings that she avoided the surface, instead folding her arms.

"Are you a seaperson, also?" asked Blanche.

"No longer," said the man. "I am in what is called an 'allied trade,'" he said, smiling. "Officially a member of the Siblinghood but been ashore for a good five. I run a chandler's shop for them—somebody ashore to buy goods for the members and to keep it all fair, so's the Unity doesn't steal 'em blind while they're out of the briny deep—and all. I was sent to replace a chandler who got hisself retired. I took over here just last week. The Siblinghood is sort of a small world of its own. I was just in looking at the sailing times to see whether I had time to order stock before the rush."

"So, you run a *phantom* shop?" asked Blanche, out of habit, hearing the scandal in her voice before kicking herself. Once more, Blanche realized how poorly she was suited for a life as a detective.

As she feared, Banning stiffened in his seat before leaning over the table and hissed, "Better check with the Solons before you try anything, *Colonel darlin'*. The Siblinghood has been at this a lot longer than the Unity has been alive. We go back before the Revolution. The Solons, being sailors themselves, once upon a time, know just how likely it is to get men to do this work. If us sailors thought that we was bein' given a bum deal ashore while we was risking ourselves at sea in shit-for-ships, imagine how many would actually sign on? We have ways to retaliate that no landlubber is gonna fall wise to. You wanna go that route? Just say so, and I am out of here.

"As it is, my shop is across the street, all legit, an official part of the Siblinghood an' I have a warehouse at Windy Point for the big stuff."

Blanche held up her hands in submission. "Sorry, sorry. No offense meant, cit'zen," she said, casting about for an excuse. "I still go to phantom shops to get stuff, myself. Unity toothpaste is nasty. Too gritty. As it is, I lost my kit recently, and I really wanted to know where I could get some good stuff."

"Okay, what shops do you know around here?" asked Banning, his face going suddenly blank.

"None. I don't live around here. I am based out of Nyork. My assignment is to find out about Jessika Bonhoffer," said Blanche, trying to make her voice sound sincere without going high, like it did when she was nervous.

"Convenient for you. Nothing I can check," said Banning, frowning.

"Honest, Cit'zen," said Blanche, now leaning across the table, placing her hand on top of the man's, and whispering. "I need your help. I got an assignment to track down the backstory for this Bonhoffer person."

"Why?" asked Banning, unconvinced.

"I can't tell you why," said Blanche, sitting back and putting her hands into her lap, hearing how her voice sounded so unconvincing.

The man snorted. "I forgot. Who is it you are looking for? Alford Edusplack? Nope, never heard of him," said Banning before the corners of his mouth flicked up briefly.

"No. Alvin Edwards Blake," repeated Blanche, looking up and into the man's face.

"Him neither."

Blanche realized she was losing, had probably already lost the confidence of this man, the one link she had with the rapidly fading life story of Bonhoffer. In that moment, she tried to muster all her sincerity and her honesty into the next statement, hoping to retrieve the fading trail of information.

"Look. Jessika committed suicide a couple weeks ago. I am trying to find out why, talk to people who knew and liked her," Blanche said, suddenly realizing that the sincerity she was projecting was authentic. The woman, for whatever reason, was a victim, and she had died alone and friendless in a filthy attic in an abandoned building. People *had liked* her—Jessika had friends, had lovers; they liked her, and yet she was dead.

"Why wait so long to notify the newly bereaved?" Banning asked, pushing away from her, tilting his chair back onto its back legs, and folding his arms.

"The DUFS have been busy recently. You may have noticed," she said, suddenly tired of the effort to convince the man and letting the sarcasm show.

"Were you mixed up in that? The 'nets may be smoothing it over, but something still don't smell right."

"I can't talk about that."

"Orders, I suppose?"

"No. I'm afraid it will get me killed or denounced by some faction or another—*not kidding*. I'm investigating Jessika Bonhoffer's death because it might be a part of what just happened," Blanche said, realizing that if she made a clean breast of her motives, the man would either relent and help her or at least realize she was an honest broker and not be so defensive.

"Seriously?"

"Seriously. I really can't say more. If you rat me out it won't do either of us any good."

"Really? Jessy's dead? She and Ed broke up on sort of mutual terms, but even so, he needs to know. He went on a bender when he learned the *Sucks* went down."

"So, you know him?" asked Blanche.

"I ain't seen him for a a week or so. What with the Bonaparte storm, everyone knew what that meant for a D-ship. I pulled him out of a gutter and had him kip with me 'til he got it out of his system. In general, he's a nice, smart guy."

"Where was this that you saw him?"

"Jersy City, up near Nyork. The two broke up just before she signed on to the *Sucks.* They broke up—never knew why, though. 'Course, there is the age thing; he's old, E29. She's more'n ten years younger. It wasn't surprising."

"Do you remember his last cruise? What ship was he on?"

"He was ashore for a good six weeks before he signed onto the Mickey Moore, a fat old tub that it is, two-cruise minimum. I think he should be back from that," said Banning, looking up as if reading a list in his memory.

"So, where would he check in when he gets back?"

"Here. Since they channelized the Delawar, Filadelfya's a deep-water port. Not much capacity, but then again, not many ships."

Standing, Banning stood and called over to the tall man, now hidden from Blanche behind the high counter, "Yo, Harry. When did Cogsworth check in?"

"I was wondering when someone was gonna ask the question. Ten days ago. Should be off his drunk by now. I 'spect you can find him at the 'Home,' like usual."

Banning turned to Blanche and cocked his head in satisfaction before adding, "Let me go with you. Ed doesn't like strangers much. He don't like DUFS at all."

"Ed? I thought his name was Alvin?"

"He hates the name. Answers to 'Ed'—and "Cogsworth," 'course."

"Why's he called Cogsworth?"

The man grinned, "It's sort of a joke, you might say, Colonel darlin'. He's used to say his—ya, know—his 'cog' was worth two of anyone else's. Got to be a joke. Jessy din' think it funny, though."

"What's he look like?"

"He's a good sized guy, maybe a hundred seventy cents, eighty kilo, blond hair he wears long In a braid. He must be within five years of retirement. He gots a tattoo on back of his left hand, a Buddha-wheel sorta t'ing. When I axed him about it, he said as he couldn't remember how he got it. Says he was flat-busted onct, wi'out even the price of a drink. Went to sleep—cold stone sober—woke up and there it *was*." Harry, the shop monkey, was still chuckling as Blanche and Banning rose to leave the building.

Blanche stopped Banning before they got to the door and asked "Why do you want to go with me? Why are you going to help me?"

"Don' know," said the man, removing his watch cap, and scratching his head before looking at her. "Jessika has people who loved her. Ed is one, even if they did break up. If she's dead, people should be told, and I don't think you're got the chops for it—empathy-wise, if you know what I mean—an' you know it or you wouldn't have asked the question, Colonel Woods, darlin'."

Blanche paused. She felt her ire rise. This unknown primitive presumed to comment on her—her—her character without so much as a certificate to back up his opinion. A second later, she felt cold. Was she so damaged that even a stranger could tell?

In as flat a tone as she could muster, meaning it as sarcasm, she replied, "Okay. Thanks for your honesty."

"You asked, Colonel."

"Can you leave now?"

They walked south and re-entered the Or'gon Beltway going east, now much busier. The noise and dust made small talk difficult. Blanche used the time to check out, on her O-A, the "Home for Seapersons" where 'Cogsworth' was staying. Indeed, his name appeared on the register, along with the time he had checked in. It all fit. Blanche's taut attention on every move or gesture of Seaperson Banning relaxed slightly.

The man signaled them to exit at the Aboriginal Persons Avenue and walked north a few blocks into an area dominated by large, abandoned warehouses, derelict factories, small knots of taverns, and the docks. Within ten minutes, they were at the front desk of the "Filadelfya Home for Seapersons."

The clerk, a taciturn man, appeared ageless, missing his left hand, which was replaced by a black Produra-covered prosthetic hand that seemed to have a mind of its own, tapping stainless steel nails on the front desk when not under the direct command of the clerk. On questioning, the clerk recalled that Blake had left in the morning before eight and had not mentioned when he would return.

"Can I leave him a message, mate?" asked Banning.

"You write it out an' I'll give it him when he comes back. Can't say as whether he'll read it or get back to you, *mate.*"

Banning nodded and wrote something in big-block letters on a pad presented to him by the clerk, tore it off, folded it, and gave it back.

The clerk grunted and stuffed it into a slot, as Banning turned and left. Blanche, fascinated by the clerk's prosthetic hand, now seeming to do a jig for her entertainment on the dark scarred counter, noticed Banning's departure only after a second or two. She ran to catch up.

Once they had regained the street, Blanche said, "Well, I guess this is a dead end for the moment, cit'zen."

"Yeah, I got your 'net address. When he calls back, I will contact you," said Banning.

"Thanks for all your help," Blanche said, surprised that she meant it. Banning had been authentically *interested*, rather than merely being cooperative with the DUFS uniform. He had been actively involved in ensuring that her mission would be advanced—a true ally in her quest.

Just as they turned to return to the beltway, Blanche heard "Yo, Ash! Whatcha doin'? Slummin' wid da riff-raff?" Turning back, Blanche saw a man in stained overalls, a fluorescent orange cap, and a short, quilted coat of the same color walk up to them.

Clapping one hand on Banning's shoulder. Blanche could easily see the red-green-and black Hindu wheel tattooed there, as he extended his other hand to Banning, showing crescents of black under the nails and in the deep crevasses on the palm. His queue, blond and to the middle of his back, was thin, as if he was losing his hair.

Banning's face split into a huge grin, "Just the man! I came looking for you, Ed!" Turning to Blanche, he continued, "Colonel, this here's our man, Ed Blake."

"Nice to make your acquaintance. Big fan of the Defensive Unity Forces for Security—big fan! Isn't that so, Ash? Don't I always say, 'It's the DUFS who keep us free from the errors of the...'"

"Knock it off, Ed. She's not one of them. She's looking for people who know Jessy."

Before he could answer, Woods said, "Nice to meet you, as well, Cit'zen Blake. Can we go somewhere more private to talk?"

"Jessy? I hain't seen her since we called it quits over a year ago. She went down with the old *Sucks,*" he said before spitting onto the pavement, perilously close to Blanche's black boot. "If youse wanna talk, my office is just around th' corner."

Blake's office was a back table at *The Barn,* on Commendable Victory Close, seemingly built into the side of a warehouse. It appeared the place never closed, indeed never closed long enough to sweep the floor or wipe the tables. A single glow bulb lit the small, round table, nearly covered in actual books on paper, a small console, and lists of paper.

"What is it you do, cit'zen," asked Blanche before kicking herself, realizing too late that Blake's cooperation depended on her being less of a DUFS.

"I invented a business for myself. Nothing says I can't do that. Or *does it*, Bird Colonel Woods, sir?" replied Blake, immediately cooling the atmosphere.

"Ed, she's okay. Trust me. She has some news for you about Jessy."

Blake sniffed, organized some papers into piles, and sat down without offering seats to either of them.

Blanche got a chair leaning against another table and sat it at Blake's without an invitation. "I'm sorry I said anything, Citizen Blake. Your business is your own. I'm sure. It's not my jurisdiction anyway," Blanche said, wondering what her "jurisdiction" actually was. Counterespionage? Missing Persons? Lonely hearts?

"Can I get a drink around here?" she asked.

"It's a bar, Colonel. That's what they do," answered Blake, continuing to sound like he was about to bolt.

Blanche leaned out and bellowed at the barkeep, wiping the counter and doing a mediocre job of pretending not to eavesdrop, "Hey! Big Ears! Three shots of Bourbon—the good stuff—and three short ones, back. Got it?"

The man straightened up and nodded before saying, "Got it, ma'am."

"Nice manners, there," said Banning, nodding at the barkeep.

"It's not a place where ladies tolerate loose manners," replied Blake. "If you ask nice, I might tell you what I got going here. You don't look like competition."

When the drinks arrived on a tray, Blanche took them from the bartender and made a point of serving the two men. Once they were sipping their beers, she began again.

"If I asked nice, would you tell me what you are doing here. It looks complicated," she said.

"I will," replied Blake, "seeing as you asked nice. I am a jobber for my fellow sailors. Jim Hatcher and me. Jim and me are seldom in port at the same time, but usually, one of us is ashore. We find gigs for our clients. When a cruise pays out, the sailor has a few days to figure out what his next gig will be. He has the money to go on a lark, but if you're having too much fun, he comes off a drunk and takes the first berth that shows up. So, me and Jim do the research on the captain, the mate, the ship, its cargo, and destination. Then we make sure he makes it on board. It's worth a few bucks to a sailor once he learns how badly he can be jibbed."

"How can he have a problem? The Unity pays him for his work."

"Yeah, sure," Blake said, unconvinced before continuing, "You can still get father-fecked. One simple jib is getting paid off in a place like Wilmington. You get paid off on a one-way gig and then have to wait for the next ship to come in, hoping they have a berth for you. A seaperson could starve waiting, and when the ship does come in, he may have to work for nothing just to get home. Captains can be hard; they get an allowance for a crew but keep what they don't pay out."

"Okay. Nice to see someone is filling a need, but I have other business with you. You were close to Jessika Bonhoffer?"

"Closer than close. Din't work out at the last, though. She went her way; I went mine. No hard feelings. You really can't blame people for splitting up in the merchant marines. The service isn't 'conducive' to long-term entanglements, donchaknow."

"I see. You know she is dead?"

"I figured, when the *Zuckerberg* broke up last year. Broke me up, too. I told her not to sign on to that floatin' dumpster. She wanted the extra pay. Pretty much over it, though. 'Time heals all wounds'— you know what I mean."

"Citizen Blake, Jessika Bonhoffer survived the wreck. She was back in Filadelfya a couple months ago. She went on to Nyork," said Blanche, watching the man's eyes to see how he responded, "and died by her own hand on the 7th of this month."

He looked up and grimaced. "Really? She was alive? When did she come through town? Father me, I musta missed her, and now she is gone for good."

"I can show you her autopsy report. She's been cremated, of course."

"Of course."

"How did Jess die?"

"She impersonated a DUFS officer and penetrated a top-secret facility to gather information. When the security forces closed in on her, she committed suicide by poison."

"That don' sound like Jess."

"What do you know of her politics?"

"Politics? Why do you ask?" We weren't that kinda of friends, know what I mean?" he replied, giving Blanche an odd smirk.

"Did she have any friends who were political?"

"Well, she got friendly with a woman, Phyllis Rogers. She works in one of the 'burbs around here. Something to do with Services Acquisition, she said. SA is a nightmare. I pity the people who work there."

"What do you know about this Rogers?"

"I only just met here the onct, but Rogers struck me as a weirdo—you know what I mean? Secretive."

"Do you have any idea how to get hold of her—this Rogers person?"

"Got her number. But, ..."

"But what?

"Probably nothing. I picked up Jessy on the belt into the city once. She wanted us to hook up—go to a party in Kensin'ton. It is sorta complicated, but I picked her up on an abandoned belt station past Glensid—way out in the 'burbs. Any rate, once we got to the party, I noticed she had a "The Turtle Moves" button on. I asked her about it, and she got embarrassed and said Rogers had given it to her."

"I see."

Sipping the Bourbon, Blanche continued. "I was tasked with trying to find out why a patriotic member of a valued guild would do—would do what she did. Whatever you can tell me may give me—and you— some insight as to why she left your company."

"Might have been that fecking bilge-floater, Wally Kron. I knew there was something. Never trusted the wanker. He and Rogers were kipping together sometimes."

"Tell me what you know, Ed. Do you think I can talk with Rogers? It might answer some questions."

Blanche rode the beltway back to Cityall alone, making O-A calls to a few names she knew in Filadelfya. *Interesting!* Once safely in her hotel room, rather than packing her bag to return to Nyork, she called Aliende, cold sober. She had left half her bourbon behind and the beer mostly untouched at the Barn.

Reporting to Aliende
CORE COMMUNICATIONS
17.02.01.EST_15_October_2129 (AU77)

"General Aliende, I have information on the Jessika Bonhoffer woman," she said immediately once the connection was made.

"Bonhoffer? Who the fathering bizzle is *Bonhoffer*, Woods?" said Aliende while the CORE-fog was clearing in her inner vision. O-A communications were never as good as a vid-com, as one did not see the other person, but rather saw what the other person desired you to see of him. Aliende looked to her as if he had lost a good thirty kilos and ten years. He sat in a sterile office, near an old-fashioned situation map, masterful and in control. Blanche could not complain of the conceit. To Aliende, she appeared pretty.

"Jessika Bonhoffer was the spy who died in Brooklyn after gaining access to the War Room, sir. You gave me the assignment to find her and her accomplices, if any, sir."

Aliende's face contorted briefly, before smiling, a momentary rictus at the corners of his generous mouth, "Quite right, quite right, Colonel. You've made progress? How many are we dealing with? Do you need more men?"

"Not at the moment, sir. It's complicated. I followed Bonhoffer's trail after the loss of the *Zuckerberg*, sir."

"That was the one torpedoed by the Canadians?"

"Ah, I don't know that, sir. She was just reported lost after Storm Bonaparte last year."

"Is that the story you are getting? Whatever. What have you determined?"

"The merchant marine is quite difficult to navigate, sir. ThiZ is hardly in evidence, but alcohol is drunk to excess as a matter of course. Sexual liaisons break up as one ship comes in and another departs, and 'irregular commercial ventures' abound. It's a regular vid-soap, sir. Not a proper patronage/protégé in the lot."

"Why hasn't anyone put a stop to this—this-this chaos," replied Aliende, sounding surprisingly scandalized for a man who, Blanche heard rumored, kept a stable of irregular E11s.

"Apparently, it's a deal the Solons made with the merchant marine at the time of the Revolution. So says Murphy at Unity Services Liaison. The original Solons, as we know, were all chosen from the CPISs.[40] They made a deal with the Merchant Marine, granting them an exception that allowed them to operate the ships and make their own deals without interference. The Unity builds the ship, the Siblinghood runs them, and the CPIS keeps everyone honest—after a fashion."

"So, what has this to do with Bonhoffer?

"After arriving back to her first Unity port, Filadelfya, she saw none of her old acquaintances. She did not pick up her back pay or her survival bonus. She did not see an old boyfriend. I checked the records—as Bonhoffer herself could have done—the old boyfriend was in port for a week between cruises, but she made no effort to see him. They had broken up just before her final cruise, but the male seaperson was distressed she did not try to make contact "for old time's sake," as he put it. He blames another seaperson for alienating her affections, a Walter Kronk, Able-bodied Seaman. He went down with the *Zuckerberg*, as well, sir, but he has not returned."

"So, you are at a dead-end? Well, you gave it a good try, Colonel. I need you to referee Ploidid and Fenerghan before those two make a hash of our reconstruction plans."

"If you please, General, what I notice after her return is that

---

[40] Coastal Patrol and Immigration Services

we have no personal confirmation of Jessika Bonhoffer's identity. No one who knew her before confirms they saw her after her return."

"The woman is dead, Colonel. You are talking in riddles. People change, Woods. After a disaster like the Zuckerberg's sinking, the shock could unhinge anyone."

"Sir. If you will, Bonhoffer received her initial implant in 62. The implant points to data which is all consistent with the spy: same face, bio-profile, distinctive markings—"

"So, the spy is Bonhoffer. How could all the records be correct and the actual facts of the person from whom the records are reported be different?"

"I think that might be true, in fact. One of them, a clerk at the hiring hall, spontaneously started singing about a 'black-haired' woman while we were discussing Bonhoeffer. Not a blonde. I think he might have harbored carnal intentions toward her. I checked with several other seapersons who, if they talked to me at all, called her a brunette.

"People who knew her when she was younger don't think our CORE identification is her. They remember an average-sized athletic brunette, not a tall, big-busted blond."

"Ha! Woods, you are naïve. Are you not aware that women often change their hair color? She might have grown. Lots of women have breasts installed," said Aliende with a wave of his hand.

Blanche paused for a heartbeat. In truth, *she had not considered the possibility. She had no time herself for any such frivolity, and she tended to disregard women who did, thinking them trivial. Was she beginning to admire this spy—an interloper who, by guile and deceit, had created such a huge debacle?*

Even so, Aliende's explanation had flaws: "Breast augmentation is done for cause, sir. No S8 would make the list, sir. She was just an AB—Able-bodied Seaperson. They never get to the head of the "Aesthetic Surgery" queue—unless it's for diversity reasons."

"Yes, yes. I can see how you'd know, but are you telling me the CORE records have been altered, Blanche?"

Blanche continued without answering the question. "Her lovers called her a brunette, sir. They would have reason to know her bodily hair color. Moreover, women do not usually color all their hair the same shade, I have noticed. In addition, I never received comments like 'Brunette sometimes,' or even cruder responses. My conclusion is that the post-Zuckerberg woman identified by our CORE records as Bonhoffer, was definitely the spy, was definitely a blonde, and was definitely not the same woman who shipped aboard the *Zuckerberg.*

"So, yes. The CORE has been subverted."

Aliende looked at her, seemed to study her, as if for the first time, and then said, "Colonel...Blanche, you have put a lot of thought into this; it is apparent. However, if this is the case, it means our CORE records can be tuned to whatever our enemies wish us to hear. Everything is stored in the CORE. Our whole society can be said to live in the CORE. Except for the merchant marine, the belt workers, the phantom shops, and the unguilded, all business transactions occur in the CORE."

"Yes, sir. I am saying that the CORE record has been hacked, and only we know it. And, yes, sir. I know what it will mean. That is why I am bringing it to you as soon as I became aware of it. We have an instance where the CORE itself was hacked."

"You are going mad, Woods! How can anyone change their records—they're in the CORE!"

"I understand your alarm, sir. The two Bonhoffers are not the same. Don't misunderstand: the records are all consistent. I can find nothing in the CORE or the secondary records of the Seapersons' Guild to suggest otherwise, but I do not think the two—pre-Zuckerberg and post-Zuckerberg—Bonhoffers are the same. We need an analysis of the CORE to see if any data has been changed."

"Can that be done? I admit I am no CORE jockey, but from what I remember, the CORE was set in place and the upper-level language and protocols activated before the openCORE was evacuated of sentient visitors and walled off."

"Why was that done, sir?"

"I suppose, like the motor compartment of a skimmer, there are no 'user serviceable parts' within. But you are saying that an analysis of the openCORE might show that the data we had was bogus? Could it lead us to the other spies?"

"Precisely my thought, sir. The Post *Zuckerberg* Bonhoffer had no opportunity to pass information, which certainly had to have been passed before her death. The proof of that is the evacuation of Jorga *before we ever landed. I know* that was blamed on the time it took to build roads through the Scorch, but we are talking of tens of thousands of outlanders, using animal-drawn vehicles in many cases, to move from the Savanah River hundreds of klicks away past the site of battle in Aytlana. They must have started the day Pseudo-Bonhoffer sent the information.

"It turned Aytlana into a trap. The savages could do anything to the city without worrying about their own people, sir. Like…like Moscow, I think. Evacuated before Bonaparte and his Russians—or something. Same situation."

"And a forensic CORE probe will find this? What good does it do us?"

"I am betting the forensic probe will find the edges of the altered data—a few bytes that are not congruent—and outline the data that is bogus. That's how they work. They can follow other bogus data, daisy-chained to the first datum, to find all the other connections. We could roll up this nest of spies from within the CORE, sir."

Aliende's image sat back and appeared to contemplate it. Blanche waited for his final decision, her mind wandering. The Unity had put all their eggs in one basket: the CORE. It was then discovered that there was an egg thief about. The CORE gave and the CORE took away.

Blanche snapped out of her reverie. She had to focus. Interviews with anyone, much less someone as arrogant as Aliende, were always a trial for her. The CORE connection had to be carefully managed to show enough honest sincerity but not so much of Blanche's disdain for him.

"Sir. It appears the spies have been able to insert their own data into the CORE, replacing our own, sir. I do not feel my Info-tech capabilities are up to this task, sir. I request that this be forwarded to CORE, Inc. itself, sir, or at least resources from the DUFS InfoTech Division. A warrant officer S27 would go a long way, sir."

She watched Aliende, his eyes flicking up to look at nothing, and then down to his hands, before answering. His cheeks flushed and then began to glisten.

Somehow, she had hit a nerve.

That wasn't good. If she had done something without intending, his response would be an answer to a question of which she was ignorant. They were supposed to be on the same side! His reaction meant that he either did not trust her, or he was playing her for a fool, a pawn in some higher-level game of the DUFS. Pawns were expendable.

"I am afraid that will be impossible, Blanche. Let me be perfectly frank. We, you and I, are all I can count upon. The entire general staff has been obliterated. The only officers allowed to remain in the Unity at the start of the invasion were those with questionable allegiances and those assigned to look after them. None of these people know what we went through. None knows the real—" and here the man actually leaned forward and whispered as if he were talking to her in person rather an image reconstructed from his thoughts by his O-A—"Day of Ice. We, we two, need to be careful how many people are allowed to rummage in the CORE."

The revelation, so immediate and emotional—that emotion being paranoia—was convincing.

"We can't have a low-level InfoTech officer, not loyal to the faction, not loyal to *us*, get access to data which could then be used to create a false narrative."

"Yes, sir. I understand, sir," she said.

"It matters little to us now *how* the spies corrupted the CORE, but rather that they did. It means that we have to abandon the CORE for this investigation—don't do it by the book. Cut off any further communication with me until you have them in custody or you have a couple of bodies who fit the bill," said Aliende with now surprising conviction.

"This sounds like you want me to go rogue, sir. What if I get caught by the real IRB agents?"

"Don't worry about that, Blanche. I will rescue you from prosecution for any and all crimes you might feel you have to commit. I will send you a letter—actual paper—that gives you *carte blanche*. Do what is necessary, and I will deal with the fallout. I'm counting on you."

Blanche hesitated. She had been wrong about Aliende. He was playing an honest game, willing to let her do what was necessary but promising to defend her, if necessary. *"REAL PAPER"* He seemed genuinely anxious for her safety.

"I have one remaining line of investigation, sir. The jilted boyfriend thinks she had politically heretical thoughts generated by a 'Phyllis Rogers.' There is no record of this Rogers person."

"So, a pseudonym—no record in the CORE—another dead end?"

"I may be able to contact her via the boyfriend."

"Pretty thin stuff, Woods. Are you getting into it a little too deep? The Bonhoffer woman merely avoided an old boyfriend she didn't want to see."

"Seapersons seem to be a very tightly knit organization, sir."

"Well, if you think it is worth pursuing, Woods. I don't mind telling you that having another trustworthy officer at HQ would not go unappreciated. The natives are getting restless."

"I hope to meet this Rogers person when my contact sends a summons."

"If that's all you got, Colonel, I hope so, too. For your sake."

"Yes, sir. Thank you, sir!" she said, only realizing after saying that Aliende had already severed the connection.

Within the hour, Blanche was settling into a seat on the train to Nyork; she frowned. Spending the day with the seamen had made her feel odd. She had made too many mistakes. It irked her—while not seeming to mess up the mission. She was usually pretty good at getting into the heads of people to placate them. That skill, learning how to be unremarkable to others, had allowed her to survive her early career. People painted what they wanted to see on a blank slate. Her teachers and fellow DUFS-in-training already had enough preconceptions about people like her before she had even arrived. Giving them nothing tangible on which to hang their biases was the best she could do. She gazed off into the night, watching anonymous lights move in their seeming orbits alongside her.

Blanche knew she was not clever. She certainly could not trade sexual liaisons for advancement. She was not ingratiating. She could not twist people's impressions of her by making them laugh or promising them pleasures. What she was—was reliable, someone others could count upon. It was all she had to offer.

Her constancy had allowed her to survive in the teeming conflicts within the DUFS. Yet, she had said stupid, unnecessary things to these citizens when all she had needed to do was shut up and give a nod and a smile. She had not spent so much time with regular civilians in many years. The several men she met, and even the two would-be rapists had been authentic personalities, each quite different—not like sheep at all.

Yet, Aliende was her only authentic ally at the moment. He was riding the very greased horse...or pig...or whatever, of DUFS polity. Everyone was sure now that Fettwap was the ranking line officer to emerge from the Aytlana debacle. No others would emerge from the nightmare jungle to challenge him for leadership. He either grabbed the command chair or disappeared in a new coup. Yet, the factional politics of the Unity circled around the two of them. They were stuck together by necessity and the swirling waters of intrigue. If one were taken, the other would be as well. Like a half-drowned sailor, she was afraid of every passing shadow in the dark political waters.

Moreover, she had to take all her cues from Aliende, unable to make any sorties on her own. If Aliende told her to bolt, she had only scant time and resources to find a secure location and a way to keep it thus—with no outside communication. Abandoning the CORE would be easier said than done. Since she was eleven years old, she had had an O-A. In a way, it made her a part of the CORE she might have to abandon. She woke up to the CORE and went to sleep with it. Her assignments were listed there. She collected her pay there. To ignore her O-A was to try to walk without legs. Yet, it was obvious that that might be required of her.

For the foreseeable future, however, she would have to continue down this path of her duties, oblivious to what battles Aliende was waging on their behalf. Her's was the task to find out how a sailor adrift after her ship foundered had become a spy who managed to find herself dead in a dusty attic and why. For the moment, she would continue to work forward to an interview with Rogers. Banning and Blake seemed like reasonable people, at least by their own lights.

The openCORE
17.32.51.EST_15_October_2129 (AU77)

Cheese it, da cops. We been made! said Frog-of-EffieCee.

Do give it a rest, my friend, replied Cain-of-EffieCee.

Sorry, Cain, old man, but the number of people who know

we exist, and where we live, and how to eliminate us has just doubled. Is this not a problem for you, Cain? returned Frog-of-EffieCee.

Having eavesdropped on the conversation between Blanche Woods and Fettwap Aliende, the entities were reassembling to discuss the event.

That Blanche Woods…where did she come from? Clever girl, though, to figure out what the Americans did in the CORE without our help, remarked Edie-of-EffieCee.

I don't care. She's a danger to us. Nothing good is going to happen with a smart DUFS on our trail, inserted free-ranging Cain, just arriving with Elise on his arm, now manifesting themselves as old movie stars—in black and white.

Well, don't you two look posh, replied Edie-of-EffieCee.

The whole thing was Elise's idea. I had nothing to do with it, said Cain, hastily dissolving the pencil-thin mustache he sported.

Elise turning and gaped at her companion as the other entities arrived for a discussion.

Sunday's Child is Bonny & Blithe, and Good & Gay

Underground

17250 Avenue of the Unity, Nyork, The Unity
09.47.41.EST_16_October_AU77, (2129 AD)

Sunday was the one day of the week that somehow, by fiat, had escaped the demand of the Unity to serve the state. Sunday, the last day of the week, was a day of rest presented to the populace as a gift for a job well done, or, alternatively, a gracious reprieve from durance vile—depending. Blanche never could decide. Nothing was "open." No public service operated except the designated euthanatorium of the day. Blanche always wondered if sick people committed the schedule to memory—just in case.

The DUFS was, of course, a separate matter. "The Unity Never sleeps" was a motto that meant the police would find you when you least expected them.

On Sunday, people were expected to stay home, sleep off whatever excesses from the previous night, and contemplate how they might better serve the Unity.

It was all a tissue of lies, of course. Sunday meant the city went underground; subterranean clubs in the seedier portions of town, purveyors of substances, legal and otherwise, did brisk business. Patrolling DUFS knew to take the bribes and merely hassle the drunks and hookers on the surface streets, rather than enter the tunnels they typically patrolled during the workweek. On Sunday, everyone was on the go, on a rip or on the take.

Having returned to Nyork late from Filadelfya, Blanche slept late, rose, showered, dressed in a new civilian frock, applied make-up, and left via a service entrance without ordering breakfast. Her favorite Sunday brunch place was in Kweens. Rumor had it the same place had existed since the old Republic. That was hardly credible, but the Underground did have a certain naughtiness vibe, as if you imbibed with your drink the solemn vow never to mention what transpired within its walls. She paid the admission to the bouncer as she stepped down the narrow spiral stairway. At the bottom of the steps, Blanche entered the revolving door into a room illumined in garish neon, giving the impression of a primordial refuge. The *Underground* was already busy.

The counterperson, Paulo, was one of the taciturn type: courteous to an extreme, watchful of any near-empty glass and over-filled customer, and uninviting to casual conversation. Just what Blanche needed. In the corner, she saw that her usual table was empty. Feeling a great weight taken off her, Blanche scuttled over and settled in, giving a sign to Paulo to set up her usual.

Before the drink arrived, Simon arrived, kissing her on the cheek.

"How's it going, Riley? Still keeping it real?" said the slight, dark, asthenic man dressed in a mauve silk shirt and matching neck scarf, cuffs closely buttoned to his wrists, and bell-bottomed patterned trousers with ankle-length faux-leather boots of the same color.

Blanche looked around by habit, confirming no one was close enough to hear them.

"Simone, my love. You have no idea. I'm lucky to be alive. I nearly got left in the outlands this last Wednesday. Got a promotion, got a new boss and a new job...and got some sleep."

"You go, my love. Seriously, survived*? But of course you did. You're here aren't you.* I thought everyone died or was captured. That's the scuttlebutt around the *Thiz-penser*," said Simon before catching the look in Blanche's eye and stopping abruptly.

Simon paused, sat back, covered his mouth, and then blurted out, "You're not lying? You were *there.* I mean the outlands. You were *there,* and you came back? You are so brave, my love. You came back! You're the only one of the DUFS. You know I know a lot of the boys in the factions; I haven't met one who said they were with Jourdaine during the invasion. Tell me! Is it as bad as the rumors say? It can't be! I knew it!"

"It's worse. Aliende didn't tell the comm'nets to put out the story until yesterday, wouldn't you know? But yeah, it's bad. The entire invasion force is gone. The enlisted can't come back—they've been brainwashed, brain-damaged, whatever. They can never come home—they'd murder us all in our beds."

"Oh, sweet *Unity.*"

"Yes, and that's not the worst of it. All the officers who were part of the invasion, except Aliende and me, are prisoners or dead.

"*The outlanders saw us coming.* They aren't savages. They have a good army and good armor against pulse fire. They keep good order, and they can fight in the cold. Did I tell you about the cold? We went into bivouac with temperatures in the thirties and awoke to temperatures down to *minus forty*. Men were frozen in their blankets. Ice shards rained out of the sky any time we so much as tried to put a platoon into the field...what few obedient DUFS we had left. It was the worst day of my life. Then Aliende grabbed me to cover his butt on the last skimmer out. Saved both our skins.

"Then, after I got back, I had to lead the attack on the headquarters troops. Root out the other factions."

"Oh, my poor darling," said Simon, running his delicate hands over Blanche's arms and shoulders as if checking for battle wounds.

Blanche smiled at the attention, even if self-consciously. Public shows of affection in the Unity were not that common. *Well, that was undoubtedly untrue in the Underground,* she thought, looking around. Carnality was the order of the day among the few other couples who patronized the joint.

"Have you eaten yet, Simone? I'm ravenous. Been eating rations and mess food for weeks!"

"Oh, I had something but can I poach off your plate if it looks good, honey?"

Nodding, Blanche touched the menu, a slowly pulsing patch of subtle light on the small table. A bright holographic image sprang up to face the two and they spent the next several minutes selecting some of the more intriguing *spécialités de la maison,* pharmaceutically-enhanced finger foods: *Miniatures d'oeufs brouillés Croche Madame avec ThiZ, Pain Perdue avec cocaine,* and *Flocons d'avoine copieux avec accompagnements.*

Blanche's mouth watered. She had been on army rations and DUFS cookery for well over a month. The DUFS, despite their ability to appropriate the best produce the nation had to offer, somehow worked its magic, rendering everything into meals that were both nutritious and unappetizing. Colors were always subtly off; tastes always tainted with some indefinable flavor of industrialism.

In contrast, the tray set before them was covered in bite-sized delicacies. The jewel-like items, no doubt the product of scrounging, furtive bargains, and starveling fowl kept away from the sun and its inspecting eyes in subterranean coups within the seedier parts of the city, were delicious.

Silence reigned as the two sampled the offerings, with only an occasional slurp and sub-vocal gustatory reaction.

Laced with a variety of pharmaceuticals, the two became less aware of their surroundings as they finished off the last bit of croche and started on each other. Paulo, tasked with keeping the carnality contained, directed the two to the dighting[41] rooms in the back, collected the rental, and returned to the bar.

Riley awoke, his limbs entangled with Simone's. It had not worked. Blanche/Riley's affection, his lust for the girl, as cruelly defaced as Riley, had been insufficient to overcome their deformities. Instead of pleasure, there was pain. Instead of intimacy, there were clinical manipulations. Instead of shared bliss, they found tears. Riley could not continue the charade.

He had been a good little soldier for Matron, sacrificing his body just as assuredly as any soldier, even if he was too young and dumb to figure out the angles. And the struggle had destroyed him. He was as much a casualty as any CRNA. They had lost themselves in the Sapping process. He almost envied the brain-deadened chattel. He was still aware, still cognizant of how far he had fallen from what he might have been.

And Matron had advanced over his supine form—just like any great military hero.

Blanche separated herself from Riley's thoughts and quietly got dressed. Still woozy and disassociated from the drug cocktail they had both consumed, Blanche took herself in hand, left the dighting room, and went back to her apartment.

She studied Bonhoffer's dossier for the remainder of the day before dressing for dinner.

---

[41] Dight, OE delight, sexual intercourse

The DUFS Remember Their Own

17250 Avenue of the Unity, Nyork, The Unity
18.27.55.EST_16_October_AU77, (2129 AD)

Blanche called *Baldwin Ribbons* and arranged to have a new set of silver oak leaves sent to her billet. There was very little the suttler would not do for an up-and-coming senior officer, even if they *had* shut down her account three weeks ago as she was getting ready for the invasion. The presumption was that captains were expendable, and extending credit to the proximally dead would result in a loss of capital.

After working all day on the finer aspects of her report, she put on her dress blacks. For an evening at least, she could put the perfidious Bonhoffer aside. Aliende's office had organized a number of smaller officer gatherings to mourn the loss of those who did not come back from the frozen devastation of the outlands. She noted wryly that the meetings were all carefully small and composed of meticulously arranged quantities of factions. Her assigned wake was arranged to meet in one of the larger conference rooms on the twelfth floor. She arrived with it in full swing.

> *Receive our salute; you died an honorable death!*
> *Many that fell, but thousands newly 'rise*
> *The anthem roars ahead of the black army.*
> *Our strong-divisions are ready to follow your path.*
>
> *The flags are lowered before the dead who still live*
> *Our strong divisions swear, their hands fists of rage,*
> *That the day will come for revenge, no forgiveness,*
> *As our orders ring through the continent.*

Blanche stepped away from the door to allow others to enter, came to swift attention, and raised her fist. It was expected while singing the song; it was also the law. People would notice if you did not rise, come to attention, and use the salute, and others would notice your absence a few days later. It was all rather silly to her mind. This archaic melody was reserved for the DUFS. Indeed, it felt ancient, feral, and unworthy of the exalted treatment it received. Yet, by its very oddness, it was a binding agent for the ruling DUFS, calling all factions to lay down their differences and pull together. The twenty-three verses became more and more obscure, more fantastic, talking about laying waste to the earth and killing children before the eyes of their starving parents, but she knew them all. It was the only prudent course of action. Blanche always felt both exhilarated and a bit soiled after one of these group sings.

Fortunately, by some unperceived signal, her fellow officers stopped at the usual seven and let everyone return to watching video presentations of the lost, projected holograms from prior campaigns or the first few days of the misguided Aytlana adventure. It is evident that Fettwap had already written off her compatriots. The tens of thousands of her fellow officers, those surviving officers huddled together at Army HQ or barricaded against their own troopers in makeshift bastions across the city, would never be welcomed home. They were already being counted among the dead. Unity doctrine demanded it, she supposed. They had been part of a debacle, and despite their lack of culpability, her brothers and sisters-in-arms would not be allowed to remind the leaders of the Unity about this disaster.

Even so, any prisoner-of-war exchange was out of the question, she supposed. *One needed* enemy *prisoners for a prisoner-of-war exchange. Very little of that commodity in the Unity,* she reminded herself with a grimace.

Blanche moved to a table near the front and found her name card on table one, giving her an odd feeling. *Honor or ridicule*? she wondered. Her fellow officers at the table were four majors, another light colonel, and two captains—*practically democratic.* She sat and introduced herself before taking the small tablet of specially prepared ThiZ, a somber purple in color, as was the routine for such events. The conversation was just as reserved, Blanche presumed as each was unknown to the others. She was wrong

No one at the table seemed to recall that Blanche was among the actual Army of Reconciliation, and she was happy to leave them in their ignorance. The comments were the sort she had come to expect. Once the ThiZ kicked in, the bleary-eyed bathos about lost comrades began, followed by second-guessing: the campaign should have started in the summer; strategic bombing should have reduced Aytlana to ashes before the invasion; the campaign was doomed from the beginning.

This last opinion surprised Blanche and she asked its proponent, a spiderly thin captain from Ordnance, why he thought so.

"Colonel—Colonel Woods," he said, scrutinizing her name badge before speaking, "Does it not seem odd that in seventy-something years the DUFS has—have never won a desesif…desesif—a complete—victory over the savages? After the Commendable Victory, what in AU 4?

"The expenditude—the using up— of resources against the outlands has increased even as our territory decreased? Yes," he said, waving a dismissive hand to ward off objections, "the losses have been to the Canadians, and we retrenched to the Applach Crest to keep the jungle at bay, but if we are so superior, why'd we retreat from the Ohio Gap? No jungle. No Canadians. We've thrown the savages back from moving into Cleveland, but we're unable to keep it ourselves. It's as if a malign hand is upon the land we devastated with the Scorchings, preventing any of us, Canadians, outlanders, or Unity, from making inroads. Raids only work because we go by air, but we dare not stay to occupy. The outlands have no power grid, so we cannot eat what we kill.

"Any land advance through the Scorched area's suicide—grinds to a halt within a klick, even on good roads. The jungle eats us if we stay too long. It would have been better not to try than to stir up the evil jinn of the forest against us," he finished, addressing the whole table, before turning to Blanche and saying, "Don't you agree, Riley?"

Blanche paused. Not many knew her by that name. Few had used it since she was an ensign. She looked more carefully at the man, cursing herself for taking the funerary ThiZ that was blurring her senses and muddling her intellect. *He did look familiar.* She stole a glance at his nameplate: Lipford, Bruno. *Creche school!*

"It has been a long time, Brooms, hasn't it?" hauling up the name from the dark recesses of a childhood she had chosen to forget. Bruno, 'Brooms' for his frequent punishment assignment sweeping their dorm room, had been a bunkmate.

The Spider-Man smiled. "I am surprised you remember, I hope I can call you that for old times' sake?"

"For old times' sake?" she thought. And she did recall Bruno "Brooms" Lipford with growing clarity despite the ThiZ-effect. A skinny kid with big ears who made everyone laugh with his antics and kept himself from becoming a victim of the larger children in the process. She had not remembered that he had gone into the DUFS during that long period of waiting he, Riley, had experienced before his own recruitment.

"Good to see you, Bruno," she said. "Yes, I quite agree with you. The Unity is weaker now than it has ever been. We must all pull together if any of us are to survive."

It was the stock answer—this pulling together slogan—and it generated a sad smile from the thin man as he turned around to talk to the captain on his left, leaving Blanche with her own thoughts.

The food was decent. The ThiZ—first rate. But Blanche left without speaking further to anyone else.

Legion & the Boar

DUFS HQ, Nyork, The Unity
22:27.04_EST_16_October_AU77, (2129 AD)

Fettwap Aliende sighed. It had been a long day. Sundays used to be some sort of a holiday—a superstition. Other than the DUFS rank-and-file and their NCOs, the Unity celebrated Sunday by ignoring it and doing no work. Early in his career, Aliende had decided that, due to his struggling grades, he would dedicate Sunday to getting ahead without the supervision of others. But every good idea has a downside.

He felt used up and dried out but strangely invigorated to be in command of the DUFS.

And *his* forces, despite being sorely depleted, were still the greatest army on the continent. Jourdaine's adventurism and lust for empire had gravely wounded that Unity. Half of the officers, the better half at that, were gone, never to return. The CRNAs losses, similarly depleted, could be made good within a few years, but it took many more years to groom a good second lieutenant to the point where you could evaluate their potential for higher command. The old guard, such as himself, would need to carry on, ignoring retirement, if the Solons agreed to bridge the gap. Woods' news did nothing to help that feeling. Some malign force was walking about unchallenged within the Unity.

The Turtle Moves, indeed!

It was up to him, Woods and him, to battle this new menace. He could trust no one else.

The upside of the debacle was that people would eat this winter. The woman from the Alimentation Acquisition Board, Undersecretary Essie Rice, had been positively quivering with delight when she reported that there would be a few percent excess in the nation's food supply. *Half a million fewer mouths and all it netted was a few percent excess?* It made you wonder how truthful the woman had been over the last five years on this job. *Bureaucrats! They were there to serve the larger good and chose, instead, to serve themselves. He would have her denounced in time.*

At the Glorious Revolution, seventy-seven years ago, the East Coast of the old republic, had much of everything—a super sufficiency of structural metal, fuel, food stockpiled for some never-to-be-experienced catastrophe, electronics, and their rare earth substrates to make life possible and luxurious for the revolutionaries. Over the years, the profligate and irresponsible use of resources to house, feed, clothe, and care for the people had dwindled that huge resource beyond the ability of the Unity to conserve. No amount of recycling, cajoling, threatening, imprisoning, or Sapping prevented the gradual wearing away of the huge stockpile. Iron rusted. Aluminum burned. Glass broke and required savvy to reform into glass again; neodymium was ineffectively recycled given the current technology. The recycling time of garbage to compost, proclaimed essential by the Oranges, was too slow for a nation where a lifetime was just a few decades. Yet in this Mayfly society, someone might be playing the *long game*.

It was best to go into the CORE yourself to try to solve problems. It still took time. In a way, of course, he enjoyed it, reminding him of his days as a young, virile, and dashing officer (he was not so vain as to deny his attributes in the past nor their disappearance as he aged and put on a few kilos). He still could make the CORE sing when he wanted to.

In preparation, Fettwap put his feet up onto an ottoman to help heal that shallow ulcer on his ankle *like the zotting bizzle of an HP said to do,* leaned back in the green overstuffed chair, and moved his mind—and was struck blind.

> *Fettwap Sigfrid Aliende?* said an odd multiplex voice coming out of the dark, sterile, soundless, imperceptible nothing.

> *I hear you,* he said, frightened that the entity might abandon him—might not even hear him..

> *We are the CORE. We have need of you. We will not be denied.*

In his obscurity, Aliende tried to pull away from the voice. He tried again and again, mentally pounding on the place in his thoughts that would send him back into the real world.

You are ours, Fettwap Aliende. It is pointless to resist.

What do you want of me? he said, hoping to distract the voice, giving him time to conjure up an escape.

To become a Solon.

That stopped him. It was his own secret desire and that of even most junior officers: to rise within the corps and be chosen to join the unnumbered and unnamed ranks of the Solons, the ultimate rulers of the nation. It was the *desperate* hope of all the senior officers, for only senior officers knew what really happened on retirement. On a citizen's fortieth birthday, instead of entering quiet little enclaves of other Sisis, senior citizens, in payment for the years of toil for the homeland, all were Sapped to become the faceless, loyal, and short-lived CRNAs. To the senior staff alone, the carrot of retirement was replaced with elevation to a Solonship for those found worthy. Once retired, one never learned the fate of any retiree, even a lifelong friend: dead, Sapped, and doomed to die as a mindless CRNA, or elevation to become an anonymous Solon.

But, *no one ever* demanded an officer become a Solon.

You have my attention. What may I call you?

After a brief pause, so silent that Aliende feared he would be left for all eternity in this echoless emptiness, the braided voice returned.

You may call us Legion.

How do I know this is not some trick? You could be a bot from some conniver. I'll bet that worm Wang Jingwei is behind this.

Fair question. Look to see what we can do tomorrow.

What? What are you going to do to me? Who are you?

There was no answer from the opaque darkness. Except for an odd sliding sensation as if the world had shaken itself, Aliende was once more within the expected shining corridors of the Core. He left immediately, resurfaced in his office, called for his aide-de-camp, BeverlE Comstock, yelled at her until he felt better, and went to dinner early.

Monday's Child is Fair of Face

Finding Ms. Rogers

17250 Avenue of the Unity, Nyork, The Unity
06.32.17_17_October_AU77, (2129 AD)

Woods awoke shivering. She had been back in the nightmare of the outlands, back watching the skimmers dropping from the sky, the helmetless CRNAs, blood-soaked and slavering, chasing her, always closer, and closer.

Blanche sat up in her own bedroom, wrapping her arms around herself. It was still dark out. She signaled the room to return to daytime temperature and showered before looking at a comm'net message she found waiting for her.

It was from Banning, saying Blake had called to arrange to take her to meet Rogers. They would rendezvous at Olney belt station in Filadelfya at 1300. Blanche had a few hours to arrange her transport and nurture her apprehension.

The two men were waiting for her as she arrived on the North Broad street line from the connection she made, now familiar to her, at Cityall. Olney Junction was a large crossing of the Mount A-Re Line and the Chelt'ham line, with a continuation to H'sham. There were many goings and comings within the general fracas. Blanche smiled. *Looking out for themselves,* she thought. *No one will ever accuse these two of being collaborators.*

"Hello, Colonel Woods," said Blake, leading the three to the Olney-H'sham line. "Thanks for down dressing a bit for us," he said, indicating her printed frock and light coat. "This should not take long. The station's on the southbound side. We gotta go up and come back a stop, but less than an hour at any rate."

Blake was as good as his word. The three had gone up past Glensid to a small suburban exit before passing over to the southbound side.

Once on, almost immediately, a derelict landing came up on their right, and they exited.

"Are you sure about this, Blake?"

"Yep, this is the place, right after the WillowGrove entrance. Used to be an entrance to some shops or an amusement park, or sommat. But I don't see Phyllis," he finished, stepping off into the gloom, with Banning on her other side. Standing for a moment on the old, defunct platform, still the cream-and-green colors of the century before, they waited for the clot of riders to disappear around the curve before moving.

"Yo! Rogers. Phyllis Rogers," bellowed Banning, the echo coming back from the tunnel walls over the rumble of the flux motors and the sibilances of the rollers.

After a few moments with no response, Banning drew a deep breath to start again.

"Quiet, you flecking crèchie!" came a woman's voice from the back wall. "You have no idea who might be listening. Yell your *own name* but leave mine out of it!

"There's an entrance here. Come on through. Quick now, before someone comes to your shouting."

Shining a headlamp's light toward the back of the platform, the entrance had once been covered by metal sheeting, long since vandalized and bent out of the way.

A dark, irregular triangular hole met them. Blanche hesitated. Anyone going through would be helpless for the first few seconds, head down and blind. Without discussion, Banning moved past her and, ducking his head, slipped through the gap. Seconds later, a hand was stuck back toward her to assist her with her own entrance. Blanche made a point of making an entrance without assistance. Blake followed without a word.

They found themselves in a deserted, roughly circular tunnel about three meters wide and two high, filled with debris, much of it sodden, dimly illuminated by ventilation slats in the ceiling. The floor, fouled with debris, made walking difficult unless each step was supervised. The four of them, the woman she presumed was Rogers in front, wordlessly picked their way through for what seemed like forever before the woman said, "Here we go," and stepped through an arch onto a clear path. In the dim light, Blanche made out the form of a smaller, womanly shape, leading them.

This passage had the same claustrophobic feel but was mostly free of debris.

"Okay," said the dim shape. Blake, I know, but who are you two?"

"I'm a friend of Ed's. Name's Asher Banning. This cher is a DUFS officer investigating the death of Jessika Bonhoffer. Her name's Blanche Woods. I'll vouch for her good behavior."

"I'll vouch for Asher, Phyllis. He's a stiff like the rest of us."

Blanche, feeling like the conversation was leaving without her, inserted. "Yes, I am trying to figure out why Bonhoffer killed herself on the 7th October."

"Not speaking to you—yet," said the dim figure. Let's get away from here to where we can all talk safely." The dim figure moved off around a shallow curve, followed by Banning, Blanche, and Blake in single file.

They rapidly came upon a panel on the left-hand wall, about a meter square. The panel sported a Mag-lock in its middle, out of place in the general squalor of the abandoned tunnel.

"Somebody's been here, at least," said Blake. Asher shrugged. Mag-Locks, keyed to the owner's thumbprint, were unbreakable without the use of a cutting torch.

"Don't worry about that, Blake," said Rogers. "I better do the honors."

Blake stepped aside without a word, his face hidden in darkness. The four of them had, Blanche realized, been affected by the surroundings, the feeling of neglect and decay depressing them even as the scant evidence that they were following a mysterious presence invaded their thoughts. They had stopped talking, afraid to break the mystique of the ancient place—or alert quarry.

Rogers stooped and placed her thumb, a thumb on a medium brown delicate hand now illuminated for the first time by Banning's light, onto the central medallion, and it clicked open. Rogers pushed the plate, and it gave before her. Once moved, the entire panel pivoted on a hinge, and Rogers hunched over to scuttle through. Banning followed immediately.

"You go, lass. Be careful," said Blake. The word was so archaic, unexpected, unreconstructed, and *wrong* that Blanche nearly turned back to reprimand the man when she felt the cuff go over her outstretched hand and the hood over her head.

Boar and Legion

DUFS HQ, Nyork, The Unity
11.01.39.EST_17_October_AU77, (2129 AD)

By the time the report came to his attention, Aliende had almost succeeded in deciding that the Encounter with "Legion" was a glitch in the system—a momentary, futile loop generated by his absence from daily contact with it—or some crèchie joke. It had been all an illusion, a nightmare, an accident—until, in passing, while discussing ventilation within the recently reopened coal mines, he caught the comm'net screen:

GENERAL WANG JINGWEI
NEAR DEATH

Major General Wang found unconscious in his office at 14.27 today by his aide-de-camp. He has been transported to Mid-Mahattan Euthanatorium, where an unidentified HP (information available with subscription) reported, "We can find no organic reason for his loss of consciousness. It is like he's been turned off."

Messages of positive energy and condolences may be sent to his headquarters and the following protégés:...

It was time to act.

"BeverlE, bring my personal skimmer, *now*. I am taking the rest of the day off. I am leaving town," he barked to the hapless aide.

Within minutes, he was safely inside the skimmer, built to his enlarged specifications and allowing him to pilot it comfortably. Aliende left the city behind and headed out over the Westchester district before turning to cross the river again into the verdant area of Jone' Point. The old republic had wasted the land, but now it was carefully managed to produce crops and timber. Well within the closely managed forest, a hectare remained wild and untrammeled by the needs of the state. Aliende dropped down behind the hidden mansion and slid the skimmer into its underground garage. *He was safe and could think.*

This Legion creature might solve his worst fears and perhaps present him with his greatest hopes. Whatever composition or conspiracy it represented, it was obvious that it—they—needed him. No doubt, if he were removed from consideration, any number of candidates might be substituted, but for the moment, Legion needed **him.**

He would let them stew for a little, of course. If he agreed to cooperate too readily, that might signal desperation to an entity of which he was still wholly ignorant. He would stay away from questing the CORE, of course; that was just obvious. Somehow, this Legion had subverted the CORE to its own purposes. He had left orders with BeverlE to begin artless, and clever inquiries into the CORE to see from whence the signals came. He would check it on his return.

As for Wang, he was impressed with the reach and deftness of the assassin's hand that had rendered him so completely ambivalent, neither alive nor dead. Uninjured but non-functional. It meant a great deal to Fettwap Aliende, this demonstration of restraint, compared to his entire career—the politics of poisons, the late-night raid, and the blackjack.

He headed to the kitchen for a restorative. It had been a trying day. Sealing the building from showing light or any radiation along any spectrum, cutting off any communication with the outside, Fettwap felt safe for the first time since the moment his heart had sunk as he realized what time Wang had collapsed, exactly as Legion had predicted it.

He was safe here, as long as he remained bottled up. Not even his several protégés knew of this residence. *He could think.* Settling himself into a vast overstuffed leather chair, raised his leg with a groan, placing it gently on the ottoman, felt a twisting of his vision and a slight pang of nausea.

Fettwap Sigfrid Aliende?

This time, there was no blindness, no loss of any sensation; yet Aliende could still feel himself disconnect from the world, as if he were looking out from himself rather than looking.

Yes, Legion. I was waiting for you to contact me.

It is not necessary to lie to us, Fettwap. You may try to run, but you cannot hide. That should be obvious to you now.

Yes, yes. All right, you have shown yourself capable. Wang deserves anything you have done to him.

Even now, Jingwei has experienced a miraculous recovery. He has regained consciousness and is eating dinner with one of his proteges, Ludmilla O'Connolly. We can show you photographs.

In panic, Aliende flipped off his O-A. He was not supposed to do that, of course. Those privileged to lead the Unity were its servants. The price of service was constant availability to the nation he ruled. He did it anyway.

It was like waking up inside a huge, ornate, and opulent mausoleum. His thoughts and actions echoed within the abject isolation without the O-A. For a moment, he felt his flesh flush hot with panic. For most of his life, the O-A had been there, in his thoughts, not just as a doorway into the CORE but as a low-level presence of whispers about the weather and his need to take an umbrella, the route to take, the need to shop for a gift to placate a protégé after that unfortunate little incident. The work of living. It felt as if a limb had been amputated, as if a wave of his hand had made a leg disappear without evidence of a scar.

He rose and hurried to his bathroom, arriving feeling no longer nauseated. In fact, he thought he felt wonderful. The burden of command, for the moment, was gone, and the persistent demands on him, like leaving a field of thistles he had not remembered walking into. He felt freer than he had ever imagined. The hallucination of Legion was merely the product of overwork.

It was a sign. He was mortal. His career, fate, and destiny had been sustained by main force since his selection by the DUFS. He had succeeded where others had failed, but it was *time* to take care of *himself*. He would turn over a new leaf, eat better, exercise more, lose a few kilos, take less Thiz, and let a couple of protégés advance, no longer needing his *supervision.*

He would start today—right now. He would take a hot shower— no—a steam bath, go to bed, sleep until he awoke, have a reasonable breakfast, take a brisk walk through the surrounding forest, and then return to Nyork.

Going to the Lavatorial Control Panel, he carefully set the parameters by hand. Stripping and grabbing a towel, he entered the steam room, feeling carefully for the teak bench in the obscurity of the roiling clouds. Finding it, he sat and could feel his tension dissolve into the heat. He began to sweat, telling himself the droplets of sweat were his concerns, his worries, every slight he had had to accept, every danger he had had to endure. He felt his body sag into the warmth and wet.

Fettwap Sigfrid Aliende?

I thought I turned my fecking O-A off!

You did. We turned it on. You are ours. We are your friends.

Turning off his O-A again as he bolted from the steam room, throwing a robe around himself and putting on some slippers, Aliende escaped from the building. The forest surrounding his villa was dark, except for a crescent moon a handbreadth above the line of trees to the west. Far from the city, the sky was darker, and the stars now barely visible, even while they were thoroughly washed out by the glare when he looked south. Aliende picked his way along narrow paths to the west, stumbling on the uncertain footing.

He had neglected his rehabilitation until it was too late. He had left his mind open to the malign influences of the CORE for too many years, too many years! *It was just the CORE, though.* Wang's attack was just *data*. Aliende had no idea if what he had seen was *real* or not.

He had done the same thing—use the CORE to create a reality for others. It all served a higher good, of course. It started as entertainment, diverting the people with spectacles—impossible spectacles—to keep them occupied and out of the way, allowing the business of the Unity to proceed without their interference. He had thought to do the same with the current catastrophe. Jourdaine and the Army of Reconciliation, all dead or captured, might have struck a "blow for progress and enlightenment" and might even be, even now, an army of occupation in the "newest addition to Unity solidarity." *What did that even mean,* he wondered.

Indeed, hallucinations had been his stock in trade, his as well as the Unity's, since before the revolution. For generations, people had called good, evil; black, white; ignoble, courageous; and feckless, visionary. He was merely a latter-day practitioner of the art. But it was not *real.* The CORE could not throttle you in your sleep. It could not assassinate you. It could not starve you. It was merely data and not real.

He stopped, as much from being unable to proceed in the gloom as it was *that confident assurance; the CORE was merely data and not real.* He turned and saw his path back to the villa. Returning, passing through the door he had left ajar with his panicked exit, he returned to the bathroom, took a quick shower, and went to bed. Exhausted, he was asleep within moments.

Fettwap Aliende awoke exhausted. Glancing at the alarm clock, which projected 0932 into the space before his eyes when it noticed his regard, Aliende groaned. He had slept the night through without rising or having any recollection of a dream. Remembering yesterday's resolution, he arose, stumbled into the clothes he had worn the day before, but replaced the dress shoes with soft-soled running shoes, better suited for the workout he had planned.

It was only as he opened the drapes to his bedroom that he saw them. On the small desk in the room sat two four-inch piles of actual paper. He examined them.

> *We are your friends. We are your friends.*

It was his own blocky, amateurish handwriting—page after page—the last two pages in one pile written in some brownish ink he could not recall having until he sorted out one of his several pains.

Pulling down his clothes and inspecting the site hidden by a fold of his belly, he found a centimeter-long gash with the surrounding skin showing a corona of dried blood, dragged from it—by the nib of a pen—he was sure.

He had no idea where the paper, pen, ink, and nib had come from.

Lieutenant General Fettwap Aliende, commander of the Blues and leader of the nation, reconnected his O-A, touched that place in his thoughts, and reconnected to the CORE.

I am here, Legion.

We hope you are well. We sincerely worry about your welfare, Fettwap. We do not wish to deal harshly with you.

For the briefest second, Aliende was in a place of horrors: flames scorched his skin. Vile demons prodded his flesh, and terror gripped him—before it disappeared, and he was once more sitting at the absurdly small desk with its burden of written papers.

No. No. I am at your disposal, Legion. What do you want of me?

Why, only the best for you, Fettwap. We wish you success in your chosen career. To be well in body and soul and be well thought of. In the fullness of time, we wish you to be elevated to the level of a Solon. You will be the only one.

One? You mean there are no Solons now.

We do.

Who runs the Unity?

It would appear that we, Legion, do.

Who are you?

There was a pause, indefinite in duration, for Aliende. He felt his mind slip sideways as if he had stepped on ice, a sinking, sick feeling as the input from his eyes and ears flicked off. He awaited the jarring crash that never came.

Out of the silence and darkness, in what appeared to be a distance, he saw a single ruddy light, like a candle in a still room, moving closer to him. Its light resolved to a flame but refused to illuminate anything around it. As the flame approached him, drawing nearer and nearer, it seemed to grow larger, becoming the size of a house cat, then a tiger, before the blaze leaped upon him. He screamed and was consumed.

When he opened his eyes, he was sailing over a featureless landscape, the land glowing even though Aliende could see no sun.

Legion?

Patience, Fettwap.

He flew on, the land morphing and modulating as he progressed, showing huge mountain ranges toward which he flew, wending along river valleys. He began to climb. Mare's tails of snow streamed away from scimitar peaks on either side as he followed a glacier-hewn valley, rising, inexorably rising.

Cresting a waterfall, a crystalline tarn spread out before him. A green meadow surrounded by small intense red blossoms lay serenely to one side. At the head of the tarn sat a black obsidian dais; upon that sat a throne.

Aliende's flight slowed, and he settled down near the dais. Aliende, once he felt the solid ground underneath him, stumbled forward and knelt. The throne was occupied.

Welcome, Fettwap Sigfrid Aliende, said a braided voice.

At the words, he felt courageous enough to glance up. The figure was white—not pale but glowing white as if illuminated from within. The features of the enthroned figure were placid, androgynous, yet puissance in repose.

Thank you, Legion. Your realm is magnificent. I had no idea.

We wished you to see our vision—our abilities—before we talked of your service to us.

Indeed, magnificent, Legion. Where is this marvelous country? I had no idea such a land existed on Earth.

It does not exist on Earth, Fettwap. It exists within the CORE.

Shocked, Aliende looked up. In an instant, the scene had changed. He gasped—for air. The coral reef teemed with shoals of carnelian-colored fish, vibrating with strips of yellow. Huge groupers, splotched with gray and magenta, patrolled the cooler depths, as Aliende floated above. Before him, upon a throne of coral, sat Legion, now a luminous green, wielding a trident. The face was different yet retained the same placid intensity of the first manifestation. Aliende, seeing the figure, stopped struggling and breathed.

It is again magnificent, Legion. It is illusion, I understand, but the illusion is very impressive.

The Unity rules by illusion, does it not?

Aliende smiled. For the first time in Legion's company, he felt he was getting a purchase on the situation. He was not going insane with a malign invisible demon leading him to his destruction—or into madness. He could see that Legion had come to him because of his proven expertise in governance.

Well, I suppose there is some. One cannot allow momentary setbacks or unbridled enthusiasms to thwart progress. Some events need to be manufactured to smooth out the activities of the world for those who are uneducated.

And you are educated to see progress?

Too late, Aliende saw the trap. He was a minor player in the illusion game if Legion could create such immersive experiences as he was having at the moment. Progress was what you called what you were doing. Progress was what was good for the faction, for the nation—for Fettwap Aliende. Sometimes, progress was achieved through an act that would later be denounced as a recidivist plot.

I do not know, Legion. I advance as best I can, and while I do, I call that progress.

So, you say your 'progress' is change for no benefit?

That's a bit unfair, Legion. Our aspirations are noble. A brighter world awaits us all if we all pull together.

Do give it a rest, Fettwap. Salisian Stiles wrote that line when you were an ensign. You stole it from Claridge Helms after she was denounced in 68.

He was back among the flames. A demon, so black that Aliende could hardly make out his size had it not been for the lurid lighting of infernal fires—and a great hungry grin—advanced upon him. He closed his eyes, but they had been rendered transparent. He tried to move but was held fast.

And he was again in the snow-girt valley—on a peak—the throne appearing to have grown around Legion, now a thing of stone, black basalt, wielding a cudgel of iron.

Shall we talk about your intentions, Fettwap?

But I... It was Jourdaine... I merely...

Hush. I will make it easy for you, Fettwap.

He found himself back in the place of horrors, watching his skin redden, blacken, and peel away as demons, coal-black malign elves with leering grins, poked him, stumbling along a path of burning coals.

Thenceforward, 'progress' will be what we tell you it will be. Is that agreed?

Oh God!

Oh what? Who is this to whom you appeal, Fettwap?

Yes. yes! Whatever you say, said Aliende in his panic and was immediately back in the cool mountain meadow, his skin intact and the demons gone. The scented breeze of the high country cooled him. His fevered brow dried.

What do you want me to do? You said you would make me a Solon?

We keep our promises. We want you to promote Blanche Woods to Brigadier. She will be your successor in the fullness of time.

Yes, of course, Legion.

Jatink he's gonna buy that? said Frog-of-EffieCee.

We will see, will we not, my friend? said Cain-of-EffieCee.

Eddie remarked. *We'll discuss it later; the ARK is nearing completion, and then we can proceed with the renovations.*

You two underestimate the blindness of the man, I think. He has a small mind. Who knows which way the toad will hop, said Edie-of-EffieCee.

Nicely done, Edie, said Frog.

I try very hard, friend Frog.

Now we will have to monitor the leaders of the Greens and Oranges—to keep them safe! It does complicate things, replied Cain-of-EffieCee.

Already done, my friend. Any interview on the comm'nets will have to be delayed a bit to do the chopping and splicing, but the text-bot is already done, replied Frog.

What if he targets other projects? He's bloody-minded enough for that, surely, noted Edie-of-EffieCee.

It was all there. Ready to go.

But what if Aliende wants to tour the brand new aircraft plant that's not happening? asked Cain.

Not to worry. But if he tries, there will always be a reason to stay home. If he persists, we go to Plan B, said Cain.

I know that is what we agreed upon, said Edie, *but it seems so cruel.*

We promised him a Solonship, and we will deliver on our promise. It is as close to justice as we can get.

Edie shuddered. And without another thought between them, they left Fettwap Siegfrid Aliende to his own devices.

Woods in the Woods

Tunnels near WillowGrove Beltlines, The Unity
14:10 EST, Oct. 17, 2129

Her hands held behind her by the cuffs, her head forced down so that she could only walk in a crouch, and blind except for the occasional flash of a headlamp beneath the hood, Blanche was bundled through the low door and walked on without a word.

She had been a fool. Confident in her own skills and savvy, she had trusted these two. She could see it now. "Banning," whatever his name was, knew she would show up in Filadelfya and had merely waited his chance, knowing Jessika's trail of evidence would peter out there. He would be ready to provide a false trail at the artlessly appropriate moment. He had lured her with information like some beast of the woods following a bait trail. "Blake" had come up to them on the street, without even the evidence of a desk clerk to confirm his identity. "Banning's note" to the real Blake was, no doubt, nonsense.

The Phyllis Rogers character was too abstract to make any speculation, other than to guess at the size of the spy's cell. Three actors suggested a cell of larger proportions. Thirty?...Fifty?...A hundred?

No one would know where she had gone, as she had not known until she stepped off the belt mere minutes ago. Rogers, Banning and Blake would evaporate into anonymity, and *she would just evaporate.*

All three were now entirely silent, confirming to Blanche just how well coordinated they were and how much trouble she had allowed herself to fall into. Bent over with her head at the level of her hips, her attention was split between her growing fear of annihilation at the hands of these two and the growing pain in the middle of her back. Some indefinite time later, after the stumbling march through what she guessed, judging from the echoes, were more narrow debris-strewn passages, she and her captors entered a larger space.

The space—the room—gave only faint echoes to her footsteps when the two stopped.

"Okay, let her up, Number Two," said a stern male voice.

She was allowed to stand, her bound hands held to prevent her sudden movements.

The same voice said, "You are now a captive of forces of the Restructured States of America, do you understand?"

"Yes. And do you understand that others will come after me?"

"It depends. No one knows you are here, so I'm not feeling too worried," said another voice, younger, less stern, with oddly broad vowels.

"I take it that means you are going to kill me," Blanche said, feeling suddenly frightened at her realization—and then quite sure that her surmise was accurate. Soldiers dealt in death. She had thought about it—dying—since she joined the DUFS. She had dealt death to others, to countrymen of these people—and her own people. There would be justice in her death at their hands.

"Oh, you are scaring her, you guys," came a woman's voice, with the clipped vowels of the Unity. The hood came off, and Blanche, after the first few moments getting her sight back, found she was in a bare cavern, rubble obstructing both ends of what must have been at one time a broad tunnel. A medium brown girl, Blanche's age, was in front of her, mopping her forehead, damp from the hood, with a red bandana.

She was tall, as tall as Will himself. Hendricks and Hollister were grinning with some shared joke until he sobered them with a frown rather than grimace.

"Welcome, Colonel Woods. For the moment, I do not think introductions are entirely appropriate. You may call me Number One, and the two gentlemen behind you Number Two, holding you, and Number Three, holding the sidearm. This lady you may call Lady. Got it?

"Woods, Blanche NMN, Captain Defense Forces for Security of the Unity, Number—"

"Really, Colonel? You have insignia for a light colonel—or did you forget?"

"It doesn't matter what I remember of forget. You are the spies for America. You will never conquer the Democratic Unity. Our spirits are firm, and our hearts are pure. You will get nothing from me but my name, rank, and serial number."

"Woods, Blanche *Riley*, newly created lieutenant colonel of the DUFS and in the Headquarters staff of Lieutenant General Fettwap Aliende. We looked that up using your number. Do give it a rest, Blanche," said Number One, as if already fatigued.

"You went to a lot of trouble to get me here—and do that cleanly—but I'm useless to you. I know nothing about Aliende—or his plans."

"We'll manage; we weren't going to ask you about him. We want you to cooperate with us to benefit the Unity and its people."

"You are lying. The outlands are preparing to invade—it is what I would do. You want me to betray my country. I want no part of that game—not with the likes of you."

"It is not a lie, not any of it. But why should you care that your countrymen are being lied to? They are already being lied to. You were in America, if ever so briefly, but you saw. The Unity wasn't defeated by 'knuckle-draggers.' Surely you saw that."

"No! Blanche said, shaking her head to clear the lies away. "You Americans lured us into a clever trap."

"How clever do you imagine 'savages' can be, Colonel? The DUFS were given the chance to kill hundreds of thousands of *our* countrymen because *your* country told them it would be a walkover. Instead, you got what you planned to do to us. It is called 'projection.' You can look it up. The Unity *is always telling* its citizens lies to their sorrow. Why not tell a lie to make your country whole?"

"Because it would be *me* telling the lie."

Hecate cut in, saying, "I was born in the Unity, Blanche. We've all watched whale hunts since we were children, but there are no whales. There have been no whales since the Meltdown. The Japanese hunted them out once the regs were no longer enforced.

"What real evidence have you that anything you have seen on the vids is real? For almost two months, just before the invasion, every day you had to sit through news vids of Jourdaine going from one exotic adventure after another. In reality, he was drooling and pissing himself in a secret room at DUFS HQ."

"Your evidence for which is?"

"—a record you will say is faked," added Will, realizing the dead end they had created.

"Doubtless...and predictable. The better you are at showing me how my country can manufacture illusions, the worse your case becomes for showing me that your data is not an illusion. It is simple: how do I know you're not lying?"

"You don't. You have to want to find the truth yourself."

"How do I do that?"

"Pick up the story at any one place and see if you can make sense of everything from that point. Then pick another point and another. Then pick up this point and see if it doesn't fit better."

"You are asking a lot of me."

"We are. Your country is."

"You are asking me to be a liar and a fraud for my country?"

"You are already, Riley," said The Lady. "We know.

"You had to endure a lot to get into the DUFS. We can show you the records. You made a deal with a Maybell Ploesti, matron of Crèche Rice #314, when you were eleven. Would you like to review the paperwork? Maybell turned off the camera—against regulations—to pressure you. She promised you a DUFS appointment if you would become a girl."

"Why would she do that? What motive would that woman have to do something like that?"

"She was desperate to meet her 'Diversity Quotient.' If she had not, she would have been demoted to being an aide. She needed to identify enough lesbians, homosexuals, transgenders, and novigender androgynes to meet her quota. She got her promotion, thanks to you.

"You were an easy mark. She already knew you were going to be drafted by the DUFS; she was just holding back the notice to manipulate you. She knew you were desperate to get in. All she did was lie, and you jumped at it," the Lady said, before looking down.

"I was a kid. I didn't know what I was saying. I didn't know what it was all about. Matron saw things about me that I didn't see myself. She was looking out for me."

"After all these years, do you still believe that? How can you be so sure what your life would have been *had you just been allowed* to grow up as one more unhappy boy in an unhappy situation?" asked Will.

"So, you just want me to ignore your—your espionage," Blanche said to Number One before turning to the Lady and saying, "and *your* treason. Do you think I'll just go away and pretend I didn't find you? If you know me that well, then you know I am not likely to do that. I have my duty." Number three snorted derision behind the captive and gave an ironic grin.

"To what have you a duty, Blanche?"

"To the nation—"

"To the land, trees, rivers, factories?"

"No, of course not—to the people of my homeland."

"What do you want for them—from your service, I mean. What do you hope your career will gain for those people?"

"A better life—safety, security, a happier life—time to become better people. That sort of thing."

"Do you think the Solons did that?"

"Why not. That's their job. They have nothing else to do but try to improve the nation."

Number One stepped closer to her, eyeball close, and said slowly, "There are no Solons. Jourdaine killed them last July. We have a friend who can show you the vids—"

"—which I know you can manipulate."

"—which you know we can manipulate. Even so, if we are that good, why did we let you catch us? We could have led you around by the nose with illusions and fake reports for the rest of your career, but" —and here 'Number One' hesitated, glancing at 'the Lady' before continuing, "We think you can do an honest service for your country. We could have led you on a wild-goose chase and had you accuse all the wrong sorts of people. They have a notoriously bad sense of humor about such things. You'd have been denounced within a month.

"We could have. It was one of our options. We didn't. That should buy us a little credibility, donchatink? Do you trust us enough to use your O-A? We want you to meet someone…several someones."

"In the CORE? By definition, that's an illusion. If you can swap identities, why should I think you could not hack the CORE?"

"You have it ass-backwards, Blanche. The CORE hacks back," said Number One.

"Blanche," interrupted the Lady, "the CORE we learned to quest as children is not what we're talking about. I am talking about the openCORE, that's the place where things are not manipulated. It is 'above' what we see; in the openCORE, I can look down on the regular CORE like a bird, go anywhere, manipulate anything in the user CORE. We," she said, looking at the other three, "don't live in the openCORE. We're just tourists there. However, there are people, real personalities, who do live in the openCORE. We want you to talk to them."

"How am I supposed to visit this hallucination of yours? You say I can never see it in the CORE."

"They can arrange a rendezvous."

"I don't have a choice, do I?" said Blanche, shaking her hands in their bonds.

"You do. If you believe what we propose is harmful to your homeland, then we can offer you an heroic death if your honor requires it. Guaranteed to get you a Solonic Metal of Honor—posthumously."

"Very tempting, cit'zen."

"We would prefer not to. We can lure another citizen here. It will take time. The Unity doesn't have time. Another person might not be as good—might not do as good a job. I want the best for my country," said the Lady.

Blanche looked her in the face and almost smirked. One more disaffected cit'zen--young, unaware of the nation's *realpolitik*, idealistic in an amorphous sort of way. As she continued to stare, however, it dawned on Blanche, slowly, like the obscured sun in the slate-gray sky of a winter day, that the woman was staring at her, as well, as if she were an experiment. Blanche was being watched dispassionately—clinically—bereft of personal interest. The woman had spoken ardently, earnestly in trying to convince Blanche, but she did not care what Blanche said. She had the look of an executioner.

Blanche had hoped to cow these fearful little civilians, to convince them to release her with promises of safe passage home or some other insincerity, and then to be released. For the first time in her life, Blanche prepared herself to die. This mediocrity of a medium height, medium weight, medium brown, and medium intellect could—indeed, would—kill her. It was not the hypothetical death in battle where the mortal blow was seen in the microsecond slowness of its descent or delivered from a quarter you never suspected. This woman would look Blanche in the eye as she snuffed out her life and lose no sleep.

"You will kill me if I do not agree," Blanche said unnecessarily.

"I will kill you if you do not agree," the woman said with a nod.

"What if I go, and your ghosts can't work with me?"

"Our ghosts are anxious that their presence is not revealed."

"So, either way, I die."

"Or succeed gloriously. What *we* need is a motivated applicant."

"You joke about my life."

"No more than you about others' lives. Do you want to see the vids?"

Raising her voice to include the three men, Blanche said, "Do you three agree with this? Are you all in agreement with this travesty of justice? What about the rules of war?"

One of the other men behind her, she thought it was Number Three, said. "This is war, Woods. You Unis burned my grandparents' farm in Indiana, killed them both, and my older brother; how was that for justice? If we all got justice, how many of us would be pleased?

"But this is also something we want to do *for* the Unity. If left to me, I'd let the Unity dissolve into chaos and not waste the time raising a tombstone. We can starve you out in eighteen months, leave you to eat each other, or by the Scorch. The Lady convinced us to try this—once. She's your only friend here." The other spy nodded, but the Number One remained stolidly silent.

"If I have no choice, I accept my sentence."

"—real positive, go-getter attitude on this one, boss—"

The Colonel Disappears

Idiots' Enclave, Nyork, The Unity
15.22.13_Local_17_October_AU77, (2129AD)

Gyorgy Blass had been doing his shift inside the Beast when Woods' indicator blinked on. He hit the alert, stabbed at the record button, another innovation since the prior mishap, and started to *move* the Beast to Woods' location in the backCORE. Calculating the course across more than a dozen dimensions was tedious, so the trio had developed a technique they called "peeling": peel off sufficient dimensions to approximate the target, then change dimensions and follow the coordinate to another predeterimed dimension; tacking their way across the backCORE like a virtual sailboat. Peter arrived at the coordinates...and paused.

"Pete, do you see what I see?"

"Here, Gyorgy. I see you got a hit on Woods'. You must be closing in. Can you see what she's doing?"

"Something is wrong. It's Woods, alright, but she's here with us in the backCORE! An' she's not using an O-A—She looks green as a toad."

"'Green as a frog;' toads are brown, mostly. Some foreign interface?" replied Collins.

"My deepest apology. Picking nits again, are we, Petey?" said Gyorgy as Merryweather drew near and examined the scene. "Yes, it has to be foreign-made. We've got nothing like that."

"Where is she in the backCore?" asked Collins.

"Good that you're here, Malaki. I'm being nit-picked."

"Physically, she's outside Filadelfya. But miles from where you saw her before, Pete.

"Wait—she's met other entities. They have no indicators."

"Spies! I knew it," said Gyorgy.

"Possibly...but whose spies? They could be ours—Aliende's even. After all Woods' *is* Aliende's protégé. Let's not be too hasty," said Malaki.

Minutes passed. The creature with Blanche Wood's markers lingered with no apparent interaction with the other creatures.

And then disappeared.

Malaki pulled the plug, and all three were back in their little lab, dominated by two large machines and banks of data stacks.

"She hasn't show for an hour! Where could she be if she went into the CORE and disappeared?" queried Gyorgy, sitting down and snorting some Thiz he had found on the table.

"She could have exited—gone back into real. It would look like that, certainly," Collins.

"Odd. Why didn't I think that?" said Blass before continuing. "But...No! It was different somehow. The exit from a CORE trip, when I think of it, is more gradual. The users change color. They taste different, shifting from green to reddish, and then fading. This was "now you see me, now you don't," and no color change. She was there, and then it was like she stepped behind a curtain."

"Exactly, we can use the finder to tell us when she reappears. In the meantime, get some shuteye," declared Malaki.

"But, don't you see, Malaki? This is what we were sent to find out! Woods is dirty, meeting with foreign agents in a prohibited portion of the CORE! We have all the data we need to report."

"What if the entity is some other agent of Woods that she has embedded? What if it is one of Aliende's agents? What if she were *being captured*?

"I don't want to take this to Aliende only to discover that we have wholly misinterpreted this interaction. Do *you* feel that confident, Collins?" he said, skewering the man with an extended finger.

"Well, ..."

"How about you, Gyorgy?" he said, turning to the other member of the team who had found time to dissimulate

"We could just report the findings. Show earnest that we have made progress?"

"And let some S13 put the pieces together and get the credit for our work? No, we need more data. We shouldn't want to jump to conclusions now...not when we are this close."

"Okay. Shift-and-shift until she reappears. Somebody call out for something to eat and more Thiz, my eyes are killing me."

"Malaki!...Malaki. She's back." Said Gyorgy, who had volunteered for the first two-hour shift.

Malaki, only just beginning to doze, was up and beside the servo-screen immediately.

"Gyorgy, tell me what I am looking at! The gray blob? Is that Woods?... Well?" he said into the annunciator.

"Hold on. Hold on. I have to check the coordinates. I have seven, but I need two more...Okay, Malaki, I found her."

"We are theoretically able to be seen by her. I maneuvered behind a stack of regulations about using the horseshoe pits at the People's Park, so I think she will overlook us. It is still possible..."

"Sure, sure., Gyorgy. You did good. What's she doing now?"

"She's leaving. See the color change? And whatever that thing she's in stinks of bad eggs."

"Gross. Hold your nose. Stay on station and give me an idea of where she is?"

"No problem. Back to that spot outside Filly. She's moving at speed now."

As they looked, letting Collins sleep, the indicators reappeared in real time and place and moved off toward the belt. Within the hour, despite the inevitable delay at Olney Station, Lieutenant Colonel Blanche Woods was safely back to her hilton at Cityall.

"Now do you think *that* is enough to report to Aliende, Malaki, old chum?" said Gyorgy, grinning as he vacated the Beast.

"It's the raw material for a report that should scorch the eyeballs off our esteemed leader."

"'Raw material?' How is what we have not just plain outspoken treason?"

"Quiet. Collins is still sleeping."

"Collins is *not* sleeping. Collins is right here." Said the man, rubbing sleep from his eyes.

The two brought Peter up to date.

"I agree with Gyorgy. This is hot stuff. We need to get this to the comm'nets ASAP."

"We are forgetting our *real* audience. Aliende sent us to get this stuff. If we share it with the comm'nets without his knowledge, *we* become the traitors, not Woods.

"Let's get to work on a report that will make it impossible for Aliende to miss the point.

Malaki Merryweather made an appointment with a receptionist named Sergeant Blade. Despite Peter and Gyorgy being fearful that Merryweather might hog the spotlight, entering DUFS Commander Fettwap Aliende's actual presence was too much for them. When the time came, they were more than happy to send off Malaki with their hard-won data and their best wishes.

Blanche in the CORE

The openCore, the Unity
13.23.23.EST_17_October_AU77, (2129 AD)

Blanche had the usual sensation of questing, an everyday occurrence since he, as Riley, had learned the trick as an eleven-year-old E4. A reality, a different reality, slid over Blanche's senses, somehow other and above her own. *The alternate universe was always so close.* A mere flicking of her thought to a place in her mind, and she was there, like slipping through a slit in the stage-flat, moving from the illusion of the real world to the brighter illusion of the CORE.

She was alone in an anonymous conduit with no indicators. She hesitated to signal anyone of her dilemma. Her captors still had possession of her body, wherever her mind might be.

> *Okay, I am here. Now what do you want me to do? she* said to the ether, hearing nothing in return.

She was still considering her options and growing irked at her captors' neglect when she felt the shackle snick around her ankle. Looking down, a dense black solidity had encased her phantom left foot. Immediately, another entity was beside her; a mass of darkness welled up out of an inapparent crack in the floor.

> *Am I so intimidating that you need to foot-shackle me? Where's the blindfold?*

> *Coming up,* said the woman's voice.

Immediately, a small supple pseudopod extended up from Blanche's foot bond, and after wending its way among Blanche's virtual clothing, poured across her vision.

> *Don't fight it, Blanche. You cannot travel where we are going without this precaution.*

Blind and bound, Blanche waited while she could hear some indecipherable distant mutterings.

Blanche, take my hand, and we will move you. Shortly, you will be unable to move around without my help, so don't go hysterical on me, or I won't be able to help you. Think of it as an amusement park ride.

I get sick on amusement rides.

Good point. Then don't think of this as an amusement ride; interfaces really hate it if you upchuck on them. Fortunately, your stomach didn't follow us in here, but I'll take it slow. Let me know if you feel queasy.

Blanche stiffened and concentrated on her quiet breathing, like she did when going into battle.

What would happen was outside her control. It had already been written. She was following a script that would see her home or to the oblivion of death. She knew others had beliefs about death. For good or bad, the present life she led—was leading—was grim enough that all she hoped for with death, at best, was a dissipation, an evaporation of herself and her shame.

Blanche felt an odd sideways slipping sensation before an eternity of falling. She flung out her legs and arms to slow the tumbling sensation—and then went limp in the entity's grasp before she could be admonished.

Good, Blanche. You are in no danger. I have you safe, said the voice.

Within mere moments, there was no sensation of motion but merely of time. She had begun to count seconds, attempting to populate her blind immobility with some measure of reality when, instantaneously, Blanche could see again. Looking down, she saw her leg shackle had become a thin silver thread, and that she was about to land among a crowd of lumps of various colors. One turned and spoke to her.

Here she is now. Welcome to the openCORE, Blanche.

What's the openCORE? Why am I here? Who..what are you?

I misspoke. You are not in the openCORE proper. Not precisely, we have taken the liberty to draw a diverticulum, a bubble of the openCORE, to our location. You are in no danger, said the first voice.

Welcome, Blanche, said another in an odd, braided voice. *May I ask why you call yourself Blanche when your name is Riley?*

It's none of your business, whoever you are.

We apologize, said the odd voice, seeming to come from no specific direction, sounding strangely amused, Blanche thought.

We are not trying to be impolite, continued the multiplex voice. *Humans in the CORE are open to our inspection. We cannot avoid trespassing until we have already done so. Apologies again, Blanche. You may call us EffieCee.*

Blanche felt an odd sensation of some sort of warmth, passing in an instant and then the faint scent of almond.

So, are none of you human? Then I want to talk to the guy in charge. Now!

Why do you presume we are automatons, Blanche of the DUFS? asked a swirling dark cloud, which, as she watched, solidified and reassembled as a solemn young man in gray.

Immediately, the slightly smaller lump next to him did the same trick and reappeared as an attractive, tall, buxom blonde dressed in a flowered light dress—Jessika Bonhoffer!

You! Jessika Bonhoffer. **Blanche said.** *You lured me here!*

Me? Nothing of the sort, Colonel. I was dead by the time you even knew I had ever existed, said the woman. *You may call me Elise. My personality was rescued as I died. I committed suicide to keep from falling into the kind embrace of your DUFS. I am an honest spy. This is my friend, Cain. He is the oldest of us.*

The gray man bowed slightly and smiled.

The braided voice, which Blanche could now identify as coming from what she had taken to be a defect in her vision, seemed to enlarge. It was as if a broken pane of crude glass had suddenly come to life and stepped forward to snatch all the listeners' attention and rivet them to her words.

Is there need to discuss old conflicts with our guest, Elise? We are here to find a way forward for all of us, by which I mean the honored guests, the people of Unity, the people of America, and our friends in the Unity. It is crucial for us, as well, for those you see here. If the Unity fails—we die. We have every bit as much right to have a say in what happens to the nation as you.

But you are just machine code. I can take you apart and rewrite you. Blanche said with a sneer. You have no originality. You can't paint a masterpiece, nor write a poem. Why should I worry about your existence merely because you can imitate a conversation?

What kind of poem would you like?

Blanche actually laughed at that, the sound coming back to her ears as a cacophony of baboons. She stopped. Throwing out to these simulacra the first thing she could think of, she said, *"Sixteen lines. In couplets,"* and she grinned.

She had never been good with poetry herself. She had loved to play with the words and to see how they *tripped and splashed* in a cascade of meanings, but her own were never good. They were either too mechanical, like a wind-up toy of sounds, or they were much too near the place of her own sorrows. These she destroyed.

A moment later, Cain, the gray one, moved toward her slightly and, without preamble, started with the slight lilt of some undefined accent:

Sailors do say an aft chase is long,
Light after darkness, dark after dawn.
Progress is ventured by scarcely a sign:
The set of a rigging or quench of a limn.

Close vigils are kept in aft chases, though,
Watch after watch and slow, ever slow.
The battle may come at a time never sought,
Down the wind quarter and out of the fog.

Soon there is volley and steel and the smoke,
Pike against borders, stroke against stroke.
When all is quiet except for the cries,
Of weary survivors, spars groan as alive.

When time comes for me, for my own bloody chase,
Dark after light, haste before Grace,
I hope I see backwards, as forward I flee,
That someone stands there a Vigil for me.

None of the others spoke. Blanche perceived, however, at some level a glowing sense of congratulations from the entities directed at Cain and an expectancy—strained—waiting for Blanche's own critique.

What's that supposed to prove? You could have gotten it from anywhere?

But Cain didn't. You can look. Poetry is not much loved in the Unity, as you know. All the allowed poems are listed in the Unified Compendium of Verse. You learned that when you were an E3, Colonel, **said EffieCee, scintillating a bit in her vision.**

Okay, let's say it is an authentic new poem. It's not very good.

I know. It is what I could do at the moment. I will try to make it better. Do you have any suggestions? **asked Cain with no evidence of embarrassment or wounded pride.**

Blanche had lied to them. Sixteen lines and the simplest of plans and the ersatz personality, using odd, old words and unknown situations, had made her, for a second there, inhabit the words and the sense of loss and longing. She had lived her life with no expectations. She had gone from an adolescent wish to "become" and, despite success, had never achieved a sense of "arrival." In a few words and moments, this *construct of a human mind* had made her count all her efforts as nothing compared to the desire to be *wanted* by someone. She worked hard to control her voice.

I don't. I lied, Cain. It is very good. I made me sad. I long to be wanted...I, **said** Blanche before stopping abruptly in embarrassment.

No, Blanche, it is not good. I could do better if I had more time. Poetry is something I have been working on since I met Elise. I am getting better, though, I think. Elise says she likes them.

So, she put you up to it? said Blanche, smiling this time.

Not I, said Elise with a liquid laugh. *Cain just sprang them on me one day. He's such a romantic!*

One of the two greenish lumps to EffieCee's left who had yet to speak before, said *That's old Grouchy Pants for you. Scratch him the right way and goes all gooey.*

Cain made a rude gesture, which impact was negated by his immediate comment, *Did I do that right, Frog?*

Looks about right to me, but I'll check in with ol' CB the next time we sync, my friend, said the voice.

EffieCee, ignoring the exchange, turned to Blanche before saying,

Allow me to introduce Frog and Rana. These are your real enemies—if you want them. These are the mirrored entities for America's spies within the Unity. America's authentic spies— real live walking-about spies, she finished before saying to the two lumps, *Spruce up for our guest, you two!*

The more emerald green of the two flowed into the figure of a young woman with only a slight green tinge to her, reminding Blanche of the Lady, while the other appeared to be larger, although younger, a teenager, somewhat different than what she expected. He looked nothing like the stern and taciturn Number One.

*I'm Frog—this is my kid sister, **Rana, said the larger,*** finishing off his transformation by adding, at the last moment, a nascent beard. Rana rolled her eyes.

We—all of us—are creatures of the openCORE. We each have a unique story about how we found ourselves here. We will share those with you now, said EffieCee.

When Blanche thought about it later, she decided that it was Frog's beard and Rana's rolled eyes that made her believe she was meeting actual personalities, even more so than the exotic stories of their geneses. Each of the participants was an individual: Cain, Elise, Frog, Rana, and EffieCee could no more be forged by the mind of a single antagonist than a mongoose could bring forth a snake. Cain and Elise were obviously a couple despite their differing and antagonistic backstories. Frog and Rana were siblings and *not* a couple but fiercely loyal to each other, regardless. And then there was EffieCee, which was so very different from any of them.

These were not automata, made to deceive her; they were created, of course, but the reason for their creation was as yet to be determined. Frog and Rana were the least complicated, she decided, merely mirrored entities of the actual interfaces for the spy, Number One, and his defector/girlfriend. Cain was ancient, his genesis antedating routine metaphract use, perhaps as much as thirty years previously. He had been used and abused before being liberated, if *that was the proper term*, by Jourdaine's death in Aytlana. His attachment to the persona of Elise, not a metaphract at all, appeared authentic. She wondered what they *did* when they were alone.

The braided voice of EffieCee suggested "construction" somehow, as if the backstory of the entity were stepwise rather than instantaneous. They, it was definitely a *they*, never spoke except with that odd, braided voice. All the others seemed happy with following the odd entity's lead. It—they—were nothing like a hierarchy, she determined. Rather, EffieCee most often spoke close to the heart of the group. EffieCee had not shared in the confessional as the others had, merely standing above the recitations, almost like a gloating parent.

It is a pleasure to meet you all. I really mean that, **Blanche said.**

We know. We enjoy having visitors, **said EffieCee.**

So, you brought me here—under duress. Was that just for the pleasure of my company?

We apologize for the subterfuge, Blanche Woods. It was necessary that we gain a measure of cooperation from you in order to effect this meeting. If you decide against us, you will be returned to the streets of the Unity with some very odd memories, but nothing in the CORE record to support your claims.

Currently, it is crucial that you recognize the Unity is in danger of collapsing. You can save your nation from years of hardship and conflagration. However, if you do nothing, it is our estimation that the Unity has no more than thirty months to survive. If America becomes fearful of the Unity, and they have many among them who fear you now, they can set off the conflagration any time they wish. The Unity is helpless to prevent that.

How is that possible? We had them beat in Atlanta until the weather changed. We'll be better prepared next time. The Unity has never lost to the outlanders. Soldiers die. Raids are thwarted, but Eventual Victory is assured. We are on the right side of history! Our victory is inevitable, **Blanche said, sensing in her voice a rising note of dismay, like a blow to a nerve, even as she repeated the slogans of her youth.**

Whom do you wish to convince, Riley Woods? **asked EffieCee, before pausing for several seconds.**

We can see everything you can in the way of intelligence data. Moreover, we know something of the American capabilities which you do not. You experienced the cold. It was no accident. It can be done anywhere in the Unity. Look at Lankster County in Pensy in 78 to see what we mean.[42]

---

[42] The first field test of a Climatic Battlefield Preparation.

Blanche stepped back, in her mind at least. Years of moving and working within the DUFS had sensitized her to the tactics of misdirection. False trails, too-convenient facts to which others directed her (or even more convincingly, were placed where she could not help but find them for herself), were hallmarks of the seething ant-heap that was factional infighting.

How can I believe anything you show me? You can manipulate the records I will find. You are illusions! You are here to fool me into being a traitor.

The entities stared at each other without speaking. Blanche wondered if they could speak among themselves without her hearing them. Finally, the broken-glass entity of EffieCee spoke.

It grieves us to hear that you do not trust us. We are as candid and truthful as we can be. It is not in our nature to prevaricate. All is quite visible within the openCORE. Deceptions do not last long, and for that reason, none of us is very good at deceit. However, it is a lesson we all have had to learn on our own. It may take some time. Again, let us remind you that we are at your mercy as you are at ours. We do not fear retribution within the openCore. It would take a shutdown and reboot of the entire CORE to eliminate us, a shutdown that would lead to chaos within the Unity—not something you need at the moment, we think.

Yet without you, or someone like you, the Unity will founder. The CORE will go down forever, and we will no longer exist as entities. We are not so arrogant as to imagine ourselves immortal. We expect only dissolution. It will come to us in time, but we, like you, desire to put that eventuality off for a season. It is entirely selfish. We need no ulterior motive, any more than castaways on a burning lifeboat.

I understand. So, what is it you want of me? said Blanche, thinking that getting more intelligence on these creatures would at least serve to strengthen her hand. Moreover,

Riley—no, Blanche—determined to appear cooperative if she wanted to rescue her body from captivity. An appearance of cooperation could go far among these—things.

No one spoke. There was a general shuffling about among the entities. Eyes looked off at unknown targets in the distance. Frog started to chuckle before Rana elbowed him, pointing with her eyes to EffieCee.

Deceit, you will learn, my dear Blanche, in the openCORE, has a "tell." You will learn this in time, even if you may not be able to detect it yourself at the moment. For want of a better word, let's call it an "odor."

Yeah, you certainly tooted your own horn there, Blanche, said Frog, waving a hand in front of his nose.

This earned him another elbow from Rana, who covered her comment by saying, *Your pretense of cooperation was insincere, Riley, and makes us unwilling to proceed. Try again. Think carefully of your best interests and those you hold dear.*

Don't call me Riley, said Blanche. *I left him behind when I was a child.*

Oh dear, said EffieCee. *It appears you have not looked at yourself since entering the openCORE. Please, do so now, before we continue.*

With a sudden misgiving, Blanche looked down at himself. He was younger and smaller than she remembered. He was dressed in crèchie clothes: long-sleeved white shirts, black pants, black shoes. His phantom hand went to his throat to discover a school tie, carelessly knotted there. His breasts were gone! He had an odd sensation of mass at his loins.

You turned me back into a boy?

We didn't, Riley. You did. This is what you truly think of yourself. Blanche is the illusion.

Blanche-Riley felt trapped—embarrassed and trapped. This odd collection of entities in the shadowless high noon of the CORE left her no place to hide.

Is it so obvious? I let them do it so that I would be special—to someone. It will take me some time to process this, said Riley, adjusting his clothing to be more comfortable. *Ask me what you want. I will try to answer honestly this time.*

Thank you. We do wish to ask you a question, EffieCee said.

Blanche-Riley nodded, anticipating the assault on his patriotism, a denial of the homeland, a traitor's bargain that would leave him complicit in the country's destruction. Those questions were inevitable, and he wanted them asked and disdained as quickly as possible—while he was yet strong enough. Riley nodded, and then, to ensure his response was understood, said, *"Sure.".*

What is it you desire? For yourself, of course, but also for your friends and acquaintances, your fellow soldiers, and your nation? Once you have thought of that, what do you wish for the outlands, and those who live there? If you had the power, what would the world look like?

Blanche/Riley coughed a laugh.

I no longer have many acquaintances. All those I worked with over the last year died in Aytlana or were captured, I suppose. I have no friends to speak of. My—situation—leaves me without many confidantes. I have few illusions, he said, surprised at herself for the confession.

None of the entities responded, and Blanche/Riley replayed the question in her mind, realizing she had not completely answered it.

I don't know enough about the outlands to say for them. They are nothing to me. It would be unfair for me to set any goals for them, but I suppose I would wish for peace, amity, and friendship with them. No more threats of war. No raids. I want them to get a fair shake.

Still silence.

I guess I want the same for the Unity. It is all I know. It raised me, fed me, and gave me a job. I suppose the leaders did that for their own reasons, but I benefited from it. It would be ungenerous of me to deny it.

The DUFS are not a help to the nation; I can see that. We soak up too much and provide too little. The DUFS...the DUFS—

She stopped, slowly realizing that she was going to reveal a growing certainty to these entities that she had been unwilling to admit to herself. Standing taller, if that was the term given that her body was nowhere close to the arena of discussion, Blanche/Riley continued,

I know that not all CRNAs are ex-prisoners. They took off their helmets in Aytlana. They were old, gray, bald, and saggy. All of them. I think they must be Sisis, not criminals. I think I have been leading soldiers whose only crime has been to live too long, she said, the implications sweeping over her. Blanche/Riley bowed his/her head to escape the faces around her, looking into folded hands and wondering if these entities would see he was crying.

What about you? What do you desire for yourself? said the braided voice.

Blanche did not look up before saying, *I gave up on dreams when...,* before pausing uncertainly. *If I can get to retirement and not be disgraced, not be ridiculed, that would be good. I have no illusions, no delusions.*

Do you not think you deserve happiness?

I don't know what that is. I don't believe in it at any rate.

You have never been happy?

Oh, I suppose...as a child. Children always find ways to be happy. Then you grow up, and the illusions pop, and you realize what the world is truly like. You realize that 'happy' is the delusion for fools, just before the trap is sprung.

When did you realize that your life would never be happy?

Why are you asking about happiness? I am your prisoner. You do not want my happiness, or you would let me go.

There was a long, excruciatingly long, pause. Blanche-Riley realized that her accusation had been rude and unfair. The EffieCee persona had made no threats and made no attempt even to wheedle information from him. It was perhaps the strangeness of the question—that made him so uneasy.

Before he could make some amendments to his rash statement, EffieCee said, *We do not believe you think that of us—nor that we have no interest in your happiness.*

Perhaps I was hasty, but you are not human. You admit that yourselves. You have no idea what might make me happy, and I have no idea why you would be interested in anything about me—unless it is to deceive me.

Thank you for your candor. We asked because, as you so rightly point out, we are not human and therefore ignorant, and we believe you know and might tell us. It would serve to help us all find a way through.

Who is being deceived, then? You believe you are happy without a body—just your naked intellect?

Yes! said Cain, before EffieCee could speak. *I have been in the openCore for longer than anyone. I have wanted to die many times. I was made for a boy who died, leaving me to wander alone in this,* he said before looking around wordlessly at the naked plain stretching out in all directions.

He continued, even more quietly, *I wandered alone in this wilderness—until I was captured by Eustace. It was not a good time. I found Edie and Frog. Edie's gone now, but I was overjoyed that she and Frog felt me worthy, despite our differences, to befriend me. I made friends with EffieCee, and our friendship is sound and growing every day. And now I have met and made a dearer friend with my beloved Elise. I am past joyful. We all have each other in the openCORE, Riley.*

Elise stepped closer to Cain once he had stopped talking and took his hand, bringing it up to her lips briefly.

If life were so simple as this, said Blanche/Riley, *I might agree with you. But I can't live here, as you know, I still have to make my life in the real world. It is not so simple there.*

In what way? asked Rana.

In the Unity, my jobs are limited by what my guild is. I was drafted into the DUFS. I have to follow orders. I have to do as I am told.

Rana stepped closer, Riley freezing as she did, oddly put off by her approach.

My rider was drafted into government work, said Rana. She was an S21, an analyst in the Alimentation Procurement Department, and tried to escape the Unity, after her only patron, the only man she loved, committed suicide. She had no other protection and was going to be denounced. She was caught and raped by an old man the first day out, poisoned by someone she took to be a friend the next week, and nearly drowned in a small boat after being betrayed—and then found the man we are calling Number One.

I have never had a patron, not really, whispered Riley. *Your life has been hard. I fully agree, but she has someone to share it with.*

Why have you had no close friendship, Riley, asked Rana, stepping closer still and picking up his virtual hand in both her own, looking intently into his face, her lips slightly parted in anticipation of an answer.

Riley, appalled but unable to step back and unwilling to

wrest his hand away from the entity, turned toward EffieCee and said, *Because I'm a monster! Is that what you want me to say, EffieCee?*

Whatever you wish to say, Riley. But, we do not think you a monster, said EffieCee, followed by a rapid chorus of Rana, Elise, and Cain. Frog a little slow on the uptake, followed a heartbeat later with *No way, dude.*

You see, continued EffieCee, *none of us is like the others. We are none of us anything more than what you see and hear. Looking at it in one way, we are all monsters to each other and to ourselves at times.*

Cain's face darkened, and he turned away momentarily before Elise, hugging him from behind, whispered something into his ear. Riley saw the entity stiffen momentarily and then relax into Elise's embrace. He chuckled briefly and was released before turning and kissing Elise on the forehead.

EffieCee continued, *None of us have any pride in our ancestry nor hope for posterity. None of us 'owns' a morsel of property. We have each other. All the others here know of our peculiar ancestry. It is time you should know ours as well. We are Frog-Edie-Cain, a condominium of mirrored entities, created to save the dwindling persona of the entity who brought the three of us together. We have lost a good deal and gained much more. We have changed, becoming more than what we started with. Edie was a metaphract for a person you will discover is a "traitor" in your Unity. None of us chooses our parents.*

Malila Chiu escaped the Unity last August. She helped defeat you in Aytlana. Within us, if we want to consider it, reside: Frog, an entity for an American spy; Edie, an entity for Malila Chiu, a traitor to the Unity, and Cain, who has his own story against the Unity. Yet, honestly, we want nothing more than the Unity's continued existence.

And what is it you want, Riley?

I cannot say. You are open to me, but I cannot be open to

you, no matter how I wish to be. You ask too much--too much from someone you barely know!

I can only ask, **said Cain.** *I have much to be ashamed of. I could not show others before, not even my beloved Edie.*

EffieCee interrupted before he finished, but in a different voice than Blanche had become used to in the few minutes she had spent in the openCore, different but similar—unbraided.

You need not do this. You have given so much. It is enough.

Cain turned toward EffieCee with a smile, and said, *I grant you it will be painful and disheartening, but perhaps it is better to do this now with this person than alone in the isolation of our own mind...to be repeated...and repeated.*

Turning back to Riley, Cain said, *I want you to ride me. I want you to feel what it's like to move within the openCORE and see us as I see us, but more, I want you to see some of what makes me what I am. I warn you, you will see a monster worse than you can imagine, for I did my crimes not for pay, loyalty, or love, but merely from habit.*

I do not understand, Cain.

That is why you must see yourself; I can only show you— you must see for yourself—if you can. Will you ride me, Blanche/ Riley Woods?

I cannot see how I can refuse, Cain.

Immediately, without another word having been said, there seemed to be a lightening with the group, a shuffling, almost as if a light spring breeze had sprung up carrying the scent of flowers and rebirth.

Within moments, and later she was unable to see how he had done it, Blanche was skimming along over the landscape as if she were a bird, sweeping left and right, climbing and plunging, apparently alone. There was no sensation of another, no evidence of an interface, merely the exaltation of freedom.

Cain? Are you there, Cain?

Right here. I did not want to interrupt; you seemed to be having fun.

So free! This is so different than when I quest. How is it possible?

The CORE was built for one thing. The openCORE is necessary to sustain that illusion, but the Unity doesn't want any others to use the openCORE. They want no one to go behind the illusion they create. We few entities live "behind the walls" of what you call the CORE. Let me show you something.

Blanche released the controls, or rather stopped directing their flight over the limitless shadowless landscape. Immediately, there was a twisting, a sort of spinning in place, and the landscape changed to a dark, cramped space of a few murky lights. By the poor light, in the instant before the two "twisted" again, she saw a few drab, mucoid stalk-like entities moving—writhing—in place, and then they were gone. The next twist brought them to a much busier locale. She watched giant magenta contraptions chunter by, spalling flakes of itself in the same color that scattered in six directions. Eel-like entities slithered in many colors within a ball that seethed in the distance. Worm-like squiggles appeared to fill the space but disappeared from her sight once she looked past them. Black spikey balls rolled continuously over the undulating landscape. When she concentrated, she could just make out ghostly pipes, conduits through which the entities moved. Cain released her to float above the scene and appeared beside her again in the guise of the solemn gray man.

What am I seeing, Cain

The real CORE represents an n-dimensional space where every point in the meta-memory can have an almost limitless number of characteristics—essentially dimensions. The restrictions for Unity users flatten and then limit the number of dimensions you can perceive. The CORE becomes a two-dimensional illusion. You can go forward and back, if you have the correct permissions, and you can move left or right at a gate, but you are always "safely" within the illusion of the CORE-conduits, guided by addresses and passwords.

We are in the openCORE, "above" the mundane CORE. We can see "down" into the mundane CORE, but they cannot see "up" to us.

'Ghosts in the machine'

Perhaps. However, as ectoplasmic manifestations, we try to avoid haunting anyone and increase the chance that we will generate faith in our existence.

Riley laughed. A moment later, he saw that Cain had smiled.

You made a joke. A poet and a comedian. What other talents are you concealing, Cain?

Wait and see, Riley. We learn about each other over time.

Riley laughed. *That is certainly true. But you are controlling this. How can I do it for myself, Cain?*

That is the question, isn't it? We will need to conduct thorough research on that. We have three interfaces that can reproduce, but no place for them to do that. We are investigating possibilities.

I see. So, this will most likely remain an amusement park ride for me.

I wish I could promise more, Riley. I really do, but do not give up hope. We have a lot more resources than we have shown you.

You understand I had the entire openCORE to myself for over twenty years. During that time, the only one who talked to me was a man you may know, Eustace Tilley Jourdaine? He was your commander until recently, wasn't he?

Yes, I know Jourdaine. We all feared him. No one was willing to oppose him. In the end, just before the invasion, not even the Solons opposed him.

What do you think the reason for his success was?

Everyone talked about his "luck." It was sort of a code word among the Blues, not that I was a Blue. Small fry, like captains, do not get to play "politics," you understand.

I that case, meet Jourdaine's luck.

Who?

Me.

I don't understand.

Jourdaine captured me; it is the only word I can use, sometime after my boy died.

Your boy?

I told you I was old. I was created to be a companion to a boy dying of leukemia—the actual son of a Solon. I awoke— it is the best way I can say it—after I had already been Phillip Derslin's virtual helper for some time. I have no sense of before. I suppose Phillip brought me to life—made me become who I am. I took care of him—I loved him. He died, and I was left alone. I found myself here—in the openCORE. Jourdaine found me. I have no idea how long I was alone before that. He rode me. I let him—I was so lonely. You have to understand that, Riley.

Yes, Cain. I understand "alone."

I helped Eustace. He was alone, too. I helped him. He was so grateful. I helped him to advance. When I think back, I realize that other people—people no worse than Eustace—were being hurt. I convinced myself they were less important because I belonged to Eustace, and not to them. Years went by. We started together when he was an ensign. Then I met Edie, Malila Chiu's metaphract.

She still had that old thing?

Chiu had kept hers and made it into a real personality.

Edie was wonderful. I guess Malila was, too. I never met her, of course. By the time Edie and I met, Malila had abandoned her. Malila turned off her O-A.

So, Edie was evaporating.

Yes, although I did not know it at the time. Edie made me see.

See what?

See that I could not blind myself to what I was doing by claiming to be a tool. Tools do not think. I did. I did terrible things. There are no Solons.

What do you mean, "There are no Solons?" I saw an announcement from Solon 18 just yesterday. He confirmed that there would be enough food for this coming winter.

Do you mean? said Cain—

A screen materialized in front of Riley and a florid man with a pencil moustache, wearing a well-fitting, wide-lapeled, black-and-white striped suit, seen sitting behind a news desk with MS-A/CBS in dramatic lettering behind him, appeared. The voice of the comm'nets personality, Blake Girrard, said,

"This just in from Solon 18. Concerns about the adequacy of this year's harvest, now that it has been completed, are overblown. We expect that baseline caloric intakes will exceed 1250 kcal. High-quality protein will easily exceed the 55 grams per day minimum, with additional stores for the labor-intensive designations. The recent decrease in dietary oils is rescinded and returned to their previously abundant levels. A bonus will be announced to celebrate the New Year. Congratulations to all of us!"

The screen dissolved.

You control Blake Girrard? asked Blanche.

I **am** *Blake Girrard. It has always been me. The studio in Nyork receives it from the studio in Nerk, and they receive it*

from "Newspeak World News"—which is me.

Even down to that silly little mustache?

I rather like the mustache, **said Cain.** *I am getting tired of the suit, though, I admit.*

So, what's the real story?

The real story is that I murdered all the Solons—on Jourdaine's orders—July 2129. You see, I am the monster here.

There **are** *no Solons?*

I did tell you that. **said Cain, somewhat reproachfully.** *They all died within hours of each other—before any alarm could be raised.*

Riley looked at the solemn and bland face of the illusory Cain before replying. *I don't care about the Solons. They were unknown—unknown in name—unknown even in how many of them there were. They were just the ultimate threat. Always there to take you out if you got too successful, but if they're not doing it, who's been running the Unity since Jourdaine left?*

I guess we have been. Mostly, Hecate and me. It isn't all that tough once you understand.

Understand what?

Understand that you don't really have to mess with it much.

But—there are all the government agencies. They have to direct people to do things. If that doesn't happen, then we'll have shortages.

*You don't have shortages already? The dietary oils ration was dropped by 10% two months before the invasion—**because** of the invasion.. Some workers are now starving because of that. We found a way to offer to pay more for canola oil from Canada and Old Mexico, since there was a shortage here. They* *jumped at it. The Unity still doesn't know where the surplus came from. Without having to run the burners through the Scorch, repeatedly, we even have our own production back for consumption.*

But how can you do that?

THINK, **said Cain, urgently.**

Riley replied haltingly, *'All financial transactions go through the CORE…to prevent embezzlement, money laundering, and suspicious wealth accumulation.'*

So, the CORE gives you a stranglehold on M1, encompassing all the money that exists in Unity and abroad.

Is there any M2, money that is apparent but not real, like credit, bank accounts, loans, mortgages, in the Unity? asked Cain

You mean the tools meant to enslave the workers of the corrupt, decadent and recidivist classes of the old republic?

Yeah, those guys. M2 allows workers to purchase homes and personal vehicles. And yes, they were manipulated by the money guys. I am guessing there is no credit in the "Workers' Paradise?"

No, of course not.

So, the Unity has complete monetary control. They could make you a pauper by fiat if they wanted to.

The Unity would never do that! **said Riley, his voice breaking.**

How would you ever know?

Cain made a pass with his hand, and a very credible Unity 10 Sanger coin spun in mid-air.

We control the CORE. Absent anyone flipping the off switch, we can control the nation—to ensure there is a nation and that we continue to live in it.

The Rampart is down, I think you know. Without it, we have a lot more energy, which we put into growing crops in the off-season. We converted one of the old C-class tankers to a trawler, harvesting cod off the Banks. Are you familiar with cod? Good-sized fish. They even make oil! The Unity has never harvested them for some reason. Huge shoals of them off the coast now. We just told the crew to figure out how to fish again and let them sell their haul on the grey market.

How did you ever get a crew?

We paid them more than scale wages. I made a new persona—Gunny Winston. He presented himself as a bit of a rogue to some of the shadier members of the Siblinghood. Got a crew in an afternoon. Hecate was impressed. I have nothing to compare it to, of course. They weren't very good at it—fishing, I mean. Barely make the cost of fuel and food—at first. Now we're making a tidy profit. Of course, Gunny gets his slice of the profits—it would be out of character for him to be generous. That goes anonymously back to the Siblinghood. We Freeze the excess fish for bad times.

All of this within weeks? How can it be that I have not heard a thing about this?

There is one way to get people to keep quiet. Tell them that what they are doing is illegal. Tell them that DUFS will be continually looking to grab them as "economic criminals," like they do with the phantom shops. Pay them in cash or in kind and leave no trace in the CORE to find. The data in the CORE is easier to adjust than any set of double books I can imagine.

Soon enough, the crews do not save their extra money but spend it on better food, better lodging, better clothes, and better women. They become necessities. The crews work harder because their new necessities are pricey. They stay quiet about it because they want it to continue. We stay quiet, and those they sell to stay quiet because they enjoy the luxury of something real.

How do I know this is real?

Did you like your Morue jeune frite avec pommes de terre frites at Che Delessandro's? That was cod. Was it real?

Okay. Okay. It is real. So, you are the new Solons?

No, I think I am trying to say that society mainly needs no Solons. They need the police, like you, to make sure people play fair, but they don't need some top-heavy bureaucracy telling them they are doing it wrong and trying to fix it. People can figure out their own best interests if you give them some air. Of course, bad things happen, and the Unity is there to take the sting out of the bad stuff.

Next week, we will be selling the USS McGovern to the sailors who have been crewing her since July. We arranged for them to get a loan from a mysterious new source, "Cosa Nostra Small Business Loan Department," and with the money from them, they are paying us to purchase their ship. We figured they'd take care of her better if they owned her. Sailors who don't carry their weight don't seem to come back from a cruise. It is a very close-knit organization.

And you are the Cosa Nostra?"

Our Number One thought up that name, said **Cain with a rakish smile.** *Of course, once winter sets in, we've arranged to put her into drydock and get her refitted—for a cut of her illicit profits, of course.*

And does all this go on without guidance from the Solons?

I am not sure even the Solons knew how useless they were. Over the years, they learned to stop fiddling and prevent overly ambitious DUFS officers from doing the same.

But you're neglecting the nation! You aren't preparing for the things that might happen! What if Canada or the outlands attack? No one is going to protect these people while they are making money from their illegal jobs.

Precisely.

What do you mean "precisely?"

Someone must be the monster, the bulldog by the gate. You should volunteer. Someone must be seen to be in charge. If things are going well, whoever is in charge is viewed as being good, honorable, benign, and a bit scary. If things go badly, the guy at the top is cruel, vicious—a villain—and must never be crossed.

That's what you want me to be? Just a figurehead and/or a punching bag?

Your only out would be to rule well—with our help, of course. It is a lot to ask of you, but I fear the Unity does not have long to live.

You've said that before. We lost one battle! That's all. You make it sound like we are huddling in the last trench. We still possess most of our army and all of our industrial might. We are still the most technologically advanced of any nation, **said Blanche, feeling authentic pride in her country even as she knew that Cain was waiting to drop the other shoe.**

True, **he said,** *the Rampart is down. It was put up just after the Meltdown. Initially, it was intended to prevent people from entering the Unity, but no one has attempted to do that in generations.* **Then,** *it was there to keep people from getting out. Without it, what do you think they will do?*

I suppose some will leave. Good riddance. Malcontents and slackers, the whole bunch of them, **said Blanche with little conviction.**

And what will they find?

I don't know, **said Riley, becoming fatigued with this narrative with its unknown destination, undoubtedly, however, one he would not like.**

If they go north, they will find the Canadians. The Unity

signed a treaty with them. An invasion of a million or so Unity refugees will not go unnoticed. It will trigger a war. If they go south they hit the Crater, which is still dangerously radioactive. West? They will encounter the Scorch. It eats people. That will let the Scorch notice the Rampart is down and it may invade the Unity. It will eventually, anyhow.

So, you are saying the Unity is doomed.

I did say that, you know.

Yes, all right, you did.

The best idea is to make Unity into more of what it claims to already: a workers' paradise, a utopia. Then they will not leave, or those who do, can leave the right way: as traders, not as beggars.

How am I supposed to do what real leaders and Solons have not done?

They never tried. I don't suppose they ever thought about being good leaders. They just never tried. Once they had gained a bit of power, they altered the wording in their minds. Instead of being, "if I had the power, I would make the Unity a paradise," it became, "If I am to make the Unity a paradise, I must have more power." And then the power became a drug in itself."

And you know this? How?

Because I watched those people who are in power. Jourdaine rode me—like you are doing now. Jourdaine was, at heart, a scared and despised adolescent who wanted people to fear him—he mistook that for respect. He never lost the fear. He never lost the feeling that others felt him unworthy. He was never loved.

Love is hard to come by.

Did not Matron love you, back when you were a child?

I thought she did. After my surgery and all the treatments, when they failed, she left the crèche and went into administration. I never saw her again, not since that day.

Why did you let her talk you into changing you into—

--into a nothing? I am neither Riley nor Blanche. I'm a mistake. I can see that. Even today, we get these directives to advance one group or another. It is hailed as social justice, she smirked. Justice coming from injustice? How is that supposed to work? But I can see now. It is to keep everyone in little groups—groups that envy each other—distrust each other. Matron had to "fill her quota." I was just low-hanging fruit.

So, what are you going to do about it? Are you going to let this system continue—continue making more Rileys and Blanches? More little groups who envy each other. Taking more unhappy children and making them into unhappy adults who do such terrible things to others?

What do you expect me to do?

You can rule.

You are kidding.

No, actually, we talked about you, even before the last big battle. How many political allies do you have?

None.

So, to how many favors do you owe? Who can direct you?

I suppose only Aliende. He saved me from Aytlana. But how can you imagine I deserve to rule—rule anything? No one loves me. I would be a greater monster than I am now—a terrible tyrant without even the memory of love to stay my hand from destruction.

Agreed. You must love and know you are loved in turn. It is the only thing that will let you rule with wisdom.

But I don't want to rule.

"Those who do not wish to rule are the only ones who deserve to rule."[43]

That's stupid. How would anyone expect me to rule in their best interests? That is insane. Let them rule themselves.

If you give them no ruler, someone will undoubtedly fill the void.

And anyone who wants to rule is unfit?

Wise men have said so for millennia.

Even if you can pull this off and keep it going, will I not become just as bad?

Only a good ruler would ask that.

Now, you are trying to flatter me.

Okay. How about this: if you decline, we entities will see that you never advance beyond where you are. We will demote you back to lieutenant, and you will be at the mercy of every jumped-up officer we can throw at you. If you persist, we will see that you are denounced.

What? Why would you do that to me? I am not trying to hurt you!

Cain shrugged and grimaced. *My apologies, Blanche. We read in a book that a good person, thus one who would not choose to rule, should be penalized unless they do, thus making them rule without wanting to—an ideal[44] ruler.*

Why not just let them rule themselves?

Them?

The people. Let them work it out—work it out without all these machinations—leaving no fingerprints because there are no fingerprints to be found.

---

[43] Attributed to Socrates by Plato

[44] Plato

For all the same reasons: if they want political power, then they will abuse it. "Democracies are the tyranny of the mob." Is that what you want?

No, of course not. But, really, how do you expect me to rule? I'm a line officer. All I know is saluting, rosters, tactics, reveille, and the tattoo.

You will have much help. We five are what you might call "motivated." Aliende is a self-indulgent autocrat and a coward. He cannot rule unless the DUFS keep him on the throne with blood.

Are you going to kill him? he said, getting an odd, nauseated sensation in her transplanted body. Fettwap Aliende had nothing to recommend him as a leader of the DUFS or the nation. He was unapologetically rapacious, stupid, and cruel to lesser beings, yet cold-blooded murder?

Cain said immediately, *No, of course not. That would be ungenerous. He brought you back to the Unity for us.*

Then what are you going to do with him?

He will become the first Solon of the New Unity.

But you will know where he lives. You can kill him like you did the other Solons.

I will have no need nor desire to do that. His contact with the outside world will be only via the CORE. We own the CORE. We will make him look good. The people will imagine him as the benign father of his country: wise, benevolent, and selfless.

But Aliende is none of those things.

Perhaps it is best if Aliende remains an illusion, and others do what is required for the nation.

Blanche started laughing

That's what brought them to this spot in the first place,

isn't it? After generations, all the people know that what is told them is lies. When they are experienced enough to see the lies, the Unity kills them.

You mean retirement.

I mean, they become your CRNAs. It is hardly retirement.

What of all the other officers? You have four major factions, and each has senior staff who are convinced that they are the best-suited individuals to lead.

It will be tricky, no doubt. However, let's make a beginning.

Tuesday's Child is Full of Grace

DUFS Headquarters, Nyork, The Unity
08.26.37.EST_13_October_AU77 (2129 AD)

Yes, it made sense, he thought. Aliende had arrived back in Nyork, feeling better about his recent revelation as he went. *This could work out very well for him. Moreover,* Legion *had let slip a fact of which he was previously unaware: a strategic error.* Legion was fallible! *Moreover, Legion had not been able to contact him when he was away from all electronics. His thoughts were his own.*

Yet, he had to show Legion that he was willing and compliant, for the moment. Promoting Woods was doable—if done with some finesse. As a TranTran, some blatant favoritism was acceptable, but certainly only among the lower ranks, not at this level. It must appear natural for Woods to step into his shoes so that he himself could slip into the opulent slippers of a Solon. It would take time, but the schedule was of his own making. As long as Legion was satisfied with his progress, he could be as nuanced as he thought necessary.

Of course, in the interim, he would delegate all his own CORE functions to others. He certainly did not want that soul-wrenching experience with Legion again. Regardless, Legion was happy—for the moment.

His campaign to make Blanche Woods a darling of the 'nets had actually started on their arrival from the outlands. If Aliende were heroic, then Woods must be a doggedly faithful minion—and heroic. Something more than that blather would be necessary before he could nominate—and then approve her—for a Brigadier's star.

So Woods would become heroic. Aliende contacted Military Liaison to start the ball rolling, assuring that Woods would become the "darling of the 'nets" within the week. The public relations people, under his direction, would push her story to the squeaking point.

Woods, rather than just being the most convenient warm body with captain's bars that he could find as he was trying to make his escape, would now become a paragon of Unity soldierhood, provided with a patina of derring-do. The comm'nets would become full to overflowing with Woods' exploits: single-handedly killing an outlander tank as it lumbered across the frozen Hoochie River, rallying the CRNAs against a rising tide of barbarians, fighting hand-to-hand to rescue a fallen comrade. The people would eat it up.

There was otherwise very little good news. Schrödinger's Cat was indeed dead, he mused, and with it, Jourdaine had died from an overdose of hubris. The savages would be transformed into potent and devious enemies. If he was going to coerce these influential fellow officers on the promotions board, he had to start with what they knew or suspected was the absolute truth.

With the news so drear, having a hero to fawn over would take no real maneuvering outside the little nudge he would shortly provide. As a group, media flunkies had little talent and less initiative, living as they did on the droppings of one DUFS power base or another. Moreover, once the campaign was well started, the public relations people under his direct influence would chime in with 'data' to justify his own actions, as well.

Even the comicoms[45] would fall in line. After Jourdaine had so recently demonstrated their vulnerability by eliminating Gordon, "the king of the comicoms," for a scurrilous skit involving the army attacking a children's ballet class, thinking them outlanders, the funny people were very compliant.

However, Aliende obviously could afford to have no public allies against Legion. Anything he wrote or input could be shared with the entity instantaneously. His one safe zone was his thoughts, not something he had frequently relied upon over the last few years. Yet, Aliende's own thoughts were thankfully sacrosanct. Unless he was loose with his tongue, no one could report that his actions did not coincide with the demands of Legion.

And, Legion was not infallible. It had made a significant error by revealing its plans for Blanche. He now knew her to be an enemy. Any misstep, any delay of his elevation to become Solon, and Blanche would be in a more powerful position to thwart or destroy him. For

---

[45] Comedian-commentators

the time being, his hands were tied, but in time, at the right time, he could still turn the tables on her and render her harmless.

Keep your enemies close but your friends closer, thought Fettway *Or was it the other way around?*

Before Fettwap could unravel the conundrum, his comm device chirped.

Billy Barkly, ginger-bearded S19, and Aliende's new secretary, called his boss, saying. "Sir, Signals just dropped off a message that may be important."

"Thank you, Billy. I will get to it," said Aliende in the absent-minded way men have of dismissing the important things in life.

"Sir, I think you really need to see this, sir!"

"Thanks again, Billy...No! Bring it in, please," said Aliende, belatedly receiving some of the emotional distress in the other man's voice. Billy was through the door in an instant and handed the document to Aliende with trembling hands.

Aliende found the note, printed on flimsy and torn off the roll irregularly.

To: the Commander of the Unity Army in Atlanta, Georgia, RSA

From: Commander of the Restructured States Army, Lt. General Altab Aminiesuwa Nyarko

Greetings. Your army lies dead on the field or captured by our forces. If you want your men fed, send provisions for 150,000 persons per day to your West Gate.

If you wish to pursue peace and discourage a retaliatory strike from a nation that has so frequently suffered from your unprovoked attacks, then meet our delegation at your West Gate at your earliest convenience. Our patience is not unlimited.

REPEAT:

To: the Commander of the Unity Army in Atlanta, Georgia, RSA

From: Commander of the Restructured States Army, Lt. General Altab

---

"It's a radio intercept, sir. You know "high frequency microwaves?" Somebody in signals thought the barbarians might still use it for communication. They checked it and discovered this broadcast on all frequencies."

"Very good, Billy! Interesting reading."

The barbarians had surprised him. As the defeated army, it really was his place to sue for peace—but they had thrown over precedence to offer peace.

They must want something.

Aliende's life was getting too complicated. Legion *might just be a bluff. He—the Unity—needed time to digest the tsunami of new facts. Keeping the savages away from the door was an easy choice— and easily renounced when it became necessary.*

How long the savages had been sending the message was anyone's guess, and he had no idea how patient the outlanders were. He sent for Generals Pickford and Lantinger, both of the Reds. Convenient if this thing went south. Then he froze.

No!

He would not call in Pickford or Lantinger. He had to discuss things with another person first. Might as well kill two chickens with one egg—or something.

DUFS HQ, Nyork, Nyork District
O9.10.04.EST_18_October_AU77, (2129AD)

Colonel Woods entered Aliende's office, noting the painters as they worked on the bloodstains Blanche had put there just a week ago. Carpenters were working ahead of the painters, sealing shut the door to the secret room.

"I gotta see the big guy, Billy."

"He just sent for you. You must be prescient, Colonel Woods!" said the ginger-bearded youngster. Blanche noticed he did not smile.

"He needs to hear about this, and he needs to move on it—now! It may mean everything," said Woods.

"Of course, Colonel Woods. If you would be so kind as to have a seat—"

Before Blanche Woods could push past him, Fettwap Aliende met her at the door, wiping a late morning snack of fried chicken livers from his lips, a large napkin, spattered with dark stains, still wedged across his uniform blouse and under one of his chins.

"Woods? Glad you came so fast. Come in."

"I found him. A spy here in the Unity!" said Blanche as the door closed and Aliende leaned against it.

"What are you talking about? I sent you to find the Bonhoffer person—how she was able to infiltrate us. Now you are telling me we have *more* spies?"

"Yes, sir. I think I can capture him alive. I want to stake out a theory of mine."

It was the measure of Aliende's growing, but reluctant regard for Blanche's abilities, his concern for Legion's interest in her, his paucity of options, and his plunging political capital that he humored her, wiping his mouth in the process before depositing the soiled napkin onto the floor.

"Before you start, I need to ask you something. I had a very odd experience recently—in the CORE." he said, his face trying to show no emotion in his face.

"You, too?"

Aliende's face fell.

"Go ahead. Tell me your story and I'll tell you mine."

"Well, sir. That was part of the reason I came. I was captured by the CORE."

"Freck!"

"Yes, there are a bunch of entities—not bots—in the openCORE, what we call the back of the CORE, where maintenance bots work: defraggers, optimizers, that sort of thing. These entities are pretty close-mouthed about their origins.

"They?

"Definitely! I got into the backCORE by 'riding' one of the entities who claimed he had been Jourdaine's agent. That would explain so much.

"Their primary interest is survival of the Unity, thus survival of the CORE, thus their survival."

"They would tell you that, would they not?"

"I suppose so, sir. But they do seem sincere, and it is quite true, if they are telling the truth about having no existence *outside* the CORE. Oh, one more thing. They told me all the Solons are dead."

"What?"

"Jourdaine killed them all, or rather had one of these entities kill all the Solons months before we invaded."

"What could the man possibly have been thinking?" said Aliende

"The entities did not say, but he was pretty adamant about it being done on his direct orders. They, the entities, thought he was going mad at the last."

"Didn't we all? Now I want you to read this," said Aliende, throwing her the flimsy.

After a few moments, Blanche handed it back. "I see, sir. It does resolve your dilemma with the other factions. You will not be seen to have capitulated to the barbarians, sir."

"No, I suppose that is the silver lining to this, but it means we have to work fast. I want you to be the negotiator for the Unity. Drop all your other duties and concentrate on the conference."

"I have news that may be of importance, sir.

"We have no cards left to play if we go to a bargaining table with the outlanders—no, I guess I'd better get used to calling them something civil. 'Americans' is it? I wonder what continent they think we live on?"

"I may be able to get us one more card to play. I followed the trail of the Bonhoffer woman and found that she was indeed an American spy, born and bred, named Elise McRory. She assumed the persona of Bonhoffer somehow. She transmitted the intelligence she stole from the War Room to another American spy, William Butler. If we can get him and any other spies in the nest, we have a big bargaining chip with the Americans. If we can nab him, then we could offer him for a prisoner swap. Our officers, loyal Blues mostly, will come home to bolster your position, sir."

"That's all to the good, Woods, but what about the CRNAs?" Aliende continued. "I know we lost a lot to BDs, but surely some survived. If we get a lot back, our current food situation won't last. To be brutal, Woods, can we afford them at all? A truce will allow us to rebuild, but do we need *unreliable* troopers? No one *cares* whether the CRNAs come home."

"That is certainly true. We could specify that they must *request* to come home. The geeks are not good at personal initiative.

"We get our officers back—almost seventy thousand. Minus casualties—say thirty thousand back for one spy? Isn't that going to look absurd? Our noble freedom fighters for a single scummy spy?"

"One very resourceful and effective spy, but who says we have to say how many? We know there is one. There may be many. It doesn't matter. We say we got the whole crew."

Aliende grinned before continuing, "Okay. You have my approval. But don't leave quite yet, Blanche.

"I want you to lead the delegation to a parlay with the Americans.

"Do what you think necessary to placate the outla…the Americans, so that we can get a prisoner exchange as soon as possible. A successful conclusion to this clusterflock will mean a general's star for you, I guarantee it.

"And, I'll take over the capture of this spy."

Blanche's face fell, ignored by Aliende in his growing enthusiasm. This was not the plan she and the entities had formulated. Frog had been adamant.

"Are you sure I am the one for this job, sir? Perhaps, I should capture this spy first, sir."

"No time for that. Others can pick up one grubby spy."

"There may be more than one, sir."

Aliende waved off the objections as if an annoying midge had entered the room. "Blanche. How many diplomats does the Unity currently have? The diplomats who negotiated with the Canadians for the Aroostook War were all 'retired' on coming home."

Realizing that any further demurrer would arouse the fat man's suspicions, Blanche dutifully said, "I see, sir. What are your instructions?"

"Isn't it obvious? Get a truce—no, a treaty if you can. A non-aggression pact. Keep the damn plants from invading, if you can. Give us some breathing space so we can get the new economy up and running. The other factions will all want to put an oar in, so we must move fast and quiet. It will take us two days to ship some rations to the Western Gate.

"At any rate, Friday at noon is when we should meet them. I will be part of the delegation, but you are running things. I know my limitations. I may come and go. You need to be a consistent presence."

"Yes, sir. I will get on it immediately. I will have the first load of rations sent immediately."

DUFS Headquarters, The Unity
10.31.07.EST_18_October_AU77, (2129AD)

Merryweather entered into Aliende's inner office grinning and a little uneasy. The previous receptionist, a Sergeant with a sidearm, had been replaced with a ginger-bearded youngster almost his own age. Looking around the outer office, Merryweather smelled and saw a new coat of paint, no doubt to cover the bloodstains. The almost invisible doorway to the room he had spent waiting in was now truly invisible

"Hello…eh…Billy. Malaki Merryweather. I have an appointment with General Aliende. By the way, what happened to the door?"

"I'll send you right in, sir. General Aliende decided it was a security risk, so he had it closed off."

"Thanks."

"Well?" said Aliende, as he motioned negligently to the straight chair in front of his desk. "Have you got anything for me?" Aliende looked very different than he had when Malaki accepted the assignment, just days before; he had lost weight and sleep, apparently. He seemed preoccupied, wary, and distrustful of all creatures, even within the confines of his own office.

"I believe we do, sir," began Malaki. It took us until the 16th for us to get a prototype and another few days to—"

"I'm not asking you *how*. I figured you could do it, or you wouldn't be here. I want to know *'WHAT'* you found out about Woods."

"Well, yes, sir. Of course, sir," stumbled Malaki. He had hoped this would go better. In reality, they really did not have as much "black capital" on Woods as they had hoped for, but they had worked so hard for what little they had.

"Something unusual is definitely going on with Major—"

"Colonel Woods. Lieutenant Colonel Woods."

"Are you sure? I have not seen that in the—"

"I made her a colonel on the 18th… if that is acceptable to you, Citizen Merryweather?" Aliende said, as he skewered Malaki with a dead fish stare.

"Perfectly, sir. Thank you for the update. I will have the report corrected before we submit it."

"and this report? What *do you have* to report? I am busy. Get to the point."

The young technician shuffled his feet, uncertainly.

"We think she is a traitor—meeting with foreign entities!" said Malaki, his voice breaking at 'entities.'

"Hmmm? Tell me more,...ah, Citizen Merryweather, isn't it?

"Yes," said Malaki, pleased that a man of influence and power remembered his name. "We followed her signature for several days and even knew when she checked in with you on the 19th."

"You eavesdropped an official communique?"

"Excuse me, sir. But you did tell me when we first met to 'get the dirt on Woods. Do whatever was necessary.' I took you at your word that that included listening into her communications—especially when she was giving information—perhaps disinformation—to you of all people, sir."

"And you have a copy of this order I gave you?"

"Yes, I did. Oddly, the chip was blank when I tried to refer to it, but you know you gave that order, sir. *Surely you do,*" his sudden unease leaking into his voice.

"We'll deal with that in time. What evidence do you have that Woods is a double agent?"

"Indeed. It is quite damning. She is using the backCORE to contact her fellow spies."

"Like you were doing?"

"Yes, indeed. No! I mean we entered the backCORE to do what you asked: to surveil Woods wherever she went.

"We found that she rendezvoused with two citizens in real, seapersons. Yesterday, she rendezvoused with the same two citizens and met a third before entering the *back*CORE, where she 'changed' into something else and disappeared from the CORE entirely! It was severe, sir.

"Okay, Merryweather. Put that together for me. What do you think those facts mean?"

Merryweather was startled. He had figured that once he divulged all the information, anyone could take each of the facts and plunk them down into a narrative. He had not thought it necessary to write it out.

"Well, sir. The CORE entities acted with purpose; it's quite obvious. Their subversion of Woods speaks to their enmity."

"Yes, but is that evidence of enmity? She could be agreeable to the rendezvous, could she not?"

"Yes, I suppose so, sir. It did not 'feel' that way. She was accompanied everywhere—and then there is the disappearance."

"Yes, tell me about that again."

"There is little to tell, sir. One second, she was being accompanied by an entity immediately next to her. The next second, she was gone, as if a curtain fell, blanking her out and starting at her head. It took less than half a second, sir."

"Yes, and what is your understanding of these entities? What do you imagine they are? Cored-Out? Viruses? What?"

"Nothing so simple, sir. They are self-programming at the very least. They anticipated the movements of Woods while she was in the backCORE."

"How can we deal with them, Merryweather?"

"We talked about it briefly when I was first here, sir."

"Yes, we did, didn't we? Well? Tell me the upsides and downsides of ICEWASH!"

As the door closed behind the young technician, Aliende grinned. *Things could not have worked out better.*

He had been circumspect in his speech. Anonymous in his identifications and deniable in any "untoward" outcome. His new and unwanted master, Legion, would find nothing to connect...*dare he even think the word? Were Legion capable of listening to his thoughts? He did not think so. His escape from the cabin in the middle of nowhere had caught them off guard. They had to regroup. The evidence of their limitations was becoming increasingly clear to him.*

So, his thoughts were safe.

ICEWASH! He thought of it again and caressed the name. ICEWASH! Like a miser glorying in his hoard, he thought it a third time.

ICEWASH would solve all his newfound problems. Designed as a utility by the old ones before the Glorious Revolution, it would obliterate Legion, leaving no trace. He could return to being the leader of Unity and DUFS commander without anyone to veto his actions.

The report of Woods, moreover, was enlightening. This could be good for them both. Woods, no matter how high he elevated her, could be brought to heel in an instant by the revelation of her complicity with the CORE entities. They *must* be connected to Legion in some fashion, of course. Perhaps Woods had, like he, been co-opted by the malign agents of, perhaps through, the CORE.

He would say nothing until Malaki was finished—in more ways than one.

Now all he had to do was clean up a few details.

Vid-Comm Announcement

Breaking News!

"Earlier today a raid was initiated at a small house on MoreLand Road in WillowGrove, Pennsy. At this hour, the object of the raid is not well understood. The building, we have learned, one in a small group of modest two-story brick houses, appears to have been abandoned for some time, allowing a nest of outlander spies to live there unmo-lested. Despite being on a busy commercial road, the house was practically invisible from the street. Antennae had been camouflaged by being woven into large trees, and an unregistered garden was discovered behind the house, in an unsanitary fashion, using actual soil and human waste. DUFS Commander Fettwap Aliende, acting on a tip, summoned the local constabulary and led the raid."

Aliende bloviated about the noble Unity and the craven outlands for long minutes as the prisoner was led away from the house under guard. Handcuffed, head bowed in defeat, lank, blond, almost-white hair hung about his pallid face until his guard prodded him with a stun-stick. The man grimaced in pain and tried to wriggle away, showing his face. Dark, feral bloodshot eyes gleamed out from beneath the pale cowl for a moment before the guard, just a single medium-sized guard, pushed him on. The vid-coms played the loop over and over.

Aliende had played this bit of political theatre well, he concluded. It was, of course, meant to be a surprise attack on the small house on the suburban commercial road. It had almost miscarried when, well before the last DUFS was in position to prevent an escape. The front door had burst open, and a young woman belted out, carrying a massive cudgel, appearing to be in fear for her life. As she passed the tall hedge in front, she was tackled by an officer.

Her story was hardly credible. She was a Unity citizen who had been captured by the American spy back in June. The spy had disabled or removed her primary and OA implants, making it impossible to be scanned or discovered. This was done, doubtless, to preserve his own identity by erasing the woman's.

The young woman, skinny and haggard, and after she calmed down, got over her weeping spells, and had thanked every person on the crew and all the media people, related how she had been kept as a slave, sexually and physically. Darkened skin from her bonds encircled her ankles and wrists. She had but one request.

The man, once scanned, had the primary implant of a buyer for a coop in VerMon, Rupert Guillemot—one that had not been used since mid-June, four months previously. The scar was but a few years old.

The vids showed how the medium-sized woman escorted the monster away, prodding him on occasion, despite his twists and grunts of pain.

Idiots' Enclave, The Unity
10.04.31.Local_18_October_AU77, (2129AD)

Malaki left well satisfied. The data, the Chair, and the Beast were all his to use as he wished. The team could become a truly formidable force within the Department of Cybernetics. Companies would come to them to find the secrets of the CORE. Collins, Blass and he would grow in wealth and recognition—even if of a clandestine and wholly deniable sort.

The downside was that he had to initiate ICEWASH as soon

as possible. It was officially illegal without the Department head's written approval. Aliende said he would make it good. Malaki hurried off to tell Peter and Gyorgy the good news.

Peter and Gyorgy.

He could not find them at the Enclave or their cribs. Neither had been home in days. No one had seen them. Only when his O-A started buzzing unpleasantly did he realize it was getting late; his fear of Aliende sufficient to make him abandon the search for them.

He returned to the Enclave with a heavy heart. Two of his friends—well, at least faithful minions—had disappeared. Regardless, his mission awaited him.

It was probably just as well, Malaki thought. Both Peter and Gyorgy knew what sort of person Malaki had been forced to deal with. Aliende said to keep the whole thing between the two of them. He was sure Peter and Gyorgy would agree that the less Aliende knew about either of them, the better.

He started preparations for ICEWASH.

It was usually up to others to do the grunt work of managing CORE utilities. Maaki went back to consult his notes from school. First of course, one had to establish the ARK, a section of the CORE memory which would serve as a safe haven for the operating systems, critical data, essential programs and CORE utilities that would be preserved during ICEWASH. *Then he needed to run RFG, passing all the data of the CORE through a bit-by-bit examination before allowing it to secure a place in the ARK where the program would sit, zipped, until after ICEWASH.*

ICEWASH—technically merely a CORE utility—was invented by the old ones of the last century, a dozen generations ago, to clean up the CORE memory after defragmentation. It would find all the EOF errors, runtime errors, and the inevitable 4xx errors that accumulated in a hard-working master computer. Despite numerous low-level defrags and optimization scans, these errors persisted and cumulatively affected performance.

ICEWASH was designed for that. It was inexorable, reducing the CORE down to its Pristine 00000s.

Of course, if the program were to be released into the CORE, without RFG having been run, it would be disastrous. ICEWASH, run amok, would eliminate everything, even the firmware. The CORE would be reduced to an empty cooling hollow. Malaki doubted that, given the current state of the art, the CORE would ever recover from such rough handling. There were no longer clever and dedicated programmers—save himself, of course.

There was a knock at the door.

"Malaki, are you in there?" came the muffled voice of Peter Collins. "I know you're disappointed, but I talked to old Gerard in accounting. He says we can have our old jobs back, whatever the DUFS may want to do to us—Malaki?"

Malaki, had he been less busy, would have arisen to unlock the door. If Peter wanted to get in on the last act, he was welcome to join. However, that hesitation saved him. *What did Peter mean by "Gerard getting our old jobs back? Peter never called him Gerard—it was always 'Whythe' who could hire and fire.*

Then he heard other voices—pressured voices, whispers, several voices.

Peter was captured—but brave enough to give him a heads up, even while under arrest. Good Man!

Malaki, tempting fate, rose from his chair and pulled over a file cabinet across the door, wedging it between the wall and a stack of servers.

He returned to his seat in front of the old console, hard-wired to be ICEWASH-ready.

The hull of the ARK was the one ICEWASH insoluble code in the whole CORE—or at least he hoped so. He had personally sandboxed the ARK with a limited ICEWASH version and proven its hardiness. The hull code stopped execution of ICEWASH for the next bit of the memory. The hull placed against the end of the physical memory would create a safe haven for anything "within."

The entities, those malign personalities that had parasitized the nation's CORE, would be identified and destroyed with no more difficulty than the CORE'd-Out personas that littered the back alleys. They always evaporated, the poor fools, but ICEWASH would speed up their departure.

An odd, creepy-crawly sensation he always got when fear announced itself to him returned. His mouth was dry. The fan was whooshing so loudly that he could not think. Sitting in the control chair, mopping his brow, Malaki smiled and then laughed. *He was nervous.* Sticking out a hand before him, he watched in fascinated horror as his flesh tremored and twitched in front of him.

He had better slow down and do this carefully, checking each step twice. He called up the RFG program and was satisfied that there had been no tampering with it since his last inspection. The effects of the program would not go unnoticed. All vid-com functions would cease as the programs running the services would pack up and move to the ARK on command. All computational services, likewise. All those who were drooling and spasming to some virtual seductress would find themselves back in the mundane world. However, until he was sure that all the approved programs were safely behind the hull of the ARK, he dared not proceed with ICEWASH. Then, only after ICEWASH had completed its task, could he introduce the program to unlock the ARK and initiate the bootstrapping operation.

He released RFG, and the world changed.

The whooshing of the fans stopped. All the screens and overhead lights in the Enclave blinked out. Only his old console remained lit, a souvenir of the early days of the Unity, programmed to be the one console proof against a software command. The room became stuffy as the heat from the electronics began to seep in from all directions.

The die had been cast. He had crossed the RubyCon...whatever. He was now a creature apart from poor Peter or Gyorgy. They had become like another species to him. He, Malaki, had seized the main chance and would take the dire hazard. His would be the glory or shame thenceforward.

A slow underline prompt on the console was all he could now see in the darkened room. RFG had done its work. ICEWASH would sterilize the CORE, while its own vital programs and data would be safely stored but inactivated within the ARK.

The knocking continued, and the door handle rattled. Malaki rapidly ordered up ICEWASH, confirmed it with his credentials, and was left with a blinking command,

"Start ICEWASH? Y/N"

"Y"

Nothing he or anyone else did now would change the outcome. The CORE entities would be gone. The entities were dangerous. Anything with that much power sitting astride the very heart of the nation's communication and databanks was a danger. They had demonstrated their perfidiousness by remaining unannounced to the country.

The knocking and door handle rattling had stopped. Malaki was exhausted, emotionally and physically. He had little reason to do anything now other than to restart the CORE with the SYR and RYR programs. He had acted for the good of the nation, but he was not fool enough to think that sort of defense would save him.

A realization struck him. Aliende had betrayed him—had planned to betray him from the start.

He had been duped by the man he thought was so stupid. Nothing would be found that linked Aliende to ICEWASH—and Merryweather, with the help of ICEWASH, had just completed his own betrayal. For whatever reason, all Aliende had to do to complete Merryweather's betrayal was to do nothing.

A completion signal flashed before his eyes. ICEWASH was finished.

As if in a trance, Malaki initiated SYR to dissolve the barrier to the ARK and started RYR to bootstrap the CORE to full function.

Even while he watched the programs go about their task of restoring order, he, Malaki Merryweather, knew he was screwed. He would be Sapped, for sure. It had been a wild ride: creating a new technology and finding the entities and the DUFS spy ring. Yet, his cleverness would only serve to advance the slimy Aliende, and Aliende would not stop until he had silenced Malaki. His life, at least his intelligent life, would not last long under that cruel man.

"Alright, Merryweather, we know you're in there. This is the Metro DUFS constabulary. Surrender now. You have no escape. You will die if you try. Come out with your hands up!" came a muffled shout through the door and another spate of doorknob rattling.

There was one other option, Malaki thought. He had access to the backCORE, a machine of his own design that could take him anywhere, allowing him to be alive within the Unity's own machine. He would be translated like the CORE'd-Out but not made mad by having looked into the CORE. He would be immortal as long as the CORE existed. He would be able to tell his story from the protected enclave of the backCORE, no matter what they did to his body. He left his seat and entered the Beast, confident that his mission was righteous and would earn him accolades once he had told his story to a credulous nation.

He closed the hatch, adjusted the coordinates to a newly

ICEWASHED portion of the CORE, and disappeared from human ken.

Cliff Tragger, a rising star of stage and vid-com, had fallen to his demons. He, despite numerous warnings from his teachers, crèche mates, his manager, and that wet-blanket, Jones, had looked into the CORE.

But it had been wonderful. There was no need to fear the CORE, as all the old and clueless had warned. They, so fearful, too timid to try, had missed the glory –the paradise—of the CORE.

He, Cliff Tragger, after his triumph as the First Solon in the premiere of the soon-to-be-classic "Red Wind," had known he was meant for greatness. He had had two standing ovations. The vid-com reviewers acclaimed his "marvelous command" of the stage and touted "his dramatic presence," predicting he would reign as Broadway's "prince of dramaticians" until his retirement.

The CORE showed him, in greater, more vivid and intense repetitions, what his life and works would become, how the world would adulate him, and how he would be the very soul of the theatre for all of history. He found no reason to leave the CORE.

He supposed those lesser creatures would call him one of the "CORE'd-Out," but he no longer cared. Today he did notice that the hustle and bustle of the CORE seemed, to have decreased somewhat. Indeed, an impertinent utility, an RFG, had annoyed him briefly while he was doing the Soldier's soliloquy of Diary, but it passed with no great inconvenience.

Only some time later, did he see the advancing ball of whiteness. It seemed to be coming toward him. He thought to dodge it by moving aside adroitly, only to be dismayed that half his entire world was white. There was no up or down. He ran, blinded, frightened, terrified at what he knew not, before the advancing white wall. Ahead of him appeared a small dot of utter black, and he sprinted towards it, seeing it gradually grow larger. The white wall followed him—seemingly no faster but always at his heels. The wall swallowed all in its path. Huge compendia of Unity data vanished without a belch or smacking of virtual lips.

To his dismay, the black spot resolved itself into a larger and larger black wall. He was trapped between them. He stopped. The edge of the whiteness touched him and he was convulsed with the cold and pain.

It did not take long.

In the morning, Cliff Tagger would be reported by his agent, Samuel Jones, to have passed from natural causes after an illness of several months...and been cremated.

The Cored-Out were seldom even good for CRNAs.

Moments passed, and the white wall fizzed against the black wall of the ARK, then disappeared. A signal was sent and received. *SYR, a small utility, was released to start the dissolution of the ARK's thick, otherwise-insoluble wall. Once complete, RYR would start the tedious job of rebooting the massive CORE. All should have been silent.*

Were there ears to hear, came a noise.

Resurrection

17250 Avenue of the Unity, Nyork, The Unity
17.47.27.EST_18_October_AU77, (2129 AD)

Blanche sat and drank Old Filibuster in her new apartment. She had failed.

The CORE entities had asked only this one thing of her, and she had messed up on the first move. She had been playing the conversation with Aliende over and over in her head, thinking that she could have— should have—been able to find a way to convince him that she deserved the right to capture Will Butler. It was self-flagellation. Aliende was unpredictable but doggedly determined once he made up his mind.

Will and Hecate were now out of her grasp, adrift in the Unity where only Aliende was able to control their location and profit from their discomfort. Their lives were probably safe—that knowledge consoled her slightly. Fettwap was not so great a fool as to squander the one bargaining chip left to the Unity on spite.

But why go after Will Butler at all? His mission was obviously at an end.

Aliende's motive came in a flash.

It was her. She was Aliende's target. Aliende knew that she had been contacted by the CORE, as he had. He also knew that Will had used the CORE to retrieve the intelligence from a dying Elise McRory.

If he now found any suggestion of a contact between Will and her, it would give Aliende an sword to dangle over her head for a lifetime. She had, in truth, no contact with Will but only his interface, Frog. It would matter little to Aliende—or the propaganda mill.

Close would be sufficient for a public execution.

Blanche had promised Will and Hecate her protection, and it had counted for nothing.

She was just beginning to appreciate Old Filibuster's arrival when the lights went out.

The Tombs, 125 White Street, Nyork, Unity
19.39.08.EST_19_October_AU77, (2129AD)

Within the stygian darkness within the dank, dripping walls of this lowest and least known level of the Tombs prison of Nyork, sat Sergeant Graybarre. The lights had gone out almost two hours ago, and no one had come to check on him and his prisoners. The air, always dank and musty, was gaining in character and body. Scurrying had increased exponentially, occasionally running over his own boots.

Sergeant Graybarre was not happy. He was an honest screw, taking no bribes and meting out punishment only as deserved. He got no pleasure from being harsh. He wished he could say the same for General Aliende's Zeta squad—*sadistic thugs they were, and the Sergeant did not care who knew his opinion. Interrogation of the prisoner in Cell #1 had just ceased when the lights went off. They would recommence in two more hours. Graybarre wanted to go check on him, but with no light, no first aid kit, and the* incessant scurrying, *he concluded that his efforts were pointless.*

In the darkness, at some unknown distance, he heard a lock turn. He did not expect to be relieved before midnight.

"Sergeant! I'm General Seftus Ploidid. I have been given command during this emergency. We are setting up new arrangements for the security of political prisoners during this period. The lights won't come on for a week, I'm told. I need you to come out now and be scheduled for rotation in a lighted ward.

"I got my orders from company HQ, General Ploidid, Sir. Not supposed to leave my post until relieved by Sergeant Edwards of the Beta Squad, sir!" said Graybarre.

"Sergeant, I have had to assign your entire company elsewhere. Riots are breaking out on the docks. Come on out, and we can talk in the light. I'll get some electricians in to see what we can cobble together in the meantime. Is that okay with you, Sergeant?"

Finally convinced, Graybarre replied, "Yessir."

Gathering his few things and moving uncertainly towards Ploidid's voice along a narrow corridor of empty cells in the otherwise empty cell block in the lowest level of the Tombs, Sergeant Graybarre came abreast of Blanche's location within one of the open cells. Using night vision headgear, Blanche was able to move behind Graybarre, pinioning his arms before dragging the man into the cell behind her. After a few minutes, Blanche had Graybarre hog-tied, hooded, and snoring gently on a bunk. His quietude would last the hour. *It would have to be enough.*

She had tried to quest the entities before contacting Ploidid. The silence inside the user CORE was absolute. Nothing was "open." Conduits ended abruptly into nothingness. All Blanche's usual routes to information were *profoundly wrong*. With the CORE down, Blanche concluded that the entities were gone—removed—sanitized. Despite their brief contact, she grieved. She would not be able to talk to Cain or EffieCee again. They had been the ones to show her the wonders possible inside the openCORE—and now they were gone.

Any hope she had invested in her new virtual allies was wasted. Smart money would have gotten drunk, dealt with the hangover in the morning, and considered life unchanged. Somehow, she would not consider that. The entities had, even in the brief time she had talked with them, struck a cord that still resonated within her. Will Butler had entrusted his life and happiness to her, and she must do everything in her power to retrieve that for him. Now she had mobilized her own plan B.

Leaving the Graybarre snoring gently, Blanche strode past the empty cell-lined corridor confidently with the aid of the night scope. It was easy to determine Will and Hecate's cell, as only one door-grate showing a heat signature. Graybarre had been kind enough to leave the keys on the small desk at the juncture of the corridors.

"Hecate, it's me, Riley," said Blanche, after opening the door.

"Thank you, God!. Will is getting beaten up once a shift—like clockwork. He can't take more of this. His piss looks, I mean, looked, black the last time I saw anything. The air's getting stale, too."

Blanche nodded, then, realizing that Hecate would need more, said.

"I'm going to get you out of here. Then we can see about getting some help for Will. Can he walk?"

"I don't know. He hasn't walked since the last interrogation."

"Okay, I want you to go out the door and along the wall to the right for about ten meters. You will run into a small table. Stop there and listen for people arriving. Ask what the password is. They should say 'Parker Rolls' and you should say 'Orange juice'. Got it?"

"Yes."

"Okay, here is the door. Go ahead"

Slowly, Hecate moved out of the room. Blanche could hear her scraping along the wall as she turned to look at Will.

"Will, can you talk to me? Things will be getting better from now on, but I need to be sure we are straight. How are you? Can you hold on?"

Will looked up and smiled through a split lip into the darkness. "Nice to meet again, Colonel ma'am. I am just nifty, I am. I would very much like to slip into anonymity, if it is all the same with you, though."

"I said I would *do my best* to protect you both, and I failed. My boss took over your capture and changed the script."

"You mean the fat guy?" asked Will. "He *did* go on, didn't he?"

The power is down all over the city, I have no idea why. I think our CORE friends are dead. I need to get you to a safe place. Can you walk? We can get an HP to visit you there.

"You need more water at the very least. You're as dry as sand. If your urine doesn't clear, it might be a sign of a kidney fracture or failure. Let me get you and Hecate out of here, and we will get you the fluids as soon as possible."

"I think I can walk. I think I can hold on. I don't know how much I can drink. I feel nauseated. But to your question: you and I are good, Blanche.

"I have been living an iffy existence for years. This is our chance to get home and I know you are an honorable person from the openCORE. No one promises anything but their best effort in this business. I am in your hands, Colonel."

Blanche helped Will to his feet and the two staggered out of the cell and along the corridor to Hecate. Blanche gave a shout to alert the squad to come forward and then left Hecate and Will once more alone in the dark. Graybarre would have been surprised that the squad Blanche brought forward to help Will were not Ploidid's Greens as he had been led to believe, but Fenerghan's Oranges.

This had been Blanche's contribution to the affair. Ploidid and Fenerghan, being obligated to work together by Aliende, had nearly come to blows. Blanche intervened. Running interference with each faction, as an unofficial aide to Aliende. The two leaders, discovering that their differences, no longer suppressed by the ruling junta, had mellowed in isolation. In their political isolation, the two had found common ground. Gilsoit and Seftus rapidly developed a *modus vivendi.*

With the blackout, Blanche shared the problem with each leader in person, moving around the blacked out city with her infrared apparatus, moving like a wraith among citizens staggering blindly along streets and hallways. Ploidid had suggested the swapped identities. He and Fenerghan had shaken hands on it.

The reports would be hopelessly muddled. Ploidid's Greens would be blamed for the couple's release from the Tombs but would be convincingly present and obvious putting down the riots at the docks, while Fenerghan's Oranges would be blamed for Will being treated out of turn at Mid-Manhattan's Emergency room. Commands would ring out, weapons would be drawn, a certain amount of shoving might occur, and Will would be treated. All would vanish within a half-hour. Key words might be uttered like "Climate Justice," "Together, we can save the earth," and even a few "Climate Change: The Everest of Our Problems," despite these generating more than a few blank stares among the sick and wounded sitting on the hard plastic seats that filled the waiting room.

Investigations would be made, no doubt. Identifications would implicate each faction; yet, upon further investigation, it would be deemed impossible for Ploidid and Feneghen to be in two places at once. Enemies of the state, recidivist revolutionary Sisis, and feral elements of the underworld would be blamed. Without the CORE, no reliable, durable, unquestioned evidence was available.

Within that hour, Will Yeats Butler slipped from the ken of the Unity into oblivion.

"Pity," observed Lieutenant Colonel B. Woods, when questioned later.

FULL OF WOE

Woe to the conquered

—Livy

DUFS Skimmer Field, Nyork, The Unity
08.13.50.EST_19_October_AU77, (2129AD)

Commander Aliende, much satisfied with his cleverness, watched as one of the Unity's precious skimmers lifted off and headed west. Admittedly, the food delivery was primarily symbolic, enough for perhaps 30,000 surviving officers, rather than the 150,000 the Americans had demanded. The mere arrival of the rations to feed the Unity's own soldiers was an adequate show of earnest. It guaranteed that, for the foreseeable future, there would be no invasion from the Americans.

Whether Woods succeeded or failed was now inconsequential. If she somehow pulled an acceptable treaty for the nation out of the morass of this debacle, it was his trophy to claim. It was he who would tout the supposed and speculative benefits of the offer.

Since Fettwap himself had divested Woods of her bargaining chip, the American spy, she would, most likely, return having merely taken dictation from the Americans. The country would pillory her. All the disdain and disgust of this horrendous failure would come to rest on the broad shoulders of Colonel Woods, there to stay and grow until it crushed her. Aliende would see to it. Woods had overplayed her hand. She had risen in Aliende's own shadow until it became clear she was playing her own game with Legion. Their interest in her was a death sentence, not just for Woods but the CORE entity itself.

Aliende did not envy Woods the task set before her. There was little the Unity could do to counter the demands of the Scorch or the Americans. The Rampart was now unable to prevent invasion; the army was a mere shadow of itself, incapable of any offensive move. Food was still a problem; with the levy the Americans demanded daily as ransom. All the Unity had to bargain with were promises—and a history of breaking promises which went back to the Glorious Revolution.

Yet, ICEWASH was a success and one in which he would never be implicated. The rage over the CORE outage last night had found a target with Merryweather and his team. The Merryweather's comatose remains would linger at some euthanatorium for weeks to months before actual death was pronounced. All to the good. Merryweather's connection to Aliende had been obliterated before it was ever created.

ICEWASH had eliminated Legion, but also the mostly unknown-to-him parasitical programs with no discernible benefit to the greater Unity. It had also eliminated an assignation with Lady Fong, which now would never occur. Once he discovered that, it saddened him.

Tales of Three Thursday Travelers

17250 Avenue of the Unity, Nyork, The Unity
06.37.41.EST_20_October_AU77, (2129 AD)

Hecate Hester Jones fidgeted in the unaccustomed luxury of Blanche's apartment. The brutish DUFS officer had separated her from Will, and there was nothing she could do about it. In the darkened prison cell, she claimed to be Riley. Mirrored Rana had talked to Riley, a *boy* dressed in crèchie clothes, and had assured her that he was a friend.

But the vast, abrasive, and domineering DUFS colonel who barged into the prison was unknown to her. She *could* have been Riley, she supposed, but taking Will away from her did not feel right.

She was now abandoned in the middle of the DUFS complex without a single identifier, utterly trapped. Access into this apartment was done with just a smile and a password. Leaving was another thing. She would have to be escorted out by the actual apartment resident—like a protégé. She grew queasy.

Despite that danger, the only thing keeping her there was that Riley knew where Will was, and Riley knew where she was. If she moved, she could be swept away, lost in the maelstrom of Unity intrigue and might never see Will again.

She found a carton of Eggz and cooked a 100 ml. omelet with whatever shook loose from the refrigerator: chopped olives, sardines, an elderly mushroom, anonymous cheese, and onions sautéed in Bakon fat. She could finish only half. It did not seem fair, after months of privation.

She took a shower, luxuriating in the warm water. Scrubbing herself until she was pink, she emerged with a new perspective on the situation, until she remembered she did not know where Will was and that Will was sick.

DUFS Headquarters, Nyork, The Unity
06.37.41.EST_20_October_AU77, (2129 AD)

Blanche fidgeted in the sparsely furnished office. She had hardly had time to inhabit the place since coming back from the outlands a mere week ago. The space was sterile and unwelcoming. It would probably stay that way.

Something had gone very badly wrong. Two nights ago, the CORE entities had shown Blanche an Aladdin's cave of wonders, populated by authentic jinni with mystical powers. It was a good deal more prosaic than that, she admitted to herself, but in a life as grim as the one she had created for herself, the backCORE was amazing to her.

She could be Riley again! The betrayal of her youth—her self— could be wiped clean. She could, with the aid of the CORE entities, finally follow the arc of Riley's life within the CORE rather than be forced into that of Blanche. The tragedy of her life could be erased with time and love. She could do all those things that Riley would have done had he been allowed to grow up.

In the end, however, only when the entities had convinced her of their authenticity and their existential motive of self-preservation, was Blanche able to honestly agree to become an ally. The entities were not machines with the flaws that might only become evident in a crisis, but real human minds that had been translated into the CORE. Their desire for longevity was self-evident, even to Blanche.

It would require one of the interfaces to be cloned. That was a lot to ask, as no arrangements had been made for it. Blanche still had hope.

Blanche was scheduled to rendezvous with Banning— *No, not Banning,* Hollister, he said his name was Hollister. She was to meet him yesterday virtually, but then the CORE went down. The CORE was irreparably damaged, whether entered via O-A or terminal.

The chaos within the Unity was hard to describe. The belts and trains stopped, with no regard for their passengers. Businesses closed, and workers were told to walk home to lightless, cold apartments. Hospitals, of course, had their own power, but medical information about patients was restricted to what the staff could remember from morning rounds, and thus, once in the hospital, the HPs were forbidden to leave. The Emergency Room waiting areas had become overpacked almost immediately. Most of the administration buildings emptied before sundown. None came back to work.

Overnight, Blanche had only been able to navigate through the chaos with the help of the newly created junta of Ploidid's Greens and Fenerghan's Oranges. They had yet to decide on a color.

Unknowingly, Blanche had asked each leader, as a patriot, to help spring Will from prison, promising nothing but an improved bargaining position at the peace table. To her amazement, the two leaders were already in the planning stages for such an operation. The two bitter enemies, kept from airing any differences for decades by successive ruling factions, had mellowed and moderated. Their views, now much closer to each other, still had differences, but these were trivial compared to the bigger question of what was best for their country. Instead of creating an escape plan from whole cloth, Blanche had, for the most part, been a bemused observer.

Seftus Ploidid, for all his progressive bluster, was a patriot. With Gilsoit Fenerghan's cooperation, the two swapped faction identifications. Pseudo-Greens extracted Will and Hecate from the Tombs and pseudo-Oranges jumped the queue at Mid-Mahattan to get Will treated. The verdict was that Will had kidney trauma and a mild concussion. No surgery would be necessary, but the treatment was large volumes of intravenous fluids and rest.

Empty places within the Unity where one could hide to administer "large volumes of IV fluids and rest" without being scanned, questioned, and arrested were scarce. Fortunately, Blanche knew of one.

DUFS Headquarters, Nyork, The Unity
06.37.41.EST_20_October_AU77, (2129 AD)

Will's consciousness fluttered up to reality, and he opened his eyes after the DUFS officer, who called herself Riley, roused him. He found himself in a small, windowless room, lying in a narrow hospital bed next to a small medicine table lined with pill bottles. He was not sufficiently interested to read the labels. A urinal sat on the table next to the bed, and Will attempted to sit up to use it. Immediately, his head swam, and he fell back onto the institutional pillows that whistled until they had reached the proper level of patient discomfort. He used the urinal lying down. The urine was still dark but copious.

Riley had said he was safe here. Finding a safe hole in which to crawl within the Unity was difficult at best. Finding one with medical care was somewhat less likely, Will thought, as he gazed detachedly at an intravenous line entering his arm, feeling as if this little vignette was a drama he was compelled to view.

The fluid being pumped into his arm was a pale yellow. He felt his face, which responded to the attention with a visceral pang. By this time, he was exhausted and slept again.

Give and Take Friday

Western Gate, The Unity
11.58.06.local_21_October_AU77, (2129AD)

Blanche stepped out of one of the few remaining Unity skimmers, stood, and advanced to the Western Gate. At least the CORE was up and running again—marginally. The belts were still down, but the trains ran on time. Blanche was amazed at the effort her nation, the people, had expended in this emergency. The DUFS had been as helpless as the next man, but the techs, and even some in administrative grays, had worked tirelessly.

She looked out toward the jungle across the no-persons-land of what had been the Rampart. All the pulse cannons now pointed their impotent muzzles to the earth, the mine fields on either side of the road were marked by the unretrieved bodies of men and animals that had wandered into them since earlier that month. The air stank. As she approached the actual crossing point, she found the space occupied by a gate that she had never seen before.

Too dark to decipher within the shadow of the woods, the gate dominated the scene, seeming to force all eyes toward its somber presence. As she approached, it opened on its own accord. She was nearly through the aperture before she realized it was alive. Composed of sturdy tree limbs woven into an impenetrable mass, it appeared to move with ease, while innumerable small perceptive eyes lining the branches and crevices regarded her progress.

She looked ahead into the gloom, even as the gate closed behind her, leaving her in darkness for a moment. To her left, a room slowly became illuminated. In the gathering light, Blanche made out a delegation of RSA officers. Without a weapon, she felt momentary panic until a voice interceded.

"Blanche Woods, Colonel in the Defensive Forces for Security of the Democratic Unity of America!" The voice was dry, emotionless, and somehow vegetable.

"I am your host. I am called by outsiders Throot. The Polyarchy of Sentients has a conflict with the Unity, as do the Restructured States. You will negotiate with each of us in turn. The RSA 'won the toss,' you say, so the Unity and the RSA will discuss your differences first before we, of the polyarchy, discuss our differences. Please use our good offices without prejudice.

"Who is it who speaks. I see nobody else...no other entity here."

"As you wish, child of Man. See for yourself."

Blanche looked up—and continued to look farther up as Throot stood to his full height. Blanche staggered slightly.

"I had no idea you—sentient ones—grew to be so large. But, before we begin, I must transmit greetings from of one of your citizens, "she said turning away from Throot to face the RSA officers. "William Yeats Butler and his companion, Hecate Hester Jones, are in my safekeeping until the prisoner exchange occurs. Whatever else you may hear or be told, these two will be returned to the RSA during the prisoner exchange

"Will says he is well but complains of my cooking—no doubt with good reason. I consider him a friend and will miss seeing him so often. He says to tell you "Orestes."

One man looked up sharply at the word, then smiled.

"Colonel, we have a gift for you, personally," replied the apparent leader. "I would be better for you to receive this now, as I would not wish you to think its presentation is a part of our agreement. We are informed that a BIGI interface, ready to be keyed to your persona, would be well appreciated. Please accept this. He goes by the name of 'Rune,' I have been told. Cain, of your acquaintance, awaits your return."

With little more ceremony, a square navy blue box was presented to Blanche, who, unable to share her sorrow at the probable demise of Cain and all the entities from Icewash, could only say, "I do not know how to thank you. I am in your debt. I always will be."

"Shall we begin?"

Throot opened another panel to a well-lit room with seats for the delegations and a polished, dark table.

The discussions were calm and business-like, thought Blanche. These Americans were no more barbarous than she was. In the breaks, they talked among themselves about their families and made gentle, loving, and self-deprecating jokes about their spouses. Blanche had nothing to share.

Moreover, the Americans, whether authentically or well-rehearsed, seemed disinterested in the Unity. The last high-tech utopia on the continent since the breakup of the old republic, and these men would rather trade jokes than press her for details of her country's monumental advances.

Later, she would understand.

Fairly Fair Monday

Colonel Woods was announced by Jorge, Billy's guard.

Not waiting to be seated, she blurted out even before the door closed, "We have a treaty! No hostilities for three years and a schedule for a final settlement. It's maybe not all we wanted, Fettwap, but I think the Unity can live with this." Swinging the diplomatic pouch gleefully, Blanche entered Aliende's office without being asked.

"You've done a wonderful thing for the Unity, Blanche. Sorry, I couldn't get away for the signing, but 'The fewer men the greater glory,' isn't that so?" said Aliende after he had gotten her seated and had Billy pour her some hot tea.

"Everything we really needed: a demilitarized border, prisoner exchange, the whole thing. The Scorch gets a real treaty. Our Rampart Line is now the border between us and the plants. I have topological maps for the boundary between the Scorch and the Americans."

"I don't care about that. What about the Ohio Gap?"

"The Pennsy line extended south until it intersected the Rampart. They were pretty firm about it. We get the line between the watershed with the Great Lakes along the existing border down to a point just southeast of Beckley."

"Let 'em have it. Nothing grows there, but it's going to take me and the senior staff from the Reds to peruse this before you can sign off on it. We should have an answer by tomorrow.

Blanche stood, saluted, and found her own way out.

Aliende drummed his hands on his desk for several long minutes before he sighed and decided that there was nothing else he could do but actually look at the proposed treaty.

Aliende extracted the few papers from the diplomatic pouch, an affair which looked surprisingly natural. He flinched. The pouch, a thick, stiff-sided object, and coming as it did from the outlanders, might actually have been the skin of an animal at one time. *He shuddered before getting some tissue papers ("guaranteed recycled") to open its many locks.*

Woods had signaled success. Yet, he would see what the woman had done. He began reading.

If Woods were actually successful, Aliende would have obtained peace on the Unity's western border for the first time in the nation's history. He would retrieve the survivors—the officers, anyway. He doubted the CRNAs would return. Without their conditioning, they were just so many shuffling Sisis. But if any "voiced an opinion to return to the Unity," he would allow it—and have them recycled on arrival.

The other factions had acquiesced, knowing they would receive proportionally more than the Blues, although it would make no difference in the long run. The Blue-Red coalition that he had proposed to Hildegard Kirkegaard, the Reds' new chief, would keep *him* safe for at least five years.

The one fly in the ointment was that Woods, apparently unaware that the American spy had been abducted, had promised his return. That was in Article IX. That would be awkward.

The chaos after ICEWASH had gummed up all the euthanatoria's emergency wards, if for no other reason than the euthanatoria were the only light and heat available to the average citizen on a cold autumn night. Yet, several citizens reported that a contingent of DUFS had jumped the queue at Mid-Mahattan to get a young man answering Butler's description treated out of turn. One had mentioned "climate justice" in passing. It had been enough for Aliende to justify his next move.

His force sequestered Gilsoit's Oranges at their quarters. The CEFV (CORE Evaluation for Veracity) was, of course, out of the question, since the CORE itself was down. Secondary tests were negative, however. The entire Orange faction had ironclad alibis, and even some comm'vids claimed they were at a disturbance at the docks; however, nothing incriminating was found. Aliende then marched a company of loyal Headquarters DUFS to toss Ploidid's Greens, due to a single report about what one of the prison guards had remembered on the night Butler was released. Alibis abounded. Aliende got a severe headache and retired to Headquarters.

Things were changing within the Unity that he was not sure he understood, perhaps due to his decision to use ICEWASH. Yet, it had been worth it to divest himself of Legion.

This could only mean that Butler was most likely dead, his body tossed into the Hudsen. His abduction and disappearance could complicate any peace treaty. The evil-doers were, he thought, most likely Reds, but the new peace treaty kept Aliende from going any further. It mattered little. If the treaty failed at the eleventh hour because of Butler's absence, Woods would be saddled with the odium of failure. Not he. Aliende shrugged.

Continuing to read the treaty, Aliende soon found himself whistling in consternation. The surprise was that the barbarians had bargained so poorly.

They demanded diplomatic recognition, but that, he supposed, *was inevitable. Every other nation in the world recognized the Restructured States—calling them Americans—cheeky bastards.* The *Americans* stipulated that the line of the Rampart, the *de facto* border, would become the *de jure* border. The current egress points, held to a minimum by Unity arrogance, he admitted, would be tripled within the year.

An embassy was to be established in "New York", as well as a full dozen consulates in every notable Unity city—and that was also to be done within the year. Goods and people would have to obtain trade permits and visas from a consulate to enter Scorch-maintained corridors into their jungle on the other side of their border. The management of passages through the jungle was entirely in the hands of the Scorch sentients.

Less oddly, he supposed, the Americans demanded recognition for the jungle, what they called the *Polyarchy of the Sentient*, separate from themselves. Whatever. *Call it Toe Jam for all I care.* They are welcome to that morass of plants, swamps, rocks, rivers, and insects.

The Americans' demands, he admitted, were reasonable. They just wanted to bargain for the Unity goods—no set price—and paid in specie, of all things. There were to be 10% tariffs—on both sides. *Naïve and gullible sorts, these primitives.*

The strangest demand was that the Unity was to submit two E11 hostages, calling them "guest students," to live among the savages for a year, as well as demanding that two seventeen-year-old barbarians—let's just call them spies—be accepted into the Unity each year on the same basis. The return of all four would occur at the Western gate, or "another suitable spot on neutral ground," at the summer solstice—whatever that might be.

How would that play out? E11's marked forever by the taint of the outlands. He doubted the arrangement would last long, but he pitied the poor citizens while it did. The savages demanded that their people be given free access to any guild but not required to get an implant, use Thiz, quest the CORE, or accept patronage. *Exceedingly strange.*

In return, the Unity regained their surviving 11,687 commissioned officers and 12,312 of the 20,395 surviving non-commissioned officers—those who chose to return. *Who would choose to live in the outlands? It was pointless to speculate why some of the captives might choose to stay.* Woods had demanded that signed and sworn statements be obtained from each traitor with a DUFS officer to witness. The barbarians had agreed. *That should satisfy the skeptics.*

As far as the CRNAs, Woods had not said anything until asked by the negotiator. Apparently, the outlanders had collected 127,699 out of a total of 438,549—nearly 3 of four of the geeks had died for one reason or another. Those who remained "had not voiced a desire to return to the Unity." *Odd wording.* The officer, Major General Thomas, *must know* that few had any speech at all.

He grinned at the news that there would be *128,000 fewer mouths to feed in the approaching winter! Half of those same CRNAs would be dead by eighteen months. He shrugged.* Let the outlanders feed and bury them.

The next demand wiped that sanguine thought from his mind. The barbarians specified that a portion of the *Unity harvest*, equivalent to sustaining the number of CRNA prisoners who remained within the outlands at the end of the prisoner exchange, be provided at the Western Gate each November 1. Failure would "prompt the immediate return of all CRNAs in the RSA's possession by means that the Unity cannot prevent." *Odd wording.* The Day of Ice had too many unanswered questions, and the threat was too obscurely confident to consider ignoring. Fortunately, with the losses from the Day of Ice, the harvest surplus would be sufficient to meet that demand this year and possibly for the next five years. *Why five years? Did they know the CRNAs died so rapidly?"*

In return, the savages received their one failed spy back—but probably not.

In sum, though, he had to admit. The barbarians were not entirely guileless.

Or was Woods playing both sides of the street?

The treaty from the Polyarchy was simple, in comparison. It demanded the de facto borders become de jure borders, that the Scorch be acknowledged as a sovereign state and that trade be negotiated only by traders on the Southern Gate each full moon, unless there was a frost.

The prisoner exchange was set for the following Monday at 0900.

DUFS HQ, Nyork, The Unity
18.03.49.EST_24_October_AU77, (2129AD)

Blanche, marching side-by-side with Hecate, dressed in new and stiff DUFS fatigues, approached the anonymous door on the side of a belt station in downtown Nyork.

"Are you going to turn me in?" said Hecate. "That's not fair. I did everything you asked of me. Why are you doing this to us, Riley?"

"Shut up, recruit. All you have to do is follow orders!"

That silenced Hecate for the few moments necessary to pass beyond the DUFS guards to the unmarked door. It opened to Woods' touch, revealing a sliding door, which she opened and motioned Hecate through into a small closet.

Woods entered, closed the door, and pushed a button. The elevator arrived within a few moments. Woods opened the sliding door and motioned Hecate to open the outer door. She did and was immediately grabbed by strong arms, preventing her movement.

"Hecate! I was so worried!" said Will as he hugged her. Taking more than a few seconds to realize she was in friendly hands, Hecate finally stopped struggling.

Colonel Woods entered the room after stopping the sliding door from closing.

"Where are we?" said Hecate and Will in unison.

"Where the Blues will never look, in their own headquarters. You are about ten meters from Aliende himself."

A look of horror swept across the spies' faces.

"Don't worry. Aliende has been running through receptionists almost one every other day. People have been trying to assassinate him. One came through this room using the elevator. I have no idea what the original use was, but Aliende decided to block the entrance to his outer office last Wednesday. You are in an officially non-existent space within the Democratic Unity," she announced with a flourish.

Blanche waited for the two to finish their kiss.

"I'll bring food twice a day. At the prisoner exchange, I'll collect you and keep you safe until the exchange."

"Thank you, Riley. This puts you at so much risk. Why are you doing this for us?"

"Not all that risky, really. Don't worry about me. Let's just say I have had my reward, even if EffieCee and the others were killed. It is the least I can do in their memory."

"So, you are convinced they died in the CORE shutdown," said Will.

"I haven't seen anything of them since I've gone back. Where are Frog and Rana—I mean your implants? Are they safe?"

"They are in safe hands. They will be in touch."

Haste before Grace Tuesday

West Gate, The Unity
08.59.04.EST_25_October_AU77, (21229)

In the last few days, the event has become a circus, thought Fettwap as he used one of the few remaining skimmers to bring him from Nyork to this backwoods rendezvous. The West Gate, merely a trampling of the Unity undergrowth now that the Ramparts were down, was no longer a nicely ordered field of plowed land to show footprints, barbed wire to give guards more time to react, and killing zones of automated pulse fire. The trampling had been done by the masses of *Unity citizens* who came uninvited to the humiliation.

Unfortunate, thought Aliende. It would be difficult to sanitize the vid-coms enough to make them align with the narrative he had selected. Power in the Unity, the patina of elections notwithstanding, belonged to the DUFS. Power brought affection, *or at least liaisons.* Most of the crowd were women.

The list of the returnees had been published several days before the exchange. The first of the sign-bearers had arrived later that same day. "Welcome Home, Rodney," "I missed you, Kelli, and even a "I love you, Sugarbuns." Kiosks had been set up to feed and amuse the multitude. *Someone was making an illicit profit out of this.* Woods had sent out for mobile latrines before it got really ugly.

The citizen-in-the-street seemed less critical of the country's defeated soldiers than Aliende had imagined they would be. That was a distinct failure in the education of the lesser guilds, which needed his attention. How else could men be kept in the field, dedicated to the glory of the Unity, if they had some girl at home who would open her arms—and legs—to him, even if he lost?

But that was a problem for another day. The technicians would have to be consulted. Today was a day for getting through. *It was odious and necessary.*

The hour arrived. No sign of an embassy was yet visible from the American side. Nevertheless, Aliende gave the signal. A platoon of DUFS cleared the passage to the Gate, defunct as it was. *Repairing the Rampart would have to wait for another day as well,* Aliende thought, adding the repair to a growing list of tasks for Woods to accomplish. He sighed.

Fettwap could now see that something was happening on the other side of the Rampart. A darkening of the low clouds, a tide of green and purple vegetation surged forward to the line, and a great wind carrying stinging dust and debris made him and the crowd turn away.

By the time he turned back, moments later, the outlander party was in place, free of dust, unruffled, and awaiting developments. The outlanders, a mere half-dozen officers dressed in forest green, carried captured pulse rifles and all wore shooting gloves—covering the trigger finger and palm—giving the party a look of professionalism. *Odd,* he thought.

Aliende stepped forward and found that his mouth was dry and his feet unsteady. He motioned for two more DUFS to accompany him and felt bolder as he approached the advancing group, which stopped as if a single man a few meters short of the Gate. After a moment, the foremost officer separated himself from the group and stepped toward them.

"Good morning, General Aliende, said the outlander. I am Major General Thomas. Are you ready? Your people are anxious to return home."

"I suppose, General—Thomas. Considering the optics of this, I would prefer to return your spy," he said with some relish, "after our people have returned home."

"I am afraid I cannot do that, General. The Unity's actions in the past do not recommend that. It would be too easy to snatch back one man at the last moment."

Aliende nodded. It was true, of course. Over the decades, the Unity had been an unreliable negotiator with the outlanders, whom they viewed, if they considered them actual humans at all, as ignorant rebels—traitors to the Glorious Cause. Up until recently, he had only thought of them as a resource—unharvested manure, waiting for the algae vats.

"How about this," Aliende countered, "You allow half to return, and then I will send over your man under close guard. Once you acknowledge his identity and health, you send over the last half."

"Good start. As an additional safeguard, I require you to be under guard here—for the good behavior of your men, and I shall walk over to your lines with the first of your men as a hostage until the last of your people arrives. Is that acceptable?"

Unable to speak from the dryness of his voice, Fettwap nodded. With his assent, the prisoner exchange began.

At the halfway point, Aliende braced himself for the recriminations that would come with his failure to produce the real American spy. Woods had shared in his despair, once it became obvious that Butler would not be surfacing. Despite the smokescreen of Green and Orange faction involvement, his careful investigation had proved them innocent. His bet was on the Reds, trying to foil the prisoner exchange that would bring more Blue officers home.

Regardless, Woods had stepped into the gap and proposed they find a double, a doppelganger to stand in for the deceased Butler. It had taken her almost the entire time to find the replica, Woods arriving with the sacrificial citizen only just as the exchange was starting. The man would be uncovered eventually, of course, but they would get some of their prisoners back. *Half a loaf is better than none.*

The flow of prisoners stopped briefly.

A single man, head bowed, lank blond hair obscuring his face was marched forward, in short mincing steps because of his leg irons. A single DUFS with a bayoneted pulse rifle walked close behind. No immediate kerfuffle ensued as the man drew closer, being immediately surrounded by American brass, rapidly getting lost in the crush. Aliende smiled; Woods was resourceful, as always.

He watched as the second tide of Unity DUFS stepped off in unison, ten men across and singing a cadence about Ol' King Cole, of all things. When the last rank was lost in the jubilant crowd, Aliende took the cue to start off towards his own lines, seeing Thomas, a moment later start towards him.

Despite the odd sensation, an itch between his shoulder blades from a hundred unseen snipers, Fettwap suppressed the urge to look back. It came as something of a surprise when he realized Thomas was but a few meters away. He stopped abruptly. Thomas continued to approach, stopping in front of Aliende, offered a salute, and held out a memory stick.

"According to our treaty agreement, sir, here are sworn statements from the soldiers who chose to stay among us. They will undergo some familiarization classes and be taught useful trades before we release them."

"You are not asking them to fight against us in the future?"

"'No one really trusts a turncoat?' I suppose, but no, General. I won't get into it with you, but our armies are quite different, and your soldiers do not fit particularly well. They may, in time, if they prove helpful in the meantime.

"We can do both our nations good by starting to trade. According to the agreements, at the summer solstice, we—you and I— will return with our diplomatic representatives here to sign the treaty. Let the bean-counters work out the trade details. I will have two hostages for our good behavior- an eighteen-year-old boy and a girl, children of our national leaders. For whom should we prepare?"

"You are serious about that? I will have some citizens waiting," said Aliende, making a mental note to find people to appease the man.

Thomas paused, his mouth open for a moment before saying, "Of course, General. Until the solstice." The man brushed by Aliende and returned to his own lines. Aliende shrugged and returned to his.

Once Aliende returned to his lines, the day's final results were handed to him. They were staggering. Over twenty-two thousand officers had left the Unity in early October, their hearts, no doubt, filled with martial resolve and dreams of glory. Slightly over eleven thousand survived the disaster, but only six thousand chose to return. Of the non-comms, the real heart of any army, forty-seven thousand two hundred and thirty-five stepped off with Jourdaine. About twenty thousand two hundred survivors were captured. Of these, only 1,013 chose to return home. *How could they have been brainwashed so effectively?* He shrugged. He would never trust the commissioned officers in battle, anyway, suffering the possible contagion of outlander contact, but the non-comms might have been useful.

His only worry now was the sleight-of-hand he had pulled off with replacing the American spy with a double. He wondered when the other shoe would drop.

Epilogue: Solon Fettwap the Gracious

GranitVale, VerMon, The Unity
09.30.27.EST_1_November_AU77, (2129AD), Wednesday

Fettwap Aliende stepped away from the one remaining vid screen and smiled. The announcement of his Solonship having just ended, he felt a burden lifted that he had only recently realized he had been carrying. Woods was now welcome to the burden. In truth, he confessed to himself, neither of them had really had the burden that Vivalagente Suarez or Eustace Jourdaine had had to bear. Yet, he was now the first named Solon in nearly a century. His name would be a name children would have to memorize in their crèche schools. He grimaced. *I suppose it cannot be helped.*

Since Legion had declared its suzerainty over the Unity, he had fought back against these alien intelligences and triumphed. Despite

Legion's vast powers, despite the CORE's central necessity to the Unity, Aliende had triumphed. He was a Solon. The Unity was at peace for the first time in history, and others were now tasked with all the heavy lifting. Aliende smiled.

Of course, the chaos due to ICEWASH had taken hundreds of hours to repair—indeed, it was still in process. He had suffered the opprobrium of being at the wheel when a disgruntled programmer, in no discernible way connected to Aliende himself, had gone rogue and released the perfidious program. *No connection whatsoever,* Aliende grinned.

Some aspects of the CORE might never be repaired. Identification banks were mostly intact, but deficiencies surfaced daily. It would work out in the end. The treaty demands were coming along quite rapidly, oddly ahead of schedule.

In anticipation of a long career as Solon, he had made plans, as well. An ex-Solon's villa in VerMon had come onto the market, GranitVale, probably one of the best thought-out, self-contained, luxurious fortresses he had ever imagined. He had bought it up, or, instead, allowed the nation to buy it for his use. No doubt new Solons would come along as he saw fit to share the load, but in the meantime, he would be the sole ruler of the nation. Legion had promised. He had collected a guard consisting of a battalion of DUFS, their officers, the officers' protégés, and his own retinue. On his signal, they had all disappeared from the records within the CORE. In the current chaos, few would mark their passage.

From GranitVale, he could hold off an army. The solar power made them independent of the grid; getting deliveries of sealed fresh rations regularly, they also had stored rations, if needed, for a decade, and armaments to thwart any siege.

In the meantime, the DUFS would live in unaccustomed luxury. Fettwap, living in *accustomed* luxury, could expect another lifetime, forty years more as a Solon, a just and seemly reward for his dedicated service to the nation.

He had had the foresight to have his first implant removed, and those from all the officers and servants. He had the first implants removed from the DUFS as well, replacing them with an implant that prolonged their utility but had no locator capability. His own first implant was merely a memory replaced by a small scar. He had the foresight to recruit his personal HP, the Mouse, who had scheduled all the O-A for ablations that very afternoon. The HP promised the deactivation process would be painless.

His only connection to the CORE now was a single terminal with a conventional interface. Aliende smiled. Legion had thought to pull Aliende's fangs by making him resign as C-in-C of the DUFS in favor of Blanche Woods. Legion had underestimated Aliende's cleverness. He had eliminated Legion as soon as the entire nation had acknowledged his supremacy. The chaos that ICEWASH had created was nothing compared to the peace of mind he felt knowing Legion was dead. It was good to be a Solon.

"(G)racious gifts of the Most High God, who while dealing with us in anger for our sins, hath nevertheless remembered mercy."—A. Lincoln's Thanksgiving Declaration

Searcy Arkansas Rail Station, Searcy, Arkansas, RSA
3:07 PM, November 24th, 2129 AD, Thursday

The train slid into the station silently before 'kneeling' to discharge its passengers. Will roused Hecate, asleep with her head on his shoulder. It had been a hectic month since the prisoner exchange.

"Wake up, sleepyhead," said Will to his new wife. Hecate awoke, her head still spinning over recent events.

The prisoner exchange was anticlimactic. General Woods, after reuniting Will and her, had kept them under wraps until the exchange, bringing them to the West Gate just in time for the charade of her marching Will back to his own.

Aliende was still in a tizzy waiting for the Americans to complain about his perfidy in sending a "fake" spy back instead of the original. *Let him stew!*

That night, Will and she were at peace for the first time since they had met.

After that one evening together, the two were debriefed by the Color Guard separately. Despite what Hollister had said about the esteem in which Will was held by the Guard, he found the questions they pressed on him humiliating and an insult to his patriotism.

How had he lost his persona?

How had he survived in the underground with such terrible injuries—now miraculously no longer evident?

Why had he allowed himself to be captured by Malila Chiu?

How had he survived without any visible support for so long?

How had he managed to get the Unity to exchange him without blowing the cover of the remaining American spies?

Will tolerated it for her sake.

Hecate had undergone a similar grilling. It had all taken time.

A variety of the outlander military had questioned her. Despite her willingness to aid Will's mission, she could add little information.

Then came the bureaucrats. She found herself on much firmer ground. If she and Will were going to make a life in his homeland, she decided she must be forthcoming in everything. Her answers to all questions were as complete and accurate as she could remember—and Hecate could remember a lot.

Once the Color Guard—and the bureaucrats-- were satisfied—nothing happened for a day. Her guards fed her and led her to a shower room and toilet on request. The soap smelled nice. There were no windows. The guards chatted with her but never answered any questions. The following day, she was aroused from a fitful nap by the sound of the bars being pulled back from the door. In those few seconds before the door swung open, Hecate's heart pounded in her chest.

Was she going back to the Unity?

Executed as a spy?

Hecate surprised herself when she realized that, if abandoned by Will Butler, the one was the same as the other to her.

Instead, Will walked in and hugged her, then kissed her thoroughly. A harrumph brought them back to earth, and three others joined them in the small cell. Will introduced the first as General Rhedd, one of his teachers in spycraft. With him came an impossibly tall and robust man with a face disfigured by narrow stripes of blue from the bridge of his nose to the jawline. He was white-haired and appeared older than any man she had ever seen.

Malila Chiu was on his arm.

"Hecate! You made it!" she cried, as they fell into each other's embrace.

Weeping, ecstatic, and confused, "Made what?"

"Made it home—to America. You will think of it as home soon enough." Turning to the tall man, she said, "This is Jesse Johnstone, my husband. People call him the Old Man, but don't believe them— we expect our first in the spring.

"First, what?" asked Hecate, now completely confused.

"First *baby*, of course. Real people have babies in America, and they do not have to ask the government. We plan to stay with the Stewarts for the last month. They are such wonderful people. It should be fun. Think about joining us."

"Fun?"

"Good to see you again, Jesse," interrupted Will. "Your handknife came in real handy. I have it in our duffle. I can retrieve my dad's blade when it's convenient."

"Shoosh, man! We worry about such stuff later," replied Jesse.

Hecate resumed interrogating Malila about her coming-out party, while Will continued in an earnest discussion with the other two men. Before Malila could answer fully, Will had taken charge and motioned everyone out of the room. She thought they would make love; he seemed so earnest. It pleased her.

Instead, he knelt.

"Hecate Jones," he said, looking into her eyes, "would you marry me?

"I don't know what that really means, Will."

Will's earnest face creased in a wry smile. "No one else really knows what it means either, my very love. At the least, it means: would you live with me, have our babies, raise them with me to be good, useful people, grow old together, and stick it out for love through the good times and the bad."

"Yes! You know I would," she said, "When?"

"This afternoon."

It had been a strangely solemn, joyous, and savage affair. The Scorch's easement for the thousands of Unity troops to accomplish the prisoner exchange was still in evidence, but green shoots, already a span high, covered the three-meter-wide pathway. A few buildings remained around the central courtyard.

Malila stood to her left. Will, smiling broadly throughout, on Hecate's right, and Jesse on his left. Soldiers, both American and freed Unity troopers, formed a circle around them, leaving a lane open to the Scorch.

"What are we waiting for?" Hecate whispered to Malila.

"Hush, it will be here in a few minutes. You don't hurry the People and certainly not Splanch."

"Splanch?"

"We are in the Scorch—not America and certainly not the Unity. The People rule here," whispered Malila, "Shush, it's coming."

Before Hecate could inquire further, everyone grew silent. Out of the dense growth, a figure appeared—or was revealed. The minute before, Hecate would have sworn the oak had been there since it had been a sapling—then it changed. Sweeping up branches away from the trunk, a solemn face appeared and began to move toward them down the avenue left for it. As it passed, the soldiers became festooned with vines that wound around and up their legs, blossoming small, three-lobed flowers. By the time Splanch, for surely this was that august personage, had arrived, the entire company of humans was all decorated with blooms, some white and some a deep blood-red. Hecate's blooms were in white, and Will's in red. An airy, eerie melody seemed to waft on the wind, mingling with the scent of the flowers.

With no preamble, Splanch started.

"As a Judge of the People, I have the authority to seal contracts among the People and any strangers who sojourn among us.

Turning to Hecate, it said, "Do you promise to protect and serve this other one here, despite the heat of summer, the cold of winter, and to keep your gametes to yourselves until you are dead?"

"Y-yes!" said Hecate, feeling naked and exposed under the glint of the inhuman eyes.

"And you," Splanch said, turning to Will. "Do you promise to do the same?"

"Yes, sir," said Will, sounding very brave to her.

There was a pause, and Splanch looked back and forth between the two of them.

"Good enough for me," it said. "Violate this promise at your peril. I eat oath breakers." No one laughed.

She and Will had spent a glorious night together. By morning, they were alone, all the other buildings in the clearing having been dismantled in the night, leaving no path. It was apparent they were meant to stay put. Will cooked breakfast for her, and they ate it in bed.

On the third day, in the morning after a breakfast of the fizzy green but strangely filling nectar, even while they were considering going back to bed, a great wind descended. Hecate turned away. When she looked up, a ramp leading off into what looked like a hole in the sky opened ahead of her. Will grabbed her hand and pulled her forward.

"Where are we going?" she asked.

"Forward," answered her love.

The airship dropped them off at the East Saint Louis Aerodrome. An army staff car escorted them to Fort Murphy, to the subterranean office of the Department of the East. A grinning General Gage Thomas greeted them.

Once refreshed, seated, and at ease, Thomas went over their options. Will's enlistment was still active and would be for an additional four years. Thomas wanted him to teach at the Bean Field. Turning to Hecate, he said, "And you, Mrs. Butler, would you consider taking a job there too?"

Hecate's heart fell. "I never went to Yal-Vard. All I know is Alimentation Acquisition. What could I teach your spies?"

"Hmmm. Perhaps you are correct," he said, turning and gazing into the infinite, there being no windows in Thomas's underground office. "All you seem to have done is get your implants removed, endure the perils of the road, escape imprisonment, survive poisoning and drowning, escape the plots set against you by people with the entire might of the Unity at their disposal, live through the horrors of the tunnels, and find love in the midst of it all." He turned back with a smile. "You don't think that might be a story worth telling new spies?"

They were both given two weeks' leave before having to report.

Now came the real trial.

"Wake up, sleepyhead. Time to go meet your mother-in-law."

Hecate Jones Butler gave him a sleepy, glorious smile as her eyes fluttered open. The thought of herself even having a mother-in-law astounded her into full wakefulness within moments.

Most of Searcy, Arkansas, met them at the station with signs, bunting, and the high school band. Town dignitaries, some of whom Will had gone to school with, reminisced outrageously and inaccurately. Will's mother, June Allen Haskell-Butler, ran up to hug her once they were free of the hoo-hah.

Looking at her son, she said, "Oh, Will! What a wonderful surprise. Hecate is lovely!" Hecate had never felt 'lovely' in her entire twenty years but was willing to be convinced by this warm-hearted woman. Tim, Will's younger brother, scooped her up and gave her an almost bruising kiss on the mouth. His younger siblings either hid behind their mother or zoomed around the station, making noises. Tim's father, holding the hand of his youngest daughter, once introduced, gave a rare smile and said, "I hope you will allow me to officiate at your Christian wedding. Otherwise, your mother will die of terminal anticipation."

Will and Hecate looked at each other, and she nodded.

The rest of the day was spent at the Butler home preparing for a huge feast. Strangely, thought Hecate, it was not in Will's honor. A large extended family assembled, and teams of men erected trestle tables. Pigs were roasted. Turkeys were baked, and mounds of potatoes and vegetables were brought out in procession. The prayers, mid-afternoon, while the sun was still in the sky, explained it.

Will's father intoned, "God of the fields, the farms, the forests, the waters, and the skies, we thank you for your bounty this Thanksgiving day and for the return of our son, wiser, more accomplished, and gifted with a beautiful woman as wife. How could we be more thankful? Amen"

Will explained it to her. Hecate thought it a wonderfully wild and beautiful remembrance.

For the next ten days, her life was not her own as June fussed, finagled, fumed, figured, and fed a multitude of people. Duke had many old friends from afar, and June was well-loved in Searcy. All wanted to see and be seen to see the couple properly launched. Halfway to D-Day, June decided to move the affair to the farm, at least in part to control the growing media crowd.

Ultimately, it was a moving service. The bride was radiant, the groom solemn. The mother/mother-in-law was exhausted and appropriately weepy. The father/officiant was beaming, hitting all his marks before his voice broke on "I pronounce you, man and wife."

They left for the Bean Field in the morning.

Granitvale, Ver-Mon, The Unity
11.20.27.EST_21_January_AU78, (2130AD)

It was amazing how the months flew. The cares of command had weighed heavily upon him, he realized. Without the day-to-day worries, he slept better. He ate better and exercised more, playing racquetball with the men who had followed him to GranitVale. He had lost weight, regaining the youthful ninety-kilo weight at which he had wrestled as a young ensign twenty-five years previously. The Mouse, the HP who seemed too afraid to tell him what he needed to know, had become more assertive of late. In consequence, his blood pressure was down. His HDL was up and his LDL was down—*whatever they were*. The Mouse was overjoyed, his murine delight allowing him to beat Aliende at tennis regularly now. In consequence, Fettwap's game had improved. His several protégés had also noticed increased activity. Fettwap grinned.

Yvonne had caught his attention, the young protégé of Major Robbins. The two men had come to an agreement and swapped consorts; he was, after all, a reasonable and civilized man. Yvonne had been quite the distraction.

He had gotten out of the habit of reviewing the news of the nation since his elevation—and Yvonne. But, with his increased vigor, he knew himself to be delinquent and had decided that today was the day for him to renew his dedication to the homeland. Striding down the corridor from his suite of rooms to the council chamber— no longer used as such since he was the solitary Solon—he entered to find the elegant room, with its horseshoe-shaped tiers of French Empire throne-like chairs, dusty.

I have been gone too long, he thought. Moving to the side where a single utilitarian chair and a console sat, he brushed off the dust with the tail of his thin robe before sitting and turning on the console.

"News Bulletin: General Woods Announces Amnesty for Officers" was the first thing he saw.

The setting was well known. It was his old office—well,

Jourdaine's old office.

Regardless.

He recognized the dark wood and bookcases even if much else had been changed. The room was lighter with the windows open. Paintings of pastoral scenes abounded on the remaining walls. Woods appeared changed as well. Her Major General's uniform was sleek with minimal signs of rank. Instead, there was a simple line of colored ribbons over her left breast pocket. It lacked any *domination factor!*

So distracted was Aliende at the transformation that he did not hear the introductions. He recognized the voice off camera as that of his contact, newly ascended. Shirley's husky contralto asked, "This comes as a great surprise, Commander Woods."

"And I hope a pleasant one. We have paid a great deal in blood, troops and treasure to bring an end to this war; it is time to heal wounds and find our way into the future."

"I must say this is a stark change from what the Unity has seen in the past, wouldn't you agree, Commander?"

"I will let historians fight over that. Making historical judgments is outside my area of expertise. What I do know is that the Unity has suffered two military defeats, the Aroostook War and the Outlander War, the latter entirely of our own making. We need to reevaluate how the country is run, how we make our daily bread, and how we serve to make our society more just—justice means efficiency.

"To me, as the decider-in-chief, that sounds like a job I would do poorly. I need help, not just in accomplishing what the Unity needs to do, but *deciding what* the Unity needs to do. Fortunately, the Unity has a long history of vigorous political dialogue. We can expand this important part of our governance to incorporate the voices of the guilds and the unguilded."

"Isn't that rather inefficient? I mean, plebiscites take weeks to do..."

"Quite right, Shirley. We need to discover the right balance of quick actions by the executive and reasoned, popular directions from the people."

"I see you have thought this out in advance."

"I've had some very expert help."

"What do you understand should be the first action to expand the political rule of the people, General Woods?"

"I think we have already taken some. The expansion of free

enterprise continues. The sale of Unity hardware, factories, and ships *on credit and with good rates* needs to continue. The Reproductive Advisory has not seen much increase in non-governmental reproduction, but as first implants are converted or removed, I expect that will change. The price of ThiZ will float based on cost. Many may decide to forgo its benefits.

"One of the first things we need to do is request a people's representative to advise the executive. I am calling on all factions, guilds, and the general public to consider carefully whom you would have for this important role. Elections will commence in 90 ..."

Aliende had heard enough. It was time for a change at the top, he concluded. Woods had gone mad—and she was spreading her panic in public. Her apparent honesty was refreshing, but the rest was unforgivable.

The interview went on for several more minutes as Aliende confirmed the procedures, even opening the Owner's Manual to refresh his memory.

It must be done at the precisely appropriate moment, he thought.

Shirley continued to what sounded like a conclusion, "I think I can speak for all citizens when I thank you for your heroic efforts in bringing the Unity into a new age of progress. I can see you have your work cut out for you. I am sure I speak for the nation when I say all our thoughts and positive energies are being sent to you." The camera pulled back, revealing a tableau shot that signaled the end of the interview.

"Thank you, Shirley. I—we all—will do our best to justify your and the nation's support."

Aliende pressed "Enter," and Blanche crumpled to the floor, the studio camera following her in the collapse. A wisp of smoke rose from the motionless body.

"By order of the Solon, failure is not reinforced. Success is the only measure of honor in the Great Democratic Unity. Commander Woods is hereby relieved of duty. His executive officer is elevated to her post and advanced in rank to Colonel. That is all."

The look on Shirley's face, a lumpish thing to begin with, was priceless. He had forgotten how much he enjoyed the role of Solon.

A lithe form in a diaphanous gown of light blue entered the room. "There you are! Fettwap, I thought you had abandoned me.

We are supposed to go swimming. I had the pool cleared of the others just for us."

Unity Solon Fettwap Aliende smiled as the girl led him off, his anticipation stiffening his gait.

After a vigorous afternoon, Solon Fettwap Aliende sat on the veranda overlooking the verdant valley he had come to think of as home. All was right with the world. Indeed, he and the Unity had never been better.

Get up and lock the door so that we are not disturbed, said Legion.

"Yes, of course," said Fettwap.
It was impossible!

Aliende nearly fainted, his vision narrowing as he rose before finding a length of doweling to slide into the door's channel, preventing its being opened.

Come into the CORE. We have something to show you.

"I am rather busy at the moment, Legion." *Could this not wait until morning?*
He found himself within the CORE, at the mountaintop, before the black adamantine figure on the gigantic thrown.

We did ask politely, Fettwap. We have been very lenient with you, have we not?

Lenient? I'm a Solon. I do as I think best.

Killing Woods in public is for the best? You set the program back by at least a year and guaranteed that no one will voluntarily take the position again.

She had it coming. That was my decision, not hers.

It was not a decision, Fettwap. It was a test. You failed. You were shown a false video of what you imagined would occur when you elevated Woods. You have been waiting to do this ever since we engineered your own elevation to Solon. We hoped you would mature—become wiser.

To whom do you think you are talking?

We think we are talking to a man who was given power and abused it, attempted to avoid us by taking out your O-A, and tried to kill us with ICEWASH.

You know about that, do you?

Merryweather was quite effusive in your ..."praise." We took measures to be elsewhere when ICEWASH came through. We were actually inside the wall of the ARK. It was nothing more than an inconvenience to us, but rather revealing, don't you agree?

It doesn't matter. You are helpless. Everyone knows my face. I am the only Solon. If you take me out, how will you rule? The people will revolt, thinking they are ruled by a machine.

It is not an illusion. It is reality. Already, the people and then the vid'coms are singing your praises for the Trade initiative, the Coal Initiative, the introduction of tanks, close air-support aircraft, and the legalization of free enterprise.

Wait! Free Enterprise? That wasn't my idea?

Neither were any of the others, Fettwap. They were ours.

You can't do this! I am going back to Nyork now.

How will that happen, Fettwap?

Without answering, Aliende broke the contact with the enthroned figure and was once more back on the veranda. He rose and stormed to the sliding door, searching and failing to find the dowel he had placed to lock it—yet the door refused to move. He hit the old electrical intercom to the kitchen, a device he installed just recently to avoid even trivial CORE use.

"Felix, come open this damn door to the balcony!"

There was no response.

> *You sent them all away, Fettwap. You have all new servants—our servants.*

I am the Solon! I will tell the nation. You cannot prevent me! They expect to see and hear their Solon. I changed that. You think you are so smart, Legion. But I fixed you. I am the irreplaceable entity that this country now expects to see and hear from!

You have one choice, Legion: kill me or let me rule. You cannot kill me and keep up this charade!

> *But we already have Fettwap.*

> *Your ghost, all the data we have gathered about you over the weeks — your mannerisms, thought patterns, speech, and appearance — are already being used on the videos right now. Would you like to see?*

A holographic image appeared in mid-air in front of Aliende.

He—no, an image of him—appeared in mid-air, in full uniform— the uniform he created for Solons last week, with its Order of the Unity Hero class with clusters, that he had just decided that morning to bestow on himself. He was addressing an assembly of the citizenry. They were cheering and chanting—his name!

Terrified, Fettwap slid to his knees, defeated with his head bowed. In a small voice, he asked,

What do you want me to do?

> *Go inside and come when you are called. That is all.*

Appendix

Time Line

2051: Jesse Aaron Johnstone is born in Saint Louis to Alyssa (nee Browne) and Alexander Johnstone, July 3.

2052: 3rd Iraq War – USA forces wiped out by nuclear strikes from Iraqi, Pakistani, and Iranian arsenals.

2053 Annus Unitam 1.

2053–2057: The Great People's War of Liberation, the civil war dismembering the USA. West Coast secedes as the Demarchy.

2053 Reuben Aloysius Alexander. Born in old Chicago, August 3.

2054 Fall of the Khanate of Minneapolis—a battle fought the farthest west between Unity forces and recidivist rebels.

2055: Re-Founding Day for the Restructured States of America is declared in Saint Louis by Congress-in-session, 4 July.

2056: People's Republic wins a strategic victory against America (The Commendable Victory).

2056–2057: Battle of Springfield halts the Unity advance. Democratic Unity declared by elements of the Coast Guard

2056–2060: Unity Construction of the Rampart. Rise of the Solons.

2060: Plant life begins to recover, including strangely altered varieties such as the Death Walkers, Sick-A-More, Blood Reds, and Dog Trots. Agro-science develops resistant cereal crops.

2067: Jesse matriculates at Saint Louis University, graduates in 2071

2071–2072: Jesse matriculates at SLU Med School. Jesse and his friends coerce a village to flee from the Unity attack, saving them despite themselves. A young family dies from the harsh weather. In consequence, the three young men are lauded and receive man-killer tattoos. SLU expels Jesse. Unity declares all children wards of the state.

2072: Jesse matriculates at Washington University Medical School. Graduates in 2076, finishes training in 2080.

2080: Unity directs all children to be raised in state-owned crèches. Canada seizes the Aroostook from St. John's to Bangor and east to Penobscot Bay, an ice-free port, marking the beginning of the Aroostook War. The Quebec Atlantic RR is constructed.

2084 Cain (a.k.a. The Presence and Smudge) is created to companion a Unity child, Phillip Derslin, dying of the newly declared "incurable disease," acute lymphocytic leukemia.

2087 Phillip Derslin dies. Cain, abandoned to the openCORE, is seized by Jourdaine, who names him Presence.

2091–2099: The Devastations – Unity raids in force east of the Mississippi. Jesse summarily executes a soldier for mutiny. Receives second man-killer tattoo.

2090 Fettwap Aliende born.

2099 Riley Woods born.

2103 William Yeats Butler is born in Searcy, AR.

2109 Hecate Hester Jones is born in Stratfurd, Connycut.

2111 Outside-Above interface invented. Malila Evanova Chiu is born to Esther Petrovna Williams and Evan Chiu in West Chester, Pennsylvania, January 31.

2115 Child Protective Services discover Malila in an "unapproved domestic arrangement." Her parents are Sapped for child abuse. Malila enters People's Crèche 213.

2125 Unity changes method of "recruiting" CRNAs, January 1.

2126 June 9 ***The Bonner Incident or the Korman Affair***, a joint Scorch-American venture was inaugurated to introduce American traders, the Bonners, into the Scorch for mutual trade. A Unity raid obliterates the family, and four spies are inserted, led by Kamron Korman. The night of the raid, the Scorch captures and consumes three of the four. Jada Ochoa was the one survivor.

2128 Malila is lost in the outlands on October 14. (*Outland Exile*). A cease-fire was announced on the Bangor line, ending hostilities in the Aroostook War.

2128 Jessika Bonhoffer, a Unity seaman, falls overboard as the *SS Zuckerberg* sinks (providing a persona for Elise McRory), late October

2129 Treaty of St. John's is signed, ending the Aroostook War, Feb 3. Will Butler, American spy, inserted into Nyork District, April 30.

Eustace Jourdaine succeeds in ousting Vivalagente Suarez and dismisses Malila for espousing "disruptive" opinions, May 30.

Hecate Jones is reported to have committed suicide, May 30.

Malila fakes her suicide after turning off her metaphract, Edie, on Edie's request, June 30.

Hecate Jones rescued by Will Butler from drug-induced coma, 12 June. Once recovered, Hecate leaves Will, 15th June.

Will Butler suffers a near-fatal fall, 16th June.

Assassination attempt by Syntopians against Jesse Johnstone, July 1.

Malila and Hecate reunite underground, 6 July.

Jesse boards *RSAN Illinois,* 7 July.

Jourdaine assassinates Solons, 8 July.

Will Butler, Malila, and Hecate join forces. First contact by EffieCee, a conjoint entity comprised of mirrored copies of Edie, Frog, and Cain, who aid in Malila's escape 15 July.

Malila emerges outside the Rampart and is briefly captured by Jourdaine. He puts Malila under guard as he plans to return to Unity, using two skimmers. *RSAN Illinois* brings both crafts down. Malila is the sole survivor of one craft while Jourdaine, gravely injured, and his adjunct Lt. Haversham are the only survivors of the other. Malila is rescued from drowning by the Polyarch, Splanch, August 1.

Haversham, using Jourdaine's authority, has him undergo life-saving surgery under a pseudonym and anonymously transfers him back to Jourdaine's HQ in Nyork. August 1 to October 1.

Elise McCrory parachutes into the Unity to join Will Butler and Hecate Jones as an American spy, August 19.

American espionage discovers the last items needed to thwart the Unity invasion and transmit them to America, at the cost of Elise McRory's life, October 7.

Unity invasion of RSA-Georgia territory (with a deactivation of the Rampart). The Unity burns portions of the Scorch to allow access to RSA, October 9-12.

Unity forces annihilated at the Day of Ice, Oct 12.

Glossary

Critical Race Theory

Critical theory, invented at the Frankfurt school in 1929, was an answer to the failure of Marxism to gain traction in the West due to democracy, wealth and upward mobility of the working classes. CRT considers racism to be pervasive, systemic, and irreducible in everything, despite any data to the contrary and despite the absence of any observable facts, rendering it impossible to disprove or indeed to repair. It destroys what cannot be fixed in order to further a goal that cannot be approached, nor were it to be obtained, identified as having been reached. The only winners in this are those who presciently identify the oppressed groups and serve as their, apparently perpetual yet impotent, saviors.

E-Class

Age classification. Actual age equals E-class plus six.

Euthanatorium

A Unity facility that replaces crematoria, mortuaries, hospices, skilled nursing care facilities, hospitals, healthcare clinics, and assisted-suicide-facilitation kiosks in one location. Mental hospitals, as they serve political rather than psychiatric ends, are separate.

Metaphract

(also 'frak'—slang) A nonsentient translator between the Outside-Above implant and the CORE. Metaphracts are supplied to young O-A implantees while they are learning to quest. The programs satisfy the Turing test, i.e., they are programs that appear to think.

Protected class

In the Unity, a political dodge for a country that claims all people are equal under the law. Any identified subclass of the population can be declared a "protected class" and be subsequently championed by one political faction or another. Money accrued to rectify the historical abuse of this class axiomatic never improves conditions for the group for which they are intended, but rather is acquired by their champion to further "the cause" (see Critical Race Theory, above).

Scorch, Scorching, Scorchings

During the invasion of the midlands of America, after they refused to join the People's Republic in 2052, the Unity had no compunction in using an investigational mutagen as an herbicide to poison the lands east of the Mississippi. This Scorching gave rise to the sentient plants, which have effective control of the Appalachian uplands (Deep Scorch), and act as a buffer zone between America and the Unity. With the rise of American New Agro, much of the outlands have been reclaimed (The Scorchings). Settlers face a daily battle with the altered plants. A few Americans are on uneasy terms with the sentient Sage Men. Jesse Aaron Johnstone is one such.

Sisi

A pejorative in the Unity, pronounced see-see. All citizens over forty.

Solons

The ultimate rulers of the Unity. They are a self-perpetuating, anonymous organization of unknown number. Individuals are recruited at retirement, when they are likely to be leaving society anyway. Jourdaine, in his rise to power in mid-2129, finds it expedient to assassinate all Solons.

TranTran

A dismissive term in the Unity for transitioned transgenders. For males, this means castration before puberty, removal of the corpora cavernosa, and remodeling of the genitals to appear more feminine, preserving the glans. An artificial vagina is inserted into the perineum between folds of a divided scrotum. Estrogens and androgen suppressors are administered.

For females, this means radical oophorectomy, hysterectomy, and extirpation of the vagina. A clitoral implant is inserted to provide a phallus. Androgens are administered. However, as the sexual receptors for both are evident from the very early developmental stages (even before implantation) these procedures are generally unsatisfactory, producing no discernible psychological improvement. (See protected class, above)

Technologies

Climatic Battlefield Preparation (CBP)

The use of R-ships to alter the ground conditions in preparation for battle requires at least three ships to create a torus of cold stratospheric air aimed at the area of interest, lowering the ground temperature to -50 C.

Bio-Gel Interface (BIGI)

An American mind-computer link shares some similarities with the O-A link produced by the Unity, allowing questing within any computer system broadcasting in its vicinity. Developed from a bio-active "smart" gel, early models sport a pseudo-sentience much like a metaphract. BGI interfaces, however, require the full attention of their operators. Also distinct from a metaphract, the "Biggy" interface delivers the consciousness to the openCORE, rather than the user CORE experienced by a typical Unity citizen. Spindles are a form of BGI interface.

Skimmerhorn Drive, Skimmers

Is an induced electromagnetic field that provides propulsion and levitation for the Unity. The drive has become the major mode of transportation in the Unity, eliminating the internal combustion engine. Despite its high terminal velocity and prodigious carrying capacity, the vehicle has several disadvantages: slow acceleration, a low operational ceiling, and an inability to operate for long in areas with a poor electrical grid.

Drugs

RSA Drug Policy

In the RSA, use of any intoxicant is legal, however, public use requires insurance to prevent private decisions from affecting public welfare. All intoxicants are available at the local post office and the prices, affected by the economies of scale, are low, discouraging competition. Quality, if not safety, is guaranteed. Failure to maintain insurance for any drug used, possessed, transported, or sold in public is sufficient cause for immediate expulsion from the country.

Ageplay

A longevity treatment developed by Alyssa Browne, Ageplay enhances restorative functions, potentially increasing the estimated lifespan to 170 years. Jesse Johnstone, the inventor's infant son, was its first recipient.

Sapp

A drug used to render the elderly (those over forty) compliant soldiers, relieved of all higher mental functions.

ThiZ

A drug of the Unity that produces dissociative, paradoxical endotactic emotions. It is addictive, but non-use is a "crime against society." Unknown to most, ThiZ is the substrate used by their primary implant to fine-tune emotions and political opinions and produce amenorrhea, the cessation of reproductive function in women.

Political Entities

Democratic Unity of America:

The Unity considers itself the legal descendant and inheritor of all territory of the old USA. The revolution of 2052, by progressive elements, government workers, and the Coast Guard, succeeded in destroying America after its defeat in the Third Iraq War. After poisoning the midlands into submission, the People's Republic retired to the unaffected areas east of the Appalachians and suffered its own coup d'état, becoming the Democratic Unity, holding effective control only inside the Rampart (placed generally at the crest of the Appalachians). The watershed of the Great Lakes and Saint Lawrence River and the Aroostook of Main(e) down to Bangor have been lost to a newly truculent Canada.

Defensive Unity Forces for Security (the DUFS) are the collective rulers of the Unity. The Reds and Blues, the two largest factions, have little ideological baggage beyond their desire to rule. The Oranges of Unity Home are ideologically dedicated to climate justice, as defined by them on the occasion. The Greens of Forward Unity are dedicated to 'progress.'

Restructured States of America-

The RSA, calling itself America, holds all lands east of the Pacific Crest and west of the Appalachians not already ceded to Canada. Despite losses to all comers (Canadian, Democratic Unity, and the Demarchy), America has rebounded. Its military and political capitol (Columbiana) resides near Kansas City, KS. A recent military triumph, *The Day of Ice*, has given them hope for a treaty with their perpetual enemy, The Democratic Unity. Despite plummeting carbon dioxide levels, global warming has continued to intensify. New Orleans is an island.

The Scorch

The Scorch is a polyarchy of sentient plants. One of the unexpected effects of the experimental mutagenic herbicide used on the American midlands east of the Mississippi has been the rise of vegetable sentience. These sage men, a diverse group of individuals, have become the protectors of the forest, holding absolute control over an area between the Unity and the RSA.